I0562026

Song of the Nightingale
Book One of
The Nightingale Saga

Matthew Johnson

Song of the Nightingale

Published by Untold Stories

Riverside California

This is a work of fiction. Names, characters, businesses, places, events and incidents are either the products of the author's imagination or used in a fictitious manner. Any resemblance to actual persons, living or dead, or actual events is purely coincidental.

ISBN: 979-8-9873724-9-4
ISBN-13: 979-8-9873724-9-4

DEDICATION

To Kenia for her heart and her kindness.

ACKNOWLEDGMENTS

I would like to thank all those who put in time and effort to make this project come to fruition. First off, to my partner and editor, Sophia Chin whose support and dedication gave this story its song. For Kenia Castenada the muse who scoured through my mess of words and straightened them out. Farah Evers for the amazing cover. For the amazing readers who take a chance on a new world, may you enjoy the music, and know you are not the monster others make of you.

Prologue

Death and Disappointment

Turn back. It's not too late.

Veena's foot slipped and she stumbled in an old wagon wheel rut scarring the road from when it had last rained. When had it last rained? An answer beyond her memory. It was difficult to remember much beyond the tumultuous years, caught in the living storm that her husband, Bryn, had doused her in. The uneven road slowed her escape, gave her an opportunity to second guess her choice. No! No second guessing. She had to press forward. Fear. Only fear of what might happen next caused her hesitation. The image of what Bryn might do to her should he find her on the road before she got much further. It would be worse, much worse were she to go back. Going back meant she'd stay with him until her death.

Tears she had thought dried under the merciless sun threatened to sting her red rimmed eyes. Once again, the meek voice spoke: *Turn back. It's not too late.*

Turn back to the pain and anguish. The beatings, bruises, bloody lips and swollen eyes. The harsh words degrading her, searing her spirit. Turn back and she'd never escape Bryn alive. Veena touched the welt on her right cheek and winced.

You deserved it!

She'd once believed it, and a part of her still wasn't entirely convinced that she could have improve the situation. Maybe kept her concerns about his drinking quiet, kept a cleaner house, faced the empty belly rather than his wrathful hands. Bryn didn't mean it, and he used to cry, holding her in his lap like appeasing a child having a temper tantrum. That was early in their marriage when the foundations were established.

Then the tenderness faded.

Always open palmed, never his fist, she used to tell herself, weeping and pressing a wet rag to her face while he raged like a bear disturbed from hibernation. He wasn't always like that. The lie slid as easily across her thoughts as broken glass across her palm. Bryn used to be sweet and caring. Comfortable. A wool sock that itched when the foot sweated. It was the fire water's fault. Nazglum's drink burned the tongue and whatever remained of her love for him. With his anger stoked, she was tinder, wilting in the flames.

Bryn was hooked deeper than an evergrow's tree roots. It was either the drink or her. The suckling on the neck of the bottle and smacking her face afterwards told her which one he chose.

One foot in front of the other. Each step carrying her away from him. Closer to Euclid city where she might find a new life. Her one regret was leaving behind her daughter.

Ivy.

Veena gripped the silver locket on its copper chain, warm on her skin above her cleavage. Besides the clothes she wore, it was her most precious possession. The one item of value that wouldn't hold any value to anyone else—Euclid wasn't a place for desperate women with limited skills, let alone a girl on the verge of adulthood. Ivy would be better off without her. To no longer bear witness to her failures as a mother, and a woman. Allowing a man to treat her worse than a dog. At least a dog would bite.

I'll come back for her. Once I'm established in the city.

The fantasy of setting up a place of her own in the big city, stitching worn out stockings—Creator knew she had enough practice darning holes until nothing remained except loose string and then it would be time to purchase new ones, or go bare footed in rough shoes, or boots—tailoring dresses for the wealthy women as they attended fancy parties, or anything at all, except for working the streets. She had a particular gift. A gift to convince people that they needed her for more than carnal pleasures. As long as they weren't abusive like Bryn—he'd become wise to her trick and beat it out of her—she could survive.

Wish I could sing away the misery of this road.

Road dust collected on Veena's worn boots. A stone rattled inside the right one, poking the side of her foot and then top, before settling on nipping her sole. At every step the stone jabbed her, reminding her that the journey wouldn't be easy. Blowing a strand of black hair from her sticky face, Veena sat on the side of the road. Dried grass rasped beneath her, poking her thighs, and she yanked the boot off. Red grooves marked where the stone had scratched her. Given enough time, her foot would be slick with blood and not just sweat. She'd seen enough of her blood spilt from little pebbles and big hands. The pebble tumbled out, clattering beside her. So small, yet such a great nuisance.

The day had flipped on her. Hot morning light waned into approaching dusk. The hazy sun slowly dipped behind the hills, its angry eye watching her.

Rubbing her foot, Veena looked around at the drought-yellowed grass and stunted trees. There would be no sleep for her tonight. Not that she expected much until she reached Euclid.

Turn back. It's not too late.

"I can't do this," she said, chin dropping to her chest and arms covering her head. The silver locket dangled from its copper chain.

She'd acquired it the one and only time Bryn took Veena and Ivy to Euclid on one of his business trips. They were in a loud and smelly market when Veena felt a tug on her sleeve. She had thought it was a thief or pickpocket and turned to smack the hand away. Instead, there was an older woman, a mess of gray hair, wrinkles, and ragged clothes. Her smile was genuine, beautiful, reminding her of Grandmother Reed.

"Here," the woman had said, pressing the locket into Venna's hand. "I saw you in a dream. You're really, real. Take this. Take it. Creator bless you and the little one." Then the woman was gone, slipping back into the crowd. Venna unfastened the silver clasp and inside was a hand drawn image of Ivy, an exact image as if she had plucked Ivy's likeness from the air and captured it on the paper. Veena looked around for the woman, but she was gone.

Turn back. It's getting late. The small, persistent voice urged, as annoying as a pebble. She wished she could dump it out of her head.

"Aren't you a little far from home," a gravelly voice said, drawing Veena from her memory. "It's getting dark and the roads are no safe place for a pretty woman to be out here alone."

Veena raised her chin. A man covered in a black robe stood a few steps from her. She assumed it to be a man, or it could be a woman with a deep, husky voice, weakened by age. Whoever it was leaned over on a gnarled staff, face hidden in a shadowy cowl. There wasn't a speck of dust on the robes, yet he, or she, smelled of a musty room. One covered in a thick layer of dirt and cobwebs. She cringed, looking for a horse or wagon or anything to explain his presence.

Late. Getting much too late.

Veena had been on the road since the sun rose. Hadn't seen anyone coming or going, though she'd hoped for a wagon to pass by so she might hitch a ride. This person, she had decided it had to be a man, since only a man would treat her like a lost child in need of protection, popped up as though he climbed from a hole in the ground like some mole.

"I'm not alone," Veena said, hoping to deter the man.

"So true," the man nodded his head. "We are never as alone as we might think. Always something watching. Something waiting."

Veena shivered at the serious deepening of his voice.

"Listen, I'm fine. You don't have to worry about rescuing me or anything," Vena said. "Unless you happen to have a carriage up those sleeves, then I think you best move along before it gets dark."

"Why would you need rescuing from me?"

Veena paused putting her boot on. The question was odd and she thought she misheard, or misunderstood him. The hairs stood up on her arms the way they did when she sensed Bryn building up into an angry brewing storm. Sometimes she was able to sooth him before it burst. All it took was a song. Men were easily persuaded when she gave them a sweet tune. Women, too. They were all cordial to her, sweet as succulents and ready to do just about anything she asked. It was her one way of surviving, until it stopped working on Bryn. He forbade her to sing ever again around him. *If you fucking hum a single note, I'll knock you so hard you'll sing from your ass end*, was his exact response.

"What do you want?" Venna wrestled the boot over her sore foot.

"Oh, you really don't want to know," the man said, shuffling closer. "Some desires are best kept secret. Besides, it's not about what I want."

"I have no coin or anything of value, if that's what you're looking for."

"Tell me, do I really look like some lowly thief? I would have to be a desperate one to wait all day on a quiet, hot road. One could die of thirst before seeing another passerby." He laughed, but Veena heard no humor in it. "Oh, how you forget about your *something* of great value. *Something* you were so quick, so willing, to give up."

"I don't know what you are—"

He pointed one finger to the locket hanging on the cooper chain. "What kind of mother abandons her child to a monster?"

The echo of her guilt sent a cold shiver down her back and her gut soured, hot bile creeping up he throat.

"Bryn had never—"

"I'm not talking about that wineskin you called a husband." The man took another step closer and the musty, neglected smell twitching in her nose turned rotten, like spoiled meat and weeping pus. "I'm talking about the ones coming to get her very soon. They will do more than beat her, oh, much, much worse. And you won't be there to protect her."

"Ivy," Veena said and hiccoughed, spitting out yellow bile. The thirsty ground drank it up. She jammed her foot in the boot and stood, wiping crumpled grass off her bottom. "This was all a mistake. I have to get back to her."

"You are absolutely correct," the man said, leaning in closer, so she could almost make out a face in the depths of the hood. He was taller than her, even hunched over. "Except some mistakes have no way of being corrected. Not everything in life is able to have a do over. What's done is done and no more fun to be had by Miss Muffins who runs away from her tuffet."

Veena's eyes narrowed.

"What do you mean?"

"You won't ever see her again."

"Don't you dare threaten my child!" The song rose in her from her belly, prickling like sweet water from a spring. A deep breath would turn it into a fountain to drown him in it. When the power of her melody struck the listener, a part of it would come back in the form of a thread she sensed, and the more people listening, the more threads were cast, winding around the listeners, and she was a spider in the web, enchanting those she ensnared. One old man shouldn't require so much power, but she wouldn't leave anything to chance. Drown him in her sorrows, let him experience the pain and anguish until he broke, the way she should have drowned Bryn.

"Such a pretty voice," the man said. Veena gasped. Instead of ensnaring the man, twisting him to her will, he caught the thread in invisible hands and gave it a strong tug. "Such a shame."

He dropped the cowl and a gruesome, pale face frowned at Veena. Round bald head, skin covered in red, pulsing welts, and half his nose was missing, chewed away by the maggots crawling from the holes where his nostrils should be.

Veena leaned back, straining on the threads and fought to loosen his invisible grip. He was too strong and she had a better chance at stopping a bull from charging. Her heels skid in the dirt and she was dragged closer to him. Veena gritted her teeth, fighting the way she had never fought against Bryn. The way she should have instead of cowering. *Ivy! Must get to Ivy!* She thrust against the taut strings with all her anguish, all her anger, and all her fear. No matter how she strained, some force kept dragging her forward.

The man chuckled and shook his head. Maggots fell into the dirt and crawled up his robes. "Too bad the song is only effective on mortals."

She tried to release the song, drop the end of a rope around a wild horse bent on trampling her, but it was tightly wrapped around her chest. Tighter and tighter, fingers squeezing her neck until the song became a strangled rush of air trapped in her throat. Veena clawed at the invisible fingers, bulging eyes pleading for mercy.

The man who wasn't a man, but rather a creature from some forgotten nightmare, grabbed her by the hair.

"Like I said, it isn't about what I want," he said, true disappointment weighed in his words. Truer than any words of affection Bryn had ever spoken to her. Veena believed him. "I would keep you in a cage so you could sing to me for the rest of eternity. But alas, we all have our part to play and yours ends in a tragedy."

His hand jerked her head to the side and a sharp pop resounded in her ear. The song cut off and her body went numb below the neck. She fell, a very long time falling, tears glistening in her dulling sight.

Ivy! Forgive me.

Forgiveness was one road she would never travel.

Gold coins rattled in the sack hidden under the front bench where Tym Lyre sat. Never a prettier sound had he heard than the song of profit. He hummed along to the tune, knowing it wouldn't last. For the moment he let it lighten his heart and mind before the sack was lightened after he'd distribute payments, and like a song, the gold would dry up and leave him chasing the next tune.

"Fucking hot day, how can you be so cheerful," Laird said, tugging his cap over his face. "I'm ruddy enough without the sun burning me redder than a pig's asshole"

"Curl your moustache into a tail and your mouth'll look like a pig's asshole." Tym slapped Laird on the shoulder.

"Fuck you and your mother." Laird swatted Tym's arm away.

"My mother's dead and you aren't my type… unless you curl your moustache."

"Tym spent enough on his lady friend back in Euclid," Slim Devon said, hooking his arms on the front of the cart, bouncing with each rut the wheels struck, though he grinned wider than a boy who discovered how to peek up a woman's dress without getting stomped on. "How much did she take from you?"

Not enough and all too much.

"Let's say she was worth every last copper penny."

"Wish I could get a room in the city." Slim Devon sighed. The boy was too much of a romantic for too dirty of a city. It would trip him up and roll him in the mud, shit on him, then rob him of every last shred of clothing. The boy would be scrawnier than a corpse, begging for food before the moon waned.

"You can't afford a room in that shithole town as it is," Laird said. "You're not pretty enough to be a whore."

"A boy can dream." He swiped sweaty black hair from his face. "A boy can dream."

"A boy can be buggered up his ass, too."

"What's this with you and assess?" Tym grit his teeth as front wheel hit a divot and jostled the entire cart.

"He ain't gotten any." Slim Devon laughed and ducked a weak jab from Laird.

No truer words the boy had ever spoken. Especially when it came to staying longer in Euclid. The lady friend was a great comfort. A proper business woman who sold sweet tinctures and smelly oils, kept fats in a jar labeled in twirly letters too pretty for the goop. In the back room, where she conducted her side business, Tym could spend a lifetime caught up in the smokey haze, dreaming the eternal dream. Smooth skin tingling beneath his rough fingers and their sweat slick bodies writing until he no longer remembered his name. Though, his sense of duty always came back, along with the heavy hand of guilt wrapping around his gut.

Bryn needed him.

Not Bryn exactly, Bryn could sit on Nazglum's sharp prick for what Tym cared for his brother. Veena and Ivy needed the coin to live on. Bryn may help make the firewater, when he wasn't busy sampling it, but he was as useful as a sponge drinking up as much as he earned. Veena and her sad eyes broke Tym's heart every time he caught her glancing at him. He longed to take her away, though, he knew better than give into the "what if" or "what might've been" impulses. Veena had her pick of the brothers and chose Bryn. Her reasons were never clear, though Tym expected it had to do with Bryn's charms and Tym being too slow and dull when he was younger. Now their personalities had flipped. Drink-dulled Bryn and time on the road and in the streets of Euclid sharpened Tym like a knife whittled the round stick into something pointy.

"What's that at the side of the road?"

Slim Devon had a good pair of young eyes. Tym didn't notice anything, until he saw several black birds flapping their wings.

"Dead animal," Laid said. "This heat'll kill anything. Look at the yellow grass and bare trees."

The closer the wagon drew, the more Tym saw, and the more his gut tightened. When the ravens shifted, he spotted an arm, a slender one all blistered and red.

"That's no animal," Tym said. He pulled back on the reins, Slim Devon crying out as his chest hit the wagon boards, and threw the brake on the wagon wheels. Tym hopped down onto the dry, cracked ground.

"What are you doing?" Laird whined. "Leave it alone. That's none of our business."

The ravens cawed their complaints, large black wings whisking up dust as they took flight. The smell was overwhelming, and he covered his mouth and nose with his arm. As much as he was repelled, he had to look. A naked torso of a woman lay partially in the grass. There wasn't much remaining to identify her—her neck ended in a jagged hole where bone and gristle poked through, dried, dark red patch staining the dirt.

I can't leave her out here.

This was someone's loved one. He would want someone to bring Veena or Ivy home, not that they would ever be caught, well, dead, on the road. Maybe it was one of the girls from Welkdsdale. Running away to the big city was a romantic idea that usually ended in tragedy. A girl desperate to escape, a girl like Ivy, would risk the journey every few seasons, never to be heard from again by her worried family. Maybe he could put the concern for one family at ease and let them grieve rather than allowing hope eat away at them.

"Oh, the smell!" Laird said from behind him and Slim Devon doubled over beside Laird, retching. "Vomit on my boots and I'll kick you in the face, Slim Dandy. Hey Tym! Wait there, ugh, how can you stand the smell."

Breathing shallowly in the crook of his elbow, Tym knelt beside the poor woman.

"Tym, don't... don't touch it! It might be diseased."

Whoever, or whatever did this, didn't leave a scrap of clothing, or bag, or—here was something. A strand of copper around the remaining nub of her neck. Trembling fingers tugged the chain. It could have been any old copper chain, but he was certain he'd seen it before. *Bet my entire sack of coin on it, and give it all away to be wrong.* The chain caught on the bone and he shook it loose. His breath stuck in his throat.

On the copper chain was a silver locket.

"Oh Creator! Bless her." The tears stung his eyes. Without opening the locket, he knew there would be a thumbnail-sized painting of Ivy. A gift from a crazy woman in Euclid Veena had mentioned. Tym's knees shook and he collapsed beside the body, listening to hundreds of flies buzzing, several landing on his warm face, and humming a hungry tune on his nose and trembling lip.

"Venna." Her name came out in a wet sob.

"Shit, boy, go get the sack cloth from the wagon," Laird said from a million leagues away. "Hurry your scrawny ass up, before the flies start eating him."

Let them eat me. I don't deserve any better.

Slim Devon stood, gawping down at her nude body, sack cloth loose in his hands. Tym growled, snatching the sack from the boy and shoving him hard enough to send him sprawling into the road. Slim Devon squawked.

"Fucking perverted bastard." Tym covered Veena's body with the sack cloth and wrapped it gently around her.

"Hey, go easy on the kid." Laird paled and held his hands out, pudgy fingers splayed, like he was warding off a punch from Tym. Right that moment, Tym was ready to tear apart everything. "You aren't taking it with us?"

"The fuck I ain't." Tym walked past him and set her body in the cart.

"The smell—"

"Bryn has to know," he said, fixing the cloth over a foot that was exposed. *More importantly, Ivy has to know.* "If you don't like it, you can walk the rest of the way to Welksdale."

"I've never seen a dead body before," Slim Devon said, looking to Tym like he was about to cry or vomit again. Maybe a bit of both. "Can I ride up front with you two?"

Slim Devon bounced between Laird and him, boney shoulder poking Tym in the ribs. He kept quiet, though Laird grumbled about the sun and the smell, tugging his cap so far over his eyes it nearly covered his nose. Tym wished he'd shove it in his mouth to stop complaining. His mind wandered to why the hell Veena was out on the road and he could think of only one reason.

Bryn.

What he did next all depended on Bryn. His excuse for letting his wife die. *Veena. My beautiful, naïve, Veena. We could have had a good life together.* He shoved it away, buried next to anger broiling inside.

The sun was a distant red ball in the sky behind them when they arrived at Bryn's house. Patches of yellow scrub grass fought their way through the dry, cracked ground. There weren't any trees to provide a refuge from the sun's blazing touch bleaching the stone foundation of the single-story house a dull grey. Paint peeled from the wooden boards that used to be a light blue, but instead had turned ashen color. Thick white material covered the windows in the house to keep it cooler inside, and even that never really worked. Tym sweated enough to stick to the walls on the visits to help Bryn bottle the firewater.

Tym hopped up the rickety stairs to the porch and pounded on the door.

"Bryn! Come on out!"

Silence responded to his pounding, longer than a heartbeat, longer than what Tym deemed it would take for a living person to answer the door. Fear seized his seething thoughts that Bryn finally broke and killed Veena and possibly Ivy, dumping his wife's body out on the road. He rattled the knob and found the door locked. He lifted his leg, ready to kick it in when he heard a gruff, muffled voice. The door jerked open and a pasty face appeared, red blurry eyes staring from the depths of two black sacks. Bryn ran a hand through his flailing brown hair, a sour smell enough to make an onion cry rolled from him.

"What! What you want?" Recognizing Tym, his cracked lips parted into a yellow-toothed smile and he stood nearly naked in soiled small clothes. He opened his arms wide enough for Tym to smell a ranker odor and avoid any embrace Bryn might feign. "Brother! You have returned from whoring! I hope you brought enough home so I can feed my family."

"Where's Veena?"

Bryn frowned, his fists clenched at his side.

"What do you mean? Why do you want that bitch?"

Bryn was bigger than Tym. Stronger, too. His brother's despicable response was all that was needed to set Tym off like a coil wound too tight. Caught off guard in his drunken stupor, Tym easily dug his fingers into Bryn's shoulders and spun, like tossing a large bag of wheat. Bryn stumbled across the small porch, feet caught up in the other and tumbled down the stairs, each thump like a hammer tenderizing meat, and he rolled across the dirt. Tym followed after, jumping from the top step. He needed to put his brother down, maybe keep him down for good. Knuckles crashed against Bryn's hard skull sending a jolt up Tym's arm. He wheeled back and smashed his brother's nose. Blood and snot spurt across Bryn's lower lip.

Bryn batted away Tym's next swing.

"The fuck!"

"You killed her," Tym screeched, not recognizing the sound coming from his throat. "You killed her, you fucking bastard!"

Bryn growled, recovering enough from the surprise to kick Tym's legs out. Tym landed on his ass, teeth clicking together. A hard fist smashed him under his left eye and he fell over. Before any more blows could fall on him, Slim Devon and Laird were holding a snarling, writhing Bryn.

"I didn't kill the bitch. She run off. Dumb fuck. Bitch ran off."

Tym sat up and winced at the welt growing under his eye.

"I found her body out on the road."

Slim Devon and Laird echoed Tym's words, lending weight to their credibility and driving home the reality to Tym like a hammer wanting to bash his brother's skull. Bryn's struggles lessened and he went slack in their arms.

"What?" the surprise in Bryn's voice sounded real enough.

Tym went to the wagon and uncovered the headless, naked body. He signaled for Slim and Laird to release Bryn. His brother lurched to his feet and Tym readied for another attack. Instead, Bryn wobbled over the wagon and stared down at the woman's remains.

"It can't be her."

Tym dug in his pocket for the copper chain and silver locket. Bryn watched it sway like a hang man's noose, touching his neck and rubbing the raw skin.

"Where's her head?"

"We couldn't find it," Tym said.

"You thought I did this?"

Tym narrowed his eyes, not bothering to give his brother a response.

"I hardly laid hands on her," Bryn said, and his voice lowered into a deep growl while he touched his head. "For reasons you wouldn't understand. You ain't married. Whoring and marriage are as different as fucking and arguing. I guess you pay for it all in the end."

"What was she doing out on the road, Bryn?"

Bryn shrugged, then spat a glob of red onto the dirt. "I don't know, but I'll tell you one thing. She got what she had coming."

Tym was too stunned to say or do anything. Bryn grinned, yellowed teeth were streaked red.

"Do with her as you will, I have had my fill."

Bryn walked away, favoring his left leg, touching his head and rattling off another string of curses. Tym shook his head, fighting back the tears, teeth grinding. His brother always was an ass, a callous ass, but this went beyond any description he could think of and he had thought and said worse to Bryn in the past. Tym glared at the middle of Bryn's back, he could easily knock his brother over and stomp out his miserable existence. Get a few kicks in before Slim Devon and Laird peeled him away, and he would've, except, standing on the porch, thin in her dirty dress, feet bare and green eyes wide, was Ivy.

Bryn moved past her as though she was a ghost or a figment of his hung-over brain. Tym wouldn't be surprised if it was all a dream to his brother.

"Mom," Ivy said in a small voice.

Tym swallowed hard, his throat dry and crying out for water. How do you tell a child her mother was dead?

Ivy pattered down the steps.

"You don't want to look," Laird said, stepping in her path, but she stepped around him and headed for the wagon where her mother's decapitated, naked body lay in sack cloth. Slim Devon hung his head, and Tym hardened himself for what was to come next. He caught Ivy in his arms, her flailing elbow striking him in the same sore area where her father had punched him a moment ago. Tym saw a flash of white and tasted blood, but he held. Held her tight like if he let her go, she would be gone, drowned in an ocean of grief from there'd be no coming back. Ivy sobbed, her voice rising as she plead, then demanded.

"Let me go! I want to see her. I need to see her, now!"

Tym held her tight against him, absorbing her blows and abuses. His own tears mixing in with hers and he sat in the dirt, Ivy in his lap and they cried together. After their tears became sobs and heaves, he stroked her tangled black hair. No child should see her mother in the horrific state like Veena. No child deserved to see their parent mutilated.

Ivy's no longer a child. Not after this.

"Are you sure?" he asked.

She nodded.

Tym got to his feet, brushed the dirt off and held Ivy's hand as they went to the wagon. Ivy's fingers dug into his palms. She stared at Veena. No sound, all was silent, a bubble of time stuck there seemingly forever. Tym's hand began to ache, her small hand wrenching his in a death grip. Then she released him, moved closer to the body and Tym tensed to grab her again. She draped the sack cloth back over her mother.

"We need to bury her," she said, hands trembling. "She deserves a proper burial."

The moon was well into the night sky and blood bitters were humming in his ears. His arms and legs and throat were sore, not to mention his bruised cheek throbbing, but they had the hole dug deep and wide enough to place Veena. Loving words were spoken, happy memories shared, and the final pouring of libations, tears, and dirt. Not once did Bryn show his face.

"Is it safe for you to stay here?" Tym asked Ivy. He didn't know what to do with a child, but he'd be damned to leave her with the likes of Bryn.

"I'll be fine," she said and nodded at the house. "He needs me."

You are a better person than I.

He handed Ivy the copper chain and silver locket. She stared at it, not saying a word and when he was about to back away, she threw her arms around his neck, kissing him on the cheek.

"If you ever want to escape—"

"I know," Ivy responded before he could finish.

Part of him was relieved he didn't have to take her away. He didn't know the first thing about caring for a child. He hardly knew how to take care of himself. She reminded him of a young Veena. Creator curse him, but his broken heart couldn't handle anymore.

Slim Devon and Laird sat quietly in the wagon, faces long and drawn. They shuffled impatiently, trying not to stare, while alternatively looking at their boots, then to him, frowns telling of their need to go home to their own quiet lives away from this shit Tym dragged them into. Tym couldn't fault them. They didn't sign up for this part of the delivery. Nazglum's balls, neither did Tym. That was the strange part about a family business. No matter how much you wanted to disown your partner, you'd have to look his family in the eye and tell them why they're going to starve.

Tym reached under the bench and withdrew the pouch of coins counted out for his brother. He hesitated and added a few more from his own pouch.

"Promise me you won't run off," Tym said, holding out the coin pouch. "Promise me."

"I won't," Ivy said.

Not exactly a promise, but it would have to do. He relinquished the purse and after giving a sad smile, Ivy turned to head back to her Veena's grave. She knelt there, the rest of the world forgotten.

"Let's go home, boys." Tym hopped back onto the bench.

As the cart rattled on the road to Welksdale, Tym looked back at Ivy, who raised a thin arm, fingers unclenching from her fist and she waved. Leaving her didn't feel right, but there was much that didn't right in the world for Tym. A concern that would weave through his thoughts occasionally over the seasons as they continued to haul firewater from Bryn's stills to Euclid, returning with a sack of coins. The concern would draw tighter as he noticed the bruises on her arms that she attempted to hide and the pain in her eyes pleading for him not to speak of them. Creator damn him, he wouldn't speak of it in front of his brother, but quietly ask if she wanted to leave. Stubbornly she would refuse to let Bryn go.

"My mother will be worried," Slim Devon said, letting out a tired sigh.

"Tell her you stopped at a funeral," Laird said.

"Then she'll wonder who we killed."

"Say she's fortunate enough that it wasn't you," Tym said and when he saw Slim Devon's eyes widen, Tym softened his growl. "Besides, you are bringing home a nice bit of earnings. Silver and gold can soothe many o'worries. Rattle the bag and she won't mention you being late or early ever again."

"Death is a funny thing," Laird said. "The young don't think of it, the old think on it too often, but we who are neither too young or too old, we don't like to see death because it takes the fun out of living."

Tym grunted.

"That, my friend, is the most profound truth you have ever spoken."

With that they fell silent again.

In the evergrows came the first song of a nightingale. Once more, Tym couldn't help but think leaving Ivy behind was a mistake.

Part I

Birds of a Feather

CHAPTER ONE:
HUNTED

The songs woke me from my slumber. Hundreds of voices singing in unison, a harmony to heal the world. They awakened me and I was called upon by my lord to hunt them all and break them one by one.

They say the pain dulls the further along time passes. Memory rewritten by more recent events and the person you lost becomes a thin gauze of an idealized singular dimension, typically the positive traits glowing in the back of your mind. A ghost slowly fading from life. Like most ghosts, the memories haunted just the same. Sparrow reached across the empty bed to find that ghost haunting her was nothing more than a vaporous dream, and she gripped empty sheets, balled into a tight fist. The empty space, once occupied by Finch, ached the way she imagined a phantom limb would ache. No balm could soothe the wound. Not even time eased the burden. Love hung heavy on Sparrow's heart.

Take a moment to grieve. Then get your ass out of bed.

Robin's motherly advice.

Sparrow stroked the cold vacant place. "Creator, wrap her in joy until we are reunited. I pledge to continue your work. May Harmony be restored and all your children discover your bliss."

She dabbed her tears and threw back the sheets. Another burden of the survivor included finding a reason to leave your bed every morning. That current reason was to destroy the Silent Men. Eradicate every one of the murdering sons of bitches. Not every reason required the purest intentions. Not when those same sons of bitches wanted to murder you as well.

"Goldy," Sparrow called and the tent flap opened. A young woman with bright golden curls closed the flap, holding a steaming cup of tea. Sparrow smiled, thanking the child. Goldy always knew when Sparrow was about to wake and had tea ready for her. It was almost as though the girl was touched by magic—she wasn't, Thrush had tested her. When Sparrow had asked Goldy how she accomplished such a feat, the girl shrugged and said, "You thrash around calling out a name and then you wake not long after."

The name Sparrow assumed was Finch, but didn't have the courage to confirm her assumption.

"I have prepared your riding skirts, boots, and a light top, since it will be another warm day. They are laid out on the trunk, ma'am," Goldy said and curtsied. "There is a bowl of oats and honey when you are ready. Would you like them in here or would you prefer to eat with the others?"

How long had it been since she last joined the other women? Since she saw another face besides Goldy and that of Finch in her dreams? Sparrow sighed.

"I think I will join the other women today. Thank you, Goldy." *I don't know what I would do without you.* More words Sparrow couldn't articulate. Goldy was the one who cared for Sparrow in her depths of darkness after Finch had died. *Murdered. They raped and smashed her. Broke every bone they could and will do the same unless—*

"Do you require assistance in dressing?" Goldy took the cup of tea, knowing Sparrow could only handle a few sips before giving up on it. Flavors bled from her world, and Sparrow didn't foresee them returning in the immediate future.

"I can manage it, today at least."

Goldy curtsied and left her alone.

The clothes felt a little loose. Goldy wouldn't say anything about Sparrow not eating enough, though she might hint at a second biscuit or extra helping of oats. Eating had become a chore when she hungered for something that she couldn't taste, and when she did get her chance, Sparrow would consume her fill, but as Thrush, knowledgeable Thrush and her odd perceptions, often said: "Vengeance is temporary madness. Once sated, it'll leave you as hollow as a rotting tree trunk."

I'm ready to test her theory.

The world outside her tent was bright and vibrant with activity. Sometimes it was hard to remember that people went about their business, no matter who had died. Death was part of the soldier's experience. They supped with it every day. Embraced it before battle and sought it out with weapons drawn, arrows floating through the air, bodies crashing, men and women screaming and calling for their mothers as their fluids splashed and innards spilled out. A soldier's death was abstract to Sparrow. Something that happened to others, since the Singers, as they were called, were above the common soldier. They had their songs as weapons and protection.

Songs weren't enough. Soldier, servant, whore, and craftsman, all were chunks of meat to be ground beneath the enemy's boots.

"There's our little morning glory, fresh from her sleep and ready to grace us with her beauty," Robin said, sitting at an outdoor table set up for meals along with two other women. *Almost like they're enjoying a picnic rather than planning survival.* Robin was a short, plump woman, always in her red clay-colored frock, always her large round eyes mocking everyone around her. Robin had taken to wearing a purple poppy in her hair because Sparrow quipped once that Robin's cheery disposition could wilt a poppy in the desert. *Nuthatch and Thrush must've helped her get it, because nothing grows in this drought dead land.* Robin adjusted the band holding the poppy in place, and continued her commentary. "Quit risen from the grave one might say, and pale as ever. Look at how her clothes sag. I swear you are more bone than flesh, girl. Eat! Your pretty, little maid has set aside a feast for your pleasure."

"The girl is a darling," Thrush said. Icy blue eyes stared down a sharp nose. Thrush was the smallest of them, but she held her head angled upward as though perched on an upper branch to peer down on them all, rather than they look down on her. Her brilliance inflated her confidence in a way Sparrow never understood, though admired. "Your ward is a bit of a bother when one is trying to have a conversation about the nature of modern youth and the Creator's blessing. She positively wouldn't leave until I gave my word that you would eat this entire bowl."

"I will have a word with her," Sparrow said. *Goldy, I don't deserve you.*

"Don't be such a ninny, Thrush," Nuthatch said, not surprising to Sparrow—Goldy and her were of the same age. Nuthatch smiled, red-lipped, black curls striped in white bouncing when she turned her head, waving away any retort with dainty whisk of her hand that was both infantile and authoritative at once. "If only we all cared so much."

"Less ninny and more nanny," Robin said. "Our morning glory has enough nannies. What she requires is the direct advice from a plump ol'auntie. Killing yourself in grief isn't honoring the memory. It's just another way to die that isn't useful to anyone, especially the one dying."

"Very wise," Thrush said, waving her spoon after slurping some cream from it. "The living serves better than the dead, though, the dead do have moralistic tales—"

"Too early for morals," Nuthatch said.

Sparrow smiled in agreement, sitting on the bench beside the younger woman. Goldy had it all set ready for her, furthest away from Robin at the small table as she could possibly go. Bowl, spoon, crème in a tiny cup and honey in a thimble. Everything was here except for the tea. *Which she served me in my tent. A lifetime ago.*

"What have the scouts reported?" Sparrow asked, stirring in the honey and crème. She would eat because eating was an automatic response, spoon dipped in bowl, spoon lifted to mouth, chew, swallow, repeat. All to keep her body and mind working toward one goal. After that one goal was reached, then she could set the bowl and spoon aside. Stop pretending the motions in this life. The other women stopped and stared at her as though they had never seen her eat. "Is it too early for scouting reports?"

"Aren't you feeling chipper! Who spiced up your tea?" Robin asked, adjusting her poppy, and then frowned. Sparrow raised a brow at her, waiting for her to continue. Robin dropped the false pleasantries. Sparrow hated how they treated her like a porcelain doll ready to crack. "Fine, if you must know. Old Bear and Whispers haven't returned to report anything."

"That's telling," Sparrow said. Old Bear had discovered Finch's body dumped in a ravine. It was the first and last time Sparrow saw the old man cry. It wasn't like them to be gone for so long. Both he and Whispers were the most reliable scouts in the Singers' troop and had served the longest. Their absence was disconcerting. "Nobody has bothered to check in on this because…."

"It isn't midday," Robin said. "Why the sudden interest?"

"Which direction were they watching?" Sparrow asked, ignoring Robin's question.

"The west road," Thrush said and Robin glared at Sparrow.

West. That's where I'll begin my hunt.

"They might be delayed because they are following a lead," Nuthatch said, trying to ease the tension. Ever the diplomat, that one. "I wouldn't read into it yet. Not until later when the sun is scorching us all. Creator, Robin, I wish you would draw those clouds overhead and convince them to provide some shade, if not a bit of rain." Nuthatch pouted, fanning her face in a delicate manner and sprawling in her chair.

"That's right, you wilting daisy, I should pop open a parasol over your precious little curls," Robin said, her mouth drawn between frowning and pouting. "One wide enough that anyone with one working eye, and a brain to match, could pin point our camp. All for your comfort."

"Would be such a dear thing to do," Nuthatch said. "Bring all this waiting to an end."

Thrush laughed and Robin crossed her arms.

"Oh youth, wasted on the young and unwise."

"If they don't return before the sun crests the tree tops," Sparrow said. "I will ride west and see for myself."

A spoonful of oats went into her mouth, tongue and teeth doing their duty. Might as well have eaten air for all the flavor it brought. She waited for one of them to protest. Thrush at least would point out the futileness of the plan. Robin would call it idiotic. That didn't mean they could stop her. All this drifting east to the mountains delayed the inevitable. She swallowed the lump of oats. Possibly her last meal. She could think of worse.

"Sounds like a splendid way to spend a midday," Robin said. "I will join you."

"I couldn't think of anything more pleasant," Thrush said. "Gives one a chance to clear their head and think about the important, meaningful parts of life."

"I think you are all mad to ride in this heat," Nuthatch said. Then she gave an exaggerated sigh. "I will go, if you must."

Sparrow set the spoon down before it fell from her trembling fingers. Their sincere attempts to dissuade her from what they perceived as an irrational decision was a thorn piercing her through the rose petals. She could almost weep from joy at their attempts, if her tears hadn't been used up on Finch.

"What about the mountains?"

"They will still be standing after our ride," Robin said. "All of us will winter there with the rest of the singers. We will design an effective plan of assault on the Silent Men. One that doesn't end with us being permanently silenced."

"We mustn't dawdle too long," Thrush said and sipped some tea. "I have sensed a strong song and I hope to discover its source."

"Yes, we know, before it is gone," Nuthatch said. "How long ago did you last sense it?"

"Three moons," Thrush said. "The strength of it… is enough to direct the course of our future."

"At least it chose our course to the mountains," Robin said, scraping the spoon around her empty bowl and staring at it in disappointment.

"Fortunately, there is one city on the way to our new perch where we can resupply for the final push up the foothills."

Sparrow swallowed and nodded. *Most birds flew to warmer climate, and here we are designing a course for somewhere cold, isolated. A place where a little birdie could go mad with her thoughts and loneliness.*

"They must either be fools or have very short memories if they pursue us anywhere near the mountains. Especially after the trap you and Robin had set for them," Nuthatch said, tapping her spoon against her empty tea cup. An older lady approached and took the cup from Nuthatch. Piper, named because she would play soft music on a reed pipe to entertain their camp. "What was it? Thirty thousand Silent Men drowned? Forty? Now that was the stuff of legends."

"You embellish," Robin said, her cheeks reddening.

Robin had protested the plan to trap those men in thick walls of vegetation, walls of Sparrow's own making, while it filled with rainwater. Called it sadistic and unlikely to garnish support from the people, or prove that singers were not indeed the servants of Nazglum. Sparrow had argued this was their one chance to end the Silent Men. As it turned out, Robin was right. The Singers had lost sympathy of the people and the Silent Men's numbers grew.

Some survived to tell of what happened. Some who have Finch's blood on their hands. Sparrow's leg began to twitch. Her chance at revenge was close.

"Nearly a full year and half later, they still track us, like dogs driven mad by the scent of a wounded hart," Thrush said.

"We run well, despite our wounds," Sparrow replied. The oats reminded her too much of paste, so she set her spoon aside. Goldy would be disappointed. *I'll make it up to her by eating a large supper.*

Piper returned with a fresh cup of tea, but Nuthatch waved it away. The old lady frowned.

"Riding with a full bladder isn't my idea of a pleasant time, Piper," Nuthatch said and stood from the bench. She stretched her back and touched her belly. "Bad enough I drank two cups. A third and I'll burst like a worn-out waterbag."

"We should retire to our tents until midday," Thrush said, watching Sparrow. Sparrow didn't move when they did. Instead, she waited at the table, watching the efficiency by which several women cleared and broke it down, loading the planks into a wagon. Their entire camp could be dismantled and stashed away in under an hour. All without her lifting a finger. *"You'll be in the way, let them do their job,"* Finch would tell her. As always, Finch was right and Sparrow would mess things up and polite reproaches would chase her away.

When the other Singers had left, clumped together and talking in their conspiratorial way—discussing Sparrow, most likely—she walked the camp. Soldiers bustled around, deconstructing tents, tying bedrolls to packs, checking weapons and a couple sparred in a circle, wooden swords clacking together. A dwindling number of those loyal to the Balance remained and recruiting was difficult. Robin had jokingly mentioned conscription, but from where? Most regions they travelled had their own lords to rule and those with standing forces were not so willing as they once were to part with any portion of fighting men and women.

People no longer remembered who the Singers were and those they met believed they were nuns devoted to the Creator, which was partially true. Devotion, but not blind faith. Most people distrusted magic and the Singers kept to themselves, buying supplies from cities where they could and fighting a hidden war against the Silent Men. The Silent Men were devoted to removing all magic from the world, that it was an abomination, and professed *they* served the Creator. Instead, in their ignorance, they were dancing on the puppet strings pulled by Nazglum and his minions. Without Singers, there would be no Harmony. No Balance. Nazglum would be free to cast his shadow over all the land.

Too many good men and women had sacrificed their lives. Sparrow wouldn't let their deaths be for nothing. The world would be saved despite its tendency to spiral toward darkness. Rather than circle back to her tent, Sparrow continued further to the paddocks. Hundreds of horses were tended in the thicket. Dry hay was scattered on the ground and fed bags tied over their muzzles. Sparrow found her speckled gray, a small mare who Finch teased in naming her Lover.

"Jealous?" Sparrow had asked.

"If you stroked me as much as you did that horse, I wouldn't be," Finch responded.

"Next you'll ask for a saddle for me to ride you and a bag of oats afterwards."

Finch blushed, cheeks turning a healthy red that Sparrow loved so much.

Next to Lover was Finch's mare, Bliss. No one rode Bliss since the death of her mistress, but she still remained under Sparrow's care.

"Ready for a last ride?" Sparrow stroked Lover's flank.

Lover snorted and flicked her tail.

Sparrow saddled the horse and checked the straps. She mounted, nodding to one of the grooms as she began her journey west. Let the others hide in the mountains, this was her moment to strike. She kept to the edges of camp, not risking the other women, or their servants, spotting her. She hadn't gone far when she spotted Goldy on a black Frison, the stallion's long black mane and glistening frame was too gaudy in Sparrow's opinion, and the Frison lived up to its name, Vane.

"What are doing?" Sparrow asked.

"You mentioned a ride," Goldy said. "I couldn't be expected to remain behind."

"Just this once," Sparrow said, though she had left Goldy behind plenty of times, especially when Finch was at her side. Of course, Goldy was younger then and easily distracted. Goldy narrowed her eyes and frowned, making her appear a petulant child. "Don't give me that look! I will return."

"I have been waiting for you to return for a long while," Goldy said, a bit of a whine in her voice.

How can I be upset with the girl? I brought it upon myself, allowing her to be my nursemaid.

When Goldy was ten, the Silent Men ransacked her village in their obsessive search for a Singer they were harboring. That Singer had been Sparrow. Goldy's entire family was killed, while Sparrow escaped. She and Finch had adopted Goldy. Sparrow was never good at motherhood and Goldy grew up into a lovely, respectful young adult.

"Where I go isn't safe for you," Sparrow said, wishing the girl would listen.

Goldy shrugged.

"No where's safe."

It was Sparrow's turn to frown. "You are being stubborn, now"

"Now?" Goldy raised her brows,

"Yes, well," Sparrow said, annoyance tightening her voice—a good shaking would set the girl straight, but it was much too late for such lessons and Sparrow doubted it would have the same impact as when she was six and scolded for breaking a clay pot, "in this case you will stay in camp. See to my possessions."

Sparrow rode on ahead, but Goldy followed behind. Horse hooves clomping on the hard, dry ground. The girl would follow her into the mouth of a ridge cat, ready to bandage her up and serve her some tea. The only way to prevent her from going was for Sparrow to stay behind as well. That wasn't an option.

"At least have the wit about you to flee when I tell you to," Sparrow called over her shoulder. Goldy gave no reply. *If she wants to die because of her stubbornness, who am I to stop her or complain?* "I can't be always looking out for you child."

"I will manage," Goldy said.

"Manage to find trouble," Sparrow said.

"Funny, that's what Finch used to say about you," Goldy replied. "'That woman would argue with love birds.'"

"Well, she wasn't wrong… and neither am I about this," Sparrow said. Lover snorted. "I wish you would stay behind."

"I am behind you," Goldy said. "Keep your eyes on the road and we'll both be safe."

Sparrow smiled. Goldy had Finch's sass and she couldn't love the girl more or dissuade her. The sun brightened overhead creating a hot glare on the hard packed dirt. All around yellowed-grass wilted, and Sparrow empathized. An over-dramatic wilt in her saddle the way Nuthatch imitated that morning wouldn't be too far off from how she felt. They had been riding much longer than Sparrow intended. Typically, the scouts would ride a league or two at most, but Sparrow had gone further, and there were no signs of Old Bear or Whispers. Something might've compelled them to go further. Perhaps they met a wild animal or thieves, or a dozen other mishaps. Didn't mean Silent Men were involved, as Nuthatch had suggested.

The girl can't be right, she is insufferable when she thinks she has a point. Sparrow was spitting into the wind and hoping for a hit. Her intuitions told her she was at least spitting in the right direction. Problem was, her mouth was dry since she was more concerned about leaving camp unnoticed that she forgot to bring a waterskin. She coughed and rubbed her throat.

Goldy trotted beside her and silently offered her a full skin.

Creator bless this brilliant child. Lukewarm water splashed into her mouth and she nearly choked.

"Careful now, don't breathe it in," Goldy said. "The trick is to take small gulps."

"I've been drinking water and harder spirits before you were out of your nappies," Sparrow said and wiped water from her chin.

"It shows," Goldy said, taking back the waterskin.

"If the Silent Men don't slay me, your humor just might." Sparrow looked around. The road sloped uphill, covered in dense evergrows still clinging to their green needles and yellowed thickets on sunburnt ridges and stone. How much longer would they ride before she conceded they were hunting in the wrong area? She would have to turn around before nightfall. "Do you think Robin and Thrush will be very upset we left without them?"

"I imagine they will be." Puffing her chest up and wrinkling her nose, Goldy gave a passable imitation of Robin. "So... you and your pretty, little nursemaid decided you didn't need us? Must I remind our little Sparrow and her chickadee of the many times the cat's claws nearly tore their precious wings off and their narrow escape when the wind shifted. Oh, but go on and get killed without us. Birds of a feather must stick together, unless one sees herself as the great eagle."

Sparrow snorted laughter.

"Point taken."

They approached a rock cropping split by the road. A sharp bend created a limited visibility of what lay beyond the bend. Stunted evergrows and scrubby underbrush grew along the sides and top, providing a little shade and temporary relief from the sun. Lover snorted and shook her head.

"Let's go, girl," she prodded Lover's sides, but the horse hesitated and Sparrow tensed in her saddle. *Lover's always smarter than me at sensing danger.* Sparrow listened to the rustling of overgrowth, backing Lover away from the sound. Dirt and pebbles cascaded down the side and a small figure stumbled out, arms flailing as she tried to maintain her balance as she slid down the rocks side, hitting the ground and tumbling on her side in a shower of dirt and dust. She landed on her belly, short legs sticking out from her dirty gray smock. Her feet were bare.

Goldy urged Bliss forward, but Sparrow held out an arm, stopping the girl.

"She might be hurt," Goldy said.

The girl wasn't moving.

Sparrow scanned the area from where she fell. At the height, she could have internal injuries, hit her head at the very least. Sparrow didn't take her eye off the thicket, wondering aloud. "What was she doing up there?"

"Might we answer that after we've helped her?"

"Something isn't right." The hairs on her arms rose in gooseflesh. It would be instinctual for her to check on an injured child. A motherly instinct, though Sparrow didn't possess that sort of compassion, excluding Goldy.

Guilt played a bigger role in her taking care of Goldy more than anything.

"I'm going to go check on her." Goldy dismounted and walked toward the girl. "I think she is still breathing. I can hear some noise, like she's crying or whining."

Sparrow caught a flash of movement up top. A glimpse of black boots and an evergrow bobbed the way it would if bent by force and returning to its position. If Sparrow had to choose a spot for an ambush, this was as good as it gets.

"Goldy," Sparrow said. "Step away from the child and get back on your horse."

"At least let us take her—"

"Now, Goldy!"

Strength flowed in Sparrow's chest, rising from her gut, and she took in a deep breath. The threads of her song ached to be released. Even the plants responded, leaning into her power and she sensed their lifeforce, embraced it.

Beneath her song she heard a child's voice. *Little bird, little bird, far from home. Little bird, little bird all alone. The cat's paw pounces, sharp claws shred, feathers are all gone and you'll be dead.*

Sparrow gasped like a cold hand had been thrust down her throat, forcing her to swallow her song. It sank into her gut, thrashing around, demanding release. Sparrow opened her mouth, but no tune, not even a melody moved past her tongue.

"Sparrow, what's wrong? Why is this girl singing?" Goldy had backed away.

The little girl sat up, golden curls that matched Goldy's, but less radiant, like it sucked in the sunlight rather than reflected it. Her face was pale, corpse-like and icy blue eyes stared at Sparrow, a grin on the girl's pink lips as she continued her song. *Little bird, little bird, trapped in a cage. Little bird, little bird, crying all enraged. The pots on the fire, a pie the master desires, but what will he have for dessert?*

Sparrow bent over, clutching her stomach, her head ached and she was certain she would vomit.

"Don't you hate it when children don't listen?" A deep voice echoed from above. "You tell them not to play so close to the ledge. Warn them that they will fall, scrap their knee, or bash their head in on a bloody stone. Yet, they still do it."

"Ride, Goldy! Go!" Sparrow said, gritting her teeth and grunting. It felt like knives digging at her innards. She coughed, phlegm dribbling down her chin. Goldy stood frozen between the girl and Sparrow. She looked over at Sparrow, dumbfounded concern twisting her face. Sparrow tried to sit up in the saddle, trembling hands clutching at the horn, but the weight of her song collapsing inward was too much and she began to slip.

"Then again, not all children are created equal." A man dressed in black armor like the segmented plates of an insect emerged from the trees. He wasn't alone. There was a woman and two other soldiers all dressed in black armor, all wearing the familiar insignia—an outline of a mouth with a single finger bisecting the middle, the way one might shush someone. The Silent Men were here. "Sparrow. I believe that is what they call you. Silly name for silly women pretending they have some significance in this world."

Goldy broke from her paralysis, stumbling away from the child. Thin arms grappled her around her legs and Goldy collapsed face first into the hard packed dirt. The child laughed, her song continuing into a third ridiculous verse. Sparrow's head wanted to explode like a melon dropped from a cliff. She released her grip on the power, gasping out the breath, panting like a dog drowning in a great ocean. Sparrow clung to the saddle, Lover prancing in a circle away from the hill. If she could right herself in the saddle, then she had a chance to escape.

Goldy! The child climbed over Goldy, gleefully lifting Goldy's head by her curls and slamming her face into the ground.

"I cannot believe the impunity in which you used to hunt and kill children of the Creator." The voice sounded closer. Lover continued to retreat from the rocky outcropping, swinging Sparrow into view of the man in the bug armor. "How we used to fear your powers like Nazglum sneaking from under our beds as children and stealing us away to some unfathomable hell. Without your song, you are not even a gilded bird in a cage. One might say you are nothing, but they would be fools to miss the value in this priceless gift."

Sparrow was too weak to pull herself up. She was trapped, but she could provide the others a warning. *I have clung too tightly.* She released the saddle and let the ground catch her. Lover's hooves thundered away and Bliss followed. They would return to camp, providing the others a warning, she hoped.

"Shoot! Kill the horses, not the woman."

Bow strings thrummed, but Sparrow worked the dagger she kept on her belt free from its scabbard. She wouldn't let them abuse her the way they did Finch. She would rather bleed herself than give them the satisfaction of brutally stealing away her humanity. Bad enough she failed Goldy, though the girl's stubbornness was as much to fault.

Sparrow got to her feet, her stomach and head cleared as long as she didn't reach for the song. The woman Silent Man closed in on her.

"You have great value," the man in the bug armor said. "I will show you."

Sparrow held out her left arm, blade on her wrist. One deep cut and she would join Finch in the Creator's bliss, whatever that meant. *I'm coming, my love.* She stiffened, hesitated in drawing the edge across and let her life blood feed the parched land. In that moment's hesitation, the flat side of blade cracked against her skull, knocking Sparrow over. The world spun. Rocks bit into her palms and there was a loud ringing in her ears. Still, she heard the child's song stuffing her the way one might shove cotton in their ears, or down someone's throat they wished to gag.

The woman kicked the knife from her fingers. She stepped aside and the man in the chitin armor stood over her, arms reaching across a great gulf

"Let me show you your true value."

Sparrow slapped at the armored hand extended to her.

"Suck on Nazglum's balls," she said.

Her vision filled completely in black. A hard, metal fist crunched into her face and her eyes rolled up. Sparrow lost all control of her bodily functions, and surrendered to the darkness beyond.

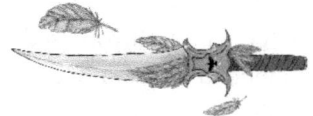

"Why do we trust her on her own?" Robin complained for tenth time, or at least ten was the number of instances Thrush counted regarding Robin's lament. Honestly, Thrush found the notion of Sparrow rushing off in the face of impending doom to avenge Finch kind of romantic, in the archaic pedantic definition of romance. The sort found in bad songs of warriors battling great evils for the favor of a lover slain by the entity. It gave a sense of purpose to the chaotic nihilistic events that occupied one's life span. A sort of snip of the string before the yarn became old and frayed, ready to snap under the weight of its seemingly long existence, though brief as a wick burnt out by the flame.

"I, for one thought, we should have had her leashed," Nuthatch said. "We could take turns holding the leash while she squirmed and snapped. Grant it she would have found a way to slip the collar the way she slipped past us this morning."

Sparrow was impetuous, Thrush agreed, though she had miscalculated how impetuous her grieving friend was that day. Measuring human emotion and gauging reactions wasn't her strongest trait. Since Finch's passing, her friend was in constant distress, exhaustingly so all the time it seemed. To abandon her senses completely and ride off alone, well, alone except for her handmaiden, though the child wouldn't be much use unless Sparrow needed tea on the road, she was troubling enough.

"The Creator endowed us all with free will," Thrush said, dabbing the sweat running down the bridge of her nose. *I wish she wasn't so free with her will, and I was less willful. These are the faults the Creator endowed in us.* "We own our actions for good or for ill."

"When I get my hands on the girl, they may act an ill-manner on her backside, but for her own good," Robin said and smacked her thigh, causing her gray mare to shake her head and whinny her displeasure.

"She might enjoy it." Nuthatch giggled.

"I doubt she's enjoying much of anything in this heat," Robin said, swabbing her forehead and cheeks with a white handkerchief that grew discolored with every swipe. She looked at Thrush, brows raised. "Anything?"

Thrush shook her head for the fourth time.

"Nothing in our current direction." She glanced over her shoulder. East. They had to go east. Here Sparrow with her insolence forced them backward. Patience would have to suffice. Patience with their grieving friend. That was the role she must play as the Coloratura in charge of this exhibition.

Robin puffed out her cheeks, blowing a sigh.

"How much further do you think she'll go?" Nuthatch asked.

Thrush frowned, a curt response prepared, but cut off when a soldier sent ahead to scout, returned, holding out a spyglass to Thrush. "Someone approaches. Two horses, though they appear to be riderless."

Riderless? A sickening sensation curdled in her belly. She extended the spyglass and scanned the road.

"Any markings on the horses?" Robin asked.

"One is black—" The soldier began.

"The other is speckled gray," Thrush said. Lover and Bliss, Sparrow and Goldy's mounts.

She reined in Snowdrop, her white mare, and watched Robin and Nuthatch rein in their mounts as well.

"Nazglum's balls!" Robin glanced over at Thrush. "What did she get herself into this time?"

Something we may not be able to get her out of.

"Are we just going to stay here, or are we going in after her?" Nuthatch said, moving her mount up.

"You are going back to camp and alerting them to a possible attack," Thrush said. Nuthatch gasped, her jaw nearly dropping into her large bosom. The girl could act incredulous all she wanted, but they needed someone to get the bulk of their army to the mountains if they wanted a chance to survive the Silent Men.

"But—"

"Do it, girl," Robin said, tossing the rose from her hair. "We don't have time for second guessing."

Nuthatch huffed and tossed her hair over her shoulder. She turned her mount, kneeing her into a gallop back to camp.

"From the way you're fingering your blades, Sparrow didn't get a chance to use her song," Robin said.

"I sensed nothing." Worse than nothing. It was like Thrush had hit a thick wall at a sprint and had been bounced back. "She could've been taken by surprise."

"How do you want to approach this?" Her lip twitching and the reins gripped tight in her hands. Thrush couldn't sense Finch after she was murdered. "Ride headlong and we may find ourselves in the same predicament. Too slow and we lose her."

It always falls on me to fix things. Thrush looked up at the clear sky. Not a single cloud as it had been that way for too long. Whatever force she came across, they needed to know its limits. There was one way they could test it.

"I have an idea," Thrush said and smiled.

"I already don't like it," Robin said.

A small rain cloud, the size of a plump sheep, moved west. *Not the most inconspicuous way to approach an enemy.* Robin wouldn't accept Thrush's proposed plan without this provision. There wasn't a moment to spare in arguing. Thrush conceded to save precious time, and hopefully Sparrow's pretty, little bottom.

Snowdrop trotted beyond the shadow cast by the cloud. Her hooves striking the hard ground was a lonely sound, reminding Thrush how exposed she was despite the cloud. One eye on the road and another on the cloud, hoping it would lead her to the wayward Singer. This part of the plan Robin didn't particularly like. The one where Thrush would ride alone, while Robin and the rest of the soldiers remained behind her by several hundred yards, off the road and moving in-between the trees. After a few grumbles from Robin and several assertive assurances from Thrush that she wouldn't put herself in any unnecessary danger, leaving leeway for interpretation, Robin reluctantly consented, which Thrush knew she would. Robin honored the role of Coloratura, usually deferring to Thrush. Except for the times she didn't.

The cloud floated steadily along, pushed by a stiff breeze of Robin's creation. The rainwater that fell from the cloud hardly struck the dirt before being instantly absorbed, leaving a darker blotch to mark its landing before it too dried up. There would be no muddy puddles to hinder Snowdrop should they require a quick retreat. Robin wanted to cover the entire sky, but Thrush convinced her it would be a tiring effort and sometimes the smallest cloud casts the largest shadow.

Besides, the small cloud could be enlarged enough to drop a deluge of rain on any possible trouble Thrush may encounter—were it beyond her powers to secure her own or Sparrow's safety. That was what she'd told Robin. Thrush had another reason for the cloud, one in which she hoped would prove to be no more than a tickle of fear, rather than a full-blown case of dread. It was a theory to why she couldn't sense Sparrow. Silencing. All Singer's trembled at the very thought of being cut off from their song. It would be like drowning in air. Thrush doubted that's what happened to Sparrow, but she couldn't count it out, entirely.

Sparrow couldn't have gone much further. Thrush gripped the smooth hilt of her short sword. Unlike some of her sisters, she didn't rely completely on her song alone for security. She could and often did fight among the soldiers, drawing blood from steel as much as she did from her song. Not everyone shared her enthusiasm for sharp edges, and Thrush couldn't fault them. It wasn't easy to sleep when the faces of those you killed up close, close enough to feel their breath as sharp metal slipped through soft flesh, piercing vital organs and creating gaps in armor and flesh to expose blood and innards to the world beyond. To be the cause of death wasn't easy to reconcile. No matter how rational it seemed to Thrush, death was death whether caused by song or by steel.

She followed the cloud, ready to use either for her sister's sake. To preserve the Harmony at any cost.

Thrush reached a bend where the hillsides rose over the slanting road. Here, it must've occurred here. Any ambush that would've surprised Sparrow had to come from a well-concealed position. To Thrush's cold calculations, this would be the perfect spot to hide a small force, archers perched in the treetops and swordsmen ready to plunge over the sides. The hairs on her neck prickled at the thought. She slowed Snowdrop to a walk. No need to rush into more trouble. Squinting for a gleam of sunlight on an arrowhead, ears pricked for the slightest creak of leather, or ill-timed cough, she scanned the tree lines. The hillside seemed to squeeze tight as she rounded the bend, and she held the reins tight, ready to maneuver a quick about face and ride like Nazglum himself gave chase.

I like none of this.

A small voice echoed from the trees. Snatches of a children's song carried to her. Thrush couldn't see who was singing, but they had to be close.

Sparrow?

It didn't sound like Sparrow's song, matured in grief. This one was young, almost a child's sweet pitched.

The world grew brighter.

Thrush raised an arm, gazing up at the sun which had moments ago been blotted out by the cloud. As Snowdrop crested around the hill, a lump formed in her throat. In the middle of the road was Goldy. Her hands were tied behind her back and ankles were also secured. She lifted her chin from the ground, eyes wide and mouth stuffed with a red rag.

Creator, Bless us!

Beside Goldy stood a woman in black. A ghost from her past returned to haunt Thrush. She recognized the woman, though the form fitting leather was new, and looked uncomfortably warm, but her disgusted sneer was unforgettable. Her desperate cries still echoed in Thrush's memory, the taste of metal and blood, choking back failure sticking in her throat like dry crumbs of stale bread.

"Looks like we caught another birdie in our net," the woman said, spear point pressed against Goldy's spine, like a bug ready to be pinned to a board.

"Where's the other one?" Thrush risked talking, though her throat was dry, parched in fear. Not fear for herself, rather for the child on the ground. Sparrow was nowhere in sight, which meant she was either dead or incapacitated.

"Out of harm's way," the woman said. "For now."

Thrush held her calm, the song churning in her gut and pleading to be released. She kept it leashed, knowing it would do more harm than good.

"Release the child, she is of no consequence."

The woman's brow furrowed and she tilted her head to the side, as though she didn't understand Thrush's demand. "You don't remember me, do you? Why would you? Considering I was a simple soldier under your command not so long ago. Then I would have followed your every word, bowing and scraping the ground, licking the dirt off your boots."

"You were never that obedient, Claire."

"Oh, so your memory is as sharp as the swords at your hip, but I no longer use that name. Claire died the moment you twisted her love into a hunk of metal and flesh," the woman said. "You want this child released and not looking like a pig skewered up for a fire, then I suggest you dismount and toss those blades aside."

Thrush noted that Claire didn't bother providing her new name. *There goes my chance at appealing to familiarity.*

"We both know that will not end in my desired outcome," Thrush said, gauging the distance between the Goldy and Not-Claire. She was a step away from the child at most. Too close for Thrush to use her song to disarm Not-Claire without hurting the girl, or before the spear's sharp point severed her spine. "So, it concludes that we must draw upon new terms. One favorable for the both of us."

"The only favorable term I will accept is one where you kneel before me and I shove this spear so far up your ass that you will be coughing up splinters."

As eloquent as ever.

"Kill the girl and there's nothing between you and meeting the Creator's judgment." The song thrummed inside her. An angry tune, demanding justice for the girl about to die. A girl who should be back at camp, packing up Sparrow's trunk and overseeing the loading of the tent. Her death would be

Sparrow's fault. Loyalty always killed the innocent.

"I have been judged." Not-Claire lifted the spear. "Now I purify." She drew her arm back, growling as she heaved it with deadly accuracy.

Thrush expected the throw, though not the target. She kneed Snowdrop into a short-lived gallop. Short-lived because the spear pierced Snowdrops chest, the mare screeching and crashing to the ground. Thrush dropped the reins and rolled from the saddle, dust kicking up into her vision. She caught a glimpse of red pouring across the white chest of her thrashing friend.

Rage pulsed along with the song. She heard, more than saw, Claire rushing toward her, sword raised for a killing blow.

This is the death you want! I'll shred you like cheese.

She opened her mouth, releasing in her rage and expecting the ground to tremble. She sensed the stones, sharp edges ready to tear through the ground at her command, but a new song, a child's banter rang from the trees. Thrush no longer had her song, it was sliced off as smoothly as a knife through butter.

A bigger problem fell upon her. Death swung down in Not-Claire's grip. Thrush drew her swords, leaned back on her left knee, and braced her right foot, crossing the swords. Locking her elbows, her arms trembled at the fury of Not-Claire's sword scraping against her two. The woman was much larger than Thrush, weighed more as well, often that was enough to win a fight, to batter an opponent into bloody submission. Strength wasn't everything in a battle. Balance and luck played important roles. Thrush sensed her opponents overcommitment in killing her, not that she blamed Not-Claire, though she was a little disappointed after all the training she had received with the Singers. Twisting to the right and using the two swords to guide Not-Claire's sword, she sent the other woman stumbling, her left flank exposed. A flick of her wrist and she could have killed Not-Claire, jamming the point under her left arm, rather than scoring the black armor hard enough to possibly bruise a rib. Hope prevented the killing.

I can bring her back. Redeem us both.

"You have grown sloppy," Thrush said, gaining her legs and crouched in *Snake Catcher*, swords poised to counter another strike. "Too eager, too impatient to kill."

"I won't make that mistake again," Not-Claire said, stretching to her full height in Heron Hunting. "I will cut you bit by bit. Each one a reminder of what you did to Aaron."

We are all fallible.

"Nothing will bring him back."

Thrush kept a shadow's length distance between them—Not-Claire had the reach advantage—circling back toward Goldy. Protecting the girl and freeing her bonds were both reasonable options, now that death wasn't as imminent. Something about it bristled the hairs on her arms. *Heron* favored quick, brutal blows, not patient hunting. Goldy gave a strange sound, like a mother quail cautioning the brood at the presence of the mir-cat. Thrush heard the snapping of dried branches, risking a quick glance to the trees. Black forms dotted the green.

"No! She is mine!" Not-Claire lunged again.

Thrush skittered back, close enough to cut the ropes around Goldy's wrists. She pressed a sword into the girl's shaking hand.

"Free yourself and then run."

Thrush slipped a throwing knife from her bodice, flicking it at Not-Claire. As expected, Not-Claire dodged it, leaving a brief opening for Thrush. *Swooping Hawk* caught the guard of the long sword, delaying a violent strike long enough for Thrush to wrap her legs around Not-Claire's right calf. Falling backward, the momentum carried the larger woman over her, sliding across the dirt.

The child's voice sang on, cutting Thrush from her own song.

Goldy was on her feet, scrambling free of the last of the rope. Dozens of dark armored Silent Men rushed down the hillside, boxing them in. Not-Claire got to her feet, blood trickling from a cut in her forehead. She growled, and again she took up *Heron* pose. Rather than wait, Not-Claire struck fast and accurately. The blade swooshed past Thrush rather than split her skull. Thrush's blade screeched across the plate protecting Claire's gut. White flashed across her vision followed by pain and the taste of blood. Thrush hit the ground, Claire's balled-fist hanging in the air past where Thrush's face had been moments ago. Dirt and stone kicked up where the blade struck, missing Thrush. Her cloak tore as Thrush spun away.

Goldy panted next to her. "What do we do now?"

"Try not to die," Thrush said.

"I'm not sure how that is going to work."

"Stab them before they stab you."

The likelihood of fighting their way out was slim, but Thrush had faced greater odds, though she had her song as a weapon and not this frustrating silence. Not-Claire was the thread tightening the circle around Goldy and

Thrush.

"Is Sparrow alive?" Thrush asked.

"Last I knew, she was," Goldy said.

"Do you know where they took her?"

Goldy shook her head.

"Claire, let the girl go and you can have me," Thrush said.

"You are not in a position to negotiate. Besides, I am under orders not to hurt the girl... too much," Not-Claire said. "She has a greater purpose. Now you, I can clip your wings and strangle you all I want."

"Not exactly the reply I was hoping for." Thrush crouched into the *Wounded Jay*, waiting for the circle to become a noose around her neck.

A bristle of steel poked at her, prodding for soft flesh to bite into. She danced away from the edges, swatting away potentially killing blows while others cut clothes, leaving behind bloody kisses to sting her flesh. Goldy was of little assistance, stabbing futilely, screeching like a child having a temper tantrum. Thrush admired her conviction, though she was vastly out matched. Then something slammed into Thrush from behind, causing her to break form and fall to the ground. Grunting beside her was Goldy, a black clad soldier pinning her to the dirt. Her face was tear-streaked and grimaced in pain

"This is where it ends," Not-Claire said, a sad look on her face, blade placed at Thrush's neck. "I had hoped for more."

The sound of hooves and men shouting caused Not-Claire to break her gaze. Around her the circle of death opened and there the magnificent blue of the Singers was visible, one round woman leading the charge.

Cutting it a little close, Robin. Thrush batted the blade aside and rolled out of reach.

"I won't have my vengeance snatched away," Not-Claire roared.

"Well, you hoped for more," Thrush said. "Careful what you ask because the Creator may grant it."

The Silent Men broke momentarily, the surge of Robin's led charge trampling the few too slow to move. Arrows whispered from the tree-lines, riders and horses screamed. Thrush countered Not-Claire's assaults, muscles aching and her breath coming out ragged. Goldy fought her way free from the Silent Man, who lay bleeding, Thrush's second short sword protruding from his ribs. Thrush executed *Lover's Pirouette*, spinning away from Not-Claire and tearing the second short sword free in a spray of red and a final death cry from the slain Silent Man. Robin and three other riders had cut the angles between Thrush and Not-Claire.

"This isn't over," Not-Claire said, retreating up the hillside with the remaining Silent Men.

"Should we pursue?" a young Singer soldier asked, bloody sword ready to give the command.

Robin appeared on horseback pale, like she was ready to vomit, which told Thrush that she was also cut off from her song.

"We ride out of here, and fast," Thrush swung into the saddle of a riderless horse, "This was a small taste of what they intend for us. We need to get to the girl before it is too late."

The number of riderless horses were greater than Thrush preferred and add in the ones who were wounded, not to mention their failure at rescuing Sparrow, the day could have been worse. She could've died as well. Color returned to Robin's face, making her less pale and ruddier, flush with the Song. Neither of them attempted to sing. They pushed their horses as fast as they dared. A long journey remained and blown mounts would slow them further.

"What was that?" Robin's voice sounded hoarse the way one did from too much screaming or crying.

"I don't know," Thrush said. "Something we aren't prepared to fight."

"I think I vomited," Robin said. "My song was there and then it was like someone stuffed a dirty rag down my throat and the cloud burst like a child poking a bubble."

I don't think you are far off.

"I was silenced, too," Thrush said.

"Don't call it that," Robin replied. "It's too much like talking about your own funeral."

They reached camp before the sun waned. Fortunately, it was taken down and ready to move. Nuthatch greeted them, searching their numbers for Sparrow. Concern creased the lines around her mouth and eyes.

"What happened?"

"The Silent Men found a way to um, well, silence us," Robin said, her face paling again.

"That's not good, not good at all. Do you have your songs back?"

Thrush looked at Robin. Robin shrugged.

"Do you want to give it a try?"

Thrush had shut herself off from the Song, fearing the nausea that came when she was blocked, though in truth she feared a more permanent block. Without their song, Harmony would cease to exist and Nazglum would be free to crack open the barrier to consume this world. Too few Sisters remained. Too few for Thrush to be a burden. *Might as well have died back at the fight.* She quieted the fear, breathing in, calming the inner turmoil, and out to remove the doubt. There the song waited, humming deep within. She slowly unleashed it, allowing the power to seek the outer-world. The earth thrummed with stones, alloys, and precious metals, all invisible to the eye. Thrush closed her eyes and smiled, allowing a moment of relief to wash over her like cold clean water after a harsh and bloody battle.

"It's there," Thrush said. "They can only temporarily block us."

"Long enough to make a mess of things," Robin said. "I suppose that is how they trapped Sparrow."

"A silent cage." Nuthatch shuddered. "I think we best be away before they bring that thing to finish what they started."

"A child's song," Thrush said, mostly to herself. "Impossible. A child cannot be that strong."

"What did you say?" Robin asked.

"Nothing." Thrush stared at the wagons loaded and soldiers milling about, waiting for orders. Some tended the wounded and others asked about lost friends. Goldy found Lover nuzzling into Bliss, her Frizon nibbling grass nearby. Every day was a fight, a struggle to maintain balance between Harmony and Discord. They all knew loss, but some losses were more difficult to accept than others. *Unless we put more distance between us and them, there will be even more names to add to the grieving list.* There was only one main road that led to the mountains and several side routes that would add days to their journey. Days they didn't have to fortify against to approaching storm.

"Let's move!" Robin waved her pudgy arm, voice raised and soldiers climbed up onto wagons, mounted horses, and they began a slow, though steady march onward.

"Robin, I think it might be best if we find a way to slow them down," Thrush said.

And tell if they have that Silencer close.

"It'll slow us down, as well," Robin said. "We won't be able to hide."

"They already know where we are going."

CHAPTER TWO:
A BAD DAY

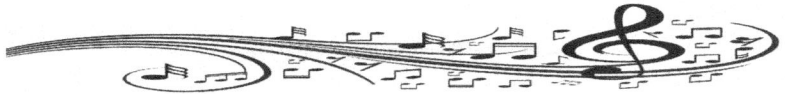

Death is permanent. Usually. When we are chosen by the Dark One, we must do as he commands at any point. Time no longer exists for us. We enter the world a few years, decades, or centuries past our life existence and must discover how to complete the task or suffer for our failures. Those first few days of discovery are bad. Really bad. Like waking from a bender to discover not only our minds fogged, but the world is stranger than when last left it.

"Looks like rain," an older man said, scratching his nose, and then digging up into one nostril. He inspected his findings before flicking it away. "If I didn't see it with mine own eyes, the ache in these ol'bones would be enough."

The black cloud was still a good distance away. Might not even pass over them, though Tym wished it would sprinkle to wash away this sticky, sweaty heat. *Too, damn early to be this hot!* There was no shade on this side of Euclid gate. No trees, no bushes, just a dry and boarded up well. Oh, and a line of about forty carts and hundreds of ragged people coming from the surrounding villages seeking work all waiting for the guards to inspect each wagon and the doctor examining each person. At a rickety table beside him another man took down information.

"What are they checking for?" Tym grumbled.

"Be nice to have some rain. Been too long, much too long without," the old man said. "Growing much in your fields? All I get these days is prickly root. Tough to chew and hell on the hands." He held up grimy fingers. Scratches, like he'd wrestled a mire cat, marked ragged red lines up to his wrists.

Tym missed having Slim and Laird with him. Laird would have a snide comment about never eating anything that would maul him. Slim would complain about the heat, hiding under a blanket to keep his delicate skin from blistering. Kid was always too delicate of a flower for this line of work. The damn fool Slim listened to his mother, choosing longer hours for less compensation at the mill, walking in circles all day, grinding away at the stone, over the glorious and slightly more profitable adventure of a liquor merchant. Tym couldn't imagine shoving a stone slab around and around all day. The monotony of it would grind his soul down to nibs.

Laird was another sad story. Abandoning Tym for work at his brother's stable, Laird had a better chance at being kicked by a horse than drudging up any excitement in Euclid. Since Bryn was a fucking sod, only good for distilling and bottling their goods, Tym had worked alone. More profit, but then he'd have to put up with people like this old man with his sunburnt smile, skin flaking off his nose and white blotches around his eyes. None of which made for a prettier wait.

Never a beautiful woman around when I wanted one.

Beyond the gate there was a woman he'd visit. Tilly was a great beauty he didn't mind spending some coin on. At this rate, he wouldn't be done conducting business until nearly nightfall. He hoped she wouldn't be asleep, or otherwise preoccupied. Not when he had such a great urge. Tym slouched on the bench, staring directly ahead. The line hadn't budged.

He perked up when the old man said something interesting.

"What did you say?"

"Cholera," the old man grinned. "Too many people coming down with the shitting disease and no one whose sick is allowed inside."

Yelling commenced at the front of the line. The doctor wiped his hands on a white apron, shaking his head. A scrawny man waved his arms around in frustration. "I'm bloody sweating cause it's hot as the Creator's balls! I ain't sick, nor drank tainted water!"

"Move along." A soldier, dressed in chainmail and the blue cloak marking the current Magistrate insignia from the house of Nymphalidae, blocked his path. Inspection was beneath the Magistrate, but that didn't mean his representative would be any less cruel to protect the profits of the city. Reputations must be preserved. The soldier rested his hand on the pommel of his sword, watching the man who the doctor deemed ill-suited to enter.

"I ain't sick, swear on the Creator," the man said, bending his knees and waving his hands over his body to demonstrate how clean he was, which he wasn't as far as Tym could tell. "Please, I beg of you. I need the work. My wife and children haven't had a good meal in days. Don't send me away, else you'll be killing them!"

Again, the doctor shook his head.

"I said move along, or you'll be the one killed for disobeying the direct command from his Excellence Magistrate, Sebastian appointed by the Butterfly Lord and Lady Chrysanthemum, third in line to the Throne," the soldier said, drawing his sword. He seemed bored, like he enjoyed threatening sick civilians as much as he wiped his own ass. A nasty bit of business that needed doing before it tainted everything else. "I do not wish to spill your blood, but I will if you force my hand."

The man spat at the soldier's foot. "A fucking pox on your cock. May it shrivel and fall off." He stumbled away, trembling in either rage or illness. "You killed us, killed my family." He grabbed his gut and ran off to the side of the road, dropping his trousers in time before squatting and a gush of brown water splattered the ground. People ahead of Tym groaned in disgust, some covering the mouth and noses with a torn cloth or buried in their tunics. Several motioned signs to ward off the evil spirit conjured by Nazglum to cure the man. Tym didn't believe the illness was caused by Nazglum, but it never hurt to be safe. He circled his heart and tapped his head before spitting between forked fingers.

"Nasty business, Cholera," the old man said. "Better cover your nose and mouth so you don't catch it."

The soldiers tied scarves around their faces and chased the man. Tym tried not to laugh while the poor fellow hopped into his trousers without a proper cleaning and stumbled away into the vast desert of scrub weed and brittle willows. If he was clever enough, and survived the day, the man would find a way into the city. Smugglers' and thieves' doors provided alternative admittance to Euclid for those able and willing to pay the price.

If I didn't pay for a forged legal document, I might be tempted to seek out a new entrance myself. I'd just be happy to get this train moving.

The line crawled along while Tym watched the sky. The clouds darkened the western sky. At the current speed, it would reach the city before he did. A few more arguments provided some entertainment. Another farmer was turned aside. He circled his cart around without a fuss, wagon loaded with hemp bags. Tym couldn't see anything wrong with the man, though his wife was panting. She had a bulge in her belly.

Looks ready to burst. Bastards are turning away pregnant women now?

Soldiers halted Tym's wagon while the old man approached the doctor.

"Purpose and occupation," a young man said, looking at Tym with as much enthusiasm as examining a dirt smudge on his boots.

Tym unfolded the permit and held it out, not like the solder would be able to read it, but the signature was the most important part. "I'm here to deliver goods to a tavern owned by Hillard Tailorson. You might say I'm a merchant and my customers are thirsty patrons at the Dripping Bucket."

Two other soldiers lifted the canvas covering the wooden crates full of Firewater. They took one of the bottles out and held it up. The liquor was clear enough it could have been water and not distilled fermented potatoes soaked in natural common weeds. Tym frowned as they pulled the seal from the bottle. This was all part of the farce. The soldiers knew who he was and what he brought to Euclid on schedule, arriving after the new moon twelve times a year for the last ten years, four of them alone ever since Veena's death when Laird and Slim abandoned him. The soldier sniffed the bottle and then took a sip before passing it on to his partner. Tym had never seen them nibble any of the grain or eat from the fruits and vegetables carted in ahead of him, but his was a luxury they probably couldn't afford.

"Any contraband you wish to declare, because if discovered inside the city's walls—"

"I know, the penalty doubles and could mean forfeiting all goods and even my life," Tym said. "Only thing I have is what you are sampling. Nothing more. Nothing less. Can I go?"

"One last question." The young man didn't seem annoyed by Tym's outburst. "Have you been in contact with anyone who has been ill?"

"Not that I know of," Tym said, placing his document away. "Why, is there some sort of plague hitting the city?"

"Trying to prevent one," the soldier said, eyeing the bottle of firewater his fellow inspectors were holding. "Move on up to the doctor and see what he says."

"I wonder what his bribe will be," Tym mumbled to himself.

The doctor sat on his stool, eyes peering from wrinkles above a cloth tied around his nose and mouth. He made a mark on a paper that Tym couldn't see, but it really didn't matter much to him, as long as it wasn't checking the no entry box.

"Have you had any chills, fever, headaches, pains in your limbs or dry mouth in the last few days," the doctor said, rambling the symptoms off rapidly. "Are you now feeling sick in your gut, chest, noise or ears?"

"No," Tym said. "Not too hot and not too cold. No sneezing and no coughing, either."

The doctor made another check mark, charcoal pencil taping the paper. Tym shifted uneasily on the bench of his cart. His legs were getting stiff from sitting so long and then having to wait longer for this guy to make up his mind.

"I have all the legal documents," he said. "If you want to check my wares, feel free to take one." The offer made him wince. Profits were leaking away. Can't get paid for what he gave away for free. He thought of it as a tax. A business tax to get him where he needed to sell off the rest of the goods. Ivy needed the coin worse than he did.

"As much as I would like to *sample* your wares, the health and well-being of thousands in the city are more important to me." He gave Tym a bored glare. "Have you had any loose stool, sour belly, vomiting within the last moon?"

The sour belly he felt now was from worrying he'd miss his delivery time. Tailorson was a bastard for keeping to a schedule. He clung so tight to his coin he could squeeze a booger from the mark's nose. Tym shook his head.

"I feel fine. Right as rain. My shit is as firm as that charcoal pencil and smells like roses," Tym said.

Again, the doctor looked up from his paper.

The smells like roses part was a bit much. I might have to back track or he'll think I'm eating some tincture to cure a disease.

"Stick out your tongue," the doctor said.

Tym stuck it out.

"Wider."

Tym opened his mouth until his jaw ached. *Any wider and it might just fall out.* The doctor made another mark.

"Do you need me to strip or anything?" Tym asked.

The doctor cocked an eyebrow.

I shouldn't give him any ideas.

To Tym's relief, the doctor motioned for him to move along. The cart rattled along the uneven cobblestones, past the large, double portcullis raised overhead, wooden doors covered in metal spikes. Once inside Euclid, the familiar moist stench of animals and people wafted through. The air seemed warmer and Tym plucked at his sweat damp tunic. Rain clouds teased in the distance, growing ever closer.

This city could use a good bath.

People didn't seem to notice. They clogged the streets, passing from one side to the next without a care that a horse and cart might knock them over and crush them beneath the wheels. Endless cursing and shouting did no good, except to make his mouth dry and face red, so he did his best to navigate around them and if they wanted to get maimed, well that was between the Creator and them.

Tym's concern was the glass bottles packed away in the back. They jostled and rattled and he prayed once or twice that they didn't break. Tailorson was a bastard when it came to deliveries. Not only about being on time, but all in good condition. Tym had seen the curmudgeonly owner of the Dripping Bucket turn away a good order of eggs because one was cracked, a ripe order of cheese that had a dent in the edges, and a barrel of malt that had "a strange odor" as he had put it. Tym couldn't lose out on one coin. Too many lives depended on this delivery, including his own.

Rain drops spelunked beside him on the cart. Large ones, the kind you took notice of when they fell, pregnant with water from the heavens. He hunched his shoulders when one tapped him in the head, like a giant finger poking him. The ground practically sizzled where the rain hit. The drought had lasted a long time, too long, and the land was like an overworked, underpaid field hand, body and tongue dragging in from the dirt and dust to swallow his way to a cool bender.

It hadn't rained in nearly a year, and it chose the day of his deliver to wet the ground's whistle. With any luck, he'd be at the Dripping Bucket, unloaded, and back on the road home—a few coins heavier—before the droplets turned into a deluge.

Like most things in Tym's life, luck didn't last more water in a leaky bucket. The sky darkened when the rather prominent, phallic-shaped tavern came into view. People were running all sorts of directions, trying to evade the down pour that ensued. There was no cover for Tym. By the time he guided the horse and wagon to the Dripping Bucket's back door, his clothes had become a sponge soaked in rainwater as well as his sweat.

It was only the start.

Shoulders hunched and wiping rain slicked hair from his face, he glared at the backdoor of the Dripping Bucket. Broken glass littered the stone walk, some old and soiled, the polish gone, some fresh, twinkling in the hooded-lantern light. The alley stank of urine and the unmistakable cloying stench of a fresh corpse. The city was a tough place to try make a living. Dying was always easier. There wasn't a body in sight, but it could have been picked up by the corpse wagon the previous night. Wouldn't be the first corpse he'd smelled or seen. Tym shook the image of the decapitated Veena from his thoughts.

Corpses and shattered glass. What is my life is amounting to? Tym dismounted from the wagon and went to check on his product, to count how many the guards took as their "tax." He lifted one bottle from the case and almost choked on the rain.

Firewater used to fill the bottle. Liquid gold that patrons of the Dripping Bucket drank like it was water of life. He set it back. *Alright, one loss is normal.* He picked up another, then another, and a fourth. One was an accident—a portion paid to the gods of mercantile and drunks. Four and more were a tragedy. Tym cocked his arm back and threw the empty son-of-bitch against the stone wall, wishing it was his brother's ugly face he was smashing instead of the bottle.

"Told you the wax was old and brittle, Bryn," he said to the imagined face of his brother who should be there with him, but wasn't because he couldn't keep sober enough to no fall off the wagon. Tym snatched another empty bottle from the crate, pulled his arm back, and launched it against the stone. Again, glass shattered, matching the satisfying high-pitched scream Tym made in frustration. Half the crates had empty bottles—the half Bryn was responsible for sealing. Like most things in life, he had botched the wax mixture and they cracked in the heat. The jostling around had caused the Firewater to spill all over the crates and be drunk up by the greedy sun. Bastard Bryn was probably inebriated on his own juice when he half-assed sealed them. Not to mention he was cheaper than a ten-pence whore giving a two-for-one special. Bryn had fucked them both good.

Tym's elbow clicked after he tossed the last bottle. The bottle clinked against the stone and rattled around until it stuck in a brown pile of what once was dried vomit or possibly shit.

"Son-of-a-bitch!" Tym cradled his right arm against his chest. He hissed, sucking air through his teeth. The pain was sharp, a remnant of when he tried to elbow a man in the groin during a drunken fight and hit a large belt buckle instead, cracking the bone. His arm had been numb for a week. "Fuck, fuck, fuck."

The Dripping Bucket's back door opened and Tym bit his lip, snapping his arm down in close proximity to the dagger at his belt. Another twinge tingled to the tips of his fingers. In a fight it would be useless and he would just as likely stab his own leg as an opponent. Hillard Tailorson's pale, dumpy face appeared followed by thin wisps of blond hair stuck up like straw, creating an expression of surprise. It was an act. Tym knew it for what it was: shrewdness. A fool would believe otherwise.

"Nazglum's nuts, Lyre! You look like your tried to arse fuck your horse and she stomped on your cock." Tailorson gave a loud bray.

Tym cringed, hiding his reaction by stretching out his elbow. Tailorson may look, and sound, like a half-wit, but he was as cut-throat as they came when it came to coin. He'd find a way to sell his mother if the asking price was profitable. That's why the owner of the Dripping Bucket bothered to buy Tym and Bryn's barrel swill at a quarter of the coin he would pay a licensed brewer. It was also why Tym stood at the back door, dripping rain and smiling at Tailorson as though he said the funniest joke Tym had ever heard, and heard again, and again, every trip he made to this shithole city.

The things one did for money.

"Only part of me that's hurt are my balls and pride," Tym said, bringing on another series of brays. *I would love to shove some down your gullet and listen to you choke on that fucking laughter.* Tym smiled, leaning on the wagon.

"What'd you bring this time, pal-o'l-buddy?" Tailorson thrust a wooden wedge under the door to prop it open. He drew up his hood and stomped in the puddle like an overgrown-child. "Got that sweet burn? People ask where I get it from and I tell them I got fire gnomes brewing it in the basement. They don't realize this place ain't got a basement. City floods when it rains, you know."

"No shit? You must be glad it doesn't rain very often," Tym said, standing in front of Tailorson, and placed an arm on the crate. Tailorson tried to go around him, but Tym blocked his path.

"Are we going to dance, or are you going to show me the product?" He was still smiling, though not one Tym trusted any more than he trusted a dog baring its teeth. He gestured like swishing aside a fly. "Move."

"Listen," Tym said. "There was a problem."

"Problem? I don't like that word. Got enough problems nagging at me from my bedside and still more singing in the barroom." Tym had seen Tailorson's wife a couple of times. The woman had a scowl to clean the varnish off a freshly polished pole whenever she looked at him. She was pretty enough to see why Hillard married her and Tym figured he could find some use for her mouth to do more than whine and spit nasty words. It wasn't his place to speak on something he didn't own, being an unwed business man.

"Seems the wax didn't seal right on some of the bottles—"

"How many?"

Tym sucked his teeth and decided to be forthright. Tell the truth and shame the shadow, his mother used to say.

"At least half."

"Half! Half. What am I to do with half," Tailorson said, chewing the word over like a tough piece of jerky. "I got thirsty customers who drink it up like it was water of life. What do I tell them?"

"Some of your gnomes drowned."

Tailorson narrowed his eyes and considered it a moment. *He's going to turn me away, damn you Bryn! Your daughter's going to starve and it'll be your own damn fault like Veena.* Tym would be lucky not to be sent home with a busted rib or three—a reminder about commitment. He reached for an empty bottle in case he had to defend himself. Then Tailorson smiled and brayed, punching Tym in the shoulder.

"Ain't you the clever mouse. Some of my gnomes drowned!" More brayed laughter. "Fine, I'll take what you didn't spill. At half the cost."

Tym's back stiffened. That wouldn't be enough to keep them fed *and* buy supplies for more firewater. Bryn would be pissed, but it would be his half the pay ought to come from, except for one reason. Tym's niece. She didn't deserve to suffer for her father's stupidity. It was bad enough she had to live alone with the smelly drunk.

In the distance, a bell struck. It didn't seem he'd been in the city long enough for another bell, but then again, he hadn't been aware of much else than empty bottles. It droned on, meaningless as time in the pattering rain.

"Is there any way you could float me an advance. I'll bring triple next time." *Seal the bastards myself, get my niece to help out. She's not entirely useless.*

"Only thing that float here is shit and rodent corpses," Tailorson said. "Neither of them worth the smell to gag on. Unless you can give me more than half a shipment of product, you ain't getting more than half the pay."

"I've been coming to you for the last three seasons, right? I've fulfilled every order, plus a little extra," Tym said, hating the sound of his pleading. Made him feel small, like when his father used to threaten to beat Bryn and him. "Cryin won't make it rain," he'd say before smacking them across the head for not completing their chores. As they fought back the tears, he'd mock them with another phrase: "Any water in a drought will feed the crops. Even your salty tears."

"I paid you for it," Tailorson said. "I'll pay you today for what you delivered. To! Day! No more."

The bell continued to ring. It pounded to the desperate rhythm Tym felt pulsing in his head.

"That's how we stand." Tym's hands balled up into fists, not that he would punch Tailorson—might as well break his hand on a stone wall to match his fractured elbow.

"Never sit on my arse waiting for a deal," Tailorson said. "I'd be sitting while they took my darling away. She ain't much, but she's all I got. No one has treated me better than the Dripping Bucket."

Tailorson chuckled at his joke. Tym noted how he ignored his wife. Maybe he ignored her in other ways and he could get the payment through a different door besides the back one. He was about to tell the greedy inn keep to take it and quit stepping on his balls, when the very same back door smashed open, wedge skittering off into the alley. Both men jumped. A boy stood in the doorway, waving his arms. He looked like a shorter version of Hillard Tailorson, only lacking his father's good looks.

"What'd I tell you about interrupting business, boy?" Tailorson asked, holding out a steel cudgel Tym never noticed.

"Da, don't you hear it?" the boy asked.

"The sound of my hand smacking you?"

"No, the alarm."

That's what the bell is? An alarm for what? Everything was too wet for there to be a fire.

"Man came running in the front," the boy continued, "said an army was marching on the city. Said another was following it not far behind."

"Shit-dangles," Tailorson smacked the wagon with the cudgel, causing the horse to whinny uneasily. "Start closing the place up. Get the men to pull up the planks in the backroom and nail the windows closed. We are in for a long storm." He started to go for the door.

"Wait!" Tym shouted, rain pounding on him. Tailorson turned and sneered as though he saw a fly drop into his firewater. "What about my pay? I'll take whatever you can give."

"I can give you this advice," Tailorson said. "Unhook your cart and get a move on out of the city while you still can. No telling what's coming down the sewer pipe, but I wouldn't want to be standing on the open end with my mouth gawping open."

Then Tailorson followed his boy back inside the Dripping Bucket, door slamming shut behind him. Tym hit the door and began knocking and shouting until his throat burned, knuckles bled, and his elbow seized up. Like the Prophet Jehovah who'd burned when the heathens caught him outside the holy city, the door remained shut to him. The alarm continued to ring and Tym understood; it counted down the seconds remaining to escape before the city sealed up tighter than a whore's knees when the coin ran out. He had to get out, no matter if he had nothing to return home with. His brother and niece would have to forgive him and figure another way to get paid.

Tym kicked the door and his toe bent at a painful angle. It ached like walking on broken glass.

Fucking day just keeps getting better.

Tym hobbled over to unhook the horse and began the ride for his life.

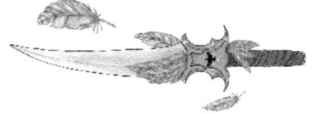

Shit! Shit! Shit!

Mud splashed and the horse slid, nearly toppling over as Tym yanked back on the reins.

Euclid's gate had closed, sealing him inside. Two iron-banded doors were closed and barred. Closer in by the gate house, the spiked-iron portcullis was dropped, like nails in a coffin. Tym was certain he'd find the same defenses at the Sunset gate. He climbed off the cart horse and pounded on the metal portcullis; his shouts drowned out by the rain cascading down in sheets. Blinking away water, he cupped a hand over his eyes while he searched the watchtower. Cloaked figures climbed ladders and lit signal fires. Quivers bounced on their hips and bows were strapped to their backs. One man stopped at the edge of the wall and leaned over. His face was obscured by a hood. Tym couldn't tell if the man noticed him from a pile of horse shit.

"Hey you!" Tym waved his arms. "Yeah, you! Ogling me like I'm your favorite sheep. Hey, don't turn away."

"Fuck off," the man said and made a hacking noise in the back of his throat.

Not like Tym would notice if he was spat on. The rain was too heavy and the spit would be another wet drop among millions.

"I need the gate open." Tym pointed at the portcullis. "I have to get out."

"I said, fuck off." The man unslung his bow and pulled an arrow from his quiver.

"Wait! I have coin," Tym said, patting an empty pouch on his hip. "I can pay you. Open the guard gate, at least, and you can have everything. I have to get home."

"I don't want to waste an arrow on you, but I will." The man notched it. "In case you're blind from wanking, we have two armies marching toward us. Those gates won't open. Not even for the Creator Himself."

Tym stepped back, watching the man test the draw. At this close a distance, the rain would do little to impede the arrow's flight. He had nowhere to stay and the son-of-a bitch Tailorson wouldn't lend him a room. The worse place to be during a siege would be the middle of the street. Same as the worse part to be during a storm. The warning bell chimed relentlessly, ringing out the moments he had to escape the siege. *This sheepfucker wouldn't let me out.*

"Last time I'm saying, fuck off." The string pulled back to soldier's ear. "My hands getting tired and soon my fingers are going to slip, planting this arrow into your thick skull."

"I'm fucking off." Tym backed away, hands held up. The man tracked him until Tym was in the saddle. He turned the horse, which gave a disapproving snort, shaking its head, water spraying him from its mane. Figuring he was far enough away and out of arrow range, he shouted: "Nazglum rot your cock and fill your woman's womb with worms."

An arrow flew past and clanked on the stones in front of the horse. She shied, nearly dropping Tym from the saddle. He squeezed his knees tighter and gripped the wet mane, maintaining his balance.

Hope he's a better shot when the army marches up his ass.

Water ran across the cobblestones, filling the gutters and turning them into rivulets. The streets were empty, except for the occasional troop of soldiers splashing along, shouting at him to "clear the way!" Even the homeless clung to the storefront eves, sullen eyes watching him. *Think, Tym, think. A city this large had to have other ways to move in and out.* Running bottles of firewater wasn't exactly illegal, not with the permit he carried and the forged signature on it, but other contraband found its way smuggled in, and not by the Sunset or Sunrise gates.

Movement from between two buildings caught his attention. Two figures, wearing patch-worked cloaks, skulked on the edges of shuttered business. A third joined them, carrying a sack. The sort of thing someone in a hurry might toss their valuables in. They headed east, away from the central road. Normally Tym would ignore them, smart enough to know when to leave well-enough alone. One reason why he survived the back-alley deals in Euclid. There was always the chance of the deals going sour and knives would flash, blood drip, and lives end. Tym avoided those situations. He was a survivor. Sometimes surviving meant going toward the danger, as much as he hated to, rather than avoiding it. He turned the cart horse and began to trail the figures, keeping at what he hoped was an unnoticeable distance. He knew where they were heading, if not the exact location.

Thieves' door. Tym heard of them, not that he trusted the watchers and their fees they would charge to use it. Thieves' doors could be run under the nose of the city magistrate, like his permit paid with good coin to keep it up-to-date. Others were more conspicuous, a door cut through the stone wall to move people and goods or an old culvert going under the wall to flush away the refuse, and possibly a corpse.

Tym dismounted and led the horse through narrow alleys. The buildings got smaller, becoming dilapidated, more like mounds of rubble covered in moldy thatch, lining the wall in discarded heaps. The three figures slipped into a shanty and the door closed. Tym waited, counting to thirty, to see if anyone would come back out. The warning bell ticked away the seconds. If it was a way out, he'd given them plenty of time to get ahead. Tym approached the shanty slowly, checking around for any possible guards. He doubted any passage was free. Everything had its price. The door was small and hung unevenly. No way he could fit his horse inside and he'd already lost the cart and a moon's worth of wages. Tym contemplated if this was the right choice. He'd be ruined without his horse and have to walk back to Welksdale.

Ruined or dead, pick your poison.

He'd have to sell her to stay in the city and probably wouldn't get more than a couple of silver, being that desperate times meant the scum would take advantage of the desperate person. The cart horse nudged him as though she knew his thoughts.

"I'm taking a peek inside, I'll be back. I promise," Tym said and tied her to a post, which was nothing more than the broken axle of a wagon wheel three quarters buried into the stone. The cart horse hung her sodden head. He wished there was a drier place to tie her up, but didn't have time to search. She swung her head away when he tried to stroke her nose, probably understanding that he didn't intend to return. "I'll come back for you."

If I can.

Tym sloshed through the water and stopped by the door, which was no more than some wood planks nailed together and attached to the frame by rusty hinges. He listened, hand on his dagger hilt. He could hear water dripping, but wasn't sure if that was more the rain outside or leaking in through the thinly thatched roof. *I could stand here and wait for the rain to drown me or invite myself into the party.*

The bell stopped chiming. That was never a good sign. Unless the armies decided to go around the obstacle in the road, rutting in the mud like happy pigs, then they would be at the Sunset gate and his time was up. Tym pulled the door outward, cringing at the metallic squeal, and walked inside.

The room was small, cramped and damp. Fresh vomit, mold and urine nearly choked him. Water plunked through the roof onto muddy straw. Wooden crates filled the place, covered in nubs of wax candles melted in place. In one corner was a pot, rust-colored and had some kind of green slime around the lip and brownish liquid inside. There were no windows, only the one door. Tym began to search the floor for some sort of trap door. *There has to be a way out. Where did those shits get to?*

Warm, earthy air sluiced through the damp coldness, and Tym stepped out of the way as a stack of crates moved, pushing inside. Two men in ragged cloaks and stained tunics stood in the tunnel behind the crates, a lantern lighting the surprise looks on their faces.

"Who the fuck are you?"

*Tailorson sent me, w*as what Tym planned on saying, but being witty in the right situations was a trick easier to imagine than to actually do. Rather than speak the words that might have stopped bloodshed—Tailorson seemed the type of man these thieves would work for on occasion—Tym hesitated.

"Um." The single, guilt-ridden word was enough to make them draw weapons: short swords, great for stabbing in close proximity. "Oh, shit."

"Oh shit is right," the first man dropped his hood to reveal a pale face marked by a black mustache which looked like a drowned rat he was sniffing. He moved to the left, allowing the man behind him to move to the right, setting the lantern down on a crate. "You came to the wrong place."

"I was looking for a way out," Tym said. All he had was his dagger. They would stab him in every major organ before he got close enough to pick their teeth. "I can pay."

"The only way out for you," Rat Mustache said, "is to pray the Creator don't throw your ass in the gutter. Because, that's where we're going to throw your corpse, you dumb fuck. Should've stayed indoors, if you can't stand the rain."

"That… that should make sense, but it doesn't," Tym said, and backed against the door. The hinges squealed as he leaned against it. "This is what happens to failed poets? How disappointing."

"I'll show you failed poet." The man jabbed at Tym, but he threw his weight against the door, the hinges screeching in protest, and stumbled out into the rain. He spun on his heels, almost falling face first into the rushing rainwater. His hand splashed into the cold water which sent a shock shivering up his arm. Boots splashed in the water behind him. Tym yanked his dagger free, the pain in his elbow a dull throb. He hacked at the rope tethering the cart horse to the post.

"Told you. I'd be. Back," he said between strokes. She just stared at him, sad eyes accusing him of abandoning her to the rain. The last fibers of rope snapped and he clambered into the saddle. He'd turned the horse in direction of the ally when a sharp sting in right calf nearly dropped him from the saddle. He hacked out with his dagger, but the man cursed and the horse gave an annoyed whinny, kicking up her hind legs. Tym hugged her neck and pressed into her as she galloped through the water, past the ally, and into the main streets. She began to slow and Tym risked a glance behind him. The pursuers were gone. His leg was numb and he found himself listing to the right. The bottom of his pant leg had turned red, dripping into the flooded street.

Tym rode on, weakness threatening to dump him, and he found himself in a familiar place. He rolled off the horse, dragging his numb leg across the cobblestone and banged on the front door of the Dripping Bucket. The name seemed more ironic than it should, and he laughed, light-headed and leaning on the door frame. He could no-longer put pressure on the leg. Soon he'd bleed out, a small red driblet in the vast rains.

The door opened after a moment and Tailorson stood.

"Man, you look like your tried to arse fuck your horse and she stomped on your cock."

"We've been through this," Tym said, or maybe he thought he did, because he toppled over the threshold of the tavern.

"Blood stains on my floor cost extra," Tailorson said.

Wouldn't expect anything less from a cheap, skinflint asshole—but the rest was lost in a red haze.

CHAPTER THREE:
CHARITY

The promise of a renewed life, to have what was taken away restored. We all want what is lost. It serves as the perfect bait. But what is offered has strings attached. A bargain must be struck. One that never favors the recipient. Many souls are caught with the promise in exchange for their desires, and so, charity comes at a hefty price and one not paid in coin.

"But that's all I got!"

Ivy Lyre pinched the silver penny between her fingers and held it out to Salinas Mathers. It looked tiny in her hands, but it was all her wealth. At least, all the wealth her father gave her and she needed the bread. They were on the verge of starving.

Mathers nodded his big head, white kerchief covering his baldness, and the wrinkles around his brown eyes crinkled at her concern. His sympathetic smile hurt; the apologetic, but I don't give a shit kind. Ivy wanted to smack it clear off his face. Doing so wouldn't solve her current problem, no matter how good it might feel.

"It cost less last week," she muttered

Mathers fat lips pouted and he continued to nod, slow and easy. He dusted white residue from his butter-roll fingers across his large belly. He was a big man, often bragged how he fought in the Welks War long before Ivy was born. He took a wound to his leg in the swamps. The wound got infected, leaving Mathers with a limp. That's the story he told everyone in Welksdale, though Ivy's father had a different tale. One that included Mathers shrieking like a child who'd found a bug in his soup, and he'd ran from the invading Trumen, slipping in the thigh-deep water and slicing his leg on a jagged rock. Saw not a lick of battle afterwards.

"Last week the miller hadn't raised the price of flour, neither." Mather's drummed his fingers on the counter, bobbing his head. "The drought's hard on everyone and I got to make sure my family eats. Can't be giving bread away, now, can I?"

You aren't starving. Ivy's own stomach rumbled. She wouldn't be able to eat until she bought the bread and got it home. No way her father would let her in the house unless she had a round loaf tucked neatly in the wicker basket.

"What about my father's credit?" She cringed at her desperation.

Salinas Mathers stopped nodding and laughed, a sharp bark making Ivy feel small enough to slip through the cracks in the floorboards. Speaking of her father and credit in the same sentence was foolish. He'd sworn he paid off all his creditors last moon. Bryn Lyre swore a lot of things, especially when he was drinking. Sometimes he just swore, mostly at her and how useless she was to him.

"Go home girl and see if you can't fish a copper or two from your father's pillow," Mathers said.

"What are you implying?" Anger welled-up in Ivy.

Mathers grinned.

"I meant nothing by it, girl."

"You did," Ivy said, slapping the counter. "You and the rest of this damn town has treated me like I'm no better than some scrawny bitch in heat since my mother passed. Where's the respect you used to give her? I won't be denied, you cowardly fat fuck."

Mathers straightened fast enough she heard his spine creak. His grin transformed into a snarl, a nasty one showing yellowed teeth.

"Get out of my shop." Mathers shot out an arm, pudgy finger nearly poking her nose, pointing to the door. He glared, eyes hot embers and jowls shaking. "I won't have you speaking that filth in here, Nazglum's harlot! You accuse me—"

His gaze shifted and Ivy sensed a body brushing past her. A sun-darkened hand dropped several pieces of copper and a silver penny on the counter.

"Give her the bread, Salinas, and quit insulting her." Crisell Farlow stood too close to Ivy. She could smell the pig-shit on his clothes, though they looked clean and freshly washed. He was younger and thinner than the baker. Also, he had a reputation for knocking a man's chip off his shoulder if he overstepped his boundaries. The valiant type of man her father despised calling him the "pig-shit saint of battered woman and animals." Crisell kept his attention on Mathers while the baker considered the coins on the counter. Ivy noticed that when greed and pride warred, the weaker man gave into greed. Mathers snatched them up and bent over the bottom of his rack where the bread was covered in a green cloth. Crisell snapped his fingers to get the baker's attention. "Not from the bottom. One from the top."

The top was where the fresh bread was kept, newly drawn from the oven. Mathers set it on the counter, eyes darting between her and Crisell. The baker gave Ivy an ugly smile, full of black pitted teeth from too much tasting of his product and not enough cleaning, and retreated to watch how she would respond to and confirm rumors through her reaction to Crisell. Ivy considered leaving the bread on the counter, opting out of the small-town gossip, but her stomach rumbled. When it came between pride and hunger, the former usually won out.

"Didn't need you to bother, Mister Farlow," Ivy said, frowning so deep she hoped he felt it deep in his thick skull. The bread was still warm as she wrapped it in a cloth and set it in her wicker basket. "I was conducting my own business and need none of your charity."

"It's not charity," Crisell said.

She understood what he meant. Especially since Crisell Farlow was one of the men her father had chased off their porch. Those who had wealth, enjoyed flaunting it, not that Ivy would understand living in the squalor of her father's home. Crisell was bidding on her like how he might purchase a sow for breeding. Ivy held out the silver penny her father gave her, the last bit of coin in and around the house.

"Here's a portion in return," Ivy said, though it hurt to part with it. She thought of all the things she might buy, like sweets or maybe a skin for water. *I'm not on the auction block for anyone in this town.*

Crisell didn't take the penny, so she set in where the bread had left a moist ring on the wood.

"I will pay you back with interest when my uncle returns from Euclid." She picked up the basket and tried to leave, but Crisell stepped in front of her.

"I can give you a ride back to your father's home," he said.

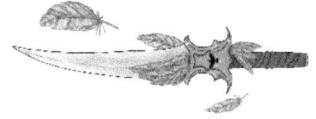

"You have done enough, thank you." Her father would want to see him as much as he desired a visit from the Sheriff or any other lawman, which meant Ivy would feel the brunt of the pain for binging Crisell or any man around. Bryn was rarely sober and hardly left the house. The only reason Ivy figured her father kept her around rather than marrying her off to some neighboring farmer was so she could fetch them food when they had coin to spare.

"But it's such a long walk and the sun is hot enough to cook an egg."

Ivy looked down at her worn clogs, the road dust covering her leggings turning them from black to brown. As appealing as riding in a wagon sounded, she didn't want to ride with Crisell Farlow or any other man. Word would get around of her rejecting Farlow's advances, lending more weight to the daughter-wife narrative poisoning the lips and ears of every man and woman in Welksdale, but she didn't want to start a new story where it ended with her as a wife to a pig farmer.

"I need to be alone, Mister Farlow," Ivy said, staring up at the almost handsome face, red-blotched and dry like weathered leather. Some simple farm girl might find him appealing, but Ivy didn't like what lurked beneath the charms. The lingering pig shit that no amount of spices could mask, or scented water could wash away. "Don't you ever want to be alone?"

"What for?" he asked, brow wrinkled in confusion like he hadn't a need to be alone a day in his life.

"To think," Ivy said.

"Think about what?" He moved in closer and she took a step back. She could feel Salinas Mathers watching her. He would tell his wife and daughters everything he'd witnessed here. Ivy Lyre rejecting a man's offer of help. Her father's daughter, and more.

"Think about how a woman doesn't need a man," Ivy said. "Because men in this town aren't worth the shit it's built on."

Crisell recoiled as though he'd been slapped.

Ivy stalked from the shop, basket swinging on her arm. People stopped to stare at her. Like they had nothing better to amuse themselves than a pissed off girl, trying to keep everyone from bothering her. Hard as she tried, it was another spectacular failure. The whispers began and she heard the same words accusing her of being strange, sullen, unlike her mother, and finally a daughter-wife.

Anger bubbled inside her and she needed to release it. To let the power churning in her gut out in song. Let her voice ring out across the village and tell them to mind their own fucking business! And they would, because like her mother, Ivy had a gift.

The fear of her father learning kept her silent. She was forbidden to sing. The hot tracks of her father's hand on her mouth, taste the blood on her tongue reminded her often.

"Ivy, wait!" Crisell clomped on the wooden walk.

Ivy kept walking. *Why is he following me? Why won't he go away?* She'd hoped if she ignored him long enough, he would. But hope was empty and often ached like her stomach when reality was a paltry meal. Crisell kept pace beside her, the pig-stink poorly masked by the lemongrass he chewed. He didn't try to touch her, at least.

"Why are you being so difficult?" Crisell asked, hands shoved into the pockets of his trousers.

"I thought I spoke plain enough," Ivy said.

"It's a ride in my wagon, not a marriage proposal."

Yet! Ivy stopped and held the basket out.

"Here. Take it."

"This is what I mean," Crisell said. "I make an offering in good faith…"

"I don't want it," Ivy said, nose turned up from Crisell. The stirring in her chest burned, aching for release. A snippet of her mother's song, one she swore never to sing, came to her lips. She sucked it back down. This was no place for tears. Not with the carrion birds circling around them. She placed the basket on the ground and continued to walk away, knowing full well her father would beat her for losing the penny and having no bread to show for it.

There has to be a better way.

Outside of helping her father gather the plants for his firewater and running errands, she had little skills. She could sing to charm the feathers off birds, but her father forbade her singing. Not long after her mother's death, she hummed a tune and a strange vision came on her about her father, face distorted in anguish while several tall figures loomed over him. Ivy had passed out and when she woke, Bryn was shaking her, forcing a promise from her never to sing again. "Lest I strangle it out of you."

The urge to sing was strong and she did her best to keep it tied down until she no longer felt the press of people watching, scrutinizing her every choice. It had passed, like momentary indigestion and she felt better, happier. Alone. Ivy was able to dream of a world beyond this cage. Where she could sing until her throat was dry and be carefree like her mother. Or the way she imagined her mother was before she met Bryn.

Ivy continued on past the single watchmen slouched on a stool at the southern gate. Simon smiled at her, hands resting on his belly considering her as much as he would a farmer leading a cow from market. Ivy liked that, not being the object of scorn or comment about the area between her breasts and thighs, like assessing the best part to eat on a chicken. Overhead in a small tower was a brass bell Simon, or whoever was on watch, would ring should there be any trouble. Ivy wasn't sure it was ever rung, because after the Welk's War, this middle-of-nowhere town was insignificant. Mostly it was a waystation where travelers paused on their way to big cities like Euclid which was a few days journey west.

"G'day, miss," Simon said and his eyes wandered from her face to her breasts and then her hips. Ivy rolled her eyes. He was older than her by twice the number of name days and had a few younger daughters at home. His wife was about Ivy's age and she shuddered at the idea of such a pasty pile of dough grunting atop her.

Maybe I should cluck and peck him. Ivy cleared her throat to catch his attention and tell him off. Simon whistled at her in a way that made Ivy shudder. Words dried up. She hated feeling like she was nothing more than meat for men. She hurried through the gates, close to tears. The events this day reminded her of the many reasons she despised men. At sixteen name days, she should've been married and a baby suckling on her teat.

The image sickened her. The whole Welksdale sickened her. Why couldn't they judge in silence and let her go about her life. Out on the road, the sun was naked in the sky, heating her skin, ready to bake her like an egg. She wouldn't make it home until after midday and her face and arms would be red.

When I tell Bryn there's no bread and no silver penny, he'll make other parts of me red, black, and blue. Part of her knew she deserved whatever beating he gave her. It was her responsibility to see they were fed for the few remaining days before her uncle returned with coin to buy actual food, and she had allowed her pride to get in the way.

"I want to disappear," she said and tried holding in a strangled whine. It came out anyway and she felt worse for it.

She hadn't walked more than a few yards when a wagon rattled behind her and she stepped in a pile of horse shit at the side of the road. The wagon stopped and she turned on the driver. "What? What more do you want?"

Crisell smiled and she shuddered. The man wouldn't leave well-enough alone. The urge to sing her frustration, dig deep into his soul and drag out his secrets and display them all for Welksdale, boiled in her gut. *Sing and I'll split your lip so your mouth flaps in two directions.* Again, her father's warning kept it bottled up.

"You forgot this," Crisell said and held out the weaved-wicker basket. Ivy glared at it, trying to figure out the entrapment. Crisell seemed to read her mind, setting the basket on the bench and sliding back from it. "No strings attached. I promise."

Ivy snatched it like grabbing a bone in front of a resting dog, and backed away.

"Now will you leave me alone?"

"Enjoy your walk home," he said and tipped his hat to her. Then he loosened the reins on the draw horse and rolled on past.

Ivy breathed a sigh of relief. At least one thing was going her way and maybe she wouldn't have to hide from her father when she got home. Maybe he wouldn't be lost in his drink and they could eat a meal in peace.

The weaved-wicker creaked, arched-handle nestled in the crook of her arm and a white cloth draped over the warm bread; the taste of melted butter was in her mouth. The hot sun stared mercilessly down, soured her tongue, and brought on a great thirst. She wished the water skins didn't leak, forcing her to leave them at home. She wished the grasslands had more homes, ones with a well she might draw water from. She wished she had a penny more to buy a sweet tea from the store in town—two leagues were far too long to walk on such a sweltering day, and silly her, denying the ride from Salinas. She wished she'd learned how to bake bread from her mother before she had died. One thing Ivy learned about wishes was that no matter how many she made; they left her thirsty.

Dark clouds teased rain, bunched on the edges of the western sky. The hot breeze on her sweaty neck told her the clouds would not bring her comfort anytime soon. Rain would only make her trip to the bakery a wasted one—soggy bread molded too fast. The drought continued to dry up the land, leaving only a few of the toughest plants to grow. Those were a sickly yellow color.

Ivy shifted the basket, its handle leaving a red blemish on her arm, itchy and stinging. The wicker chaffed in her hand, but it was her burden to carry. The bread had to last the two of them until the week's end when her uncle would return from Euclid city. He took a load of Bryn's firewater to sell to a tavern and they should have enough coin to, as her father put it, "buy a giant, golden pot to piss in."

Ivy would settle for new shoes, ones without the soles worn through, and some sweets. Dust covered her scuffed clogs and the hem of her skirt. Dirt clung to her pores. She shuffled along, thinking of the cool stream behind her house to plunge her sweat-slimy toes and aching heels. Smooth stones lined the edge for her to skip along the surface, two hops, maybe three. Anything to keep from her father's sight.

She had other chores to complete. Soured milk to churn into butter, scrub the stills so they could fire them up and prepare the next batch of firewater. They were also running low on mint and fireweed. It would be another long day with very little time to loiter. Then the rains might be here. She could almost hear the thunder.

Except it wasn't thunder. The clouds were too far away. Ivy looked over her shoulder in time to see several horses bearing down on her. She froze, the wicker basket falling from her hands. The riders split, horses rushed by close enough for Ivy to smell their musk, view their powerful muscles moving beneath the brown flesh and the leg of the rider, a black boot pointed out, close enough to kick her.

"Get out of the road, dumb bitch." An angry, disembodied voice growled at her. Dust wrapped around her, and she squeezed her eyes closed, sneezing.

When she opened them again, the riders were gone.

So was her basket.

"Oh shit!"

Ivy searched the road and, after the dust settled, found the wicker basket several paces up the road. She ran to it, hoping her day wouldn't get worse, setting her back to being both a penny short and breadless.

"Creator, no!" Ivy squatted by the squashed basket. She picked up the pieces of the bread, moaning at the grit mashed into it. Her father was going to kill her. She started to cry. They had nothing left to eat. Nothing to sell, either. Except for her. She'd rather starve than become the property of any man, their mass crushing her into non-existence.

"I hate men." She sat at the side of the road, plucking off as much grit from the intact pieces as she could, tears wetting her cheeks. Wrapping the remains in the cloth, she abandoned the broken basket and stomped on home, fantasizing about meeting the bastards who nearly ran her down. She'd demand they pay for the bread, or steal their saddle bags when they weren't watching. They'd have coin, or maybe food stashed away. More than likely she'd never see them again, and even if she did, she wouldn't recognize them. It happened too fast and she didn't see their faces in the dust and horse legs about to trample her.

Dumb bitch! That voice she wouldn't forget.

Temper heated, sweaty hair hanging in her face, she arrived home and was surprised to find four horses in her yard. The front door was wide open. Loud voices shouted from within.

"You had three moons," the same voice who had called her a bitch shouted in her home. "Three! That's three more than you deserve, Bryn."

Ivy took off her clogs and approached on tippy-toes. The nearest horse, a large gray one swung its head in her direction and gave a warning whinny, upper lip pulled back to reveal teeth that could bite her face off. Stealing the saddlebags was out of the question, not if she didn't want to get stomped on worse than her bread.

"It's coming," her father said. The usual hard edge in his voice softened. "I swear on my wife's grave."

Ivy shivered. Bryn never backed down. Not when Sheriff Gareth accused him of holding out on taxes, which he was, and trading contraband, which he did. No proof was found to put her father in debtors' prison, since he buried the coin behind the privy, close enough to the shit that no one who could smell would nose around. That coin was long gone spent, it never lasted when her father got an idea on how to, as he put it, "rise like a turd in sweetwater." Listening to Bryn's pleas was like hearing the first stones grind under her heel before her feet gave way and she'd tumbled down a steep hill. She was tied to him and when he fell, she would go down as well.

"You'll be joining her soon enough," Bitch Man said, following it up with the sound of breaking wood. At least she hoped it was wood.

"Listen," Bryn pleaded. She imagined him down on his knees, an unfamiliar position for him, unless he was digging up the coin from ground. "A few days. My brother's bringing back a huge payment. You'll get your cut then."

There was silence and then someone grunted.

"Double," Bitch Man said. "Or next time we take our cut of flesh."

Boots clomped to the door and Ivy froze. Four men stepped out on the porch. The lead was shorter than the other three, clean-shaved and almost pale, black hair tapered on the sides and ending in a rat's tail. The others wore various stages of beards the color of mud, ranging from stubble to full on fur, and they had similar features looking like a bear fucked a warthog. They were frightening in their size and ugliness.

"What do we have here?" Bitch Man said and grinned, revealing a gap tooth wider than her finger. He leapt off the top step and landed with as much grace as shit falling from a horse's ass. Stubble Beard laughed and he shot a look over his shoulder, silencing the bigger man. Ivy took a step back, waving away the dust. Bitch Man circled around her, tugging at her skirt and tried to flip it up. "Never knew Bryn had himself a lovely… lass. Might be we use you as collateral."

"Keep your sticky hands off me." Ivy grabbed her skirt and held it down, dirt from her clogs marking it up.

"Or just use her," Stubble Beard said and thrust his hips. "She looks like a fun ride."

The other two laughed and Ivy flushed red.

"Not now," Bitch Man said, "we wouldn't want to damage the goods. Decreases the value. She's worth a copper penny or two, unless she's unbroken. You unbroken, girl?"

"Fuck off," Ivy said, her lips trembling. The song floated under the surface of fear and disgust. She sounded small. She hated sounding small. Her entire life was spent curling around the will of others and being forced into their shadows.

"Sounds like an invitation, Stephone," Fuzzy Beard said.

"Mouth like that, she's probably been broken in," Bitch Man, or Stephone as he was named, said and licked his lips in a way to turn Ivy's stomach. "I would love to teach you a thing or two more for your trade, but it breaks my heart to tell you, me and the boys got other places to be. Business and then pleasure. That's how it goes in this game, but we'll be back later and then we can discuss both."

Stephone whistled and twirled his fingers. He winked at Ivy before mounting his horse. The other three leered at her, moving past, and Stubble Beard pinched her bottom, and laughed when she jumped out of his reach.

"Be seeing you around, lass," Stephone said and spun his horse around.

Ivy wanted to melt away. Run out behind the house and follow the stream to wherever it ended. Her legs trembled and she took a step. Then a voice rooted her to the ground.

"Ivy! Is that you out there?"

Her throat went dry and for a moment she couldn't respond. Then she took a breath.

"Yes, Da," Ivy said, surprised at how even her voice was compared to the rest of her.

Bryn filled the doorway, hunched over. His red-rimmed eyes wanted to consume her, and his arm pressed against his gut.

"Hurry your ass in, girl. We need to talk."

When Ivy's mother, Veena, was alive, the house was warm, bright, windows cast open allowing in light and sweet scents of lilac and blood-heart blossoms. Vibrant colors flowed through the small rooms, fresh flowers cut from the fields, stacked in plain, glass-vases. Birds sang, the wind sang, she sang, music filling their lives, and life was beautiful. That's how Ivy chose to remember it, though the memory was shiny around the edges from polishing away the tarnish of screams, slamming doors, breaking glass and shuddering cries. The vivid colors were black and blues and purples encircling red welts. The scent of old piss, fresh piss, acrid sweat dripping from drunk, feverous skin, scrubbed clean with lye and lies whispered in the middle of the day, night, or whenever her father was in in his fussy huff.

Fussy huff. That was what Veena had called it when Bryn drank too much and began smashing, yelling, and hitting anything in his path. A cute name, a way to soften the blows of a man caught up in rage like a flash storm full of thunder and lightning anger, striking whatever had the misfortune to draw his attention. Veena would send Ivy out of the house, saying, "Your father is in his fussy huff, go play in the fields," while she bore the brunt of the anger. Ivy would return to a house in shambles. Veena bent over in silence, cleaning up broken glass, wood, pride, and dabbing blood and snot from under her nose.

Ivy loathed Bryn.

After all, it was his fault Veena was dead, though Ivy never spoke those words aloud. Not if she didn't want him to wring her neck like a squawking goose.

Ivy dreamt of running away, stowing under the canvass tarp in the cart while Uncle Tym road into the city. Euclid was a big place, or so her Uncle Tym described as "a maze of wealth and depravity". If you got coin, you ate and had a place to live, but if you were poor, you begged in the streets. Ivy was very poor and possessed no trade of value. She couldn't cook, sew, or even clean well enough to keep a house for a wealthy merchant. She had nothing to sell except for what was between her legs, and she wasn't about to sink that low. Better the shadow she knew in this small, cruel town. Besides, she could sense Bryn's fussy huffs, like smelling rain before the first drops fell, and would usually disappear out into the fields. Unless he pinned her in place, a bug squirming beneath the bird of prey's talons. Like how he perched by the doorway, glaring at her as though it were her fault those rogues were about to cut him up. Walking away would result in far worse consequences for Ivy.

Bryn went back inside and the unspoken expectation was for her to follow.

Ivy did, back straight, chin high. A little dignity before he beat it out of her.

The foyer that served as a dining area and sitting room had the trappings of a fussy huff interrupted. A chair was up-ended, the splintered end of a wooden leg lying beside it. The table was askew, clear liquid spilled on the yellow-stained top. Cupboards were opened, dishes dropped onto the counters, and broken glass glittered on the floor. Worse was the lingering stench. Sweat and piss and fear. Bryn shoved the table back in the center of the room and dragged over a chair, creaking under his weight as he dropped into it.

After a moment of silently staring through her, as though she were a ghost haunting his thoughts, he spoke.

"You heard." A statement not a question. No way to lie, not that she could lie to him. He scrutinized everything she said and did, the way he examined the stills for impurities before distilling his firewater. Those were the only things he paid much attention to because he was full of both impurities and firewater. Ivy nodded anyway. He ran a hand over his face, smearing blood from a cut over his left eye down his cheek. "That's the situation we're in."

"Who were they?" Ivy held her clogs tight against her skirts and the crumbled bread in the other hand.

"Some assholes from a shithole." Bryn winced as he shifted in his chair, arm pressed tighter against his gut. "Or maybe it's the other way around. Doesn't really fucking matter. They think they can steal from us, the greedy bastards. I'm going to tell you, girl, they don't know a thing about us Lyres. We ain't a bunch of pushovers. When your uncle returns, we'll handle them."

"How much do you owe?" Coins. It always came down to coins. They were constantly cut by the rough edges of coins.

"A pittance," Bryn said and his eye twitched as it did when he understated what he owed others and embellished on what others owed him. Little meant too much and any hope Ivy had of not going another moon without being hungry sank into the floor—rooted to the room's rotten floorboards. The bread, dust speckled and grit filled, was too heavy and it fell, laying in a crumbled heap between her and Bryn. His eyes narrowed on the crushed bread.

"What did you do?" Bryn didn't have to stand to make her feel small.

"I didn't—"

"I give you a simple task." The chair fell behind him and Bryn stood, holding his gut like he wanted to vomit or shit his pants, both were not unreasonable. "Buy bread and bring bread home. And you bring me this…."

Bryn stepped on the crumbled bread. He stood taller than Ivy by a head, but seemed to take up the entire room, leaving her no space for her to breathe. The hand came down quickly, slapping her cheek and Ivy's head jerked with it. She stepped back, clogs thumping on the floor. Her ears rang from the blow.

"Useless spew! Why did your mother curse me with such an emptied-headed beast!" The hand wacked her other cheek and warmth spread across her aching jaw. Ivy dropped to the floor and covered her head. Hot tears stung almost as much as Bryn's abuse.

"Those men did it!" Ivy shouted between gasping cries. "They almost ran me down and crushed the bread."

She waited for another blow, but instead Bryn stood there, frowning while he turned over her words and searched for the lie in them.

"Nazglum nut sucking sons-of-whores." Bryn turned away and lurched across the room. He spun, the fury of the fussy huff storming on his face, only it wasn't aimed at her. "They almost ran you down! While you were walking home on the side of the path?"

Ivy nodded, wiping snot from her nose, a red streak marked the back of her hand. She may not have been at the side of the path, but she wasn't in the middle. Leaving out the small detail would be enough for Bryn, especially since he was already in a fussy huff over the assholes from shithole.

"Did they touch you?" His voice dropped and when Ivy didn't respond immediately, it boomed. "Did they touch you!"

"Yes."

"Where?"

Ivy pointed at her bottom where Stubble Beard pinched her.

"Fuck'em," Bryn said. "They ain't seeing a single penny for molesting my child."

He continued out of the room, leaving Ivy sniffling on the floor.

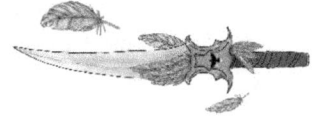

Ivy straightened up the room as best she could, sweeping the broken debris and tossing the chair out to be made into kindling—they were down to three intact chairs, not that they ever had company besides Uncle Tym. Her father's snores told her he was sleeping off the fussy huff, which he usually did, waking up in a sullen mood and expecting food to be ready. The problem this time was there wouldn't be any. He'd crushed what little bit of food Ivy had salvaged.

Not a penny remained to purchase anything else. Her stomach grumbled and she opened every cupboard door. They were all empty except for spiderwebs and she hadn't gotten to the level of hunger where spiders were appealing.

I'd rather eat dust than have them wiggling in my throat. Ivy grabbed a rag and stuffed it in her shirt. She needed to clean the dried blood off her face. After catching her reflection in a glass, her face had swelled and turned a dark purple, almost black. Uncle Tym would see it and maybe question his brother. That was a fantasy Ivy held onto more than once, but again, she would be disappointed. More than likely Uncle Tym would furrow his brow, make a joke about being careful not to run into things, and return to the business of firewater.

When did I become my Mother? Her bottom lip trembled at the horrible idea. She wouldn't make the same mistake and be driven from her home, no. She'd rather die at Bryn's hands than be another victim raped and murdered at the side of the road.

The sun was still hot, the yellowed-grass sharp on the soles of her bare feet. Ivy made her way to the stream beyond the back of their property. Her father used to farm and make a good living, enough to keep her mother and herself fed, clothed, and satisfied—well, as satisfied as a girl living in an abusive household could be. Then the drought came and the land refused to yield anything more than crabgrass and other nasty weeds. None of the edible kind. Bryn gradually sold off the livestock and his tools, leaving him with only the stills. No matter how hot it grew, people still had a thirst for their firewater.

It was illegal for her father to make the foul drink, but city folk didn't mind where it came from. As long as he didn't try peddling it in Welksdale, no one paid him much mind.

Thin, twisted trees lined the bank of what used to be a wide stream. She'd skip across it on four good sized stones, when she was younger, balancing on her toes to keep from falling in and soaking the hem of her shirts. Seasons of drought thinned out the water so she could hop over it in a single leap. Ivy waded-in to water up to her ankles and dipped the rag. She dabbed her face, wincing at the pain, removing the worst of the blood. She spotted a berry bush and plucked the black fruit, heedless of the thin thorns catching her sleeve. They were tart, but nothing tasted sweeter than they did, teasing her empty belly. There weren't more than a few handfuls, but Ivy had a pang of guilt over not leaving any for her father. The painful twinge on her cheek helped her get over the guilt.

His fault we are poor and starving, reduced to scrounging old berries. Lazy old bastard should get a job in town. Shovel shit from the stables or maybe even work for Farrow. Bryn would get along with the pigs, since they were close enough kin.

The image of her father slopping through mud and shoveling out stalls brought a smile to her face, though it hurt to do so. Not far up the stream, she found another, smaller bush and gathered some more berries, tying them up in a wet rag. She splashed along back to the house. She placed the rag, open on the table so it would dry and not get the berries moldy, and listened to her father's snores. He'd never notice if she disappeared. Not until he was hungry and she wasn't around to run to the town store or pull together scraps from the cupboards.

Ivy went to her small room, sat on her straw-stuffed mattress, and opened the lid to her trunk. It contained the few pieces of clothing she owned, much of which was faded and thread worn. Beneath them was a false drawer. Ivy opened it and took out a locket on a copper chain. She unclasped it and there inside was a painting of Ivy her mother made when she was four name days old. It was her only gift of value and her mother had always worn it. On the day she was murdered, her killers stripped her body, leaving behind the necklace as the singular identifying feature for Veena. It held no monetary value, so why would anyone take it? It was the only thing of value for Veena that she carried with her when she escaped the abusive home. Her killers left her by the side of the road where animals had gnawed flesh to the bone. She was bloated and beyond any distinguishing marks, except for the necklace.

The murderers were never found and since Veena was on the road to Euclid, Bryn wasn't a suspect, although it was his cruel words and heavy fists that drove her out of the house. Ivy wondered what life may have been like with Veena still alive. The rumors about Ivy being her father's bed warmer would not exist, that was a fact. What else might have changed? Mother kept track of the money much better than Bryn. They never went without food and Uncle Tym would visit rarely since she hated the firewater trade he had going with Bryn in Euclid city.

"Nothing but thieves and scoundrels drink that poison," her mother once said.

"I guess you're hitched to both," Bryn replied, holding up his glass of clear liquid. It had a cinnamon-scent to it and clover.

"What's a scoundrel?" Ivy, then nine and playing with a cornhusk doll asked, oblivious to the tension.

"Not a nice person," her mother replied.

"Shut your face woman and quit poisoning my daughter against me." Bryn had that wicked thunder in his voice, like he was ready to begin storming.

"I wasn't," Veena said.

"You were, always are." Byrn stood up, swaying on his feet. "It gets so's a man can't make an extra coin so's his family has nice things. You like nice things, eh, Ivy?"

"Yes, da."

"Well, you mother here don't think we should have nice things." Bryn slammed the glass down on the table, causing Ivy to jump. "Says they come from scoundrels. Not nice men, like me."

"But you're nice, da."

"Hear that," Bryn said to her mother. "She thinks I'm nice."

"A father's voice is the be-all to babes," Venna replied and Ivy sensed she was being sassy with Bryn. Bryn never liked a sassy woman.

"What'd you say, woman." His fingers flexed in and out of fists.

"Ivy, go play in the fields."

Ivy slid from the table and was walking to the door, when her father's voice halted her.

"No, Ivy. Stay here. Your mother needs a lesson in manners and respect." Bryn loomed over her and Ivy saw the fear in her mother's eyes. "If she don't learn from me, she won't learn from no one."

That was the first time Ivy witnessed Bryn lay hands on Veena, but not the last. Sometimes she played in the fields and others he had her watch the "lesson." Veena tried to remain strong, though she broke under his thundering force and fists, whimpering and bleeding and covered in darkening red welts. Ivy wasn't allowed to cry or make a sound, otherwise he'd lift her skirts and smack her bottom after he was done with Veena.

Ivy shook herself from the unpleasant memory. It was getting hard to think of anything good that happened in her life, like sweet milk that had soured and turned her stomach. She lay on her mattress wondering how much the copper chain might be worth.

Might not buy a single piece of bread and butter. She kissed the locket and looped it over her head and let it slip onto her chest. *It's worth the world to me.*

CHAPTER FOUR:
TROUBLED TIMES

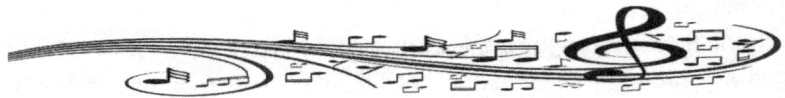

When events spiraled closer to plunging into the cold dark waters of oblivion, I was there. When the fires of war were nothing more than dry tinder, I was the spark to ignite the fire, the wind to stoke the flames. Since surrendering my being to the Dark Lord, there has never been a troubled times that I hadn't been the one to instigate.

"What if Uncle Tym doesn't return?" Ivy asked the next morning. Typically, she avoided asking Bryn questions since his response usually was incoherent at best, or a threat at the worst. Her stomach rumbled and ached, putting her in a foul mood where she didn't mind "poking the sleeping bear" as her mother would put it. The gritty bread was gone and so were the berries. She was reduced to drinking water and daydreaming about pastries while her ribs poked through her sides.

"Huh?" Bryn muttered from the straw mattress he placed in the corner of the room. Easier to pass out on than walking the five feet to his actual room. "My brother always comes back. *Always.*"

"Say that he gets arrested or thieves attack him on the road, steal all his coin." She skirted close to saying, killing him and leaving his body stripped by the roadside, but that would be a poke too hard and might put the bear into a fussy huff. She really didn't have the energy to flee the house or put up with her father's harsh punishment. "What would we do?"

Bryn grunted, considering his response. What he said didn't surprise her.

"Sell you," Bryn said and rubbed his eyes. "Get a few coins for me to eat on for the entire moon when we try again with the firewater."

"No one would buy me," Ivy said, wearing disgust like a thread-bare sheet, patched by distrust and doubt. Her father preached her worthlessness so often she had believed it and marveled at why men would look in her direction at all. Then again, they would stare at a skinned hog hanging in the market, mouth salivating at the red flesh, stinking and fly infested.

"Maybe not all of you," Bryn said. "They would pay for an hour's time.

You got things a man wants. Even that pig-fucker, Farlow, desires a woman occasionally. It would be a way for you to earn your keep."

"I earn my keep more than you," she said under her breath.

"Speak up, child," Bryn said, voice becoming low. "You have something to say to me, say it loud, not like some whimpering bitch's welp."

Ivy regretted speaking, especially since his words were needles digging into her, and she drowned out his words by humming. The regret turned into a vibrant sadness, one which spread like tendrils of smoke, wrapping around a thought, not her thought, but one hanging like a moth-eaten cloak in the room. The thought rang true in the way any emotion was true. Fleeing from her the moment she touched it, though a solid picture formed. Vibrant blue against a black backdrop, an image of her mother holding flowers and laughing like she had no care in the world. So very young and beautiful, a love burning the way one might hold the sun, distant and yet warm on the skin. The very image of her should glow bright enough to blind her, but it remained black and blue. "I love you, Bryn. I refuse to die for you." Her mother's voice. "I'm never coming back. Never—"

"Enough!" Bryn's voice boomed and she cringed, the back of her head smarting. Ivy's ribs smashed against the edge of the cabinet and she grabbed hold of it to keep from falling over. "Told you never to sing. Don't you listen!"

"I wasn't—"

Hands gripped her shoulders and spun her around. Bryn's brown, blood-shot eyes, wide and bright with fury, ate her up. Smelling of fermented yeast and rot, his breath was hot on her face. Yellowed-teethed bared behind dry, split lips.

"Told your mother the same thing." Bryn shook her. "She didn't listen, neither. Can't stand the sound of your screeches, tearing me inside out. Trying to get into my head. You don't know me. You never will." He turned her again to the cabinet, forcing her to bend over. "You want a lesson. I'll give you one you'll never forget." A heavy hand struck her bottom and Ivy bit her lip to keep from crying out. "One you will not forget." Three more *whacks*, each fiercer than the last sent a flash of pain and humiliation through her.

"Get the fuck out of my sight, you useless gnat!"

Ivy stumbled from the house and fell in the yard, tears forcing their way from her hot eyes. She gasped wet breath, staring at her father in the doorframe. He spat on the porch and slammed the door. Ivy crawled along the dirt. Hair tumbled in her face, clinging to her damp cheeks. He hadn't beat her like that since she was ten and snatched a copper penny to buy a sweet in town. He whopped her so hard that when her mother finally intervened, he unleashed a series of blows on her. The next day Veena was gone.

The guilt rose up in Ivy again. *Shouldn't have provoked him. He can't control himself.* Words her mother used to say while pressing a cold cloth to her swelling eye.

"I can't..." But she knew she would stay. At least until her uncle returned with coin. She stared at the dirt road, the heat dried cracks and a warm breeze swirling the grains around. If she left, she would die like her mother, but if she stayed, things would get worse for her. "I won't let it happen."

Ivy dragged herself from the dirt, the stinging in her bottom sharp and she limped down the path to the stream. The sun had risen, a cloudless hot stare, the air heavy, sweltering. Biters swarmed the water of the stream. They'd feast on her, drawn by the sweat, their needles piercing her and leaving red welts that itched and bleed when she scratched. Ivy stripped off her leggings and stood barefoot in the ankle-deep water. Again, she wished it could wash her away, carrying her to a place different from here. Instead, she sat down on a smooth stone, the coolness soothing her warm bottom.

She spent the day hunting for anything to eat, picking sweet grass to chew, to take the edge off her hunger. More dried fruit, like desiccated corpses, covered the thorny bushes. She kept to the shade over the stream, waving at the gnats and blow flies humming around her ears and eyes. The minor annoyance was nothing compared to spending the day indoors with her father. She found some sweet mint and cinnamon bark, plucking enough to carry back home. The midday slipped away and she watched the fields where a rather gaunt deer nibbled the yellowed grass. Its ears twitched and big brown eyes stared at her.

I don't mean you any harm.

Ivy sang, her voice trembling on the verge of tears. The deer tilted its head, legs braced to run.

If I could switch places with you, I would. Let me run free.

Then the predators would hunt her. There was nowhere safe. She ended her song and the deer bound away, white tail flashing at her as it disappeared.

The moon rose on the edges of night when Ivy returned to the house. She tip-toed up the porch and opened the door. Bryn would be asleep, she hoped. Not a single light glowed in the house. Fading twilight revealed the chairs and table. A warm breeze blew through the window. Edges of parchment flapped, held in place by a coin. A silver penny.

"That asshole," Ivy said and lifted the coin. The parchment had words scribbled on it. She took it to the window and deciphered the words. *Moor bred. Dont fuc up.* Ivy crumpled the note and let it drop. He'd said the penny he gave her this morning was the last. *And I'm a fool for believing him.* Where there was one penny, there might be more. She would take the fat baker's advice and look under her father's pillow tomorrow.

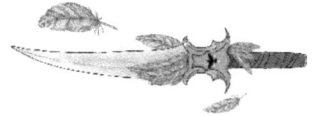

Ivy waited for Bryn to make his morning visit to the outhouse before entering his room. He'd be gone for a short time, enough for her to search around his coin stash. Dust covered the curtains, enough to make her wonder if he had drawn them since her mother left. The room smelled musty and was warm, a single bed occupied the corner and a chest of drawers was across from it, also covered in a layer of dust. Ivy went to the bed first, pinching the sweat and drool-stained pillow in her fingers and lifting it enough to slid her hand beneath. Something sharp pricked her finger. She yanked her hand back and saw the bead of blood. Ivy hissed and sucked on it. She picked the pillow up again a saw the knife with a handle bound in leather. Beside it was a red stain. A single spot. It looked fresh, fallen from her finger.

"Damn it." She looked around the room for anything to scrub the blood off. Cold water and salt worked best—this she learned from experience. There wasn't even a bucket of water in the house and Bryn would notice his sheet soaking, since he never washed them.

The door knob rattled.

Ivy looked up from the red, incriminating spot. If he saw it, or when, because it was large, almost a thumb print pressed into the sheet signaling that she had been there snooping around, he would probably break her fingers or possibly her arm.

She hustled from the room, standing by the counter and pretending to watch out the window. When Bryn walked in, her heart was pounding. He would know. How could he not know? She wore the guilt like a fresh bruise on her face.

Blurry-eyed, Bryn looked at her. His brow knit together.

"Thought you'd be half-way to Welksdale." He scratched his arm and stretched. "You got my note and coin."

"It's not enough," Ivy said, focusing her thoughts on the cost of bread. The anger at the single silver coin Bryn reserved was enough to layer over her guilt. Better to fashion a cloak from thorns than to let them see you naked.

"What do you mean, not enough?" His lips pinched together. "It was enough for the last one you rolled in the dirt."

Ivy thought about mentioning Crisell Farlow providing the extra copper pennies. That would be taking a big stick and whacking the bear square on the nose. Not something Ivy needed at the moment. *It's small. He won't notice the blood. Might even think it was his own.* She closed her eyes, forcing the worries into the background so she could think. Then she blurted the first words to dace off her tongue.

"Mathers took the rest on credit."

"Did he?"

"Said it wasn't his fault the drought drove up the price of flour," Ivy said, mixing in enough truth to make it believable. "I told him next time I come for bread that I would make up the difference."

Why are you withholding coin? Letting us go hungry? These questions wouldn't get what she wanted, which was the coin. She sucked on her lower lip, waiting to see how Bryn would respond.

"Miller Brown's a cheatin Gaenite," Byn said. "His goddess failed him so now he's taking it out on us hard workin, Creator's children. Alright, I got a few more copper pennies, then we are dry. You hear me? All gone. No more for rainy day funds, not a bloody cloud left in the sky."

"Yes, da," Ivy said. "I'll make it last."

"Your uncle should be rollin and rattlin in any day now." Bryn moved past her and into the room. Ivy held her breath, praying he didn't see the blood. "Unless he got caught up with some woman."

Bryn went silent and Ivy waited for him to talk about his brother whoring, wasting good coin and making him angry having to wait. There was no more talk.

Creator bless me, he's seen my blood! He'll come out and demand to see my hands. Ivy tucked her injured finger in the hem of her skirt. The slice burned and it was still bleeding. He'd accuse her of trying to steal from him. The worst part about it was he wouldn't be wrong, and she'd suffer for it. The memory of the hand smacking her the previous day stung and Ivy began backing to the door. *I won't let him hit or humiliate me again.*

Bryn came from the bedroom, fists closed.

"What's crawled across your grave?" He asked.

Ivy's mouth opened and closed. The song clawed at her throat, scratching away to be released. Bryn wouldn't hurt her again. The song would see to it. Do what her mother was unable to do.

"Don't worry," Bryn said. "Uncle Tym won't disappoint. I was only teasing about selling you." He opened his hand and six copper pennies were neatly piled against his palm. "Get us some sweet milk while you're there and a new water skin. Don't want you dying of thirst before you get back."

He gave her a smile; one she was used to seeing as a child before the drink stole him away. It was the flower pressed into her hand as a reminder that she was a beauty yet to bloom. The cornhusk doll purchased from the store when Ivy was ill. "Happiness helps you heal," he'd said.

For a moment she could almost forgive him.

"Thank you," Ivy said and took the pennies.

Bryn stroked her hair and bruised cheek with the back of his hand.

"You're beautiful, like your mother," he said, voice catching in his throat. Then he turned away and slunk to his room.

The heat was worse this midday than any day in Ivy's recent memories. She would wilt were she not already dragging, worn clogs scrapping the hard dirt. The wide-brimmed hat shaded her face, though it didn't do much for the rest of her. Her dress, lightest she owned, was an annoying weight and clung to her sweaty skin, chaffing her under the arms and other tender places. Also, her feet ached. She imagined them as swollen waterskins about to burst at the seams. Callouses on her toes seemed to grow like ant hills and burned all the same as if she stuck her winkies, as her mother used to call them, into their nest. Ivy was never more grateful than when she entered Welksdale. Even Simon's lascivious gaze, taking her measurements around the form clinging dress, couldn't spoil her mood. The fool was in the tower above her, grinning down as his eyes tried to seek deeper into her cleavage.

"How's Lavinia, Simon? Heard she started her moon's blood." Ivy grinned, brimming with satisfaction when Simon mouth rounded in a stupefied gawp.

"Wouldn't know a thing about it," Simon said and turned his attention to the bell. Taking out a rag, he polished the brass surface. "That's a mother's duty."

The sharp emphasis on *mother* brought a sting to Ivy's heart. She touched her mother's necklace she wore, a kind of talisman to having a better visit this time. When Venna would come to town, Ivy had tagged along. Being so young, Ivy never noticed how awful the people were. In fact, they were polite to Veena, full of smiles and hat-tipping. Occasionally they would offer her a bouquet of flowers and Ivy would get a sweet from the general store. Young men and women would beg her to sing and she did, until Bryn caught word and forbade her to sing in public. After her mother's death, everything changed and the town became full of sneers and whispered gossip about Bryn.

"It's a father's duty to keep his woman-folk happy," Ivy said, and Simon polished the bell harder until it gave a dull jingle. "I don't think yours would like to know how your eyes wander where your hands can't."

"Save your sass for your own father," Simon said, waving the rag at her. "I'll none of your tongue here, so keep it silent else I'll toss you over my knee and give you what you got coming."

"Touch me and I'll snap your fingers."

The rag quit waving, flopping over his fist, and Simon gawped at her again. Ivy didn't raise her voice, but kept a sincere smile. She didn't think she could hurt Simon beyond a few scratches, though she wasn't going to let him know.

"Get on with you, girl," Simon said and mumbled *Nazglum's whore* while he turned his back on her.

"Good day to you, Simon," she said adding more sweetness in her voice, enough to gag a bee, as her mother would say. Satisfied by his grumbling and shoulder shrug, Ivy continued on her way.

The road into town was empty. She couldn't blame anyone not wanting to be out in the hot sun. Though, she could sense eyes following her from windows. Curtains swayed and figures seemed to blur in the haze whenever she glanced in their direction. *Let them stare*, she moved from the road to the wooden walk under shop awnings, *not my fault they live miserable, boring lives that I'm the most interesting thing in it*. She wondered how they might react to her should she begin singing like her mother once did. Would they treat her better? She knew she could force them to treat her better.

Was that how mother got them to like her? Did she manipulate them through her song?

It felt wrong, but then it was no different than when Maddy gave out freshly baked cookies to the townsfolk who voted her husband Sean Tailor as Lumin Mayor and Speaker for Welksdale. His opponent Salinas Mathers closed up shop for a full night and day, refusing to sell bread to those who took Maddy's cookies in exchange for the votes, calling it bribery.

"He was just angry Maddy's cookies taste better than his sweetbread," Bryn said, after he was shown the door. "He'll come around once folk realize they don't always have to chew their bread, but can drink it." That's when he bought a keg of bitter-ale and drank a few loaves by Ivy's count, maybe more since she didn't know how much bread was in a mug.

Ivy made her first stop at the Trading Post, a glorified name for a general shop that sold items from hemp twine to candies and secondhand boots. A grey-haired woman, Ms. Water, whose head barely reached above the countertop watched her like a pigeon spotting a crow around her nest. Ivy picked up a reed basket, blue kerchief, and water-bladder from various shelves. Ms. Waters gave her a yellow-toothed smile and "How are you, dear?" after Ivy pulled the copper pennies wrapped in linen from a pocket sewn inside her dress.

"Will be better when the heat breaks," Ivy said, repeating what she had heard others say.

"Won't we all. Creator bless us." She kissed her knuckles and pressed them to her forehead.

The heat struck her again once she left the Trading Post and she forgot what it was to be cool. Her throat was dry and the next place she visited was the town well. It stood at the center of Welksdale. A rounded stone wall covered by a steel grate to keep critters from falling in and dying, poisoning the water with their decomposing corpses. Ivy tugged the grate away, setting it on the ground. She peered in and saw deep, dark emptiness. Her heart sank at the idea that the well was dry. It wouldn't be the first, and many a farmer lost their livelihoods because the springs shifted and they had to follow it to start over again. Ivy dropped a pebble, watching the darkness swallow it. A hollow *kersploosh* echoed back up.

"Sounds kind of low."

Ivy screeched, the sound amplified by the stone and jumped, nearly teetering into the well.

"Woah, miss." A strong hand caught her arm and steadied her. "You don't want to go swimming in there."

"You scared m—" Her voice dried up and her temper cooled. The man holding her arm wasn't someone she recognized. He was older than her, but not by much, maybe a season or two, and had nice eyes that looked into hers, holding concern rather than taking the momentary distraction to stare down her cleavage.

"If you are thirsty, I could get you water from the bucket." He smiled and she smiled back, nodding her head. Words stuck to the roof of her mouth. "Step back and I'll get you some."

Ivy watched him adjust the old wooden bucket hanging at the end of a rope, testing to make sure the pulley still worked. "Right as rain, which I hope we get soon." He turned the winch, his hand larger than wooden handle. The bucket slowly disappeared down the stone gullet. It seemed to take forever, and she listened to the wood scrapping against stone and squeak of the pulley. Muscles bulged and shifted rhythmically beneath his tunic. The mud-stained boots and his sun-darkened skin spoke of him being a farmer, though he didn't smell like one. No pig or cow shit stench. Not that he wore perfume, either, but had a light musk that smelled of hard work and dried grass. He noticed her staring and stopped turning the winch.

"Want to give it a try?"

"Sure," Ivy said, her cheeks turning red. She had done this dozens of times, but he made it seem so effortless. The crank wanted to slip from her sweat-slick hands, crashing the bucket into the water, and he caught her elbow, to stabilize it. Then he backed away, motioning for her to continue. She held the handle tight, knuckles white and arms straining. The bucket continued on its path, until there was a familiar *plunk!* The bucket, weighed by rocks, sank into the water.

"It feels so low," she said.

"The drought," he said and took the handle from her and reversed the motion. The rope re-coiled on the pulley and the bucket came up faster for him than she could make it. He took her water bladder and filled it for her. Ivy drank from it, the water cool, and tasting of minerals. Sweetest pull of water she had in a long while.

"Good?" He tipped the bucket, filling his own water bladder.

"Yes," Ivy said. She wanted to say more. Ask his name, but he adjusted the wire grating over the well, tipped his hat to her and disappeared up the street before her tongue loosened from the roof of her mouth. The encounter was strange, refreshing, and a bit frightening. Any other man in town would ignore her, or offer help in exchange for more from Ivy—she would tell those fuckers to sit on a stool leg and spin around like a sundial. Even if the words weren't stuck in her craw, she'd would like to have asked him his name and where he was from. He wasn't from town, not with his good manners.

Da would have chased him away like all the rest. Except, she might want to follow him. Find out where he lived and maybe stop in for a visit. It would be nice to have a place to escape to in case—

She shook her head. *Quit being a dumb bunny, you don't know anything about him. He could be worse than the Fugly Brothers*—a name she had associated with them since they were fucking ugly, that she doubted their mother could even love them. It didn't matter, because she missed his name and chances were, she wouldn't see him again, especially if this were the first she saw of him. He might live on one of the outlying farms far away from Welksdale. A loner who came to town for what supplies he couldn't stitch or grow.

"Get a hold of yourself, girl," she said, slipping the water bladder into her basket. "It'd been another disappointment."

Creator knew she had her fill of those.

Salinas Mathers glared at her when she entered the bakery. Streaks of white flour shone on his sweaty forehead and swiped at them, leaving behind trails like warpaint. The shop was warm, filled with a comfortable scent of yeast and fresh bread. Too bad Mather's sour face ruined the homeliness, though, he was closer to matching her father's angry stare than he'd imagine.

Ivy marched up to the counter and laid out the coins.

"I trust the price of bread hadn't increased more than this in the last few days."

"Surprisingly, no," he said and gave her a knowing smile. "Found some coin, after-all?"

He was reaching for the bread at the middle of the rack, when Ivy cleared her throat, drawing his irate attention.

"Top rack," Ivy said and added another copper. "A bottle of sweet milk, please."

Mathers stared at the coin and grunted.

"Must be nice to be able to splurge. How'd you come across the small windfall?"

"None of your concern." Telling him her father had squirreled away coin would add to his jests about finding it under his pillow, which she was certain was where he'd kept it, and possibly more. "Celebrating the return of my uncle from Euclid."

Most everyone knew about Bryn's and Tym's firewater trade, which was why the Sherriff showed up to collect his taxes. When Uncle Tym came back from the city, folks turned awful nice, that was until the coin dried up like a stream sinking through cracks in the sand. Then it was back to being a bug that shat on their meal. Lying wasn't something she enjoyed. Tym would be back soon, if he wasn't already at the house while she sweated on the road to town, and she was tired of fighting for decency. Didn't matter it was a mummer's dance, a day without struggle would be worth a moonful of prayers.

"Have him come on by once he's settled," Mathers said. "Tell him the Missus will whip up some sweet rolls, just the way he likes."

The smile he gave her was as genuine as a silver slug, looked real enough but was worthless. Ivy wrapped the bread up tightly, seeming to consider Mathers' response. She'd never deliver the message to her uncle, whether he returned or not. Mathers went in back and returned with a glass bottle of sweet milk. Ivy twisted the cork off and sniffed its content to make certain it didn't turn rancid, before stuffing the cork back in. Mathers raised his eyebrow, a signal if she was satisfied with the contents.

"He'll be by soon enough, I warrant," Ivy said and tucked the sweet milk beside the bread. It'd be warm by the time she got home, but a quick dip in the stream would cool it enough.

"Good to know. Safe travels home, little miss," Mathers said, leaning on the counter. "I heard an unpleasant pack of rouges have been riding up and down causing trouble for the good folk who travel from here. Sheriff has his men out, but they haven't caught up to the ruffians. Might be best you had an escort."

The Fuggly brothers, causing trouble so close to town? Maybe Bryn speaks the truth about them. If they touch me, he'll never pay them.

"Thank you for your concerns, Mister Mathers, but I'll be just fine." Ivy touched the necklace.

"Don't go ending up like your mother." He sounded sincere enough, much like an apology would after she kicked him in the groin would be "sincere." Mathers smiled, challenging her to say something so he could continue his petty rudeness. A turd tossed into the sweet cake that was their business banter.

The song rose up in Ivy's throat like bile. Despite her father's warnings, she took in a breath of air and was about to release it when the door opened. Kally Smither walked in, wearing a simple smock that bulged at the middle. She gave Ivy a curious glance, then turned her nose up, and went to the counter.

"I'll make certain to tell Uncle Tym of our exchange," Ivy said and left the shop before he could reply.

Her good mood dissolved like dropping a cube of sugar into water, or in this case, a mud puddle. The water skin sloshed against her left hip and the basket swung in her arm, hard enough where she could bludgeon the next person who annoyed her. Her chest hurt where the song sat, demanding her to release it from its cage and delve the fat baker, force him, groveling to his knees or make him choke on a loaf of bread. *Wild imagination*, her mother always said. She'd sing, but it would do no better than annoy Mathers. He'd probably laugh at her and tell her to beg somewhere else.

Ivy passed a cobbler store and stopped. Sitting in a display window were a pair of boots, Ivy's feet ached staring at them. Her toes curled up like worms shriveling on a hot rock. The boots looked so soft her feet would melt into them. Walking a hundred leagues in them and it would be no worse than walking one. Her blisters would apologize before leaving the soles of her feet.

She pressed her face closer to the glass, and gasped. Reflected there were four horses moving up the road. Stephone and his band of Fugglies rode up to a hitching post and dismounted. They hadn't got any prettier since last they visited her home. Ivy didn't dare move, pretending to admire the boots. Her breath fogged the glass, coming in heavy, hot bursts. She remembered fingers pinching her bottom, slimy eyes sliding over her, toads eyeing a tasty insect, tongues wagging nasty thoughts best unsaid outside a bed chamber.

Don't move and maybe they won't see you.

That plan went the way of shit in a drawer full of other shitty ideas. Stubble beard pointed in her direction and mentioned something about a sweet ass to Fur Face. His voice carried across the road as he intended. Subtle as a hammer ringing on an anvil. All four Fugglies leered in her direction. Stubble thrust his hips back and forth, earning a few chuckles. Ivy realized she was bent over way too far. She straightened slowly, acting as though she hadn't noticed them. The cobbler's shop front door was a couple steps away. She could easily walk inside and ask about the boots she would never be able to afford. Out-of-sight, out-of-mind. Then she'd hurry on home, maybe find someone with a wagon willing to lend her a kindness.

Kindness was something lacking from her life, and seemed all dried up.

"Where you going?" Stubble shouted and she saw him crossing the road. "Hey, I'm talking to you. What's your name, beautiful?"

Ivy pushed open the door and searched for the owner, hoping there might be someone bigger than the Fugglies outside. Her stomach dropped. There was a single man, the Cobbler, Lethe Cobble, sitting on a stool and squinting at a shoe he turned over in his hand. He was small, smaller than her. A thick needle and thread held between his lips. He took the needle out, tongue wetting the edges of his mouth.

"Can I help you?" Lethe squinted at her; fluffy tufts of gray hair swirled around his head.

No! She wanted to scream her. Stubble beard would break this man in half before he could do—what? Stick him with the needle?

"I'm… looking for a pair of shoes." She heard the heavy sound of boots stomp on the wooden boardwalk outside the shop.

"You've come to the right place." Lethe stared down at her clogs and frowned. He looked back up at the basket and sniffed the air. "I only trade in coin, I'm afraid."

You haven't been afraid, not yet, but maybe you will.

"How much are those in the window?" Ivy asked and jumped as the door opened. She didn't have to turn around to know Stubble beard was behind her. She could smell him, a concoction of horse sweat and horse shit.

Lethe clucked his tongue and shook his head.

"More than you can afford, Miss Lyre."

"Lyre!"

Ivy squeezed her eyes shut. The worst possible thing Lethe could say in that moment, he said.

"Thought I recognized that beautiful ass," Stubble beard said and moved in closer. "Fingers have been itching to knead that dough."

"Sir, I'm going to have to ask you to leave." Lethe stood from his stool, but he was half a head shorter than Ivy and thinner than a hitching post. She'd seen crawling lizards, more dangerous than him, hiss and spit at a hawk before it was snapped up in its beak.

"Mind the shoes, ol'man, or more than them need stitchin'," Stubble Beard said, very pleasant for a man making a threat. Almost tender.

To his credit, Lethe didn't back down.

"Unless you plan on purchasing, commissioning, or otherwise looking for your boots to be repaired, then back out on the street!" Lethe waved his needle at Stubble Beard. Then he said something else that made Ivy bristle. "That goes double, and I know you are lacking funds, Miss Lyre, so on your way."

"But—"

"On your way," Lethe said, making shooing gestures. "Don't make me involve the Sheriff."

You should involve the Sheriff! These men are dangerous!

Lethe would no more listen to reason than discount his hard work.

Ivy wanted to snatch the needle and put it through the withered old man's eye, give him a closer look so he didn't have to squint so much. He was shoving her out with someone who intended her harm. Whatever happened to her, he was complicit, and Ivy would never forget.

"You heard the old fella," Stubble Beard said, placing a hand on Ivy's shoulder. "Let's talk outside."

"We have nothing to say," Ivy said, shrugging his hand off. She hurried to the door and shut it before Stubble Beard could follow her. Weighed down by the basket and water bladder, she had one opportunity to escape. She dropped the basket, but it didn't hit the ground. Instead, Stephone caught it while Stubble Beard stepped in front of her, blocking any chance she had of running.

"What have we here?" Stephone asked, rummaging through the basket. "Bread and sweet milk. Seems like the nice fixings for a picnic. Only thing missing is the meats."

"My father will have whatever money he owes you," Ivy said, snatching the basket back from Stephone. "But, if you lay another finger on me, he won't pay you a single copper, do you understand?"

Stephone grinned at her. The kind of smile that made her skin crawl because it went only as far as the corner of his mouth. His eyes and posture told a different story. One of getting what he wants, no matter the violent outcome. The boards squeaked behind her as Stubble Beard exited the Cobbler shop. His hands returned to her shoulders, guiding her further away from the store. Ivy stiffened, but was compelled by his strength. She glanced around for anyone to help. The streets were empty, except for the five of them.

"You come along, quiet like, and there won't be any need for paying debts," Stephone said. "Won't it feel nice, helping daddy pay off what he owes?"

"It'll feels *real* nice," Stubble Beard said and the other Fugglies laughed.

"Shut the fuck up." Stephone punched Stubble Beard in the arm, causing him to lose his grip on Ivy. "Don't want to terrify our lovely accomplice any more than she already is."

"What do you want me to do?" Ivy thought she knew what they wanted, but the term accomplice didn't fit the frightening narrative in her head. She'd tear their throats out before she willing give in to what they wanted.

In her fearful state of mind, she forgot all about the song.

"Come along and you'll see," Stephone said.

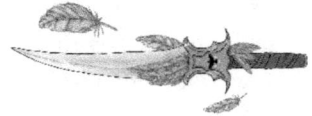

"You want me to do what?"

The five of them huddled on the boardwalk a few paces away from the Welksdale Exchequer, where the good Sheriff deposited the taxes he collected, before the Duchy came to collect and then the King's collector took the royal share from Duke Carval. At least, that was what her father used to complain about. Ivy knew very little about how the coins passed hands and things were paid for in the Kingdom. What she did know was that she didn't have enough coin for a comfortable pair of boots.

"Go in and distract the guard," Stephone said.

"But, there's two," Ivy said.

"Then distract both."

"All you got to do is pretend you dropped something and bend over. Waggle that ass a bit and all eyes will be on you." Stubble Beard moved his hips from side to side, looking like he was trying to shake off a turd rather than being sexy.

"Jeph," Stephone pointed at Stubble Beard, and swung his finger to Furry Face, "and Harry, here, will make sure they can't draw their weapons and make the place messy. You can pretend to be held up as well so they don't suspect you."

Ivy rolled her eyes.

"It's a stupid plan," she said.

"How?"

"Lethe saw Stub, I mean Jeph, come in the store and he threw us both out," Ivy said. "I don't mind what you do in town, but they'll know, or suspect, which is as good as knowing for them, that I was involved. Then they'll send the Sherriff and I'll be the one sitting in the prison cell waiting for them to convict and then hang me."

"Or you could come with us," Harry said.

"We only got four horses," Jeph said. "Be better we smack her around some and then tie her up, she'll get a better excuse, no matter what they think."

"Smart thinking." Stephone patted Jeph's shoulder.

Ivy held up a hand. "Wait a moment. I don't like that part of the plan any better than the first. Why do you have to include me in it at all. Seems like I'm more of a hinderance to your long-term goals."

"Thank your father," Stephone said. "He owes us more than he'll be able to pay. Especially with the interest."

"I'm not interested."

"Not like you got much of a choice."

There's plenty of choices. Ivy frowned. All she wanted to do was to take her bread basket and water bladder and go home. She'd never thought her father would be a better choice of a companion, ever! They outnumbered her four to one and they were too close for her to do anything, not even run. Besides, they had hold of her basket.

"Fine," Ivy said. "We'll try it your way."

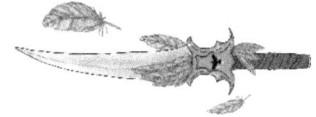

Her palms were sweaty, slick enough to leave a wet mark on the pouch the Fuggly Brothers had gave her. A few coins jangled inside it, nothing much, two coppers—her cut of the job, though they'd probably steal it from her after they tied her up. No bruising they'd agreed on, but she wasn't sure she could trust the word of thieves. She squeezed the edge of her dress to dry her hands, but it didn't help much. They continued to pump out water and her heart was the crank.

This is what a fly feels like when caught in a web…if they had hands. They might have tiny hands. I never took the time to study. Do they sweat? I guess it doesn't matter when you are going to be eaten by a spider. Gross, eating a sweaty fly.

She scrubbed her palm on her leg. It was beginning to itch. *Good luck coming your way,* or something like that was what Bryn would say anytime his palm itched. She'd thought it was bed bugs and how could being bitten be lucky? The basket and water bladder were stowed away by the horses. Bryn would be worried about her, well, about the bread and sweet milk. He'd be angry at her for coming home with warm milk. If she made it home. She'd welcome his hard fists to this moment of uncertainty. Bruises healed, but dead was dead.

Focus! She bit her lip. *You have a task.*

Drop the pouch, bend over, waggle her ass, and get the guards' attention. What if they weren't interested in women? Well, that would be the Fugglies' problem.

The Exchequer was a small place, lacking the typical box windows, which would make an easy target to break into the place. Light shone through four rectangular slots over high up from the floor. If someone somehow reached them, broke the thick-paned glass, they would be able to stick an arm or leg through, nowhere near the door. Adding extra light to the place were four sconces, making the room hotter than it should be, and gave off a burnt wax odor.

Two guards, large men dressed in the Kings color of dark blue, to remind the people of Welksdale who they worked for, stood by the door. Both were relatively young, had short swords on their hips and armored in chain mail. They wore identical bored expressions. Ivy recognized one as Ghelian—he often accompanied the Sheriff when he tried to intimidate Bryn for taxes, not that Bryn was ever intimidated enough to pay. "Can't get blood from a turnup," he'd say. "But you can keep digging."

Ghelian's eyebrow raised at seeing her. *Great! Another witness to my crime!* She smiled, hoping it didn't appear too fake. She tapped a nervous finger on the pouch. The Fugglies gave her a count of twenty to get the distraction before they moved in. "Swinging more than our dicks," Jeph had said, "Make sure you duck if you don't want to lose your head."

She had used up five already.

"Can I help you?" Maurice Coppersmith asked. Welksdale appointed titheman, or royal thief, as Bryn would call him, frowned, stared at her, quill held over his ledger open. Black ink spots stained his well-manicured fingers.

"I…" Ivy stopped tapping the pouch. Six, seven, eight, each beat a thudding in her ear. She breathed, took a step, just enough to give them a good view of her backside, a step away from the violence about to happen. A step closer to being an accomplice in the robbery. "Urm…"

"Spit it out, child, I have work to do." Coppersmith waggled his quill.

Ivy swallowed. Fifteen, sixteen, seventeen. She tossed the pouch onto the floor, a rather obvious action, one that should incite suspicion in a person trained to spot suspicious behavior. No one said anything and Ivy rolled her eyes. Rather than bend over to pick it up, she turned, catching Ghelian's eye.

"You are about to be robbed," Ivy said.

They reached for their swords an instant before the door opened. Stephone, Jeph, and Harry froze, gawping at the guards. Knives gripped in their hands, swords in the guards, they were outmatched.

Stephone's surprise turned into a deep growl.

"We've been betrayed."

Maurice screeched, ducking behind his desk. Jeph and Harry threw their daggers at Ghelian and the other guard. The blades clattered off chainmail, sliding harmlessly across the floor. One spun on the wooden floor boards in front of Ivy. She reached to pick it up, but Ghelian stepped back and kicked the handle. Ivy squealed, sidestepping Jeph's sword which bounced off of Ghelian's bracer. Jeph coughed, the air rushing from him when Ghelian punched him in the gut, not once, but twice, elbowing Jeph at the base of his neck. Jeph dropped like an old sack of potatoes.

"This is for pinching my ass." Ivy kicked his jaw, knocking his teeth together. Her toes crunched in her clog, but the pain was worth the satisfaction of hearing Jeph howl.

Ivy rushed for the gap in the fighting. She slammed into another large body, which replaced Jeph. Stephone swung a wooden club, and Ivy lunged past him, taking a boot to her ribs. She cursed and rolled over. It was no worse than the beatings her father had given her. She saw the guard whose name she didn't know bend over, blood coughing from his lips. A look of surprise and pain on his face, which turned white, while he slowly sank to his knees.

Someone tugged her hair hard and her head jerked back. The last Fuggly stared at her. Clean shaven mouth twisted in either lust or anger, like he was about to bite into a roasted pig flank. He held a knife over her face.

"Squeal, little piglet," he said, spittle spraying her face.

Ivy didn't give him the satisfaction. If he was going to cut her throat, she'd die with some dignity.

"Fuck you," she said and formed her fingers into claws. She racked her nails across his cheek, missing his eye. Her head slammed into the floor, and for a moment her vision was filled with white stars across a vast black tapestry.

"You'll pay double for that," he said and lowered his knife, the sharp edge nicking her chin. "Going to slice open your cheeks and stick my co—"

A meaty thump knocked the Fuggly over. Standing over him, arm cocked and jamming forward into his face was Crisell Farlow. His fist slammed into the Fuggly's face two more times and then he offered his hand to Ivy. His knuckles were scrapped and bloody, but there was nothing more welcoming to her in the moment.

"Come on, let's go," he said.

Fuggly moaned, but didn't make an attempt to get up. Ivy took Farlow's hand and he pulled her up. He placed an arm around her waist and guided her off the boardwalk. "I have my cart over here."

"Wait!" Ivy broke free and went to the post where the horses were tied up.

"We don't have time," Farlow said, glancing back over his shoulder.

"Take these to your cart," she handed him her basket and water bladder. "I'll be there in a moment."

The horses eyed her warily. Ivy untied three of them, avoiding nipping teeth, before Stephone stumbled out of the Exchequer. He wiped something from his forehead, either sweat or blood and pointed at her.

"Get away from our horses, you betraying bitch!"

"Go on, move," she made shooing gesture at them, but they bobbed their heads and made annoyed snorts at her, staying in place. She thought by freeing the horses they'd naturally flee from such cruel, ugly masters. They wouldn't budge. "Fine, but don't say I never gave you a chance."

People began to empty out of the various stores, gawking at the commotion. No one intervened, but they watched, soaking up the scene to gossip about later. Ivy rushed past them, as they watched her in wonder, stepping out of her way.

"Come on, Ivy!" Farlow was seated on the bench of his cart, hand on the break lever.

Ivy ran, her side aching as she tore in breath and hopped onto the cart. Farlow caught her hand, yanking her into the seat. Then he threw the lever down and snapped the reins to get the cart horses moving. Not far behind, Stephone stood by his horse, shaking his fist at her.

"I'm coming for you, bitch!" Stephone made a rude gesture with his hand. "I'm going to fuck your corpse!"

Ivy sank back onto the bench. The cart jumbled along quickly to the edge of town. Simon sat in his chair, oblivious to the action down the street. He narrowed his eyes and leaned forward when the cart stopped in front of him.

"Why aren't you ringing the bell?" Farlow pointed at the brass bell, sunlight gleaming off its polished surface.

"It's for warning of trouble." Simon said, folding his arms.

"Don't you see what's going on?" Ivy wanted to grab Simon by his fat face and twist his head so his eyes weren't on her breasts, but on the trouble down the street.

"No," Simon said. "Did Lizza Waters faint again?"

"The Exchequer is being robbed!" Farlow gripped the reins, knuckles white to keep from whipping this town idiot.

Ivy glanced over her shoulder, expecting to see a cloud of dust, the tell-tale sign the Fugglies were after them. They weren't, but there were a lot of people on the streets. A scream rose up, and Simon jumped from his chair, squinting his eyes at the action.

"Ring the damn bell!" Farlow growled out the words.

For once Simon did something other than scratch himself or run a rag over the bell. He grabbed the rope and grunted, tugging on it with all his weight. The bell chimed and the horses shied from it. Ivy clung to the bench to keep from being tossed off. Farlow gave them the lead and they were off, away from the screams, shouts, and fighting.

After they had cleared the town and Ivy was sure they weren't being followed, she relaxed and sat up on the bench. Her hands began to shake, realization of how close she came to having her throat slit. Mathers would have choked on his drool if she had died the same way as her mother, probably think himself a prophet when it was just her shitty luck. *And shitty men.*

She looked over at Crisell Farlow. He was intent on watching the road and paid her no attention. *At least there's one man who isn't shitty.*

"Want me to take you home?"

I'm coming for you! I'm going to fuck your corpse! The threat rang in her head. The Fugglies knew where she lived. Ivy shivered despite the heat. She couldn't go home, not if the Fugglies somehow escaped Welksdale. They'd come after her, but where else could she go? What would they do to her father? It was his fault they even knew anything about her. His stupidity that nearly got her murdered.

"No," Ivy said. She wanted to add, *fuck him*, but she figured her tone was enough. "Can I stay at your place, for at least the night?"

Farlow stiffened; the horses slowed as the reins tightened. Ivy wanted to laugh at his surprise, but swallowed it down, covering her mouth. She didn't want to embarrass him and be set out on the road.

"Do you think that is... wise?" He turned his head and the pained expression on his face was comical. "People will talk."

"People always say stupid shit. You hear the stories about my mother, father...*me*," Ivy said. "Blessed Creator, they have other stories to blather on about after what happened at the Exchequer. Unless you want to take me all the way to Euclid to find my uncle, I have nowhere else to go."

"Alright, but answer one question first."

"Go on, ask it."

"What were you doing there? I don't think your father paid a single coin in taxes for at least two harvests."

"I was minding my own business when those assholes corned me at Lethe's place," Ivy said. "They threatened me, laying out two choices: help them create a distraction, or they would kill me, leaving my body on the boardwalk plain as day."

The last part she made up, but the intentions were there, if left unspoken.

"I promise you," Farlow said, putting a hand on her arm. "I'll never let them hurt you."

Ivy pulled her arm away and Farlow frowned. A spike of fear went through her. He'd put her out now and she'd have to walk home. Or they'd catch on the road. Like those other men caught her mother.

"Sorry," Ivy said. "They hurt me and—" Tears prickled in her throat. She hated them, but they served their purpose.

"No, no worries." He turned forward. "I understand."

They road in silence the rest of the way to Farlow's pig farm.

CHAPTER FIVE:
FIRE AND WATER

The world will burn. Fire is necessary. The seeds of renewal will not open break free from their tomb unless the seals are destroyed. From the ashes rises the Tree of Shadows, its fruits the sorrow of those who refuse to bend their knee to the Dark Lord. Yet, the Songs of Singers wet the soil and extinguish the fires. It is their Song we must burn out.

"The rains have stopped," Claiborne said, standing in the vestibule of the shadow cast dining room. She took too big a gulp of air and coughed into her hand. The smell of death had yet to clear out despite the cool breeze wafting in the window. Fresh shit and urine odor—marks of the newly deceased—were confined to these walls, and blood streaked the floor where the last occupants, a head shorter, were dragged out the back door and laid flat by the outhouse. Claiborne passed them on her way up to the house. Flies had discovered the bounty and were happily consuming their meals. Man, wife, and child, murdered in their home because they happened to be in the wrong place at the wrong moment when the Silent Men required a temporary base of operation. In a way, everything was temporary no matter the operation. Claiborne didn't agree with the method, but she wasn't one to argue the results. Dead was dead and there was no bringing them back. *Can't unspill the milk back into the cup,* her mother would say. In this case, can't unspill the blood or sew the heads back on. It wasn't by her sword or her orders.

Those belonged to the man gazing out the window. Cacophony, commander of the Silent Men, and not anyone to fuck with, since he was easily pushed to violence. After what he'd experienced, the lone survivor of the Green Valley flooding which killed over twenty thousand soldiers and was renamed Silent Lake, well, Claiborne figured he had come by it naturally. Or unnaturally as the way those women twisted the ground and manipulated the sky to rain and rain and rain. Cacophony's black cloak split like a pair of wings, the seam revealing his chitin-like armor beneath, twitched in the breeze. At his hip was a large blade, nearly as tall as Claiborne. She'd seen him wield it like it was no more than a wooden stick, striking with such brutal force, nearly cleaving men in half. Probably used it to end this family with no more care than stepping on an ant hill.

Claiborne chewed the side of her cheek, waiting for a response. Arms crossed, her middle-finger and thumb tapped together the way an irritated wasp might twitch its wings before it struck out.

A child's song drifted from one of the dark corners, singing about rain and death mixed up in a language she couldn't understand. Her eyes drifted. *Don't look!* Claiborne dropped her chin, staring at the dark red stain on the floor. He hated it when anyone so much as glanced at the girl. The last person to do so had his eye plucked out. "You want to stare! There, get a good look!" he then tossed the bloody orb in the girl's direction. No one dared watch, but the song stopped, replaced by a suckling noise.

A fly buzzed, lapping at the blood. At least something benefitted from death.

"Yes," Cacophony said and cleared his throat. He almost sounded sad and she wondered if his response was to her statement or a conversation he was imagining. "Yes, it has stopped. I do have eyes, First Sword, and ears. No more pitter-patter on our heads or the roof." Cacophony took a deep, rattling breath. "The air smells fresh, clean, purified, the rain having washed away the battle gore. It's almost like I am walking in a field of newly bloomed posies."

Cacophony turned around and his black boots stepped into a red puddle, the fly buzzing angrily away, but not quick enough as Cacophony snatched it from the air. A small movement from his gauntleted-fingers and then he opened them, a small speck dropping to the floor. He took another step, leaving behind a minted bloody footprint.

"The parched soil drinks it up after such a long thirst." Another bloody boot print, closer to Claiborne. "Why even the old bones of this house soak in it, you can almost hear it sigh. Dry, dusty throat clearing to have one last say before the sun shrivels its lips cracked lips, silencing them. Our time in the sun is short and we all return to dust. Some much sooner than others."

He was a giant insect looming over her, his armor making him appear larger than the man inside. He was still a man, she told herself, no matter the horrors he committed. Otherwise, she was no longer a woman, but something just as terrible as Cacophony. A dung beetle whose only purpose in life was to eat shit.

Claiborne didn't flinch. She stared at the cracked window over his left shoulder. The girl giggled, a sound that was more terrifying than her song. Claiborne shivered, imaging how a skeleton grinned, showing its boney teeth, but not in mirth.

"Tell me, First Sword," Cacophony said, the segmented plates scraping together as he rested a hand near his sword, the Silent Prayer, he had named it. "Tell me something, anything, I need to know that I cannot see or smell or taste from this house. We all understand what it means when the rains stop. The child knows, even the goddamn horses know. Which brings me to the point of this conversation. Either you have brought me a corpse, or the damned women evaded you. Oh, I do hope you brought me a corpse, or two."

We have plenty of corpses. Not the one you or I want. She settled on a way to phrase the words that wouldn't end with her head rolling across the floor. When she opened her mouth to respond, the girl gave a high-pitched laugh like she was screeching with a bunch of children in the fields as they plucked wings from butterflies.

"They live!" The girl's laughter simmered into giggles and she twirled her doll around and squeezed her to her chest, then up to her ear, listening to a conversation only she was privy to. In a conspiratorial tone, she told them, "Glorian says they are close, but far away. So close, yet so far. Two little birdies huddling in their nest waiting for the storm to pass and then up they go again!" She tossed and caught her doll; Glorian, a fucking strange name for an ugly straw thing.

Claiborne's fingers pinched together, restraining her fists from punching the girl. It wouldn't be the first time she had punched a child, but she was certain it would be her last. Bad enough she sensed Cacophony's disappointment. Black muslin covered the lower half of Cacophony's face, hiding part of his expressions, leaving the bump of his nose visible. His eyes were enough to speak his thoughts. Dark brown and wet, they narrowed. Madness stormed in them with enough intensity to suck her in, a funnel cloud slurping up everything in its path, leaving behind a wake of ruin.

Claiborne had faced worse, and survived.

"We don't have the women, living or dead," Claiborne said, continuing her response like she had never been interrupted. She squared her shoulders and swallowed the lump in her throat. Better to stand firm in the storm and wait for it to pass than to slink away and drown under a rock. "But they didn't escape."

Cacophony leaned in, his breath smelling of onions. He ate them raw because they purified the blood. *Purify the blood, purify the soul.*

"Where are they?"

"Holed up in the city. Scouts say they set up position for defense behind the walls," Claiborne said and almost choked on her spit when Cacophony made a strangled noise that could be laughter and stepped back from her. "I have the men cutting trees and crafting ladders now. There are not enough guards to cover the length of the wall, but the soldiers who follow the women would bolster their numbers, making it impossible to breech by nightfall. We will cut off food supplies and poison their water source. Digging in for a siege would be the best course of action and it should be over before next snowfall. I also have both Sunrise and Sunset gates monitored, intercept parties are ready to detain them should they try to leave the city, then we can—"

Cacophony placed a cold, metal finger over her mouth to silence her. It was almost intimate, possibly even followed up by a kiss. She'd seen his level of warmth once and that was merciful enough. Rather than get angry, she remained quiet.

"Find me carts. At least a dozen," Cacophony said and removed his finger from her lips. "Cover them with hides and load them with pitch barrels. Soak the walls in it."

Claiborne hesitated to reply. He wanted to burn the city. A hasty response to the women taking sanctuary inside the walls. She glanced at the bloody prints on the floor. One looked to have been made by a small hand, fingers splayed and pressed in fear. As if they were forced to hands and knees.

"What about the citizens?"

Slaughter happened on both sides of the war. Mostly small towns and villages were put to the torch because they allowed safe passage to the women. An entire city, well, it was a first for Claiborne. A direct assault was dangerous and costly—it would prove easier to turn the citizens against their invaders, blame the women for the army at their doorstep. Cacophony's patience only lasted for so long. He wanted a quicker, more brutal approach, akin to burning the forest to kill a couple pests. The idea left behind a bitter taste.

Killing the women, one particular annoyance who always evaded her, would go a long way to sweetening her tongue.

"They have chosen to walk the Shadow path." He lifted a black gauntlet and flexed his fingers into a fist. "We shall show them the light, and it shall burn them."

The girl's song grew louder, and Claiborne heard snippets of *Burn, burn, burn the old men down*, sung at the sowing festivals to call an end to the Old Man Winter and spread his ashes on the field to bless the new growing season.

"Yes." Cacophony moved to the girl in the shadows. He knelt and the girl ran into his embrace. The light from the window shown on her face. Pale skin like porcelain, making her blue eyes glow like cold fires and she clutched the rag doll to her ear. "We will burn all of them down."

The girl smiled at Claiborne and an icy spike pricked her gut. She clenched her thighs to keep from adding to the mess on the floor. Claiborne snapped a salute and spun on her heel to leave.

"One more item, First Sword." Cacophony was on his feet, blocking the view to his daughter. "Have my carriage brought up. We have to be close to the walls to keep that damn woman from using the rain to put out the fires. Then we will have the little birdies trapped in their wooden cage."

Little lover! Oh, where is my life? My heart? Are you pouting again? Sparrow lifted her head, eyes blurry and looked around for the face she had grown to love. A face that was as warm and beautiful as the sun. Finch burned in her vision. The soft, sweet sound of her words, healing her. A bitter balm to curl Sparrow's tongue, dry and raspy against her teeth.

Don't be sad. I am here with you. Slender fingers touched her breast over her hair. *I live on as long as you remain alive.*

Sparrow went to touch the hand, but it was gone. Dissipated the way her tears might soak in the dry, cracked ground. No! No tears. She couldn't drown in sorrow. She was alive. No, kept alive. Chains rattled when she shifted her arms. They weren't very heavy, nor restrictive. They kept her from stretching her arms out, wrists clasped together. She was in a strange house with a strange odor. Like rotting meat. Flies buzzed around a broken window, glass twinkling in the hazy sunlight peeking through the clouds.

Let's see where they took me.

She tried to get to her feet, but the chains on her ankles wouldn't allow her stand or do more than hunch over. There had to be vine or root somewhere she could call on to assist her. She reached for her song and instantly regretted it. Her stomach cramped and bile crawled up her throat. The weight of the chains dragged her down hard enough, her teeth clicked together.

A door opened and a large man dressed in dark armor, almost like a bug's shell, filled the doorway. He stared at Sparrow over the veil covering his lower face. Sparrow recoiled from him.

"Our little birdie is awake," he said.

"I want to play with it," a young girl's voice said, and then the girl stepped around the man.

The one we saw in the road. Except...

Except, she was not a little girl, but more like one of those soulless creatures she and Finch encountered in Devon's Meadows. More terrifying, because those former residents were nearly mindless creatures, unlike this little girl. Her blue eyes glowed with a malicious mischievous light.

"Not this one, sweetie," the man said, and stroked the child-thing's head. "We have use for her, remember?"

The girl pouted. "Glorian says so."

"If Glorian speaks it, then it must be truth," the man said.

Who is Glorian? Sparrow didn't dare speak. Bad enough they watched her like cats planning out how they were going to make a meal of a single bird. They didn't kill her outright, like they had with other Singers, but that didn't mean they didn't have a worse treatment than what that did to Finch.

"Pretty birdie with clipped wings," the girl sang, *"try to fly and you die. A bird with no wings is no bird at all, but a song that is a scream, and death awaits unseen."*

Sparrow felt the song worm its way through her chest, trying to draw her own song. She constrained it before it overwhelmed her in sickening pain. It was a struggle, like wrestling a bear, or how she imagined that would be.

"Enough, child," the man said. "We don't wat her to suffer, yet."

The girl huffed, then ran off, trailing an eerie stream of giggles. The pressure in Sparrow's chest released. She took a breath and coughed.

"I apologize. My daughter can be a bit... eccentric." He didn't sound apologetic to Sparrow. "You must wonder why I haven't had you completely silenced?"

"It crossed my mind," Sparrow said.

"Sometimes I find one must enter the aura of evil to do a greater good, but

I have a vision," he said. "Perhaps we can strike a balance between you women and my soldiers of light. A kind of peaceful service that will re-establish the Balance, restore Harmony in your words. If you are not too far gone, that is."

"You're the ones bringing Discord," Sparrow said, finding strength in her anger. For all she knew, this bastard could have been the one to have Finch raped and torn apart. She sat up, chains rattling. "You're tearing a hole in our reality, ushering darkness in to fill our world!"

"All perspective," he said, unmoved any more than a child having a tantrum, which angered Sparrow more.

"I will never work with you." She mustered as much spittle from her dry mouth and sprayed a dribble at him.

"You have yet to hear my offer."

"I don't need to listen to the snake's hiss to know it will bite," Sparrow struggled to stand, to face this man and beckon death on her feet. *Let him kill me now, so I can be with you, love of my life.*

"Fair enough." He backed from the room. "Perhaps at a later time."

The door closed and Sparrow sank back against the wall. Tears rolled down her cheeks. *They won't drown me in sorrow. I will have my revenge or death take me.*

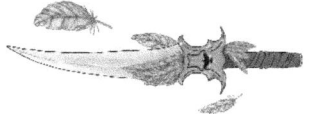

Tym woke up in a strange bed. Not a first for him, though he preferred waking up beside a warm body, soft and full of curves. He didn't even need to know her name—this made things easier when he slipped away from the city and returned to Welksdale. He wouldn't even mind a hangover, nothing a little loving couldn't cure.

A glance around the room told him he was in the Dripping Bucket. It had the familiar moldy straw smell and dark patches on the ceiling where the thatch had leaked, warping the wood over the ages. Stretching his stiff body, he discovered the rejections of even the simplest pleasures in life. It was more than a simple rejection, but an outright assault on his dignity and a reminder of how life was cruel for a single man trying to make his way in the world. When he moved his leg, an intense burning pain ignited in his right calf. He bit his lower lip and sucked back a loud curse.

Fucking sleeping on a bed of nettles! God damn city and its trash! Cheap ass tavern and fuck you Tailorson for abandoning my firewater. Probably all ruined, unless you took it, greedy bastard!

After gripping the mattress in sweaty hands, the pain began to fade, lost in the noise of his outrage. He tossed back the sheet, noticing the bandage wrapped around his lower leg from knee to ankle. Red blotches stained the top sheet covering the mattress, from the stiffness of the straw, it wasn't the first time blood marred the bed, but still, it was his blood now. *That'll cost extra.* Tailorson wasn't one to spend coin unnecessarily. He'd make Tym pay double for a new sheet.

Tym slipped on his vest and patted the left breast where he kept his small pouch of coins. It was flat, the pouch missing. *Son of a bitch stole it!* Unless he lost it in the flight for his life, which nearly cost him his leg, but a quick pat down of all his clothes told him it was gone no matter the thief. *Wonder how he'll take it when he finds out I have no coin. Might have fake outrage that he couldn't double dip me, thieving bastard!*

Coin was the least of his worries. He was still in Euclid. There was an army on their stoop. He could be stuck in the inn for days, maybe even moons during a siege. Tym had heard tails about men eating rats and sometimes their own children once the food ran out.

Or even unwanted guests. I bet he triples the price of rooms to gouge the last bit of coin before we shrivel up into corpses. Tym worked his way into a sitting position. One where his right leg dangled over the edge of the bed and his left stuck out, unable to bend due to the tight bandage and the firestick in his leg. Riding would be out of the question. He'd have to hobble his way out of the city. Give Tailorson the slip and find another way out of the damn city. Beginning to feel like a sticky web and Tym was the fly.

A bit of light shone in through the window. The storm had ended, at least. He wouldn't drown or die of lung rot.

Tym walked-hopped over to the door, trying to keep pressure from his right leg, without success. Each step was like a knife pricking his calf. Sweating and gritting his teeth, he leaned on the door frame, carefully opening it so he didn't lose his balance. Muffled voices came from down below, rising sharply in anger.

Someone is upset. Probably found rat hairs in the bread.

"Creator knows we don't want the bastard catching us with our breeches around our ankles," a woman said.

Another voice replied, softer, but stern.

"Seems we're past the ankle point."

"Our arses are hanging in the wind," replied the first woman.

Not about food, but a close second would be sex. Seemed an odd argument to have in the common rooms, especially since Tailorson's wife would be hanging around with their son. She'd glare a hole into the floor and sink them all to the dark below.

"Question is, what do we do next?"

Tym always had that question hanging around his neck. A pretty necklace that became a steel choker forcing him to do what he had to in order to survive. He shuffled to the banister and leaned over. Three women sat at the long table, surrounded by men in dark blue uniforms. One was short and plump, her hair mussed up and reddish-brown curls flopped around her wide shoulders. Another was much thinner, small, and had a sharp nose on such a small face. The third was younger, very pretty, though she waved a fan in a way to display her annoyance. The rest of them had the look of soldiers, battle hardened, the kind that had killed a man or two. Or a dozen.

Seems the army breeched the gates while I slept.

"I felt something stir." The sharp-nosed woman placed a hand over her heart and tilted her head, looking out one of the windows. "It was strong, stronger than anything I've felt in my lifetime."

The hesitation and awe he heard in her voice wished he could see what she was looking at. Everyone went silent, waiting for her to say more. Tym noticed then that the table was empty, except for mugs. From the view up here, the mugs had a yellow sheen to it. Not his firewater, then, but ale. Knowing Tailorson, the supposed good kind of ale meant to appease the invaders. More froth than barely. Looking at the harsh yellow reminded Tym he needed to piss. An occupying army inside and invading army at the gates of the city, it was any wonder he felt the need to do anything, except run. Run like a rabbit from the desert dog, snarling and nipping at its heels.

"Are you sure?" the plump woman asked, drumming her fingers on the table.

The urge to urinate occupied Tym's thoughts, wrestling with curiosity. He wanted to know what these women wanted, but at the same time he had to go back to his room or piss himself. *I'm sure they wouldn't appreciate being dribbled on.* Taking a step back, his leg stiffened and then buckled. *Fuck those thieves! I'm going to fall and then piss myself and it'll be their fault.* At the last instant he grabbed the banister.

"Without a doubt, it came from the east, a great shock rattled my bones before I was cut—"

The wood creaked.

Heads looked up. *Shit! They know I'm here.* He clenched his bladder tight.

Two men in dark blue uniforms began to ascend the stairs. No telling what they would do to him, and he really didn't want to know the answer. Tym hopped back to his door, the soldiers reaching the top of the stairs. He'd shut the door and leaned against it when they began pounding, demanding to be let in.

They were bigger than him, and even with two good legs he wouldn't hold out long. Tym scanned the room for anything to prop against the door. Every object was either too large to move or too small to serve his purpose. The only escape was a window. The way his leg burned, he had a better chance of falling and snapping his back than climbing down. The door bounced, sending a flash of pain through his leg and a trickle of urine stained his small clothes. Tym groaned, knowing he was going to be stuck in a mess of things real soon. Another hard thump nearly sent him to his knees. They would have the door open and find him weeping in a puddle of his own urine. Not the high point of this visit to Euclid.

"I'm opening it," Tym shouted, bracing for another strike. "But before I do, I want your word you will do no harm to me."

The thumping ceased and Tym strained to listen against the wood. Anything they said was lost to him.

"Your word," Tym repeated.

"By the blessed Creator you are safe from us," a soldier said.

The oath sounded sincere, but if the man worshipped Nazglum, it was an empty skin promising sweet wine. Not that Tym had any other option than to trust the man. They could splinter the wood and skewer him like a pig for roasting before he could squeal. Taking a few calming breaths, Tym lifted the latch and allowed the door to swing inward. Two soldiers waited, hands on hips, close to their sword hilts. They both appeared young, but their eyes told of an age beyond seasons. What they have suffered, Tym could never understand.

"So, are you going to kill me?" Tym asked. It was better to get the tough questions out of the way.

One soldier laughed.

"It's not us you have to worry about."

They went to grab him by the arms.

"Can I at least piss here before I piss myself there?"

The soldiers nodded and let Tym go about his business. He was grateful for this small relief. A minor win in everything he'd lost.

How low I've fallen when the highlight of my day is not pissing my trousers.

They helped him hobble down the stairs, taking their time rather than tossing him. Grant it, Tym was taking much longer than he normally would, playing up the injury. As he descended, Tym began to rethink his choices. Every one of them from the time he left home with cheap wax sealed bottles to the two women staring at him like he was an interesting worm they would like to peck apart.

Never stood a chance once I stepped foot into this damned city.

"Who are you and why were you spying?" The plump woman asked as way of introduction.

Tym stood before the long table, a guard on either side holding his arm to keep him from running off. Not that he would be running anywhere with the pain in his calf. The soldiers served more as someone to lean against, pillars more than actual guards, at least to Tym's imaginings. *A spy!* He almost laughed at the idea that he could be a spy. Sitting at the table, scrutinizing him like a tribunal were the three woman and another seven soldiers dressed in dark blue uniforms. The woman who asked him the question pressed her thick lips together like slabs of pink meat. Her cheeks were round and large brown eyes glared at him. Though she seemed small, filling up the chair with her pudgy frame, a bird with her feathers puffed up against the cold, she was frightening. Tym believed she could tear his balls off by reaching down his throat.

The pudgy woman raised her eyebrows, signaling she waited for his response, though lacking patience. It was a direct, easy question. One in which Tym could fabricate a believable lie. Believable lies held threads of truth and as long as he didn't try to weave a complicated picture, Tym would be fine. Besides, he wasn't a spy.

They must have really inept spies where they're from to be caught so easily.

"I'm a merchant," Tym said. "I'm here to make a profit. I heard the shouting and went to see what the fuss was about. There's an army approaching the city, you know. An army is bad for business. Well, most business."

He smiled his most charming smile, one that won over many a woman.

"Where are your goods?" the other woman asked beside her. She was thinner, sitting rigid in the chair, delicate fingers placed on the tabletop. She seemed frail where a sneeze would knock her over. Her sharp nose was turned up while she assessed him. Small, round eyes that were strikingly blue. Bird Beak, he decided he would call her, just not out loud.

"Lost them." A simple walk out the back door would tell if Tailorson took the bottles of firewater or left them in the cart. Tym figured the greedy bastard would have them lined under the bar, ready to pour. There were few patrons not in uniform in the common area. The presence of an occupying force was bad for business. Why they wanted to occupy Euclid was beyond his ability to reason.

"You have blood on your leg," Bird Beak said, an accusation.

"A cut." Tym cringed at how foolish it sounded, but better to state the obvious. Giving away too much information would make it worse on him. Especially since talking about the thieves' door wouldn't help prove his innocence. Who else but thieves and spies would use such an entrance and exit?

"From what?" Bird Beak pressed.

Tym swallowed, trying to think of a logical explanation beyond the sword blade. He could blame his horse, or maybe how he was robbed. Before Tym could respond, Tailorson pushed through the doors from the kitchen, carrying a tray of steaming vegetables and broth. Behind him came his wife, a scowl on her face.

"Damn fool fell on my stoop, leg bleeding everywhere. I had to mop the floors twice and they still got a stain that won't come out unless we tear up the Creator-damned wood. This wood is expensive. Comes from the Welken woods, which no longer stands because the loggers accidently burned it all down. Now the wood costs a lordly sum. Lordly sons-of-bitches, and this bastard bleed all over."

Not really a choice. Tym grinned, happy to have the distraction.

"Don't know how you'll ever pay it off," Tailorson added. He set down his tray in front of the women and his wife placed hers, holding golden ale. Not the firewater, Tym noted, which meant the wagon could still be outside, unloaded.

"Wait until you see the bed," Tym said. "I think you'll have to add it to my tab."

"Mayhap," Tailorson said. "Or mayhap it's all prepaid by a generous donation."

Bastard got the firewater! Tym tensed to strike the innkeeper, demanding his fair price, but the soldiers tightened their grip on his arms.

"What do you know of the Silent Men?" the plump woman asked, grabbing a mug of ale and sniffed it. She took a sip, grimaced, and set the mug down.

"They are quiet," Tym said, thinking it was a strange sort of riddle.

She squinted and seemed about to say something when Bird Beak interrupted.

"We're wasting time with this idiot," she said, nodding to a soldier. "Put him irons. We can question him later. Do you have a cellar we can store him, master innkeeper?"

"I do," Tailorson said. "It's full of provisions and might be flooded from the rains."

Bird Beak waved away his concerns.

"Set him some place dry."

"You told me you didn't have a cellar cause of the rains and flooding," Tym said.

"I tell people lots of stuff," Tailorson said. "Some of it is true."

"Put me back in my room," Tym said and held out his leg. "I'm not getting far on this."

"The cellar," Bird Beak repeated.

Tym began to struggle, but they yanked his arms behind his back. Cold metal scrapped his wrists, clicking together. He couldn't let them put him in the cellar. No telling what would be down there. The guards began to drag him and there was little he could do to resist. His calf burned, fresh blood seeping through the bandage.

"You can't go tossing my cliental into the cellar," Tailorson said. "This is my place you are staying in and he is a good paying man, most-the-time."

"Move out of the way before we take you, too," the soldier said.

Tailorson gave Tym an apologetic look and stood by his wife who continued to scowl, but placed an arm through his.

No more firewater for you lying, cowardly bastard! Of course, Tym may not even be around to make or deliver the firewater. Nor might there be a place left in which to deliver it. This was all a lose-lose situation, the kind of cards he was dealt, the kind to make you cut your losses and go home, happy to have a little clink left in your pouch.

"I'm no spy!" Tym said, thinking that was what a spy would say. "I make and sell firewater—"

A fist landed in his gut, doubling him over.

"Shut your mouth, before you swallow your teeth."

Tym went limp, trying not to cry, not to piss himself, though, that was too late. A warm wet stain appeared in from of his trousers and dribbled across the floor. The soldiers treated him like a sack of potatoes, a leaking one, lugging him across the Welkenwood floor, leaving behind a thin, yellow trail. Tym slackened, becoming as heavy as he could. Dead weight, and the soldiers grunted, stooping a bit to keep their hold on him.

"They have both exits covered," Tym heard Bird Beak say to her companion. "We have no choice but to dig in and fight. Might be a siege, a long one, though the walls are not as strong as I'd hope."

They need a way out. Tym recalled the city guard on the wall saying two armies approached the city. *They're trapped worse than me.*

"I know a way out," Tym said, but they didn't hear, or chose to ignore him. "I know how you can get out of the city!"

They were close to the door leading to the kitchen. Once passed those, he could shout his voice raw and only the rats would hear him. Then the furry critters would come for him and he'd be stuck in chains trying to stay afloat, as Tailorson suggested. He tried to dig his heels in, but it served only to create more pain in his leg.

Bird Beak looked at him, and he could tell she was weighing his words. Before she could respond, the plump one put her hands on her hips and scowled.

"Get him out of here, I can't think with his blathering."

Tym was carried past the kitchen and into a back room. They could slit his throat and toss his body out in the alley, no one would be the wiser or really miss him. Except his brother and niece. Though, he suspected his brother would miss the coin more. They set him against a wall and lifted a trapdoor.

"You could let me go," Tym said. "I won't say a word about you guys being here."

"Keep talking and I'll drop you down instead of using the stairs," one soldier said, while the other lit a lantern. Then they guided him to the stairs and helped him down.

Fucking liar, Tym thought about what Tailorson said about not having a cellar. *Guess I'll get to see his gnomes after all.*

The cellar was flooded, water rising up to the soldiers' boots. Tym complained about his leg, but it got wet and it irritated his cut. The soldiers dropped him on top of two barrels, positioning him so his feet dangled above the water. If he fell, he might drown with his hands chained. They began to climb the stairs, carrying the only light source with them.

"At least leave me the lantern," Tym said.

The one holding it chuckled and shook his head. The light slipped away into a small patch on the stairs, then the hinges squeaked and the trapdoor shut, leaving Tym alone in the dark.

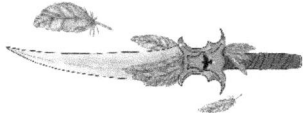

Soldiers stalked the walkways, stiff and alert like rats standing on their hind legs, searching for the cat they scented. *Nearly under their noses.* At the rise in the road, Claiborne sat on her black destrier, observing the defenders through her golden-case spyglass. It was a gift from her dead lover Arron. He'd purchased it from a merchant who said it belonged to the great Captain Such-and Such from an army long dead and forgotten. The gold was real, and she might've had it melted down for coin, but the spyglass worked better than any she viewed through. Objects hundreds of yards away appearing as though they were in front of her nose. She figured that was the reason the spyglass had survived for so long.

The watchfires no longer burned. Overhead, the sun shone bright and the storm clouds miraculously swept away. The soldiers could see her if they had a solid spyglass, not that she cared. It's not like they could call for help. There wasn't a King's garrison for leagues out here on the fringes of civilization. This city was an oasis, and the soldiers stationed there were the last drops of water the Silent Men would mop up.

A nice morning for slaughtering people. Sip on a sweet glass of wine while the enemy's blood ran thin across the rain-soaked streets. Every day was a good day to die when nothing remained to live for.

On the northside of the wall, she counted three dozen city guards and another score of men wearing the dark blue uniforms of that bitch, Thrush. More manned the two towers and she was certain hundreds waited behind the gate. Another beautiful butchery lining up the same way her father lined up hogs in their pens before dashing their brains with his hammer. *The woman will squeal for their children. The men for their women.* It would be a mess of human pleadings and tears and curses cut off, giving her such a headache. Anticipating the ending was the hardest part, because it never went as envisioned. There was always some fuckery afoot. No matter how carefully she planned. Both gates were watched and there wasn't room for them to escape.

Unless they learned how to fly. The thought drew a rare smile from Claiborne. She'd seen plenty of devastation those women could create using their song. Flying would be a new one.

She collapsed the spyglass, and turned at the sound of rattling wheels and the clomp of horses rolling up behind her. Four draft horses, sleek black coats and powerful frames drew the giant black carriage, which was the size of a small house. She'd been inside it. There was room to fit eight people with plenty of elbow room. The coachman quietly drew back on the reins. He wore a simple black robe, hood drawn up to his pale face, clean shaven, and sunken eyes. Brody was his name, though she didn't know how she'd learned it. The guy never spoke. He rarely displayed anything that could remotely show he was alive and not some conjured beast, summoned to be Cacophony's carriage driver.

That would be a horrific punishment.

A childish verse rang through an open window. Claiborne recognized it as burning bridges and kings. She shuddered at the tiny voice meant for more innocent rhymes about flowers and rainbows, not corpses and funeral pyres. Then again, she wasn't the ordinary child.

The carriage door opened and Cacophony started to emerge. He grabbed hold on the railing meant to tie down luggage on top of the carriage and, using his upper body strength, lifted and swung his legs up. Armor creaked and the carriage swayed to the left under his weight. His boots heels caught the carriage top, allowing him to straighten his arms, forcing the rest of his body to follow. He stood, a towering figure surveying the walls. Claiborne marveled at how big he was, the chiton-like armor shining black under the sun, cloak fluttering in the breeze like agitated wings.

"They choose a poor nest to hide in," Cacophony said, and rested his hands on his hips. A warrior readying for a battle he wouldn't enter. He wouldn't be needed, not if the men were successful in their endeavors. "Everything in place, First Sword?"

"Yes, sir."

Six wagons were loaded with oil and covered in thick hides, providing a canopy to protect five soldiers, also carrying shields over their backs, that would push the carts. Horses would be killed before they got within two hundred yards and in order to start the fire, especially since the walls were soaked from the rain, the carts had to be shoved right up onto it and then ignited. Too soon and the oil would burn the cart to ashes before it reached the destination, including those who pushed it.

The men looked at her, nervous, excited even. They didn't complain or refuse the orders, though their lives were put in the most peril having to approach the enemy with highly flammable substances. If dragons were real, they'd have a safer time crawling up in one of their mouths. Firewalkers were what they were called. The life expectancy of a Firewalker was brief. They did it because the women inside the walls took something from each of them, something that not even the Creator could return. Claiborne would march side-by-side with the men, grunting and sweating in her black armor while arrows thrummed dangerously close, had she not been promoted to First Sword. Everyone had their part to play. She had once served in Thrush's force and witnessed the damage the women had caused firsthand, including an unforgettable, and unforgivable, gruesome death when Thrush experimented on a man with her song. A man Claiborne loved more than any person in the world, but didn't know it until he was gone.

"Let's fire it up," Cacophony said, a rare display of excitement in his voice. The men looked at her and she shook her head.

"Wait until you get to the walls," she said. Then she raised her sword and motioned it forward. "Put your backs into it! Faster the package gets delivered, the quicker you come back to breakfast."

"*Old men are burning; the graveyards are churning,*" the girl's song grew frantic and the joy she projected made Claiborne's skin crawl. "*Spew out the dead, kings conquer met and all are left in ashes, ashes, we all fall down.*"

Over the first rise the carts experienced no problems. Once the road leveled out, mud became an issue. The wagons slowed, wheels sinking in and boots sliding. If they hadn't noticed before, the defenders on the wall knew what was coming. Arrows clanked against the wooden sides and landing in the road. One hit its mark when a man slipped, exposing his leg. A lucky shot, Claiborne knew, observing the action though her spyglass. *Unlucky for the man it hit.* The other pushers left him behind, a victim of more ill-fortune when another arrow struck him in the face, silencing his screams, and he went still. The first casualty of this battle.

Always has to be one poor bastard to earn that title. That's one she hoped never to acquire.

The Firewalkers were under three hundred yards away from the wall, arrows raining down in a heavy wave, over-shooting in hopes to slow them further. The wagons were too far for the defender to open the gates, risking a rallying charge, but not close enough for accurate shots. *As long as they didn't use fire, the wagons should be fine.* The canvass had been soaked in water and would resist all but the most stubborn flame. One spark, though, and the whole thing would go up in flames. The goal was to reach the walls, then the soldiers would rip the canvass and douse them with oil.

"Shit on a stick," Claiborne slapped the spyglass in her palm. Streaks of fire were mingled in the next volley. Those that struck the canvass sizzled out, but one wagon continued burning on the side.

"They've caught on fast," Cacophony said. "Something a little birdie told them"

"Fucking Thrush," Claiborne said. Not much she could do to trick that woman.

"I suggest a different tactic next time."

"Yes, sir." Claiborne ground her teeth. *Letting the ground dry for more than a few hours would be a novel idea.* They were committed and had to either complete the task or abandon the wagons. Retreating wasn't an option. Push through and pray they made it to the walls. Prayers, Claiborne learned long ago from much wiser soldiers, long dead, were not a good strategy for winning, and usually were saved for the dying.

The carts plodded along at an oxen's pace. Arrow accuracy improved the closer they got to the walls. Claiborne frowned, grinding her teeth until her jaw hurt. One wagon was entirely in flames. The five Firewalkers pushing it grabbed their shields before the flames overcame them. They scattered, dodging arrows and seeking the nearest wagons. Two fell, and another hobbled to cover.

"One wagon burned, sir," Claiborne said. *They're not at a hundred yards.* "Another caught fire."

"Is it lost?"

"The men still push." Push or die at this point. The wagons were too far apart and too close to the arrow fire. They'd end up corpses in the road before gaining cover. Not that Claiborne expected them to survive this mission. Very few came back from assailing the walls. Those who did were Creator blessed. At least until the next battle.

"Good," Cacophony said. "Have a detachment circle around and watch the Sunrise gate. We can't have them fleeing the fires."

"Already in place, sir."

Once the rains had ended, Claiborne made certain a dozen of her best marksmen covered the only other means of escape. The thin brush and scrub trees provided enough of a hiding place for them, should the singers poked their heads out, they would get an arrow in the ear for their troubles. They didn't have enough men to surround the city and it would spread her ranks too thin. The scouts reported the two main gates were the only way a large army could enter or exit.

Cacophony grunted and the child changed her song to sing a ballad about a soldier whose family was murdered while he was away. *Who is teaching her these things?* The girl wasn't her concern. Burning the city down, that was her focus. With four wagons of oil remaining, and one more than likely to go up in flames, catching the wall on fire seemed unlikely.

I need the gates open. Once they do, then the city will belong to us. And Thrush will be mine.

It would be easier with proper siege equipment: ladders, catapults and sappers working the walls. Easy wasn't fast and Cacophony has been trailing these women for a very long time. She'd fought several battles against him, until she was taken captive. His tactics were fast and brutal, narrowly missing capturing Thrush and Robin countless times. Here they had an advantage. The women were trapped and helpless, unable to use their songs. Failure in these favorable circumstances would lead to very painful consequences for Claiborne. She shifted her shoulders, the scars on her back itching at the thought of steel barbs slicing into her flesh.

The remaining wagons reached the pinnacle of the hill and began to gain some speed. They would need it for the last twenty yards of steep incline to reach the base of the walls. That's when the sting of arrows would be most ferocious. A hail of death and flames fell from the walls. Claiborne held her breath and watched. All four wagons were burning and smoking. Momentum worked for them and the wagons reached the rise at a good speed. The first touched the wall, then the second, third and fourth. Blocks were placed behind each wheel to secure it in place.

"Contact made," Claiborne said.

Two Firewalkers tore the cover off each wagon while the others used large shields to protect them from arrow fire and falling debris. The archers no longer used fire arrows, which would make the job of lighting the oil much easier. This tactical reserve spoke of Thrush's touch. The Silent Men's torches were lit and tossed into the wagons. Each blossomed like beautiful solinade flowers under bright Sower's sun. Smoke puffed up and the fire began to lick the city walls.

The gates opened and dark blue armor poured out. Dozens of them split to the sides like water striking stone. They attacked the remaining Firewalkers standing between them and the blazing wagons. The Firewalkers fought bravely, but were outnumbered. They delayed Thrush's soldiers enough for the blazing oil to spread from the wagon to wall and the soldiers couldn't get close enough to pull them back. Buckets of water poured over the sides of the wall, but it was like spitting on a hot rock. Thrush's men tried to dislodge the burning wagon, and Claiborne smiled as they backed away, running back behind the burning walls.

Claiborne collapsed the spyglass and nodded to Cacophony.

The men gave their lives, but the gates were open and the walls burned

"We won't need watch fires, tonight," Cacophony said. "Phase two, First Sword. Get the men ready."

"Yes, sir," Claiborne said. Phase two was her favorite phrase. It meant her sword would bite flesh and drink the blood of those who hurt her beloved. Nothing made her happier than killing those who stood by and watched the monstrous woman twist Arron into something inhumane. One thing would make her happier. Killing Thrush. Wringing the neck of that cunt's song who ruined Claiborne's life. She turned to go, but Cacophony called her back.

"Oh, and First Sword."

"Yes, sir."

"You will lead the assault."

The words were sweet music. Claiborne bowed and tried not to skip back to the lines. This would be a wonderous day. Creator bless her, it will be a day of her release.

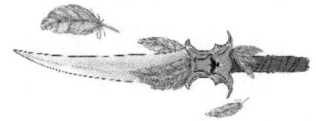

A rat squeaked. Tym couldn't see it in the dark, but he heard its skittering legs behind his head. It moved quickly, and didn't sound alone. *Fucking disease*

carrying assholes. Stay away from me! He didn't want to call attention to himself by shouting at them. Bad enough they smelled his bloody leg. *Would they try eating me alive?* He'd heard stories about rats chewing on an infant's face in the crib. Had an acquaintance who swore his deformed ear was caused by a rat whispering to him at night. Guy was wasted on firewater and whitecaps most of the time, so who knew what could be talking to him?

Tym's worst fear was being forgotten down here in the cellar. The water stank and the wood under his ass hurt. If he tilted forward too much, he could fall in face first and drown, especially with his hands chained. Nothing worse than the helpless feeling of not being able to catch yourself if you fall. Sure, as water was wet, he was fucked.

Drowning, eaten by rats, starved, thirst. So many choices in ways to die. He figured he'd drown rather than die from thirst. The brackish water would be mighty appealing to a parched tongue. He shuffled his numb ass cheek. *No falling asleep, either, else I'll fall off and drown.*

The odds of drowning seemed to be gathering the consensus.

Fucking rains. Fucking Euclid. Fucking Tailorson.

If he got free, Tym would make certain all of Tailorson's patrons knew that the gnomes in the cellar were actually rats.

The planks creaked and Tym heard boots thundering overhead. Voices spoke rapidly, but he couldn't make out what they were saying. Shouts followed and what he swore was an interesting string of curses. The first nearly audible words he heard sounded like, "the walls are burning."

Couldn't be what he'd heard. After all the rain, no way the walls could catch fire. The shout was carried across overhead and repeated so often, there was no doubt that was what the excitement was about. Except, it could be the inns walls and not the city. That's more likely what he heard.

Fire! Fucking Fire. That puts starvation and thirst out of the running. If the rats are smart, they will be long gone before everything goes up in flames. When it came down to it, he'd drown himself than burn up, though he'd have no choice, passing out from the smoke and a plunge into the shallow depths.

Seems drowning was the clear winner on the "how will you die, Tym Lyre" guessing game. The one regret he had was leaving his niece behind. Ivy was counting on him to bring back coin so she could eat. She will be very disappointed if he didn't come back. She might think he'd abandoned her, like her mother. Although, her mother got the worse of it by some fucking strangers along the road. Death by drowning didn't seem so bad when the alternative was being raped, mutilated, and decapitated to have the strangers dump your body by the side of the road.

When to do it? That was the big question. He couldn't just shove off, not when he could still breathe and maybe, though the chances were looking worse than a crusty sore on a whore's nether regions, maybe escape this dank hole.

Start screaming! Remind them I'm down here!

Tym drew in a breath, the stench of the water nearly choking him, and coughed. The floor boards creaked and it sounded like a dozen feet moving overhead.

No, don't abandon me here!

A raspy noise crawled from his throat and he leaned forward, trying to create space, allowing air to pass from lungs to throat. He tottered on the edge of the barrel, losing his balance. A loud thud sounded close. *I'm going to fall in! Drown! No stopping it now.* The trapdoor opened, allowing in a crack of light. Tym saw it. Then landed face first into the cold, bitter rain water. He took a quick gasp of air before plunging into darkness, blotting out his eyes and ears. He sank, knees striking against something hard that turned him onto his side. His lungs burned and demanded to take a breath. His head remained submerged and he gasped, blowing bubbles and tasting the bitter water.

This! This is how it ends!

Movement began to stir the water and he saw light on the surface of the water, a surface so close he could see it beyond his nose. Hands gripped him and he was yanked from the darkness into the dull light cast by a lantern. Tym gasped, coughed, and spat out water.

"Nearly killed himself," a man's voice said.

"Get him up! Might be our only chance."

Soaked-hair hung in his face and they dragged him, slogging through the water. They sent him on the stairs, half shoving and half pulling him up. *I understand what a dirty sheet feels like dragged through a hard wash and beaten on a rock.* He sat in a puddle, grateful to be somewhere dry.

"Up!" Rough hands grabbed him under the arms. They led him, stumbling through the kitchen, leaving behind a long, wet trail. His boots squelched and water pattered on the floor. The walls, he noticed, were not covered in flames. They took him to the common room where the women watched him intensely.

"You know a way out?" Bird Beak asked.

Tym nodded. He began to shiver, the cold prickling his skin.

"Because if you don't," Pudgy said, "we all die."

"I see you are reconsidering my offer," Tym said, fighting a smile. "Guess you don't want to burn in this little cage you put yourselves into."

"If we burn," Pudgy said, stepping forward, rattling keys. "You burn with us."

She unlocked the chains and they clattered to the floor.

"Good thing I'm not into dying at the moment." Tym rubbed his wrists. "Who is coming with us?"

"Everyone," Bird Beak said.

That'll be a fucking tight squeeze. Tym nodded. All he had to do was find the door again and let them worry about the rest. How hard could it be?

CHAPTER SIX:
SONGS OF SORROW

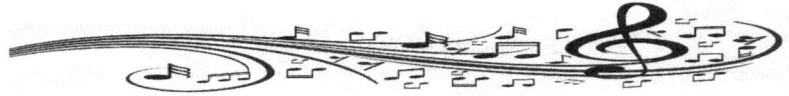

Their Songs have broken the world. They believe they heal it, sealing up the portals piercing the veil between death and life, creation and destruction. All they do is bring sorrow, delaying the inevitable conclusion. Like a candle that runs out of wick, so light must fade into darkness. The shadows will elongate until his fingers wrap around the world.

When they reached the first wooden fence post marking the Farlow Farm, Ivy wrinkled her nose. The smell of dry grass and pig shit was strong, strong enough to gag a maggot. Crisell gave no indication of noticing, which annoyed Ivy since she could taste it in the back of her throat. Being around it on a daily basis, she figured, would deaden the senses to it. *I guess a person can get used to anything.*

"Are you alright?" Crisell asked.

"Um-hum." Ivy sat rigid on the bench, a hand over her mouth and nose. She didn't smell much better, covered in dirt and sweat. Ivy looked at the drought damaged land. The lack of rain left it scarred. Cracked dirt, yellowed grasses, and stunted bottlebrush shrubs. Dust kicked up under the horse hooves, the cart's wheels, swirled around on the breeze. It had become a world of dust. Dying, but refusing to lie down. How did anyone live out here?

"I'm guessing you'll want a bath and a bite to eat," Crisell said. "When was the last time you ate?"

Ivy shrugged. She couldn't remember the last real meal that didn't consist of whatever she scrounged from the trees and berry bushes. Her clothes fit looser than before, that much she could tell. Her stomach growled at the mention of food. A warm bath was a luxury she'd not been afforded in a long, long time, not with the heat making even the thought of a fire unbearable. The stream behind her house served enough to clean the dirt and scrub away the crusty layers.

"My sister will help you with whatever woman-type things you'll be needing." Crisell eyed her. "Think she might be the right size, or close enough to find a dress for you. I'd have my mother draw you the bath, but she'd just as likely boil you and scrub your skin to the bones."

"Thank you," Ivy said. "I'll be staying only one night. You don't have to go through the trouble."

"Would be worse trouble if I sent you home and those men laid hands on you," Crisell said. "I'd not rest easy knowing I allowed it to happen."

"My father," Ivy said. "He needs to know what's happened."

"I'll send Jacob later on once I figure the roads have cleared," Crisell said. "He can give a good enough report once I tell him. Boy is as sharp as a steel trap; never forgets a single word I tell him and knows when to stay quiet. We'll have him say you were attacked in town, but are doing fine, staying over at my place until the morning. After chores, I'll take you home directly myself."

Ivy could imagine her father standing at the door, red-rimmed eyes squinting, fists balled ready to strike Crisell dead for a liar and a thief. How might he react to this Jacob fellow Crisell planned on sending? What might say when he hears about the dangers his daughter faced? *He won't come searching for me on his own, tell the truth and shame Nazglum.* Would be better for all involved if Ivy went home on her own.

"That's awfully kind, but I'll be walking at first sun. That way I'll not take up any more of your time."

Crisell grunted.

"You say that now," he said, giving her a grin. He was almost handsome in the boyish charm. Under different circumstances she could allow herself to enjoy his company. "Just you wait until Ma makes her griddle cakes. Your mouth will be watering and you'll not want to go nowhere but to the stove for seconds."

They turned down a single lane. Hog pens lined the path containing a dozen pink and mottled colored pigs of various sizes ranging from nearly as big as Ivy to ones that could fit into her palm. Snouts raised and eyes followed them, a serenade of snorts and squeals welcoming them home.

"How many are there?" Ivy tried to tally up the heads, but there seemed an endless line of them.

"Over a hundred," Farlow said.

"That's a lot of pigs."

"I am the largest provider of smoked bacon in Welksdale. No one has finer."

Looking at all the curious faces made her sad to think they'd wind up on someone's plate. Bryn didn't eat meat, said it made his stomach ache, so Ivy wasn't raised on it either. Mostly they ate grains, fruits, and anything else they could scrounge up around the farm.

"You ever try smoked sausage?"

Ivy shook her head.

"I don't eat meat."

Farlow gave her a funny look.

"What's your father feeding you? Bugs?"

Ivy had no response. She didn't want to argue. Much like the pigs, she was trapped in a pen not of her making and there was always someone, some man, standing on the outside, holding a knife to her throat.

"I didn't mean to offend."

"It's alright. There's plenty of death in the world without me adding to it."

Farlow nodded.

"I see your point, though I don't understand it. I'll make sure there's extra potatoes and greens for you and spare the sausage."

They passed a two-story house, where a gray-haired woman slouched into a chair. A white shawl covered her shoulders, and she held a glass in her left hand. She squinted at Ivy, frowning deep into her jowls. Her head turned slowly, the frown never leaving, staring at Ivy, scorching her with disapproval.

"I don't think your mother is very glad to see me," Ivy said.

"She'll have to learn to be nice," He pulled back on the reins, slowing the horses. "She's been cantankerous since father passed. Believes everyone is looking to take her children away as well, leaving her alone to ferment in her bitter thoughts."

"I don't want to take nothing from nobody."

"Don't waste your words on her." His smile was gone. "She doesn't listen to anyone but does and says what she wants. Ignore her. She may hiss like a snake, but she's harmless."

Most snakes have fangs that hurt, poisonous or not.

"It's only you three?" Ivy took in the vast amount of land. Most of it was fenced in and covered in yellowed grass.

"Besides Jaccob," Crisell nodded to a boy raking up grass and dried dung in an empty pen. Swirl of golden-red hair curled on his head, the back of his neck was red above the brown tunic's collar, and his black trousers was covered in dust much like everything else. "He belongs to the Harborsons down the road. I employ him from time to time, to keep his family from running out of food. So, yeah, we are three." He looked at Ivy; the boyish charm returned to his eyes and smile. "But we are always looking to add in a fourth, despite mother and her withering glare."

Ivy's cheeks flushed. She didn't want to be the fourth, third, second, or any number. Except one. One seemed very nice and it meant not having to worry over upsetting others. Crisell let the cart approach closer to the barn, then stopped the horses. He offered his hand, but Ivy ignored it, coming down on her own. Crisell didn't say anything, going about his business of unhitching the horses and leading them into the barn. This could be hers. The barn, two-story house, hundred pigs and a cantankerous old woman scaring folks from the porch. It all sounded like a lot for such a simple girl, but Ivy found she had no more desire to be a part of it than she had to eat a pig.

"You've returned early." A woman not much older than Ivy stood at the side of the barn, pitch fork in hand and strands of straw covering her dress. Her hair matched the color, and her face held the ruddiness from being in the sun. Myah Farlow smiled at Ivy. "I see you brought a guest home. Mother will be very pleased."

"No, she won't," Crisell said. "Mother can glare from her rocker until the sun burns out for all I care. I had bigger problems. I couldn't get everything on my list."

"Distractions." Myah leaned on the pitch fork, grinning at her brother.

"If you call the robbing of the Exchequer and the molestation of a young lady by the same thieves, then yes, I was distracted." Crisell shouldered a sack of flour. "Would you be so kind, dear sister, as to carry the other to the house."

Myah shrugged and set the pitch fork aside. She was tall and thin, but strong. She shouldered the flour like it was a bag full of air. She walked beside Ivy while they followed Crisell to the house. Myah leaned in, the smell of sweat, hay, and pig nearly overwhelming Ivy.

"My brother fancies himself a hero," Myah said.

"He did cold-cock a guy who held a knife to my throat," Ivy said, and wished she hadn't. A humorous gleam entered Myah's brown eyes, and Ivy knew she gave her more fodder to tease her brother.

"Crissy was always good at speaking with his fists," Myah said. "He was a champion puncher going back to when he was yay tall." She held a hand at her hip level. "Always whopped the arses of the other boys when they insulted practically anyone. Nearly got himself thrown in irons and caged for beating up the Ferris Mather when he called our father "a mud rolling, pig shit dealing son-of-a-bitch.""

"Enough stories, Myah," Crisell said.

"Father had to pay a fine and you worked at the bakery for nearly a moon, sweeping up and running deliveries while the bastard Ferris healed." Myah pressed on. "Never did fight much after."

"Boys grow up," Crisell said, boots stomping up the wooden steps. He paused long enough to consider the woman in the rocker. "Mother, got you some more flour like you wanted."

The older Mother Farlow continued to glare at Ivy. She drew back her lips to reveal a set of pitted, yellowed teeth, and spat on the porch in front of Ivy. "Should've left the weevils behind," she said in a raspy growl.

"Be nice, mother, I won't have you insulting our guest," Crisell said.

She shot him a look of disdain. Boney hands gripping the chair's armrest as she tried to shove herself into a standing position. Her arms quivered and she remained seated. "Or what? You'll hit me?"

Crisell moved past her into the house.

"Don't work yourself into a tizzy, Mother," Myah followed. "He's never raised a hand to either of us. He forgets his manners. This is Ivy."

"I know who she is," Mother Farlow snapped. "Her kind ain't welcome in my house."

"What kind is that, Mother?"

"The kind to twist a man, like the bitch that whelped her."

Ivy bit her lip to keep from snarling a bunch of obscenities at the senile old woman. She tried on a smile, discovering it was too much effort and settled for a tight-lipped scowl. The rumpled bag of flesh would only revel at an outburst, proving her right that Ivy didn't belong there. A strong hand closed over her shoulder, prodding her forward.

"Excuse our Mother," Myah said, shutting the screen door, "she has a bitter tongue from swallowing too much grief."

Ivy understood grief, since her mother was dead, but kept that comment to herself.

The farmhouse was well-furnished, better than Ivy's home. Several large, comfortable-looking chairs covered in plush, floral-patterned cushions occupied the main room beside a modest hearth. Logs were piled ready for a fire. Baskets of yarn and half-crocheted garments sat next to one chair. Long, gold needles, thicker than Ivy's fingers, poked out from them. Over the hearth was a portrait of a man standing next to a seated version of a younger Mother Farlow. She clutched a baby in her lap while on her left-side stood a rather serious looking boy.

"Those were the happy times here on the farm," Myah said. She set the sack down and clapped her hands together, setting up a fine dust. Ivy saw how short Myah's nails were, dirt caked into the crevices. They were not the dainty hands of a pampered woman. Ivy wondered if Myah killed the hogs, or if Crisell was the one to do the bloody work. "I don't remember much, because that's me right there." She pointed at the baby. A surprised expression on the infant's face, like she either made a big mess, which would explain her mother's tight smile.

"It's a nice painting," Ivy said.

"I'm going to burn it when mother passes," Crisell said. He stood at Ivy's left side, very close and framing the boy's face between his long fingers. "Look at how big my nose looks. I wasn't that ugly as a child. Father paid way too much to have this painted by some hack with stiff brushes."

"Good thing you grew into that nose." Myah poked him in the ribs. "I'm going to start supper. Want anything special?"

"I guess we are going meatless," Crisell said and Myah raised a brow at him.

"You don't have to on my account," Ivy said.

"Won't be a problem." Myah gave Crisell a look that she couldn't understand. Then she was gone, leaving Ivy alone with Crisell. He stood too close, and Ivy took a small step to her right, picking at her sleeve. He frowned, scratched his head, and then gestured down the hall. "There's a room in the back. It has a small bed, water basin and bucket. Pump's out back if you want water to wash up, but you'll have to wait if you want it heated. Myah will boil a pail full once diner is going."

"Thank you," Ivy said. "I think I need to lie down."

"That's fine, too," Crisell said. "Stay off the porch, until Mother has grown used to you being around. She forgets sometimes whose been living here and who visits."

"You get many guests?" Ivy asked.

"A few," Crisell said, then added, "none like you," before he slipped out the front door.

She didn't know how to take the last comment. Was he saying she caused a problem? Their mother already despised her for some unknown reason, well, unknown to Ivy at least. Why would Crisell bring her here knowing his mother would disapprove of Ivy? He might be regretting his decision. Ivy regretted getting up this morning. Nothing but trouble since she got to Welksdale.

Town can burn down and I wouldn't shed a tear! Though, that was not entirely true. There was the man who helped her at the well. A nice smile to go with his strong arms, not that any of that mattered, no, he was kind enough to help Ivy when so many watched her struggle wearing their smug grins. Nazglum take them, but not the one kind man.

The bed in the back room was bigger and in much better condition than the straw matted palate Ivy slept on in her home. A hand stitched quilt was pulled up over two down-pillows. Ivy lay on it, her side aching where she'd been kicked by Janus. She tugged at her dress, revealing the bruise on her ribs. The bone wasn't broken, which Ivy counted as a good fortune. She rolled on her back, staring up at the slanted ceiling. Not a single cobweb hid in the corners. The farmhouse was kept rather clean despite the pigs outside. Even then, she could smell them beneath the hint of mint and rosehips. Still, it was much better than the cloying stench of vomit, sweat and cinnamon she had gotten used to with Bryn. Ivy yawned and stretched her aching muscles. She closed her eyes for a moment. Sleep snuck up on her and transformed the aches into a strange dream of red and screams from people she didn't know. A sword fell among the bodies and blood splashed over and over, until it created a thin rivulet of red. Ivy tried to warn them of the incoming death, but they stared at her, no through her, like she was nothing more than a ghost in their dream, rather than the other way around. So real was the dream, she didn't know she was asleep until her eyes opened. When the light pricked her, she wasn't sure was she was entirely awake, or if this was a continuation of the same nightmare.

Standing over her was Mother Farlow, squint-eyed, lips twitching to show a few remaining yellowed-teeth. A single word mumbled from her, sounding like cat coughing up a hair ball.

"Whore," Mother Farlow repeated, much louder. Her breath stank of rot and mint. A wrinkled hand fell on Ivy's mouth, worse than a mildewed rag. In the other she had a golden knitting needle, sharp point aimed at Ivy.

Ivy slapped the hand away from her mouth and rolled to her side. Gnarled knuckles grazed her back and there was a soft thump in the mattress.

First a knife to my throat and now a crochet needle!

Rage bubbled inside, rising from her gut and burned through her chest, begging to be released. For all she knew, letting it escape would result in her vomiting over the front of her dress. *Too late to worry now.*

It started as a hum, rumbling in her throat and then became a full song, one she'd heard her mother sing in a distant memory before Bryn split her lip and silenced her. No one would silence Ivy. Pressed again the wall, Ivy watched Mother Farlow yank the needle from the sheet, followed by a puff of wool. The Old Woman snarled, lunging at Ivy. Golden point flashed, missing Ivy's left breast and stuck again in the mattress.

Ivy kept singing, lost in words she didn't understand, though the emotions were raw, like peeling back finger nails to the bloody quicks. Mother Farlow froze, face slackening. A dark hole formed in the space between, filled by visions of a younger woman, the same woman holding the infant in her lap in the painting. The younger Mother Farlow dug nails into her palms, standing outside some story in Welksdale, head turned to watch a man standing at the back of crowd of people. The man looked familiar, similar to the one in the painting, though less gray, and he wore a smile, leaning in. The younger Mother Farlow caught a glimpse of the girl, fuzzy to Ivy, but the hate coming from the woman was hotter than grabbing a burning brand.

The image clouded in smoke and a new one appeared, the same man coming home late, a faint smile on his lips. He looked up and saw the younger Mother Farlow, the smile slipped away, a dirty kerchief tossed into the laundry pile. He said nothing, passing her, but he smelled different. She didn't ask, knowing it had something to do with the singing girl. The hate returned, dipped in jealousy and wrapped tightly in heartache and betrayal. Another image, an older Mother Farlow, whose hair has lost all its luster, turning from golden-yellow to gray, wrinkled folds rutted in frown lines. She was crying, beating her fists against her boy, the grown-up version that Ivy recognized as Crisell. Mother Farlow screeched, "Told him to stay away! She was no good! I told him!" This flashed red and Ivy's face appeared, jumbled in the emotional stew. The golden needle bobbing in and out of her eyes while Mother Farlow screamed and cursed, lapping up the blood and gray matter.

The song changed, taking hold of Ivy and she struggled to control it, the way a person might struggle with a wild horse, rearing its back legs and teeth nipping at everything in its path. It commanded Mother Farlow to take the needle and jam it through her own eye. The older woman's hands twitched, raising the needle, sharp end aimed at her right eye. Part of Ivy wanted to stop struggling, to sit back and observe if she would actually follow through with putting out her own eye. Her rational part knew how terrible it would look to Crisell and Myah. Their mother alone in the room with Ivy, a golden needle waggling from her eye socket.

Ivy clamped her mouth shut, cutting off the song. Mother Farlow's arm kept bending at the elbow, crochet needle maintaining its deadly course.

"Don't!"

Ivy grabbed the blunted end and wrestled it away from the old woman.

Mother Farlow blinked, straightened so fast her back made popping noises, and drool slid from the corner of her mouth. She blinked, her vaped expression crinkling into disdain, then loathing.

"Nazglum's hhhh," her raspy voice rose in treble, shaking in time with her hands, "hhhh, whore! Nazglum's whore! Evil! Eeeeevilllll!"

Mother Farlow lunged at her, which was more of a slow fall to the bed. Her nails racked down Ivy's leg, leaving long, burning scratch marks and she yelped. Ivy wacked the wrinkled hands, using the needle as a rod, but Mother Farlow kept coming at her, tearing at her dress.

"Get off!" Ivy smacked the scrambling hand, but Mother Farlow hissed at her.

The bedroom door banged open.

"Mother!" Myah ran into the room and grabbed Mother Farlow, struggling to pull her off from Ivy. The older woman couldn't have weighed much, but she put up a fight, elbowing her daughter in the chin hard enough to send them both reeling backwards and crashing to the floor.

Mother Farlow kicked and fought but ended up succumbing in the end. Chest heaving and spit flying from her mouth.

"Whore! Stealing my... my," her rheumy eye moving to Ivy's hand, the correct word registering on her face, "needle!"

"She was trying to stab me with it," Ivy said, curling her legs beneath her.

"You brought this Nazglum's whore here!" Mother Farlow glared at Myah. "You brought this evil, black magic to spoil my house! Steal my children! My needle! My husband!"

"What's going on?" Crisell appeared in the doorway.

"I never knew your husband," Ivy said. "I hardly know your children."

Or want to. She kept that part to herself.

"She bewitched me," Mother Farlow began to tremble and Myah hugged her. "Tried to get me to stab myself."

"Don't be silly, mother," Myah said. "You were having a bad dream."

"One where she tried to impale me with this," Ivy said and tossed the golden needle on the bed. "See the holes she put into the mattress."

Mother Farlow sobbed into Myah's shoulder.

"She was having one of her episodes again," Myah said. "She didn't mean to hurt you."

"You weren't here." Ivy slid her feet into her clogs. "I need to go home."

"But supper is almost ready," Myah said. "She'll be calm soon enough."

"You don't have to go," Crisell said, almost pleading.

"I can't," Ivy started and got choked up. She pushed passed Crisell on her way to the screen door. She made it half-way down the steps when the door banged open behind her.

"Wait, Ivy. Please."

"That's the second time someone has tried to kill me today, and I won't wait around for a third."

"At least have supper first."

Ivy's stomach rumbled at the thought. It quickly soured at the idea of breaking bread at the same table as the woman who called her a whore and tried to turn her into a pin cushion. Next, she'd use a fork or plate or anything else.

"I can't," Ivy said, cringing at the sound of her voice. "I need to get home. Bryn'll be upset I'm late as it is. Are you going to take me, or do I have walk?"

"Wait until I hitch up the horses, it'll only be a few moments."

Ivy waited beside the barn, listening to the pigs snort while they rooted around the feed troughs. *So much simpler the life of a pig. Eat, roll around in mud, snort, and eventually end up slaughtered, like the rest of us. Doesn't matter the plate we end up on.* She cupped her elbows, trying to keep herself from trembling. She didn't know what happened back at the room, except she was certain the old lady was ready to put out her eye because something inside Ivy wanted her to do it. Bryn always told her, "Don't sing those rotten songs 'round me. They are terrible and singing is a terrible thing to do to a person." Ivy thought Bryn didn't like her mother's voice, but now she understood her singing wasn't bad, but what it made others do, that was what Bryn feared.

Ivy wasn't entirely sure she disliked it, either. Only the fact she couldn't control it.

"Can't let that happen again," Ivy said and glanced to the house. Mother Farlow stood by the front door, glaring out at her. She just had to sit in her chair and it would be a full circle, with Ivy leaving.

The door opened and for a moment, Ivy thought the old woman was going to chase after her, calling her Nazglum's whore, thief, and accusing her of using being eeeeevilll! Ivy didn't know what the song was, but it didn't feel like magic, evil or not, but being possessed by another creature. Myah came down the stairs, holding a wrapped plate in her hands, the basket with bread and water skin.

"Couldn't have you running off without your things," Myah said and smiled. "Or leave hungry."

Her nose prickled and she resisted the wet sob wanting to escape her pursed lips. She almost gave in, telling Myah she'd stay. The sound of horses and the cart leaving the barn settled the matter.

"Thank you," Ivy said.

Myah placed the objects in the cart and then hugged Ivy. Strong arms surprised Ivy and the scent of cooking was more pleasant than the pig shit.

"Don't let mother spook you," Myah said. "Come visit again and I'll make certain she is down for her midday nap."

Ivy thanked her again and climbed on the wagon next to Crisell.

"Be safe," Myah said, waving as they made their way past the line of pens.

Piggy eyes watched her leave indifferently. She could have never existed for them and they for her. They sat behind their wire, biding their time before the knife cut across their throat to end their journey. It was a sad way to view the world, but one in which Ivy understood as being the most accurate depiction since her mother died on the road, body beaten and throat slit from ear to ear.

I should never have come here.

A pig snorted at her, probably thinking the same thing. Not that they had any choice in the matter.

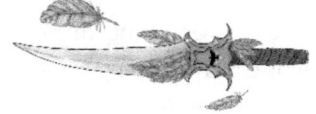

The cart rattled out onto the road, jostling Ivy. Her teeth clicked each time the wheels bounced over the ruts. She'd prefer using her two legs to get around, but her home was far from Farlow's farm. It was growing late—the sun had a red cast, bleeding across the sky. Bryn would throw a fit. *Might find myself sleeping outside for the next night or two.*

"She blames your mother for my father's death," Crisell said. He didn't bother to look at her, facing forward and quiet most of the trip. Ivy didn't mind the silence. With all the yelling and screaming happening around her since the morning, she welcomed it. "I don't know how Veena could be involved, I mean, my father was found outside of town, neck twisted like he'd fallen from his horse. Mother said it was still that Lyre, ugh, woman's fault."

Ivy could imagine all sorts of words Mother Farlow used in place of "woman." She'd called Ivy a couple of them already

"How old is your mother?" Ivy was trying to reconcile the woman in the painting to the one who attacked her. Assuming Crisell was six or seven full-seasons old, and his mother nearing her thirties at the time of the sitting, that would place her close to sixty at most.

"Fifty-five," Crisell said. "Though she appears older, mostly because she has had several seizures after father's death. Twelve episodes in total, coming as regularly as rain, well, when it used to rain. Myah and I didn't think mother would live out the winter. She would hardly eat or drink unless coerced. Her hair went white, body shriveling up like a living corpse. Then the episodes stopped, leaving her aged. Withered." Crisell swallowed hard and his voice went scratchy. "Most of the days she sits in her chair on the porch, staring off at fields, hardly saying a word. That's why I was surprised to see her reacting so…"

"Bitchy?"

"Yes, that is a good way of putting it," Crisell said

"I guess I bring that out in people." Ivy laughed, though the truth of it hurt. "How did your father know my mother?"

"From the stories I heard, your mother used to sing in town, to amuse the folks. Father mentioned how Venna Lyre had the prettiest voice in Welksdale. Enough to make the nightingales weep." Crisell's hands tightened on the reins. "Mother was jealous, though I don't think they spoke more than two words in passing. My parents had this huge argument, and he never spoke Venna's name again, at least not in my hearing."

If the visions Ivy had were true, Mother Farlow had plenty of suspicion her husband was doing more than talking to Ivy's mother.

"He was way older," Ivy said.

"We Farlows get more attractive when we age," Crisell said. "Besides, it's not uncommon for a young, pretty girl to fall for the dashing, older gentlemen."

Ivy didn't take the bait.

Her mother was married to Bryn. Bryn who hated her singing. Bryn who'd get into one of his moods, his fussy huffs, and storm at her, heavy hands thundering and harsh works crackling. Ivy couldn't find fault in Venna for wanting to be with a different man, one who said she had a pretty voice. If Mother Farlow suspected, then it wouldn't be too far off to think Bryn may have suspected the affair as well.

"Would make sense why my father dislikes you," Ivy said.

"Not for other reasons."

Fucking rumors again!

"None I can think of, except you're an ass." Anger swelled up in Ivy. Crisell was starting to sound like every other gossip in Welksdale. "Not your fault, I suspect, just part of your nature of being a man."

Crisell chuckled. "I guess I deserved that."

"And more if you believe every fool word spoken in town."

"And more." Crisell nodded. "I apologize for being an ass, despite it being a part of my nature."

Ivy smiled and rolled her eyes. She wasn't used to anyone apologizing or admitting they were wrong. She glanced at him, to see if he was making fun of her. But he gave no indication, casually holding the reins, though the horses kept their path. He had nice features, dimples in his cheeks, but Ivy was sure he'd make a good husband to some other girl. Not her. Not in Welksdale. Not anywhere she couldn't be free of Bryn. Of her mother's ghost.

A sickening feeling settled into her gut as the outline of her house appeared in the distance. There was something moving in the front yard.

"Stop," Ivy said, grabbing his wrist.

Crisell wrinkled his brows.

"Not expecting company?"

"My uncle, but he'd have one horse and a cart," Ivy said. "Looks like there are four minus any cart."

"Want me to turn around? Head back into town and inform the Sheriff?"

The idea sounded wise, safe, but she knew why there were there. If anything, this time it was her fault. She couldn't abandon Bryn to whatever abuse they'd give him on account of her betrayal. Even though she could still trace the bread crumbs of this fucked up situation to Bryn's selfish and idiotic choices, she held the crust and it was best to chew on what was on hand rather than choke on it later.

"Let me out here," she said.

"I can't," Crisell said. "They tried to kill you,"

Ivy didn't want to argue. She looked down at the hardpacked dirt, sliding closer to the edge of the bench. It would hurt, landing while the cart was moving and as long as she cleared the wheels, then she should survive. There wasn't any soft patch of grass, though prickly weeds grew well. She twisted her body as far as she could, set a hand on the bench to shove off, and bent her elbows. Before she could launch, Crisell reached over and grabbed her arm.

"Don't do that!" His grip was firm.

"I have to," Ivy said. "Let me jump. Or stop the damn cart!"

"How about I get us a little closer so you have less distance to run?"

Ivy nodded.

"What if these men have already hurt your father?"

"Then we have to help him."

"Couldn't we come back? Get some help? What can we do against four armed men?"

Ivy didn't have an answer. She knew in her heart that if they left now, when she came back, they'd find a corpse.

"I will think of something," Ivy said.

There's a way. The song pulsed in her, wild and savage. Ivy kept it in check. No one had to get hurt.

Crisell pulled back on the reins and threw the break lever forward after the cart settled. They were close enough to see the porch and be seen by anyone looking out from it. Since there wasn't any hollering or commotion, Ivy figured the Fugglies didn't bother with a lookout. That meant they'd all be inside.

Ivy slid from the bench and hadn't taken more than a few steps when Crisell was beside her, clutching a large knife the size of her forearm. It could be mistaken for a short sword. She raised her brows at it.

He shrugged. "Makes it so I'm not easily robbed."

Looking at the knife made her aware how woefully unarmed she was. They'd be outnumbered two to one, weapon or not, but she couldn't stand helplessly aside. The Fugglies hurt her and she'd not let them harm Bryn, no matter how much of a drunk asshole he'd been. At the side of the yard where the gravel met yellowed rag-weed, they halted. Loud voices came from within, followed by somethings breaking.

Seems we were in this same spot not too long ago.

The horses stood idly, nibbling on the dead grass. Ivy spotted the hilt of a weapon sticking out from one saddle blanket. The same horse that nearly run her down. It's whip-like tail flicked and the beast whinnied, stomping its rear hoof. "Shhh," Ivy whispered, not knowing anything about horses, but hoped she sounded soothing.

"What are you doing?" Crisell hissed.

Ivy flinched, reaching for the hilt, and got a face full of the tail smacking her like a gnat. She spat out a muddy taste, ducking another lash. "Trying not to get trampled," she muttered and grabbed the hilt. For a moment it didn't want to budge. Then the horse jerked and the sword pulled free, flat side sliding over its rump. The metal blade thumped on the ground. It was close to her height in length and heavier than she expected. The horse gave an angry whinny and tried to stomp on her. Ivy jumped back, dragging the blade through the dirt. Once clear, she gripped the hilt in both hands, managing to lift it easier. The tip wavering in front of her, scrying trembling circles in the air.

"Give me that," Crisell said. "Here, take my knife."

Ivy didn't bother to argue, handing over the sword and taking the knife, handle first.

Screams started.

"Stay behind—" Crisell didn't finish the sentence before Ivy was up the stairs. Running with sharp objects was something her father berated her for, but by the sound of his screams, he would have to forgive her this one time.

Ivy didn't see the first man when she rushed through the doorway. The knife point pierced his right-side, passing through brown tunic and struck bone. The man's head turned, and she recognized Jeph sporting the welt on his cheek where she had kicked him. Jeph shrieked and twisted, pulling the knife from Ivy's hand. A dark red blotch spread on his tunic and Jeph spun around, reaching for the hilt, but ended up tripping over a broken chair leg. He crashed sideways, the same side with the knife sticking out, jamming it further in.

"Sorry," Ivy said, eyes widening at all the blood. Jeph whimpered and shuddered on the floor.

Three heads turned in her direction. Harry and the other brother she didn't know his name, less-Harry, maybe, forced Bryn down on the table while Stephone held a pale sausage and a knife, both dripping red onto the table. All three looked from Jeph, to her, back to Jeph as though surprised to find her appear. Jeph was most surprised, she could imagine. His face paled and brown eyes had a glassy sheen. She had killed him, or near enough that he wouldn't last long. Blood bubbled from his lips and the dagger point poked through his tunic under his breast. The brown material darkened in a blossoming flower.

A gasp came from behind her. Crisell stumbled back a step, sword sagging at his side, staring from Jeph, to Ivy's empty hands, and back to Jeph again.

"You stabbed him," Crisell said.

"I—I didn't—"

Someone chuckled, drawing her attention back to the table where Bryn was stretched across. Ivy took in sharp breath when she realized Stephone wasn't holding a sausage, but one of her father's fingers. He grinned and it would have been handsome except for the gaps between his teeth and a crooked nose that looked like someone took a hammer to it.

"Run, Ivy," Bryn grunted. Pain and fear contorted his face. There was a cut above his eye and his cheek was swelling from where someone struck him.

"I think I like this better." Stephone dropped the finger. It bounced off the table and onto the floor, like scraps for the dogs. "Come here, Ivy, and let me prune you some."

Fear rooted Ivy's legs to the floor.

Bryn wrestled free an arm, the one with the hand still intact, and managed to punch Harry. Harry stumbled, allowing Bryn to attempt to sit up, but an elbow to his gut settled him back in place.

"Hold him still," Stephone said and pointed the knife at Ivy. "If you want your father to remain in one piece... well, relatively in one piece." He shrugged and chuckled at his error in phrasing. "Then I suggest you keep doing what you do best and ignore orders. Running won't end well for him, or you. But you, Pig fucker." He jabbed the knife point in Crisell's general direction. "You can go on your way. I'll even let you keep the sword since it belonged to him." Stephone nodded to Jeph who continued to leak blood like a punctured waterskin. "He may not be needing it after tonight."

"Walk on out of here." Crisell lifted the sword, gripping the handle in both hands, holding it like a cleaver. "Before anyone else gets hurt."

"Seems he got more balls than I figured," Stephone said, "other than hitting a man with his back turned."

"All them pig balls he ate," Harry said and guffawed, making a noise like a wet sponge slurping up water.

"We'll feed him some more, after I cut them off his bloody corpse." Stephone grinned.

Crisell clenched his jaw, face pale and arms tensed to swing. There wasn't much room to maneuver, and she was certain he'd hit her just as likely as a Fuggly.

"You nearly killed me with your horse." Ivy balled her hands into fists. She wouldn't be able to fight them off and was more than certain there would be three more bodies to add to Jeph's, but she sure would go down trying. They'd never stop coming for her, no matter where she ran. "And tried to kill me in town."

"Seeing as how you killed one our companions, I think you got more than your due back." Stephone took a step toward her.

Ivy flushed. Jeph's silent gaze stared past her, his mouth slack, and head tilted to the side. He could almost be sleeping. But he wasn't. She'd killed him surer than if she'd squashed a bug under her clog, even if it was an accident.

Harry made a quick move, lifting a wooden mallet from the table next to Bryn's prostrate form. He flicked his wrist, the mallet turning end over end, passed near Ivy's head, and she ducked. A meaty thump followed by a louder thump and a groan told her it'd hit its mark. Crisell sprawled on the floor, blood flowing from a gash over his brow.

Stephone took advantage of the distraction and crossed the short distance in a couple of quick steps.

"Got you!" A strong hand wrapped around her arm and yanked her into him, allowing him to pin her against his body, smelling of old onions and horse. His stomach was hard and felt like she hit a wall. "Listen here, girl—"

Ivy brought her knee up to his groin, but missed, bumping into a meaty thigh. Her head rocked back hard as a hand smacked her across the face, dropping her to the floor.

"Bitch!" Stephone came at her, knife arm drawn back to stab her.

Ivy stared him in the eye. The power bubbled, thrumming in her throat. She knew what to expect from the Mother Farlow experience, and gave in.

Her mouth opened and words flowed out in song. Her mother's songs were sweet, sometimes sad, but always soft. Ivy found comfort in her songs and would sing them, the verses disappearing as time moved swiftly along and she forgot the words, but never the beautiful sound. What raged from Ivy was nothing like what her mother sang. It was dark, commanding, flowing from some deep, untapped reservoir.

Stephone tensed, knife slowing its path to her and stopped, frozen like some stone statue chiseled in an absurd pose. No blackhole opened, like with Mother Farlow. Instead, the song sank into him, delving him and dragging up dark thoughts of murder and lust. Visions of maiming her, cutting her face up with the knife and then forcing his smelly body over hers, hurting her while exerting sadistic pleasure and control over her. The way his mother used to manipulate him, spank him when he was a boy. Rather than hurt him, he got an erection. Like the one bulging in his pants at the idea of harming Ivy.

"Confodite!" She didn't know the word, but it was a command she repeated in a verse of equally unknown words. Stephone's arm bent at the elbow, wrist tilting to his inner forearm and Ivy watched the knife plunge into his chest, Stephone's face caught in fear and pleasure. He grunted, repeating the same motions over and over again, red blooming with each stab. After the sixth plunge, Stephone dropped the knife, face slackened, and toppled over.

"Nazglum's nuts!" Harry shoved away from Bryn, nearly tripping over his own feet, caught himself and looked to the only escape. The problem being Ivy was between him and it.

Her song shifted, maintaining the dark undertones and the power grew, hungry for more and surged outward, encompassing both Harry and Less Harry. She saw dual images of the men beating up an old man. Watched them break scrawny arms and laugh as they dangled a coin purse in front of the old man's face, leaving him to die in his home. They took turns bending the man's wife over and grunting. The lyrics in the song changed, becoming more brutal.

"Offoca!"

The men barged into each other, rattling the table, and wrapped their fingers around the other's throat. They squeezed, eyes bulging and faces turning first red and then blue from exertion. Wet, gurgling noises escaped bruising lips. They both fell over, hands still gripping the other's throat. Legs jerked as the men seized, kicking the table. They became silent, the occasional spasm jerking their bodies. Soon, even that ended.

Ivy stopped singing. She sank to her knees, feeling like a rung-out rag. The song left her empty. Then she saw the fear in her Bryn's eye. He sat up on the table, the nub where his finger used to be, pattered blood onto the scarred floor. His mouth drawn tight, looking at Ivy like he never saw her before or preferred seeing her now.

"They won't hurt you anymore," Ivy said, voice low and matter-of-fact. Jeph, Stephone, Harry, Less Harry, dead. All dead. She had killed them. She should feel something? Deep down there was a thrill, but that wasn't right. Taking joy in killing others was wrong. Wasn't it?

"Get out," Bryn said. He sounded small, a frightened little boy.

"But—"

"Out!" Color darkened his pale face. He trembled, grabbing the first thing—the back of a chair was the only item in reaching distance—and tried to throw it at her. He succeeded in knocking it over on top of Stephone. "Get out of my sight!"

Something tore inside of Ivy. She had saved him, and he was sending her away. Tears burned her eyes. "I did this…" For you, she wanted to finish but he was on his feet, and moving to another room.

"You're not my daughter," he said. "You're… you're, I don't know…something else."

Then he slipped away, leaving a bloody trail, and slammed his bedroom door, leaving Ivy alone with the corpses she had made.

She wanted to follow him, beg him to understand, plead that she didn't know what she'd done, to convince him she was the same innocent little girl who cooked, cleaned, and ran errands for him. Who killed for him.

Did you expect anything more? Her mother's voice. The answer was obvious. She couldn't stay, though the power rolled inside her belly, demanding to be set free.

Crisell groaned. He touched the wound, winced and stared at the blood on his hand.

"What happened?" He sat up and made a sickening sound, leaned over and threw up a thin stream of yellow bile. "Did… did you do this?"

"Yes," Ivy said.

"What are you?" He leaned away from her. "Some kind of monster?"

It was all too much. The smell of blood, the fear, and the abandonment.

Ivy ran out into the yard. The horses whinnied. How long ago had they nearly trampled her in the road? How long when she saw them in the town, the Fugglies forcing her to rob the Exchequer? Seemed like ages. She tried to use the song to calm the nearest one. The horse shied away, rearing back on its hind legs when Ivy got too close. She couldn't sense anything from the horse, but the thrashing forelegs were enough to warn her away.

They can sense it in me, that I'm not right. Tym had yet returned from Euclid City. Maybe she could find her uncle returning from Euclid City. Convince him her father was murdered and nothing remained at home for them. Euclid was west. She didn't know how far, but she would walk until she dropped. Crawl there, if she had to. Her father never wanted to see her again, well, she was done with him, too. Crisell feared her, and she couldn't blame him for that, though it didn't hurt her any less. All men wanted was to use her, betray her, or kill her.

"They can all go to the shadow!"

CHAPTER SEVEN:
ESCAPE

No one escapes life alive. The ultimate payment for living is the final end where the last breath is taken and the heart no longer beats. All is silent. The Songs provide a false sense of hope, or control. They may drive me away, but I cannot be defeated. I am but a sliver of the power the Dark Lord possesses. None may escape him. In the end, all must be judged, but only he can truly save you.

"You better not be lying," Robin said, jabbing him in the side with her thick finger. It was like being poked by a stubby piece of wood and Tym grunted. Robin followed it up with another jab. "Or we'll string you up on the walls where you can roast."

The alarm bells chimed, beating time in Tym's head, a bit quicker than his heart was pounding. Smoke rose from the Sunset gate which he was certain would crumble before the night was over. Crowds of people migrated to the Sunrise gate. He wouldn't be surprised if they did the job of the besieging army and knock it down. The one thing worse than a scared mob, was an angry mob, one desperate to flee like rats piling out of a burning silage. They would gnaw and scratch until they dug a hole wide enough to scramble through, and into the claws of the cat waiting for them. Tym had heard horrific stories of towns burning in the Welk's war and he didn't want to stick around to witness a city eat itself.

"I want out just as bad as you do," Tym said, hobbling along the uneven cobbles. Each step was a fresh bolt of pain in his calf which he swallowed to keep from squawking. Worse was the bitter taste that clung to his tongue. Close to death, he could literally taste the rank water from the wine cellar. His clothes were still wet and they began to chafe. He picked at his crotch. Tailorson refused to give him a dry set of clothes, claiming they didn't have time for him to put on a fashion show. Tym tugged at the sopping trousers, pulling them from his dangling parts that were already starting to itch. "My livelihood may be gone, but I still got my life and that is something I value."

"We'll be the judge of that," Robin said.

The pudgy woman was intimidating and being surrounded by hundreds of her foot soldiers didn't do anything to diminish her stature. Only her quiet, sharp beaked companion seemed more dangerous precisely because she seemed to study him and calculate his every weakness, which to him were too many to count. The third flicked her hands in annoyance, like all this was an annoying inconvenience to her fragile sensibilities. The flow of fleeing citizens broke around them. Some running empty handed, others carrying bundles. People were smashing numerous business windows, breaking down doors, and looting the places.

Two men fought over what appeared to be a woman's dress. It tore at the seams and they fell to blows, tussling in the street. A child cried under the eve of a haberdashery, his mother was sprawled out in a puddle of blood that people slipped in, but they kept walking, oblivious to either woman or child. She was just another bump in the road to step over. An old man, nude except for a sack cloth girded around his loins held his skinny arms up to the sky, crying, "Repent! The Creator's judgment is upon us! REPENT!"

A little too late. I'm a damned man as any other around.

This was the madness of humanity shrouded in a thin veneer of civility, gone once the rules had changed. Tym knew it would only get worse once the invaders got inside. Then the slaughter would commence and women's dresses, jewelry, gold coin, none of it would matter. There would be more children left crying over dead mothers in the streets.

"We may encounter some difficulty once we get to this place," Tym said, looking at the buildings and trying to remember which ally led to section of hovels covering the Thieves' Door. He was certain there were others, but he'd look very foolish knocking on every hovel to find the right one.

"Difficulty?" Thrush frowned.

"There might be others who share in our idea of using the same route of exit," Tym said. *Or trying to profit from it.* He couldn't imagine the same guys who cut him would put up much of a complaint when he showed up with an army, in fact, he couldn't wait to see the surprise on their greedy, ugly mugs. He might use a clever line like, *remember me, you little bitches,* or a favorite of his, *a kicked dog will only cower for so long, before it bites your fucking face off.* The second seemed a tad too long for an entrance line.

"These others…. friends of yours?" Robin poked him in the ribs again.

"No." Tym grit his teeth. He tried to hobble to the opposite side of Thrush, but for such a short woman, Robin had a long reach, jabbing him again in the opposite side, like keeping a petulant ass on the same course. *I may be an ass, but I'm not stupid.* "More like annoyances."

"Just get us there and we will make sure these annoyances are not an inconvenience," Thrush said.

Getting there proved to be the bigger challenge. Tym tried to remember the structures where he'd spotted the men. This part of the city, all the buildings looked the same. Squat, three stories with undistinguishable signs, dirty stoops and cloudy windows, some broken and boarded over. No one was looting these ratty holes, not that they held much of value. People rushed on past to the Sunset gate, but his neck hairs prickled, like they were being watched.

"Turn there." Tym pointed at a narrow ally. At this stage, any narrow ally would be good enough. This one he thought might be familiar. Tym usually trusted his gut instincts, and this should be no different, especially when he needed them to be right. Once beyond the buildings, he was certain he could identify which hovel was his escape.

"Better be no surprises waiting for us," Robin said.

"No, no surprises," Tym said and gave his most friendly grin, which he was sure was a grimace, which regarding the circumstances of the pain and annoyance, was the best he could do.

Creator bless me let there be no surprises.

They could only move two abreast down the ally, Robin taking point and Thrush and Tailorson following. The innkeeper and his wife and son joined them on their exodus. The constant question from Tailorson's boy. "Where are we going?" "Will we be safe?" The glare from the glamorous Ms. Tailorson each time she responded, like she was accusing Tym of bringing this catastrophe on them. *I'm in the same shit as you, only I got us a way out, maybe.* Robin kept her hand close to her wide hips. A sword was belted and the scabbard swayed, clinking off the side of the building, reminding Tym of the consequence of his failure. The alley's ripe smell of old piss, sweat, and cooked onions tickled Tym's nose, he'd almost preferred the cellar stench. Broken glass glittered in the dying light, along with discarded boots and torn small clothes—some bloody and others stiff from various fluids. The shadows lengthened in the ally, but it was relatively short, and they emerged on a narrow street. It was empty, freshly washed by the rain. More buildings clustered in worse shape than the ones they passed. Tym could see the wall rising over the rooftops. Dark smoke blew across, adding the acrid stench of burning wood.

"We are getting close," he said. *Close to what, though?*

Robin grunted, gesturing for him to move on.

The street was empty. Tym hobbled forward, his muscles stiffening in his right leg as he tried to keep as much weight off the left. Lying down in the street and waiting for someone to trample him almost seemed like a good idea. He could pretend to be dead so they wouldn't kill him, but he didn't think fire would care if he was living or dead, just another object to feed.

He spotted movement in the ally two buildings away.

"There," Tym said. "We need to go that way."

"I saw them." Robin drew her blade and shoved Tym behind her. "Wait here."

Robin moved faster than Tym imagined her frame would allow. She leaned on the edge of the building, peering around the corner in a few heart beats. A hand touched his shoulder and Tym yelped, stumbling on his injured leg. Thrush gripped his shoulder, keeping him from planting face first into the uneven cobblestone. She gave a sweet smile that seemed more fitting a cat about to pounce on a bird, than it was for her.

"Aren't you going to help her?" Tym asked.

"She can handle herself," Thrush said.

Robin slipped around the corner. There were some harsh words, that turned to shouts, then screams that ended abruptly. Robin reappeared, wiping her blade on a torn piece of cloth. She waved them closer.

"See," Thrush said.

"Seems like they didn't know you," she said, sheathing the sword.

"Of course, they didn't," Tym looked beyond, saw two slumped forms. "I don't know this part of the city."

Pressure on his inner arm as Thrush squeezed made him hiss. "But you said you had a way out."

"I do," Tym said. "I meant that I don't do business this side of the main street."

"A man of discerning taste," Robin said, scowling. "Hurry up and get us out of here."

"I'm doing my best."

"Listen."

Tym heard nothing but the rustling of men marching behind them.

"What?"

"The bell has stopped," Thrush said.

"Which means."

"The men have abandoned the bell tower," Robin said. "The gate has fallen."

"Then we better hurry," Tym said and began to hobble down the ally, ignoring the two fresh corpses like he would a particularly nasty pile of trash. It ended in another street, this one closer to the east side of the wall. Tym chewed his tongue, trying to distinguish one pile of heaped crap that served as homes to the less fortunate, and less savory, from the one he wanted. There was a post where he tied up his horse, but he didn't see anything like it here.

"Which one are you?" He mumbled to himself. Euclid was a quarter of a league long, at the very least and there were dozens of choices. Part of him feared they went too far south. They had overshot it, but that didn't seem right.

"Well?" Robin gave an impatient nudge to his ribs.

"Um. It has to be here," Tym said. "It's in one of these, ugh, houses."

"Which one?" Nuthatch asked, whining in his ear.

"I don't know." Panic gnawed at him.

"What are we looking for?" Thrush asked

"A place with boxes, or maybe tables, stacked against the back wall. I was in a bit of a hurry, so I don't remember the details," he said, trying to assuage their angry glares. "Behind it was a door leading out of the city."

"A Thieves' Door," Robin said

"Yes."

Robin sighed and left Tym standing beside Thrush. Foot soldiers filled up the streets, more coming from the ally like a long snake emerging from its hole. Robin went to the first one, said something Tym couldn't hear and the soldier nodded, passing a command back. Dozens of foot soldiers spread out and began kicking in the doors to every hovel Tym could see. Some places shuddered and collapsed, the men clearing away before they were trapped under the rubble. People fled from others, caught up by soldiers. One man slipped past, pale and scraggly beard, eyes shining in fear and smelling of soured wine. Thrush caught his arm and he tried to twist away. Fear gave way to pain and the man dropped to his knees.

"What do you want?" Snot leaked from his nose and spittle flew from his mouth. *Poor bastard, just trying to eke out a living and found himself caught up in death's jaws.*

"The way out," Thrush said, calm and smiling. "Do you know where we can find it?"

The man lifted an arm and pointed further down.

"Show me," Thrush said.

"Please, don't hurt me." The man gave a big whimper.

"If you help me," Thrush said. "I will help you."

"Yes," the man said and coughed.

Thrush whistled and Robin responded in kind. A sharp cry went around and the foot soldiers ceased demolishing the hovels.

"We have a better guide to take us to where we want to go."

Tym realized that the value of his life just went down in price.

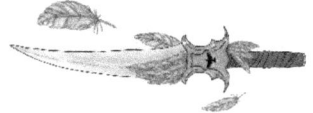

The overturned wagon wheel which served as a post where he'd tied his horse jogged Tym's memory. He'd been in such a hurry to leave his last visit, that it was any wonder he wanted to be there now. In fact, he wasn't sure where his horse went during all these chaotic events. *I hope she finds her way out and avoids ending up in some cooking pot.* He had lost his cart, the firewater, nearly a leg, and now his horse. This was turning into the worst two days ever. The way events were flowing against him, these could be the last two days he'd see.

And they weren't pretty days. No, he'd seen more shit, smelled more piss, witnessed more death than a lifetime's worth. His biggest regret was leaving his niece with his asshole brother. Everyone knew Bryn was abusive, yet no one did anything to help the poor girl out.

If I survive all this, Tym hobbled up the street, *I'll make things right.*

He'd led the group several hundred yards north of their destination. If Tym had remembered which shit hole building in the biggest dump of the city, they would be further south. Then he would have seen the line of people shoving and pushing to enter the place he narrowly escaped from with his life. A dozen armed men kept watch, knocking people down and chasing them off if they caused too much of a problem, or didn't have the right payment.

Not only did he see them, but they saw him and the army he brought. The organized chaos dissolved into one big rush for the door. Two people at most could pass through in the same instance, but dozens had clogged it. Tym didn't blame them, because he would do the same to flee an army marching up the street.

Swords struck flesh, slicing through the unarmed crowd. Severed limbs dropped into the street, blood sprayed, guts dropped and people screamed, shoving harder until the makeshift door cracked. One thug slipped in the blood and was trampled under the mass of people. Others were stabbed, sliced, hacked, corpses shoved aside until no one was left.

Tym saw children, crying and clinging to their dead and dying parent, stabbed and chopped by the thieves, completing the family unity. One man grabbed a little girl and dragged her away, kicking and screaming into the hovel. Tym shouted, "Hey fucker, drop her!" He tried to run and take back the girl, but his leg buckled and he bent over, spewing hot, stinking vomit.

"This must be your first human shit show." Robin clapped him on the back. "Fear turns everyone into animals fleeing a forest fire."

"They killed all those people," Tym said and burped up more bile.

"Now we are going to do the same to them," Robin said. Those words seemed oddly comforting to Tym.

Thrush shoved back her petticoat, revealing two of the largest knives Tym had ever seen. She twirled them expertly around and winked at him. Then she led the charge into the remaining four thugs who were busy robbing the corpses instead of making a hasty exit like their smarter companions. Two dozen soldiers followed her.

Robin harrumphed. "Such a showoff."

The thugs noticed the trouble coming at them and like the brave men they were, they scrambled over the bodies and made for the exit. One of Thrush's daggers took the lead man in the throat and he fell, creating another obstacle for the trailing three. They cursed and tripped, fought to unsheathe weapons, getting more tangled in the mess they'd created. Thrush's second dagger flew, narrowly missing one man and thudded into the check of another. His head snapped to the side, blood spraying and he dropped. By then, the soldiers were on the other two, and it ended in squeals and squeaks, more bodies to add to the pile. Tym didn't know if he should be horrified or give a cheer.

"We need that place secured," Robin said and pointed to more soldiers who joined the ones already in front of the hovel. They cleared away the corpses from the entrance, tossing them like lumps of sacks full of rotten potatoes. Tym tried to hobble along, but Robin grabbed him. "It's not safe for you to go. In fact, you will wait here with me until everyone is outside these walls."

"Why?" Tym moaned. "I honored my word and got you here."

"This guy got us here," Robin said jerking her thumb at the smelly, half-drunk with watery red eyes. "You nearly got us lost, walking the maze until the walls fell in on us. As your reward, we wait to make sure there's no more surprises or details you missed."

Tym's heart sank, watching line after line of soldiers enter the hovel, praying that they kept going and didn't stop, praying the invading army wouldn't reach them before he made his exit, and a final prayer that nothing bad waited for them on the other side. Robin motioned for their stinky guide to follow the queue of soldiers, and Tym had a moment of envy, wishing he was inebriated out of his mind so he could pass all this off as wine fumes.

Worse was the smell. Voided bladders and bowels mixed in with blood and innards on the outwards. Tym gagged, thinking he'd never be able to see slaughtered meat again, let alone eat it, without the smell filling his nose like water sucked up by a drowning man. Smoke thickened, dropping ash in tiny flakes.

"Shouldn't we be going now?" The line of soldiers was thinning. Soon there'd be no one left on this back street but Robin and himself. Unless the army chasing them came pouring down like locusts devouring crops.

"When I said we were the last, I meant it." Robin looked at the sky, brow furrowing. She sighed. "Not a single cloud. Not a damn thing I can do to save the city."

"What do you mean?"

"All of it will burn," Robin said. "That's his way."

"Whose?"

"Cacophony."

None of it made a bit of sense to him. He shut his mouth and willed the soldiers to move quicker. His legs were aching, near trembling when the last one finally passed through. Tym heard the distant sound of fighting.

"Looks like it's our turn," Robin said. "Can you walk?"

"I will crawl if I have to," Tym said and he half dragged his leg. Fresh red blooms appeared on the bandage. There was nothing he could do about it, except hope it didn't fester and cost him the leg. *Another terrible payment for a terrible visit. Hadn't I paid enough?*

The hovel was dark, but enough light from outside showed the crates tossed aside, wooden planks broken. Another corpse was sprawled among the wreckage, just another piece of trash cast aside. The back wall had a hole in the wall like he remembered. A breeze blew through smelling, old and musty and something else. Robin hurried through and Tym followed.

"Careful," Robin said, "there's another body here."

Tym's boot toe kicked something soft, which squelched as he eased his injured foot over it. He continued down the tunnel, hands brushing the walls to keep his balance. All the time his footsteps echoed, and his mind formed images of soldier running in pursuit. That before he completed his escape, they'd grab him, maybe skewer him with a spear or sword. Another body to add to the pile ready to burn in the entombment of Euclid. Then he saw daylight, or twilight as it was becoming. He stumbled out of the tunnel, caught his foot on a rock, and dropped to his hands and knees. What he thought was a rock, was another corpse. Tym squeaked, dry and raspy. His throat burned from the vomit; his tongue soured.

"Here." Robin stood over him, extending her hand. He took it and she pulled him up, allowing him to put some weight on her and off his leg. They were clear of the wall, heading into the sparse woods away from the wall. In the dying light, Tym saw the flames rise from the Sunset gate, smoke pluming the air. Tired, exhausted, almost unable to go on, he sagged in her grip.

"Set me down," he said, but Robin half-carried him.

"We're almost there."

"Where?"

She grunted. "You'll see."

They walked long into the night and Tym thought he'd collapse on top of Robin, but she was strong, and in the end, he was being dragged along more than walking. They had cleared the thin trees and circled around the city and further up the road. There waiting were mounted soldiers and covered wagons.

"Nazglum's nuts!" The second army had somehow beat them outside the city and now they were caught.

"Ha!" Robin hefted him and made him stand on his two legs. "These are our troops."

"What?"

"You didn't think we would be foolish to keep all our eggs in the same nest," Thrush said. "Do you plan on staying or coming with us?"

"I'm going wherever you go," Tym said.

"Then get in the wagon before you slow us even more."

Like that, his luck had turned and the terrible day he spent in Euclid was left behind, burned away. He clambered inside one wagon, laying on a soft blanket, the night didn't seem so bad. Losing his livelihood didn't seem so bad. Not when he still had his life.

All about perspective.

Sure as the pain would return to his abused leg, he figured he'd be paying for it all, long after the night had ended.

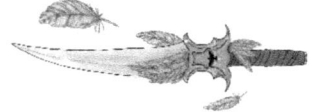

Claiborne entered the city through the burning gates. Spiraling flames billowed thick clouds of smoke. Sweat beaded on her forehead, her hair clinging to her skull. She moved away quickly enough before her hair caught fire. As it was, the heat baked her in her armor. *Like sweetbread ready for a feast.* Bodies smoldered around the gate, human beans cooked in a tin can. Despite the wet cloth over her mouth and nose, smoke stung her eyes and they watered. Not enough to obscure the carnage she found once entering the city.

Nothing like sacking a city. Claiborne swept aside a blade and stuck the attacker in the armpit, bursting his heart and watching him slide to the blackened cobblestones. *Burning buildings, soldiers running every which way. They're ants. Little ants to be crushed beneath my boots.* She stepped on a soldier who was crying for his mother. Men often did when they were dying, reverting back to some fetal quality that disgusted Claiborne. She silenced his pleas with a quick downward thrust though the gap in his chest plate. Arron had cried when he was dying— for her, not his mother. Claiborne couldn't go near him. The horror he must have seen while his body twisted into a hideous creature. Twisted by Thrush and her fucking song. In those moments, death becomes another little pleasure in life to be grateful for.

An arrow skidded off her right pauldron. She swung her head in the direction where it had flown from and spotted a man ducking beside the building, fumbling for another arrow. A hairsbreadth closer, or a shift in the wind, or even an involuntary twitch, and she would be choking on the arrow. That's the way it was in war. Luck was the difference between living to fight, or drowning in your own blood. Nothing for her to get angry over.

Not my day to die.

When the archer showed his face again, she had an axe ready. Arm cocked back, a motion she had done hundreds of times, hitting chunks of wood or straw dummies. A simple flick of her wrist and snap of her elbow, released at a chest level with a straight arm. Technique was important. Head and handle spun through the air. The sharp edge hit the bow and sent the arrow wide where it impaled another city guard running at her flank. The guard double over, clutching at the arrow sticking out from his gut. Luck had chosen him rather than her. *Never dice, save your luck for the battlefield.* That used to be her and Arron's mantra, before Arron gambled away his life. Claiborne finished off the screeching city guard with a chop to the neck, nearly taking his head off. Removing a man's head wasn't always necessary, though it was an effective way to make sure he was dead and couldn't slither up on you unexpectedly.

The key to enjoying the sack of city was to survive the initial contact with the defenders, much like all the social engagements Claiborne had experienced. There was the awkward meeting, feeling out the opponent, then the riposte of banter and awkward silence that followed as you discover only blood was in common. But even then, some blood glistened brighter crimson. She reached the edge of the building while the archer tried for a third time to kill her. Third times the charm, she heard it said, but the man proved that axiom to be false. Her sword cut through his string and opened his bowls.

"What's worse than eating a plate of fried liver and kidneys?" The man didn't respond, having a sword buried in your gut would make it rather difficult to find the right words. "Eating your own shit."

He stared at her in complete shock, the way a person hearing an offensive joke might widen their eyes and drop their jaw—she was never good at landing them anyway. His intestines snagged on her sword when she yanked it out, trailing sausage links plopping at his feet where she shook it off. He muttered something and screamed, trying to pick up his innards, but it was too late. Much like a bad joke, he fell flat on his face.

She looked around, but there was no one else to kill. She figured most would be retreating to the Sunrise gate. Knowing this didn't lessen her disappointment. Her hope was to trap one or two or three of the little birdies, three birds with one city. That would no doubt bring great pleasure to Cacophony. Unlike other armies which looted a city, taking away whatever riches and women, men, children, to be used as pleased, the Silent Men left everything to burn: people and possessions.

"The Creator provides," Claiborne repeated the mantra, wiping her blade on the dead man's cloak.

Skirmishes would intensify the further they pressed the Singers and their remaining troop against the far gate. They might find refuge in some buildings which would prompt a tedious search. A city this size, she figured, would have over two thousand buildings, not counting the ones on fire. Could be morning and half the city burned down before they thoroughly searched every nook and cranny. If they tried a desperate escape out of the Sunrise gate, then they'd be dead a lot sooner. The thing about walls were that they protected the sheep as long as the wolves were kept outside, but once the wolves got it, well, the mutton was on the meal plan. Roast mutton.

"Third Sword!" Claiborne pulled down her rag and called to a big man who'd come from a building that was smoldering. He wore a wet rag, hood was up, covered in gray dust or ash. He carried a large ax, great for unlocking stubborn doors.

"First Sword," he saluted, "building is clear."

"Split the men into search parties of five," Claiborne ordered, "start with the buildings on the main street, then fan back. Make sure they have a spotter and a runner for the larger pockets of resistance. Tell them not to engage the women alone. Their voices may be silenced, but they are still reputable fighters."

"The buildings around the Sunset gate?"

"I will have eyes on them. If anything moves, they'll kill it."

"As you command, First Sword." He saluted and moved off, then went off to organize the soldiers into cordon parties.

One thing she admired about the Silent Men was how efficient they were. No bulking at orders. Not that they had much of a choice. Once you made your mark on the paper, you were marked until such time as death released you, or the Silent Men were no longer needed. Their current success rate at hunting the Singers, or lack thereof, meant they would be in service for a very long time.

She didn't mind. It's not like she had any family waiting for her. Most of the men and women who joined the Silent Men did so because they had no other ties holding them to one place, or because the ties they had were severed by the Singers. Many had a personal interest in clipping the birdies' wings. Claiborne dreamed of crushing Thrush in her fists, squeezing her thin neck until those brown eyes bulged and her lips turned blue.

"First Sword."

She spun and saw a small boy dressed in black trousers and tunic like some perverse shadow. He possessed neither armor nor weapon, not being of age, yet, though the light fuzz under his nose showed he was nearing the age. For now, he served as messenger, and this one had a brooch pinned to his left breast in the shape of a black, shiny bug. Cacophony's personal messenger. The boy held out a folded piece of parchment. Claiborne took it, frowned at the four words scrawled across it. *Come to me now!*

Claiborne shredded the paper, letting them fall to add to the cobblestones.

"Take me to him," she said, not having to say who. What Cacophony had to say wouldn't be good. Interrupting her search of the city wasn't good at all. She had a strange stirring in her gut that she had failed, but wasn't sure how. Not when she had just begun this hunt. There was no way the birds could have flown the nest. She had them, dead on and ready to fry up.

The boy led her back up the hill where they first watched the carts ignite the walls. Cacophony's black carriage sat ominously, a single black cloud to spoil an otherwise perfectly clear sky. The sun had nearly set, leaving a reddening bruise behind. Torches were set up around the carriage, yellowish light shimmering against the glossy black doors and shuttered windows.

Two honor guards, mostly for aesthetics rather than actual protection, stood at attention, spear butts on the ground, and shields slung across their arms. On their shields was the symbol for the Silent Men—an outline of a mouth with a single finger bisecting the middle, the way one might shush someone, or as Claiborne always saw it, a cock pressed against the lips. Either worked for her, but she kept this amusing observation to herself. The guards eyeballed her, forgoing the salute and not bothering to challenge her. She was First Sword, answering only to the big man, Cacophony himself. Not that she had any say in what the guards did or did not do, because they also answered directly to Cacophony. Like estranged cousins, they neither spoke of nor acknowledged the others' existence. It would stay that way as long as she remained in Cacophony's good graces. Otherwise, they would become very intimate like kissing cousins, with Claiborne kissing her ass good-bye.

The boy left her and climbed up to the seat beside the coach man on the carriage's top bench. A team of four black draft horses flicked their tails and bobbed their heads as Claiborne approached the carriage. Sometimes she would cut an apple into four sections and feed them. She had no apple, since carrying one into battle seemed a bit presumptuous. Who had time to pause and crunch into the crispy flesh when there were people to kill?

Claiborne rapped her knuckles on the carriage door. Her dark reflection, a shadow on the glass. She waited, pressing her fingers together, fighting back the fear, anger, and disappointment of being pulled from battle at the moment of her triumph. She had those bitches where she always wanted them. She could almost taste their blood on her fingertips.

The carriage door swung open and Claiborne took a step back. She knew better than to approach without invite. That would be a good way to punch your ticket to your own death. The strong smell of onions wafted out and a strained voice beckoned her.

"Come in, First Sword."

Claiborne grimaced. She hated tight enclosures, though the carriage was larger than most, it was still too small for her liking and smelled of a sanctified tomb. Ducking her head, she entered and slid on the bench across from Cacophony, careful not to knock knees. It was warm inside, the leather almost sticky, and she leaned back as far as the seat would give. There was a clicking of flint and a lantern hissed. Claiborne made a strangled cough, spotting the girl sitting so close to her. A finger's length closer and she would be sitting on the girl's lap.

Muslin covered the lower-part of his face and chitin-armor still donned, Cacophony narrowed his eyes, watching Claiborne. She wanted to fidget, but there wasn't room to maneuver, not without touching either the girl or her father. It was like a child's game of poison where you didn't want to get tagged, because you'd be dead and out of the game. Claiborne wanted very much to remain in this game. At least until she killed Thrush, then everything else was negotiable.

"Claire." He spoke her old name, a name she hadn't used in a long time, nearly another lifetime ago. A name from a brighter period in her life, when she believed in justice and the naïve idea that people deserved it. The name of a dead person, lost when the light went out of her world. Fuck, she wished she could wax poetic and not sound like such a nit.

"Claire," he repeated, muslin wrap puffing out like a sigh. "You know why

I chose you?"

This was a rhetorical question. One which was answered many times and no longer required conversing over. He knew, she knew, Nazglum twist her titty, but even the girl could recite the response, though she remained eerily silent. No singing, no giggling. She sat with the doll in her lap, smiling up at Claiborne, making her skin want to crawl away to some dark hole, her bones not far behind.

"To hunt," Claiborne said, keeping the answer simple. Simple was best when you didn't know the intentions of the one asking. Although, she could guess. It was in his dead stare.

Cacophony nodded.

"To hunt." He leaned forward, hand on Claiborne's legs in a way more intimate than she wanted. "To catch the woman who ruined your happiness, the one responsible for the deaths of thousands, no, hundreds of thousands, of good people. An abomination of the Creator's creation, perverted by Nazglum's touch." His hand slid up her thigh. She sat stunned at the unexpected and unwanted affection.

"I…I have her," Claiborne said. "Trapped."

"Is she now?"

"The city is surrounded and on f-fire." His fingers dug into her inner thigh.

"Old news," Cacophony said. "I want new news."

"We are conducting a building-by-building search for the women," she said and swallowed. "I was going to press deeper into the city, looking to cut off any escape from the Sunrise gate."

"Gone," the girl said and giggled.

Claiborne ignored her. She spoke to her doll and could mean anything, even reciting Claiborne's fears. The girl had an uncanny ability to speak the unspeakable locked in Claiborne's heart. There was no way the women could escape.

"It's standard procedure to start at the front buildings and work our way inward, to spiral back, preventing them from changing positions between the gaps in the net." The words were coming automatically. He knew the procedures, he understood how to hunt for hiding enemies. What he wanted from her, she knew, was to get over her denial and look at the glaring problem. *Fuck!* Somehow, she missed an important detail. "The… the net…won't work."

"Why?"

"Because their army is too damn big to hide in a city this size."

Cacophony nodded and patted her leg.

"I don't understand," Claiborne said. "We had them trapped inside, the Sunset Gate fired, the Sunrise one watched. Did anyone report from Sunrise?"

Cacophony shook his head.

"Glorian says they're gone," the girl said, standing the doll up and holding it with the straw-stuffed arms out to the side like it was being crucified.

"That's not right," Claiborne said, feeling the need to punch the child, a fatal mistake, but anger was nipping at reason, and she needed to lash out. Instead, she punched the carriage wall, causing it to shudder. *There's no way they could've escaped!* Claiborne glared at the grinning child. "She's lying! I had them trapped."

"Glorian is never wrong, my dear." There was a touch of sadness in his tone. "It doesn't matter the how or why of it, just that the women have once again alluded you, which has become a rather bad habit of late."

Claiborne wanted to blubber it wasn't her fault, that she had done everything she could, but the city was too big to watch everything at once and still sack it properly. Such protests were for the weak, and would fall on deaf ears. Might as well shout at the doll. The results remained the same.

"Is your heart still in the hunt, Claire?"

"Yes, yes, it is." It beat rather hard in her chest at the moment and that was where she desired to keep it. "There's nothing more I want in this life than those women dead." She watched his hand reach under his wing-like cloak, adjusting a strap that could hold a knife or a flask—not once had she seen him drink. *I'm going to die here.* Which was no worse than dying in a burning city, except she would leave her lover's memories behind in disappointing fashion. "I won't fail you, again."

"Fail me." Cacaphony sat back, clucked his tongue, and brought his hand from his pocket, fingers closed in a fist. "Fail me. Huh? Is that what you think you did?" He turned with his wrist and opened his hand. Claiborne saw a dried flower, white petals flattened and a splash of pink on the edges. "Failure is when you are dead." He lifted the flower to the lantern. "A woman once promised me a kiss if I got her this flower. I climbed the tallest tree, reached out to the furthest branch, my body tensed and ready to fall. I plucked this flower and climbed down. Only to find her father waiting for me. He beat me, tossed me in a hole. The rain began and the hole filled with water. I thought I would die, huddled there in the cold, I could have given up. But I climbed out. I lived." He moved the flower closer for Claiborne to scrutinize. "I never kissed that girl, but I did keep this flower as a reminder of what I had to do to survive. I gave it to my wife. It was pure white back then. The pink is her blood, faded after many years, but it used to be bright scarlet the day I found her body."

He gestured with his hand.

"Take it, please."

Claiborne let it fall into her gloved hand. It was light, almost insignificant, but the weight of it caused her arms to tremble. Her brow furrowed. She wasn't expecting any of this.

"Thank you."

"Don't thank me," Cacophony said. "It is a reminder for you."

"A reminder."

"Failure is death." Leather creaking as he eased back against the cushions. "Those women will be dead by the next moon, or your blood will darken the petals."

"*Pretty ladies in gowns, dressed for a ball, skin pallor as fresh fallen snow,*" the girl sang, "*go a dancing in moonlight on graves marked by stones engraved in their name. Pretty ladies in shrouds, wait for Death's hand. He'll dance them to hell where they'll never be heard from again.*"

The song raised gooseflesh on her arms and she leaned against the carriage door.

"Isn't she wonderful," Cacophony said, a thickening in his voice, making it sound wet and ready to crack. "She sings like an angel, if angels existed."

"Beautiful," Claiborne said, the word hollow and she stared at the flower. Her blood could glisten on the petals. Death was thirsty, she knew.

"This is what makes life worth living," he said. "Such beautiful music. The Creator blessed our world, but we must remove Nazglum's taint before we lose it all. That's what you and I have in common. We both lost someone we deeply loved to those abominations. I mean to honor my wife, the pink on the petals, to purify it once again."

"They will be dead by the next moon." Claiborne folded the petal in her hand and slipped it in a pouch attached to her belt. "Then I will return the flower to you."

"Yes, yes," Cacophony nodded. "Now leave before I tear your heart out and place it in your hands as you watch its last beats. Then you can tell your love how you failed him."

Claiborne shoved the door open, ducking her head and then jumped out from the carriage. The door slammed shut. The guards didn't bother to look at her as she marched down the hill to the City of Euclid. Fire consumed the gates, the walls, blazing among more buildings. She shouted for her soldiers.

"Orders, sir?"

"Call back the troop. Keep the gate sealed. Let it burn." Fire light glowed in her eyes. "Let it all burn."

CHAPTER EIGHT:
LET IT RAIN

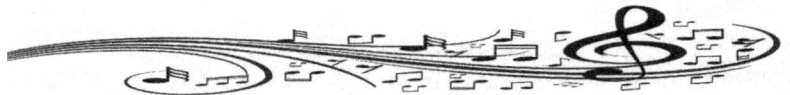

The rain I missed the most trapped in Oblivion, kept from feeling anything, my mind suspended in a long, drawn-out dream. The rain with its sweet release from the heat of a long Sowing, to wash away the dirt and sweat. To feed the depleted wells and slacken thirst. The first drops on your tongue before the start of a battle. This world was dying of drought brought on by the constant draw of life from the Void. Oblivion hungered. It thirsted. Blood would soon rain, swelling the land.

Rain caught Ivy out on the road. Clouds had snuck over the night sky, blotting out the moon and stars, until she was walking blind. Large cold drops washed over her, a miserable way to end a miserable day. Just when she thought she was ready to cry, to throw herself in the middle of the road and smash her fists into the hardpacked ground until it cracked opened, swallowing her whole, or until her hands fell off leaving bloody stumps, her anger boiled over, leaving no room for tears. How dare her father toss her out! How dare Crisell stare at her like she was some creature raised from the shadow! She'd saved their lives. Ungrateful bastards though they were, they would have died unless Ivy saved them.

Fittingly, the sky cried for her. Buckets and buckets. Enough to soak her. She looked around for shelter. At this rate, she'd die from exposure before she made it half-way to Euclid. Uncle Tym would come riding back and find her body lying on the side of the road, mirroring her mother. A drowned little country rat without a nest to call her own.

Creator bless me! Is that…. A light flickered in the distance. Ivy slogged along, her legs churning against mud. The closer she got to the light, the clearer the outline of a barn and house. She didn't know whose place it was, nor did she plan on knocking on the door. It would be difficult explaining what a young girl was doing alone on this rainy night and carrying nothing but the clothes on her back in the storm. Best she could hope for would be dry straw to curl up in.

By the time she reached the barn, she felt like a worm trying not to drown. Drenched, mud-covered her clogs and tights up to her knees. She didn't know what was worse, melting under the sun or being pounded into sludge by cold rain. In less than a full-sun-turn, she went from sweating to shivering, her teeth chattering in rhythm of the falling rain. The front entrance, a heavy sliding door, was closed, latched, and had a metal lock to prevent thieves from breaking in during the night and stealing livestock. It also kept Ivy out in the rain. She groaned, her teeth chattering louder.

There has to be a way in. She glanced at the house and shook her head. There would be no one she trusted out here. *Alone. Got to keep moving before you catch your death of cold.* Ivy shuffled along the edge, keeping under the barn's roof eaves where the rain sluiced down, splashing mud up her legs. She found a side door that didn't appear locked. She wiggled the latch and it opened. It was dark, smelling of dry hay and old shit. A cow lowed and a goat bleated. *A perfect place to get murdered in.* Die outside, wet and alone, or risk being killed in a dry, warm place. The choice was clear. Ivy shuffled along in the dark, seeking a pile of hay, or maybe a blanket, to cover up in and wait out the storm.

Her shin hit a hard, immovable object. Pain jarred up her leg, like a hot poker slammed into her bone, forcing her to sit down. It hurt so much, she believed that she broke it. Broken bones would be a wonderful ending to a horrific day. Ivy sucked back a cry and rubbed her shin. The combination of mud and wetness chaffed her skin. How could she survive the road to Euclid when she was about to die of cold and rain and broken bones in a dark, smelly barn less than two leagues from her home? She would end up like her mother. Body stripped and bloated in a ditch, flesh gnawed by animals, almost beyond the point of recognition. They identified her by the necklace containing a painted image of Ivy, a gift from a strange woman in town.

"She'll be a special one," the woman had said, at least according to her mother. "Keep this trinket and she'll always be safe."

Ivy believed Bryn when he called what the woman sold her mother as "fool's prophecy." It didn't prevent her mother from being murdered.

The pain quit shrieking, quieting into a dull throb and her wet clothes trapped the cold against her skin. She shivered, wanting to strip out of her clinging clothes. What a surprise the farmer would find in the morning, a naked, frozen girl slumped over probably inches from warm hay. She tried to stand, but her leg protested. She crawled, dirt and straw clinging to her hands, right hand reaching out in front of her, so as not to bash her head. Metal tines scraped across her knuckles. Ivy cried out and sucked the injured hand.

Bloody barn will be the death of me. She wrapped her arms around her knees, too afraid to venture from her spot. *Might be better off braving the storm.*

A rattling sounded by the front. *Rats?* No, it was the scraping of a key in a metal lock. Ivy froze. The crash of rain grew louder as the barn door opened. Cold wind rushed through, setting her teeth to chattering no matter how hard she tried to clench them. Light from a lantern shone through the dark. Ivy sat still, hoping it would pass through when a figure draped in a cloak hung the lantern on a hook. The edge of the light reached her skirt, which she snatched back into the shadows.

"What have we here?" The cloak dropped, revealing a young man's face. Damp black hair matted on his forehead and his face was caught in shadows. "Seems we have rats. Big ones from the look of it."

He didn't sound concerned.

If he knew what I did… what I can do, he would run as far away from me as possible. The song remained quiet and distant. She couldn't access it even if she wanted to at the moment. What good was the power when it worked only when she was threatened?

"Not a rat," he said, taking a step closer. She recognized his face from earlier in Welksdale. He'd helped her draw water from the well. "A wet mouse?"

"Mah…mah… my name," Ivy tried to talk, but her teeth chattered too hard. She had never felt so cold in her life. "Ivy."

"Ivy." The man stopped, considering the name. "Ivy Lyre? Didn't your mother die…."

Ivy nodded.

"I'm sorry. My name is Danial. I always say too much," the man said and crouched down. His forehead crinkled, concern filling his brown eyes. "I don't get many guests. They are as rare as the rains, lately. Looks like you got washed up from the creek. Let's get you inside the house and out of those wet clothes."

Danial's cheeks flushed and Ivy almost laughed at his embarrassment.

"I didn't mean—"

"Yes," Ivy said. She extended her hand, but Danial just looked at it. "Hel… hell… help me up."

"Oh." Danial took her hand. It was big and warm, unexpectedly gentle. He stood, allowing her to use him a counterweight to get to her feet. "Just head up to the porch. Door's unlocked. I got to feed the animals."

Ivy prickled with annoyance that he wasn't going to help her further. Couldn't he see she was in pain? But he grabbed a meal bag and started filling it with oats. *Men are stupid.* No other explanation was needed.

"An…annyone else," Ivy stopped talking and pointed where she thought the house was located.

Danial shook his head.

"I live alone, but I got a nice fire going." He held the scoop, dripping with oats and Ivy waited for him to say more. "Oh, once I'm done with the animals, I'll make you some warm tea."

"Th…thank you." Ivy wrapped her arms around herself and headed back into the rain. Danial seemed strange, strange enough that she should keep walking. He was also kind, and sometimes a little kindness was all that kept the world from burning down. Also, she would miss out on being warm and dry. She didn't know what lay beyond the farm, but she knew it would be more mud and the clouds went on beyond what she could see. Her uncle wouldn't travel in the rain. If she found walking difficult, then the wheels of the cart would get stuck making it impossible. When the rain passed, she would continue on to Euclid.

Water splashed her clogs while she ran-shambled for the porch, the pain in her shin competing against the driving cold and wet, Ivy nearly lost her footing a few times and went sprawling in the mud. Creator blessed her one thing wet right and she gained the porch still standing. She knocked on the door, making sure Danial wasn't lying about being alone. No one replied and she entered. A light, musty odor and decay struck her first. It was short-lived, there and gone. Warmth drew in, her cheeks glowing. Danial also didn't lie about the fire. It crackled across the small room. There was a table, empty except for a cup and a book. Two chairs were at opposing sides of the table. Beyond that, the room was sparse. A ladder went up to a dark loft beside the hearth. Ivy sat on the floor in front of the hearth. She stripped off her clogs, holding her feet out to the fire. Her legs were still cold and wet. Ivy began tugging her leggings when the front door opened. Danial frowned at the muddy prints.

"Sorry," Ivy said, rolling the coarse material over one foot.

"Nothing to worry about," Danial said, though his facial expression told a different story, a tight smile like her father got before the angry explosion. He shrugged off his boots and set them by the door. "Easy for me to clean up."

"Do you have a towel?"

"I said I would clean it up," Danial snapped, not yelling, but not exactly conversational, either.

"For me," Ivy said, trying to keep a calm voice. The song broiled beneath, whispering to be released. Ivy kept it tamped down. No one else needed to die, she had filled her quota on that butcher's tab.

Danial laughed, a loud, tight sound. Much like a hammer striking metal about to shatter.

"I got something for you." He walked in her direction. Ivy took a step back, reaching for a poker. He was bigger than her, but a sharp metal prong to the eye would even the odds. Danial walked past her, climbing the ladder to the loft. "It's not much," he said from above, shuffling things around, "it used to belong to my mother, and she was near your size."

"What happened to her?" Ivy asked.

"She died." The ladder creaked and Danial climbed down. "Same as father. Lung rot."

"I'm sorry," Ivy said. *Been saying it too much, starting to lose any meaning.*

Danial turned and held out a white sheet in one hand and a blue dress in the other. "This to dry off," he held out the sheet. He smiled normally, a handsome one, and appraised Ivy. "This to wear while your clothes dry. Yes, it will fit."

Ivy took the sheet and Danial kept standing there, smiling at her.

Ivy coughed.

"Are you feeling sick?" Danial asked.

"No," Ivy said. "Just used to privacy when I strip off my clothes."

"Oh, yes, yes, sorry." Danial turned his back to her.

Ivy waited while Danial stood there.

"Let me know when you're done. I'll get some tea brewing."

Ivy rolled her eyes. Too cold to care if he stared, she peeled out of the soaked dress, expecting Danial to turn and peek at her. But he didn't.

"Do you keep it next to you when you sleep?"

"The sheet? Of course, I do."

"I meant the dress." It was a light blue color, probably meant for Creator Day strolls and picnics.

"I keep it in a chest at the end of the bed," Danial said. "Seemed a shame to get rid of it when someone could find some use in it. Seems I made a good choice."

Ivy was still too wet to put the dress on and finished wrapping the sheet around her.

"All done," she said.

Danial turned back around. Again, he smiled, fire light shining in his eyes.

"You are pretty," he said with all the emotion of appraising a sheep. Ivy wasn't sure how to respond. She was used to crude comments, leering looks, and groping hands. Danial seemed sincere and she trusted that even less. "Put your clothes by the fire and you sit here. You'll be dry in no time."

Make him go away, the song whispered. Ivy pressed her lips tight, trapping the song. She couldn't let it get out of control, no matter how much it swelled in her. She placed her wet clothes by the fire and sat down, watching him add water to a cast iron kettle, and then set it on a hook over the flames. Danial opened a small cupboard. It was mostly bare, except for a few items. He brought out a cup and some dried black leaves.

"What were you doing out in the rain?" Danial asked, crinkling black leaves into a metal ball full of holes and placed it into the cup.

"Walking," Ivy said. "I was on my way to the city."

"Didn't you see the storm? I can smell the rain before it comes." Danial sat at one of the chairs by the table. "It's sweet, sort of, like a flower before it goes sour. Or blood. Fresh blood right after the knife slits the goat's throat."

"That's ah… vivid," Ivy said and gave a strained laugh. She glanced at the poker.

"Is it?" Danial's forehead wrinkled. "I guess it is. Are you hungry? I have some bread and cheese."

Ivy's stomach growled. She hadn't had a decent meal in… she couldn't remember the last meal. There were plenty of chances, she was forced to abandon meals, some crushed, all ruined by the Fugglies. The knife jabbing in and out of the eye socket, spraying blood and flecks of bone and gray matter. It was enough to kill her appetite. Almost.

"Both," she said. "Thank you."

He cut off a chunk of hard bread and a lump of even harder cheese, setting them on a plate before handing it to Ivy. She chewed fast, nearly choking, and forced herself to slow down. She licked the crumbs off her fingers, staring at the empty plate.

They listened to the rain thrum hard on the roof and windows. Ivy was grateful for the fire, even though Danial kept stealing glances at her, scrubbing his hands together. When the kettle got hot enough, he poured her tea.

"I don't usually have guests." He handed her the cup, taking the plate from her.

"Why not?"

Danial shrugged.

"No one comes out my way and I don't have any friends." He gave a shy grin. "I'm not the sociable kind, my mother used to say. I hardly ever go into town unless I need things I can't make or grow, that's where I saw you by the well. The girl with the bucket of water."

"Sounds like a name of a painting," Ivy said.

"Oh I… I don't paint," Danial said, "I got no artistic bone in my body."

"What do you do out here by yourself?"

"I grow food."

"That's an art all on its own," Ivy said. "My father couldn't grow weeds."

"No, but he makes a mean bit of firewater, so my dad told me," Danial said. "'Don't you touch that stuff,' my father says to me, 'it'll make your eyes bleed out.' And I ain't never touched the stuff."

"More-than-like, it'll rot your gut and not your eyes," Ivy said.

"I ain't never touched it." He held up two fingers, kissed them and touched his place over his heart. "Water and tea are fine for me."

She sniffed the cup. It was strong and didn't smell poisoned. Not that she would know. She tasted it. Bitter black licorice. On the rare occasion she drank tea, she was used to having some sweetener, but didn't want to ask. He seemed a simple man. Simple tea would be the best she got, which was better than nothing.

"Whelp, it's getting late and the sun rises awfully early." Danial raised his hands and let them smack his legs. "I don't have an extra bed for you to sleep in, but you can have my blanket."

"That'll be fine," Ivy said. She grimaced as she took another swallow of tea. *I'll be on my way, as soon as the rain stops.*

"Sleep by the fire." He pointed at the floor, like telling a dog to stay "It'll be warm most of the night."

Ivy eyed the poker, again. She would keep it very close.

Danial went around and turned down all the oil lamps, leaving the red glow of the hearth fire to light the room. It was comforting, much better than sleeping in some musty hay in the barn, but she was still worried. Danial was a stranger and she was alone where no one knew where she was, not that she had any other options or that anyone cared. He stood by the ladder, looking at her. His long shadow cast on the wall made him appear more menacing. He grinned at her and then clambered up the ladder. A moment later a wool blanket flopped down.

Danial's head peered over the edge. "Sleep well."

Ivy put aside the tea, then took the blanket and retreated back to the fire. She dropped the sheet covering her and put on the dress. Simple though he may be, Danial had a good eye. It fit well, a little loose at the bosom, but it would work until her own clothes dried. Glancing up at the loft, she heard soft snores. She took the poker from its stand, placed it next to her as she rolled up in the blanket and listened to the rain. Sleep evaded her. The visions of the Stephone stabbing himself over and over, squelch of the flesh opening for the knife, blood splattering and then squirting, haunted her every time she closed her eyes. Her own father sending her out, rejecting her after she saved his worthless life. Crisell cringing away from her like she was some creature going to bite him.

Nazglum take them both!

Ivy did what she had to because no one else could. They would all be dead, if she hadn't used whatever this power was inside her. What would they do with the bodies? The Fugglies were fugitives who robbed the Exchequer, there might be a reward for their capture, but she did murder them. As far as she knew, murder was a crime in Welksdale, fugitives or not. Would the Sheriff be looking for her? She tossed round, these worries keeping her awake long after the fire burned into glowing embers. Rain thrummed on, and she remembered the song from her mother that she sang when Bryn was passed out. It was like their secret.

"Shhh, don't tell your father," her mother would say, touching her lips with her fingers that smelled of mint, "let sleeping bears hibernate."

Ivy mimicked her, pressing her own tiny finger to her mother's soft lips.

Tenderly, her mother would sing and Ivy would sink into her pillow, the warmth of the blanket wrapped around her, and her mother's touch, pressing into her such sweet images of gentle breezes, sweet flowers in the meadows full of birds and soft grass. The sun glowing, and dimming into night. The stars she wished on in her dreams. Ivy drifted off easily then, hearing her mother's voice, and she did so at the strange house, caught in a half-sleep.

Safe, secure, the song so close, whispering, *wake up.*

Wood creaked. A figure loomed close by her head.

Ivy grasped the poker and swung it around, the rod striking something hard and meaty.

Danial screamed and grabbed his leg. Ivy swung again, a glancing blow off his head. He created a heavy thump as he fell over. Ivy scrambled to her feet. She held the poker over his face, ready to ram it through his eye or beat him senseless.

"Why'd you hit me?" Danial asked, crying like a little boy. He placed a hand on his head and screeched. "I'm bleeding!"

"You're lucky that's all coming out of your head," Ivy said. "Did you think you could hurt me while I was asleep?"

"I wasn't going to hurt you." Danial whimpered. "You were singing in your sleep and I… I had to listen to you. It was so sweet, yet sad, like you were calling my name over and… Owie! You broke my head. See! Bleeding!"

Ivy lowered the poker slowly, caught in cold, numb horror. She was about to kill another person not long after murdering four. *Am I becoming a monster? Anyone who crossed my path ending up hurt, or a corpse?*

"I'm sorry." Ivy dropped to her knees and gathered up the blanket. "Let me help you."

"Keep away!" Danial rolled into a protective ball, crying loud. "Go… go!"

Ivy stood. She grabbed her clogs, but they were wet. So were the rest of her clothes. The rain hadn't stopped either. *I have nowhere to go.* She looked to the door and then back at Danial, who was lowering his arms. In the dying embers, his face was a mask of blood. He leaned back on his elbows and grinned up at Ivy, looking like some evil creature of Nazglum, Lord of Shadows. His tears turned into maniacal laughter. He stood up, wobbling.

Ivy reached for the poker, but Danial shoved her back and kicked the poker behind him, stumbling in the process. Ivy landed on her bottom, rolled onto her back and put her hand under her head before cracking it on the hearth's stone. Her knuckles scraped it and they began to burn.

"You want to hurt me, more," Danial said, taking a wobbly step. "Mommy said girls like you would always hurt me. God-bless-it, she was right."

He reached down, unsteady on his feet and ready to topple over on her. Instead, he grabbed her ankle. Ivy kicked, but he held on tight, pulling her closer. The song built and she let out a frustrated scream. Danial twisted her leg.

"You won't go away," he said, jerking her ankle and Ivy flopped over on her belly, dress riding up her midsection.

"I'll leave!"

"Liar!" Danial dragged her closer, running a hand up her thigh. "You'll just come back. Bring others to laugh and beat me."

Danial lifted her off the floor by her leg and sent her tumbling across the room. Ivy smashed into a chair, the air knocked from her lungs and her left side ached. She heard uneven steps coming across the hardwood. She looked up to see Danial's lumbering form coming for her. Ivy tried to sit up, but the pain wouldn't allow it. She opened her mouth to scream, but started to sing instead. It erupted from the pain in her side, rising from her belly and spewed from her throat. Images of Danial holding her head and twisting it, the way he killed his goats. Less suffering than a knife splitting flesh and quicker than the slow bleeding.

Danial stopped several steps from her.

Don't kill him.

The song hardened and she watched Danial lumber to the wall and began to bash his head against it.

No! Don't kill him!

Whoomph of meat on wood louder than the rain. He grunted and slammed his head again.

Stop!

The song softened and Danial no longer hit his head. She delved him and found the image of a young girl. Pretty and dark haired like her. Pain, anger, confusion clung to her in a shroud. Ivy witnessed three older boys shove Danial down and kick him while the girl cried. They left him, bruised, half-alive, swearing they would finish the job if he was seen around their sister ever again.

A great sadness fell over Ivy.

"*Sedeto*" repeated in the verse. Danial wobbled away from the wall and sat down on the floor. She sensed the tight control she had over him. She could force him to walk into the hearth, standing there until he became a blaze of fire and smoke, or lay down while she stomped his face.

Danial went prostrate.

I have complete control. Ivy stood up, her side twinging, and she shuffled over to Danial's side, singing softly. His eyes were glassy and wet. He wept, staring up at some empty spot on the ceiling. *Fascinating!* and tried out a few combinations of making Danial raise his right arm and then his left. The song knew the right words to use. She stopped singing and clarity returned to his eyes.

"What happened?" he sat up, wincing and grabbing for his head.

"You fell," Ivy said.

"Who are you?"

"A friend," Ivy said, not knowing what to say. "Someone trying to help you."

"Thank you," Danial said, wiping at his wet eyes. "Thank you. Thank you."

The wind picked up, rattling the door and windows. It grew in intensity and Ivy expected it to settle down, like taking a breath before blowing again, but it pounded harder. Ivy stepped back, covering her face as the front door burst open, flapping on splintered hinges. Rainwater flew in on the wind, sprinkling Danial and Ivy blinked water from her eyes.

A woman, short and wide in girth, filled the doorway. A flash of lightning illumed her for an instance and Ivy's hairs stood on end, as though the lightning came from the woman. She stepped inside, followed closely by another person holding a shuttered lantern. They both had cloaks covering their faces.

"Are you sure this is her?" the short, pudgy woman asked.

"Yes. She is strong," a woman's voice from the one holding the lantern. "I sensed her all the way in Euclid."

"Looks like we caught them at an inopportune time," pudgy woman said.

"Who are you?" Ivy asked. The song felt distant, like a bucket dropped into an empty well.

"We are here to save you from impeding death," pudgy woman said. "Unless you want to stay here with your boyfriend and figure it out on your own."

"He's not my boyfriend."

Danial laughed.

"You will come with us," the woman with the lantern lowered her hood. A sharp nose filled her thin face. Her eyes told Ivy she had no choice.

I guess I found my way out.

A covered wagon waited for them on the road. About a dozen, to be closer to the truth. Behind the wagons were more horses than Ivy had ever seen in her life and a long line of soldiers stretching as far back as she could see. Exposed to the rain, they all huddled under their cloaks, the horses had heads drooped and tails swishing miserably. Ivy empathized. After spending a short time in the rain, she was as miserable as a honeybee discovering her comb had been raided.

The short, pudgy woman was called Robin, and her companion, the one who said she could sense Ivy all the way from Euclid, was Thrush. They hushed her when she tried to ask questions and hurried her to a middle wagon. Heads popped out from the closed canvass, but it was too dark to identify faces. Not that she would know anyone, except for maybe her uncle Tym. No one said anything to her, so she kept her head down and moved as quickly as the sopping ground afforded her. Two soldiers helped Danial limp along. Once under the cover, they bandaged Danial's bleeding head, wrapping him so the upper half of his head was covered. The gash across the bridge of his nose still seeped blood. He didn't appear to remember their fight, but her side reminded her with every jolt from the wagon.

"What's going on?" Ivy asked.

Robin and Thrush looked at each other. The lantern glow illuminated pale faces unmarred by wrinkles. Thrush had sharper features, small, dark eyes and her lips pursed together, while Robin was rounder, lusher, her red lips set in a knowing smirk. Thrush raised thin eyebrows.

"You found her," Robin said. "You tell her."

"Tell me what?" Ivy was beginning to wonder if she hadn't made a mistake trusting these women. The very fact they were women—she'd had her fill of men hurting her to last a lifetime—was the singular reason she was in the wagon. Also, they knew about her song which was very persuasive. *On second thought, that might not be a good thing.* They could be kidnapping her, or taking her to experiment except for the fact that they had a look of refugees escaping some larger calamity.

"Oh, alright," Thrush replied and folded her arms. "You see, Ivy, a tremendous army led by some lout calling himself—"

"You mean, asshole," Robin interrupted and Thrush turned her nose up and huffed, giving the impression this was a routine among them. "Some asshole warlord calling himself Count Thundercunt, or something, decided he no longer wanted Harmonic Manipulation to exist in the world, so he is hunting us down. Killing anyone who has the ability."

"His name is Cacophony, though I think it's his clever idea of showing he opposes us," Thrush said and sniffed.

Nazglum's balls! Not another man looking to hurt me. Haven't even met the fucker yet and he wants to kill me!

It was too much for her to absorb all at once. She was a saturated sponge, her hands already bloodied. One phrase stuck out to her. It had the feeling of both being in control, like the one pulling strings, as she had with Danial, but she sensed it meant she could be used.

"Harmonic Manipulation?" Ivy asked.

"Harmonic Manipulation is what we do," Thrush said, speaking in a way she might to a child. "We use our songs to change the world. Manipulate it in a way suited by our gifts. Each singer is unique, which creates a balance in the world. Containing the Shadow Lord in his prison."

"Magic," Ivy said, glancing over at Danial. He didn't seem to be listening and Ivy was glad. The less he remembered about her singing, the better.

"That's a rudimentary way of putting it," Thrush said.

"Mister phony cock," Robin said, eliciting an eye roll from Thrush, "is destroying every city, town, and village trying to get us."

"What about Euclid?" Ivy asked, heart thrumming at remembering how Thrush mentioned the city. "My uncle is coming home after making a delivery."

"No one is coming from Euclid," Robin said.

"Why not?"

"Euclid doesn't exist, anymore."

God no! Where will I go now?

She tried to fight the tears stinging her eyes, but they fell, dampening her cheeks and she sank back against the bench, listening to the rain. Tym was here one way out of Welksdale, and now that was gone. He was the one man she could trust, the only one who hadn't made any demands on her, also the one who left her to suffer with Bryn. Part of her wanted to know why he allowed Bryn to abuse her. She would never get a chance to ask him.

My safety and well-being are in the hands of strangers.

"Hey, love," Thrush said and touched Ivy's knee. "Many people fled before the battle. I'm sure your uncle will show up."

"Will this phony cock come for me?" Ivy asked. She held little hope that she might be overlooked. She was insignificant enough, a girl living on the fringes of civilization, a tick buried in the ass-end of a dog. She wasn't a warrior, barely understood her song.

"I'm starting to like you." Robin smiled at the repeat of the name she coined.

"Unfortunately, yes," Thrush said, responding to Ivy's question.

"He has another person sensitive to the Harmonic, like Thrush who can sense the gift in others. Seekers we call them," Robin said. "When you use your song, it sends out vibrations this other, I think it's a woman, typically the power manifests in women, though we were never able to find out who was doing it, will track you."

"So, I just never sing again," Ivy said.

Thrush clicked her tongue.

"If only it were that easy."

"Sometimes it just comes out whether you want it to, or not," Robin added. "Like passing gas or sneezing."

Ivy nodded. Danial said she called him from her sleep, which meant she hurt an innocent man, like a creature from the sea singing sailors to their doom. It would betray her sooner or later. Ivy would never be safe…unless there was a way to put an end to the hunter.

"Couldn't Thrush use her ability to find this other Seeker and kill her?"

"We tried," Robin said, fists clenching her skirts. "That's why they nearly caught us in Euclid."

"The power I thought I felt from Cacophony's army, came from you."

"I don't understand," Ivy said.

"Sometimes we are born with more than one skill than our song," Thrush said. "I can sense the Harmonies, but I also manipulate the ground to draw up the strongest metals and forge the strongest weapons and armor. Whomever Cacophony has tracking Harmonic Manipulators, she can cancel out harmonies as well."

"Making our songs useless," Robin said.

"And it weakens our soldiers," Thrush said, her nose wrinkling and she looked as though she could spit. "Because I forged their weapons and armor, our greatest advantage becomes our weevil in the granary. The bindings I weaved around the steel have deteriorated."

"There's no way to stop him," Ivy said, wondering if she should jump out of the wagon now and head home to try her luck with Bryn.

"None that we have figured out."

They went quiet. The ceaseless dripping on the canopy sounded like fingers tapping for her attention, malicious hands to drown her in more sorrow. Ivy felt more trapped than she had ever, even when facing down the men cutting up her father. *I would have been better off in their hands.*

Danial shifted on the bench, sticking his head out and then drawing back in. Ivy gave him a questioning look.

"I wish the rain would end," Danial said. "I want to hear the nightingales sing. They have such pretty songs. Like you, Ivy."

"That would be my doing," Robin said. "As long as it rains, then we are safe."

"What do you mean safe?" Ivy crossed her arms, leaning back against the bench. It was all so much to absorb. "Don't you have to continue singing for it to rain?"

"Not exactly," Thrush said. "The power is in you, like a muscle that must be exercised to grow stronger. The more you exert it, the more control you gain. Once you learn to master it, you only have to charge things with your Harmonics, then it will continue to resonate in a sort of echo. Yes, it'll grow weaker over time and you have to give it a little nudge to recharge the echo."

"Aren't your rains slowing us down?" Danial asked.

"But more importantly, it's also slowing them down, worse," Robin said, speaking in a tone as though explaining to a child. "They not only have to contend with a mud sodden road, but one that's been nice and churned."

"Couldn't you make it flood and drown them?"

Robin gave Thrush a sad look.

"We tried it once," Robin said. "It didn't work then, and it won't for certain work now."

"We would need somewhere to trap the water," Thrush said. "He won't fall for that again."

"What happens when the rains stop?" Ivy thought she knew the answer, but wanted to hear it from the woman's mouth.

"Then Cacophony is close and we fight."

Fight! All I want to do is sleep. She leaned back on the bench and closed her eyes, listening to the rain and wishing it would continue for a very, very, long time.

Tym woke up when the wagon stopped. His first thought was they had arrived at their destination and Euclid City awaited. Then he realized Euclid was a large bonfire and they were running, or in his case, riding for his life.

At least I escaped, a look at his bloody bandage and he shook his head, *well mostly intact.*

His leg ached, stiff from holding it stretched out for so long, and when he moved it, a cramp seized him. Tym kneaded his thigh and calf the way a baker would dough, pushing his fingers into the muscle and sucking back his whimpers. Crusty blood tugged at his hairs, adding to his discomfort. He moaned, moving his leg in a position that didn't burn, cramp, or otherwise make it seem like it was falling off, and he realized, he wasn't alone.

Tailorson cleared his throat.

"Good, you didn't die," he said, "though you look like—"

"I know, like I tried to arse fuck my horse and she stomped on my balls," Tym said. "Except my horse is missing and someone else stomped on me."

A titter of laughter and disapproving grunt came from Tailorson's boy and wife respectfully. She swatted the boy while frowning at Tym. The boy rubbed his head, glaring over at him.

"I'm glad you were able to keep up," Tailorson said. "Not many people made it out of the city before the gates were breeched, but your quick thinking saved some of us and for that you deserve a pat on the back."

Tailorson smacked him hard.

Tym remembered the people slaughtered because these women showed up unexpectedly with their army. Bodies piled like felled trees. The dead children bleeding beside their parents. What kind of men would do that? Dead men, for sure, because Thrush and Robin killed the thugs, clearing a path for their own escape. Would they have acted any differently if the unarmed people stood in their path instead?

"Where are we?" Tym asked.

"Don't know, it's dark and raining, but I think I see a single light," Tailorson said, lifting the flap and the sound of rain grew louder. The drought lasted for so long, he never thought he'd see rain again, but now that it was here, he hoped it would go away. "Making a delivery, maybe? Doesn't seem we'll be stopping long."

"Why's that?" Tym listed off all the houses on this road to Euclid, or where Euclid used to be. There weren't many residences left. The drought forced most to abandon their homes. A few stubborn ones refused to leave, like Bryn, keeping his niece basically hostage. He swore one day she would take off and he'd never see her again. *Not end up like her mother, Creator willing.* They were not at Bryn's place, he was certain.

"From what I hear the other army is still after us," Tailorson said, lowering his voice. "I say us, because we are part of this caravan and there's really no place to hide. I hope they warn the people living out here on the fringes so they don't get caught by surprise."

"You think that other army, the one chasing us, will kill the people in these homes?"

"Might take everything worth carrying and burn the rest," Tailorson said. "Heard it happen plenty of times. Think about what they did to Euclid. These people have no chance."

Tailorson made a convincing point, as much Tym hated to admit it. He grunted and took up watch at the canvass opening. The rain was cold, dripping on his fingers as he kept it peeled back. They would never escape the other army if the women stopped at every home along the way to warn people. The obvious solution would be to send runners, but this place held some special interest. He saw the woman leave the farm house followed by two others. Tym couldn't make out their faces in the darkness before they were loaded in another wagon. His wagon gave a jerk, pushing his arm out into the rain and soaking his tunic sleeve. Then it was moving again.

"Would you shut that please," Tailorson's wife said. "You are letting in a draft."

"No worse than the crotch deep water you'd set me in earlier," Tym said.

She gave an exasperated gasp, looking to Tailorson. Her husband shrugged.

"Cover up," he said.

That earned him a cold stare. This was one of the many reasons Tym was glad he never took a wife. When a woman got too demanding, he could walk away, or run in some cases. The only woman Tym thought he could run to, instead of away, married his brother, which always baffled Tym.

Never try to figure a woman out, his father told him and Bryn, *you'll hurt your head. Best to nod and do your own thing. Less trouble that way.*

The best to come of the union was his niece, Ivy. Though even that, he supposed, was a half-truth. He couldn't imagine Ivy being slaughtered like those other children in Euclid. Her mother was dead, but Tym would make certain Ivy wouldn't be, so he endured the icy stares and annoying sighs and complaints about being cold, and how it might be the death of her.

Tym wanted to shout back that her complaining would be the death of them all. He took his father's advice and nodded every time she grumbled. At least it kept him awake. The sound of rain made him sleepy and the occasional jounces jolted him awake. He was lulled into another slumber when he sat upright. A thought niggled him and he opened the tarp again. Even in the dark, the surroundings became familiar. A homecoming of sorts.

"Hey!" He slapped the side of the wagon. A soldier marching close looked at him, cloaked soaked through. "We need to stop here."

"Can't," the soldier said.

"My brother and niece live there." Tym swiped wet hair out of his face. "They need to be warned."

"No more stopping," the soldier said, lacking any sympathy. "Orders are to march on through."

The house was getting further away. Tym saw the windows were dark. Of course, they would be sound asleep inside, probably hoping the roof didn't leak too much and flood them out. Not that it would matter when the sun rose.

"Come on, at least send someone to warn them."

The soldier ignored him,

"They'll die!" Tym tried to get his injured leg up to lean further out the wagon. "That's my brother and niece in there."

"I'm sorry, but we cannot break rank."

Jump, crawl through the mud. Shout, yell scream. Get them out. Tym wanted to do all of that, but he couldn't get his leg to move.

"You stopped at that other farm house! What the fuck's so special about them?"

"I can't answer that," the soldier said.

Bryn's house was getting further behind.

"Do this for me and I'll see you are well-rewarded." Tym was pleading, his voice breaking. "I would run over there myself, but my damn leg won't let me."

The soldier no longer listened him.

"It's your fault," Tym was shouting, his throat burning, "they'll die because where you walk, death follows. Nazglum is laughing his balls off."

He felt Tailorson's hands on him, pulling him back inside the wagon.

"Hey, don't get so worked up."

"That's my family," Tym said, tears stinging his eyes. "They're all I got."

"Well, maybe they'll hear the parade and come out to see what's causing it," Tailorson said. "Not every day an army marches through your streets."

Tym sat back, hands covering his face. Part of him wanted to believe Tailorson. That Bryn and Ivy would hear the noise of the wagons, splashing of the boots, and decide to leave out the back door. There wasn't anything else he could do. *Creator watch over them.* At the next stop, he'd steal a horse and ride back if he could. If the other army didn't beat him to it. Tym never felt so hopeless and worthless than he had at that moment.

From the corner he heard Ms. Tailorson singing. She smiled, one that was reserved for guests who she didn't like and put a bug in their soup.

Fuck her and fuck these armies. The house was no longer visible. *I'm going back for them.*

CHAPTER NINE:
CAUGHT

When my betrayal was first found out to King Callius, the shock on his face was pure horror. Fallonbrooke was collapsing, overrun by hordes of Tainted., his lords demanding his surrender which would eventually lead to his beheading. His last act as king was to place me in a pot of boiling oil. Even then, his revenge was hollow. I survived, protected by the graces of the great Lord Nazglum. So, I sow the seeds of darkness, and nothing will ever be as painful as that moment I was caught, nothing sweeter. Melt my body, but my soul is eternal.

The white flower pressed against her skin, rubbing against the black tunic under her armor. Rough on her left breast, it reminded her of calloused hands trying to gently squeeze her the way he might milk a cow. The dry petals kept scratching, irritating Claiborne, but she refused to remove it, any more than she would remove the last indentations left by Arron's teeth or the warmth where his fingers last touched, or his dying screams ringing in her paralyzed ears. It'll all fade away, eventually. Cacophony's gift was his way of telling her, get the shit done or die. A promise painted in dried blood on the white petals. The past was dead, and so would she be. No matter the outcome of this chase, Cacophony would kill her, if she didn't die in battle or by some other horrific means. Since the day he had captured her, Claiborne was on borrowed time, a high interest, high stakes loan. One day, she'd have to pay up. Each breath was a bonus, a credit against the greater sum.

She rode her destrier on the rain sopped-road. Mud splattered up her boots and she kept him at a steady canter, at the head of her column.

Death wasn't high on the list of things Claiborne feared. She'd seen enough, and had dealt a fair share to others, to know it was just an end. Often it baffled her why people struggled so hard to live, when obviously their life was shit. She'd seen a man who'd had his arm cut clean off, pick it up and try to put it back on. Blood spurted from the wound like squeezing a lemon, but he'd kept on poking the damn thing, crying about how it wouldn't fit. Once he bled out, he dropped the severed piece and glassy-eyes staring dumbfounded over why he couldn't put it back together.

Claiborne felt the same way when Arron was twisted in that singer-forged-armor created by Thrush. Blessed Creator, his screams sent rivers of pain coursing through her chest, waves drowning her in hopelessness and she couldn't breathe while that Nazglum-damned women kept on singing, shaping the armor, *re-shaping* Arron.

He had begged her to kill him. His hand, which no longer resembled a human hand with five fingers, knuckles and folds able to bend and grip, but some lump of molten iron and flesh, reached for her. She couldn't move. Rushed along in the torrent of pain and revulsion and guilt, her lover's pleas gripped her and she blamed him. The damn fool! Fucking idiot! He allowed this to happen, not just to himself, but her as well. Tears swelled her eyes, kissing her cheeks. She wanted to bend, to break, to plunge the knife she held over him into a vital place, end his suffering and wallow into her own. Courage squirmed away from her.

Love makes cowards of us all.

Had she to do it all over again, Claiborne would have slit her lover's throat and used the same bloody knife to murder Thrush. In the end, Arron went silent, and she wasn't sure if the metal filled his mouth and crushed his lungs, or if he remained alive, conscious, sustained by the malignant magic in the song. Someone else did the deed she should have done, driving the knife into him. She'd buried him all the same.

Rain rattled on her armor. The cloak over her head soaked to the roots on her scalp. She couldn't wait for it to end, to dry up, and for everything to be brown and dead once again. The black carriage was spacious enough for her to travel in comfort, if being around a creepy, singing child, who wasn't really a child but some other creature inhabiting a child's body, and her insectile father was a comfort, then she'd be a queen of the ants. The flower rubbed again, and she adjusted it, keeping it from falling over her nipple. She was happy enough in the rain.

"First Sword," a soldier approached, boots squelching in the mud. She slowed her destrier to a halt, the horse baring his teeth at the soldier, Mallet, who kept a wise distance. He snapped a salute, water flicking off his arm. "We found another occupied house."

The Silent Men didn't bother with a search of domiciles, typically since it slowed progress and yielded little. Claiborne made an exception this time. The birds had escaped the trap set for them and she wanted to know how. The plan had been nearly flawless, except for the very fact of the unknown circumstance. These often led to defeat, or losing her targets. No more room for error existed and she needed to be prepared for the next time the Silent Men "trapped" the Singers.

"How many inside?"

"One man."

"Bring him to me."

The soldier saluted again and hurried away. In a few heart beats they had a sodden, sorry-looking fellow who had bruises on his face and clutched his left hand where a finger was missing. He shivered, head staring down at his feet. Claiborne remained in the saddle, off to the side while the columns of Silent Men marched past.

"What's your name?"

The man spat on her leg.

Why do they always have to spit? My horse also spits and he is much nastier than these guys.

Claiborne kicked the man in the chin, the metal tip of her boot connecting in the meaty part so his teeth clicked together and his head rocked back. Fortunately for him a soldier was there to catch him or he'd end up splashing in the mud.

"What's your name?" She asked calmly. Getting upset would only give him courage to resist more.

"Bryn." He growled it as though growling would intimidate her.

"Alright Bryn, tell me something," Claiborne said. "Did you see another army pass by?"

Bryn nodded.

"Any towns, villages, shitholes in the direction they were going?"

"Nearest town is Welksdale. No more than a couple leagues away."

It often surprised her how a simple kick in the teeth could loosen a person's tongue.

"Any walls or other fortifications?"

"Just a small gate to keep out the road scum." Bryn looked up at her. "You didn't happen to see my daughter?"

Daughter? The scouts said the women stopped at a farm house, but there was no one inside.

"We've seen no one, Bryn."

His shoulders sagged.

"We got in a sort of argument and she took off."

Family disputes always bored her.

"Have you ever been to Euclid?"

"No, but my brother was there selling some goods."

"Then I'm sorry for your loss."

"What do you mean?"

"The city no longer exists." Claiborne loosened the sword in her scabbard. "Seems they sided against the Creator and like all those on the wrong side, burned."

"You burned it?" Anger sparked in his voice.

"Fire is the only way to purify," Claiborne said. "Since you were so cooperative, I'm going to do you a favor."

"What?" Bryn squinted an eye.

Claiborne's sword swept out, cutting a neat line across Bryn's throat. Bryn clutched it, blood flowing through the rain, reddening his tunic. His lips worked, but no sound came. He dropped to his knees in the mud, gazing up at the rain, or her, or maybe even the face of the Creator. They never told her and she never asked what they saw.

"It's the small mercies that lead to redemption," Claiborne said and heeled her destrier back on the muddy road.

"Oh, what now!" Robin moved to the rear of the wagon and pulled the cloak over her head. The rain came straight down in large drops, rolling across her shoulders. Ivy shivered and huddled beside Danial against the wet cold. "What's going on out here? Why aren't we moving?"

Ivy knew she wouldn't want to be on the receiving end of her wrath. The woman didn't need swords or knives to cut a person. Her words were sharp enough to carve chunks from their flesh. Ivy wondered what Robin might've been in a different world where songs didn't make it rain, pull metal from the earth, or manipulate a person's mind. Maybe she would be a mother, screaming at her children and nagging her husband, though Ivy couldn't see what man would be able to stand such a strong personality. Robin wouldn't be the kind to let a man push her around let alone lay a hurtful hand on her. Or maybe she would be a soldier, leading men into battle, barking orders and threatening to cut off balls if they didn't run faster.

The soldier, a young man with thin features and eyes wide enough to fall into, gave a sharp salute and retreated a step. He cleared his throat several times and seemed to swallow the words he planned on saying.

"Spit it out!" Robin growled and the man took and the soldier took another step back. Ivy couldn't help wincing, either.

"There's a town ahead, ma'am," he said. "Do you want to re-provision? Or should we march through?"

"You stopped us to ask that!" Robin huffed. "Buffoon, we march until the rain stops."

"Do we really have to fight, then?" Ivy asked.

"Unless you want to die," Thrush said. She had a small blade in her hand, running a stained cloth over it, the smell of oil strong in the covered wagon. Ivy couldn't imagine Thrush hacking and slashing. She seemed so calm, a book better suited for her hands than a device for maiming and killing. Thrush gave Ivy a sad smile. "The odds are not in our favor."

"When have the odds ever been in our favor?" Nuthatch asked.

"That's not all," the man said, and Ivy could tell he was trying not to shuffle his feet. He stood rigid, but looked beyond Robin, not really seeing anything, except maybe his own demise brought about by Robin. "No one is answering our call at the gate. It's barred."

"Use your head, man," Robin said. "Find a way in."

"Shall I break it down?" the soldier asked, not sounding eager about the task.

"The town's people may not react kindly to us knocking their gate open," Thrush said.

"The town's people might shit themselves before actually doing anything to stop you," Ivy said. Thrush paused her polishing, giving her an unreadable expression. "I almost died when some assholes tried to rob the Exchequer and no one raised an alarm. I survived because one man risked his life to help."

"There always has to be that one hero," Nuthatch said. "Did he die in the process to complete his hero complex?"

Ivy shook her head.

"Creator bless me." Robin rolled her eyes. "The incompetence will be the death of us. No, don't break it down, we want to leave some obstacle in the way of the cocksucker. I'm sure you can figure another way in. It doesn't look too formidable for your collective brains to conquer."

"It will be done." The man saluted and hurried away. Ivy didn't blame him—she wouldn't want to disappoint either woman.

"Is there any way we could go around the town?" Ivy may not like most of the residents, loathing more than a few, but they didn't deserve the same fate as Euclid. People deserved a place of peace. They were not warriors. The last war they fought in was decades ago and those men who lived were older now. She doubted many could use a sword anymore. They had lives to carry on with unmolested. She glanced at Danial who stared at her in silent awe. She looked away.

"It wouldn't be worth the efforts," Thrush said. "Cacophony would cut through the place and catch us much sooner."

"Is your town always left unattended and indefensible?" Robin asked, drumming her fingers on the bench.

Fat, lecherous Simon usually occupied the post when she went to town. Eyes undressing her and a speck of drool on his wet lips. He could ring a bell, she supposed, though what his other duties on the watch entailed, Ivy didn't care enough to ask.

"I've never been here after dark, so I don't know."

It wouldn't surprise her to learn someone was asleep at their post.

"It's a wonder the place hasn't been overrun by thieves," Robin said, and sat back on the bench. She sucked on her lower lip, loud, exasperated noses breathing through her nose. "You didn't live in the town?"

176

"No," Ivy said. "We passed the house I lived in a while back."

"'Lived'?" Robin raised a curious brow.

"I don't want to talk about it," Ivy said.

Robin grunted.

"We all have our scars," Thrush said, tucking the oil-cloth under her bench. "How long have you known about your song?"

The question caught her off-guard. How much did she want to reveal to these women.

"It's alright, we all have stories about discovering our Songs," Nuthatch said and her voice lowered. "Some are not always pleasant."

Ivy took a breath.

I guess my fate in in their hands, might as well try to get something useful from them.

"My mother used to sing, but my father hated it. He ugh, discouraged us," Ivy said, remembering the bruises on her mother's face. "I wasn't allowed to sing, not even hum. He'd get mad." *Really mad.* "So, I didn't sing until it sort-of-happened today, I mean yesterday, everything is jumbled up and I'm exhausted."

"You always obeyed your father?" Thrush studied her.

"I was afraid not to," Ivy said, anger rising up. Why was this woman baiting her?

"He was a fool," Danial said. "You sing pretty. Pretty as the nightingale."

"Yes, well we all have our reasons." Robin gave Thrush another silent, knowing look. The wagon lurched, knocking Danial against Ivy. He blushed and slid away. "Looks like they found a way in without bashing their heads against the wood."

As they cleared the gate, she noticed the sentry tower was empty. *They're asking for the invasion. Maybe it's the rain. I wouldn't want to sit out in the cold.* Ivy peeked out at the buildings. She couldn't believe that she had been there less than a day ago, buying supplies and nearly dying. It amazed her how life could be dull one moment, struggling with hunger pangs, and flip so quickly that hunger would be the least of her problems. Of course, she wouldn't be here if she hadn't been forced from her home by Bryn and Crisell.

"Men are so stupid," Ivy said.

Robin nodded her appreciation while Thrush frowned. Nuthatch gave her an encouraging pat on the arm. Danial sat in a quiet stupor, hands hung between his knees and stared at the floorboards. Ivy wondered again if maybe she hadn't wiped his mind out, like blowing chalk from a slate. Then again, there wasn't much written besides loneliness and pain. Here was an opportunity for Danial to start all over again, find some happiness, should they survive. *I could tell him to run off and hide out for a few days until the storm literally blew over.* She wasn't entirely sure she had any power over him. It was beyond her ability to tie her power off like Robin and Thrush. She didn't even know how to tie a knot with string. Danial could become confused or get lost...not that Ivy should care, but she did because sometimes men needed saving from their own stupidity.

And it was mostly her fault he was the way he was.

Maybe.

The dark buildings caught her attention. All these people lived in town, but no one stirred. The rain covered the sound of horses, wagon, and men. No one made any unnecessary noise. They could pass on through and not a single resident would wake until they smelled the fires. By then, it would be too late. Like her Uncle Tym, the residents of Welksdale would be trapped, victims of the cocksucker burning down everything to get to the women, and now her. She would be responsible as well. Too many deaths for her to carry on her conscience.

"Are we going to warn them?" Ivy asked.

"If they haven't noticed us yet, then they deserve what they get," Robin said.

"You could send some men to the homes—"

"And start a panicked riot! The streets are narrow enough without fleeing citizens clogging them up."

"So you are going to roll on through and leave more bodies behind?" Four corpses she had left back in Bryn's home. One by her hand and three by her song. She hadn't mentioned them to Thrush or Ivy. She had no idea what they might do to her.

This is different. I can do something about it.

"It'll slow him until we get to the mountains," Robin said.

"That's a rather callous way of putting it," Ivy said. "Many of the men in this town fought the Trumen during the Welks war and won. They can help you fight this cocksucker."

Robin snorted laughter.

"I do appreciate the sentiment, but a handful of men more used to sticking hay with pitchforks than handling a sword wouldn't last longer than a sneeze against what this cocksucker has with him. An entire city guard was no match. He burned them out like rats in silage."

"Warn them," Ivy said. "Give them a chance to fight or run."

Thrush laid a hand on Robin's arm before the woman could respond.

"Who can you talk to that can organize a quick exodus?" Thrush asked. "By quick, they have probably until the sun kisses the sky, perhaps less time."

"That won't be long enough," Ivy said.

"You can stay here if you want," Robin said, arms folded and leveling her stare on Thrush, who didn't seem to notice.

"She can't," Thrush said. "We need every one of us we can find."

The "us" Ivy understood to mean women who had the Harmonic power. Singers like Ivy, and her mother, when she was alive.

"How many more of us are there?" Ivy asked, though every second she sat here asking questions seemed a second wasted on getting the Welksdale people roused and moving on out of the town. She had to know, had to convince these women to help her.

"We don't know." Thrush pursed her lips together, making her more bird-like. "Counting you, we have nine left that we do know about."

"Eight," Nuthatch said.

Thrush frowned at the younger girl.

"We don't know for certain—"

"We do know what Cacophony does to the Singers he finds," Robin said, the anger and annoyance flushed from her voice, replaced by sorrow.

"Why are we so important?" Ivy asked.

More important than others?

"Without us, the world loses its harmony," Thrush said. "When Harmony is gone, then the darkness takes over. Nazglum will enter and corrupt all life."

"This Cacophony is a servant of some sort to Nazglum?"

"Yes, but not in the way he believes. The Silent Men are also bringers of balance," Robin said. "The damn fools just think that by killing us, they will prevent the corruption. Nazglum's Whores they call us and have been waging war against us for several decades."

She'd never heard of Singers and Silent Men, or far off wars for the protection of the world. So many questions swam in her head that boiled down into one word.

"Why?"

"Because men want to kill what they don't understand," Thrush said. "They fear the power we have, but it wasn't always like this. We were the branches from the same tree. The Silent Men were named the Brotherhood of Creation and we were the Sisterhood. Together we fought whoever Nazglum corrupted to act as his agents. Men and women were promised eternal reward for serving, creating a blight on our roots that eventually split us apart."

"Cacophony thinks he is serving the Creator by killing women like us, but is in fact serving Nazglum?"

"She is quick," Robin said, rolling her eyes. "Are you done with the history lessons?"

"Wait, how many were there in the Sisterhood before the break?"

"Seven hundred and seventy-seven," Thrush said. "Enough to spread out across the world, acting as protective conduits."

Seven hundred and seventy-seven, and only seven or eight remain. Half the number in this wagon.

"Thrush here is the last known seeker on our side," Robin said. "Which is why we cannot stay. Even if it means sacrificing you, Ivy."

"No one's being sacrificed," Thrush said.

"Finch, Sparrow—" Nuthatch listed names until Robin glared at her.

"We do what have to in order to preserve Harmony," Robin said. "You know this, Thrush."

"Which is why we must protect the gifts that the Creator has given to us."

Ivy almost laughed. A gift. She doubted the men she killed saw her as a gift, and Bryn called her many names, but the word gift never crossed his firewater chapped lips.

"Why did you come?" Ivy asked. "Why not hide?"

"Like I said before," Thrush folded her hands, "I was sent to find others who have discovered their abilities. It was a necessary risk to preserve our future."

"Cacophony has his seeker and it won't be long until he finds those of us who remain, holding the tentative threads of Harmony in place," Robin said, staring out at the rain. Ivy noticed the dark clouds had begun to thin. "Nazglum will corrupt the world, but on the bright side, we will all be dead and not there to experience it."

What will it matter if there's no other people left to protect? Even if many are assholes, there are children here, and someone has to look out for them.

"I have to try to save the people of this town." Ivy stood up from the bench and almost tumbled over, catching hold of Danial. Directing her speech to Thrush she added: "If you think that I'm so important, that my Song can help you maintain Harmony, then I suggest you help me. Otherwise, don't talk to me about how important we are to the world, when you are allowing parts of it to burn at the whim of a madman."

Danial got up, shoulders hunched to keep his head from hitting the canopy.

"I'm coming with you."

Ivy smiled. *At least I won't be alone.*

"You aren't going to get far if you fall and break your fool heads," Robin said and looked to Nuthatch and Thrush. The first shrugged and the second gave a slight nod. "I hope your bravado pays off, otherwise you'll fuck us all over."

Then Robin leaned out the cover and shouted for the wagons to stop. They slowed and Ivy climbed over the back gate, feet splashing in a puddle. Robin tapped her on the head.

"You have ten ticks to rouse the slumbering fools," Robin said. "Then we leave."

"Don't make me have to hunt you down," Thrush said. "I'll take you with us, kicking and screaming if I must."

"Thank you. I won't be long," Ivy said, then ran along the side of their column stretching down the main street. Danial followed behind her. *I have no idea what I'm doing, but waking people up shouldn't be that hard. A child wakes his parent with enough noise.*

There was no better noisemaker in town than the alarm bell.

Welksdale! Tym hadn't seen the shabby stone walls and wooden palisades in what seemed to him a full moon. Horses, wagons, foot soldiers, all marched through the open gate. It was never meant to fend off an army, not of this size. When the second army arrived, Tym knew the walls would be as good as tinder, and the rest of the town nothing but ash before the next moonrise.

Tym didn't plan on sticking around to watch another place burn. Steal a horse and double back to Bryn's home, rescue Ivy. That was the extent of his plan. If the second army had beat him there? Well, he would ride north and mourn for them. *I got to try. Can't leave them. Bryn can go suck Nazglum's sack, but Ivy. I owe her that much at least.*

When the wagon's slowed to a crawl, weaving through the narrow streets, Tym gathered his courage. *The drop isn't so bad. It's mud, it'll be soft. Tuck and roll and you'll be fine.* He lifted his injured leg and immediately his calf screamed. It burned, threatening to burst the wound open again. Tym leaned on the wagon's gate, sweating and gritting his teeth. He shuffled his left leg, the right refusing to cooperate. All he needed was for it to buckle when he most relied on it, and turn him into a muddy, bloody lump crushed under wagon wheels.

"Where you going?" Tailorson asked.

"Business meeting," Tym said and groaned. "Word of advice. Fuck your wife and not your patrons. We'll all be happier that way."

Tailorson laughed and his wife began to berate him. They fell into a huge argument, and Tym was again happy he avoided marital bliss.

As much fun as it would be to listen to this exchange play out, I got to go.

Tym hung halfway out, arms trembling as he lowered his legs from the wagon. The ground was further away than he expected, and his left leg buckled, the fucker betraying him when he thought it would be his right. The only thing that kept him from being trampled by the trailing horses was that he clung to the gate with every ounce of remaining strength. His left foot dragged in the mud, and his boot was pulled off his foot, bare toes sinking into the muck.

Shit! Shit! Shit! His arms were never as strong as he wanted them and his right elbow began to cry out. Like every part of him wanted to end his existence. Tym grunted, lifting his upper body enough to get his legs back under him. The wagon was slow moving enough or else he'd been ripped away, becoming nothing more than road debris.

Almost got—

The wagon abruptly stopped. Tym slammed forward, his chest hitting hard enough to knock the breath from him. He let go of the wagon, coughed, and rubbed his aching ribs. Another ache to add to a body's worth. *I swear I need a week in bed.* Tym stumbled away, moving to the side in case the wagons began moving again. He searched for his lost boot and found it under the horse behind the wagon he just left. Mud squeezed between his bare toes and the rain did its best to pound him into the dirt.

"Don't you move, I'm just getting my boot," Tym said to the horse. The driver watched him; the bastard did not bother lending him a hand. Tym snatched his boot, avoiding an annoyed stomp from the horse and gave the driver a salute. "Such a great help. I'll never forget your kindness."

"I have my orders," the man said. "Not my fault you fell out of the wagon. Might be better if you stayed inside while we wait to continue on. Otherwise, you'll miss out."

"Thanks for the warning, worthless pissant." Tym walked away, slipping in the mud, and collapsed under a leaking eave. Never met a soldier worth his steel. They were either blind rule followers, or mean assholes looking to punch or fuck whatever came their way. Shaking the mud off his boot, and trying to scrape the worst from the sole of his foot, Tym leaned against one of the buildings. No way he would clear it all off, not without a proper bath. He forced his foot back inside the boot and would deal with it later. More pressing matters were at hand. Like finding an unattended horse.

He was about to cross the road when he saw two figures exit another wagon. Swiping rainwater from his face, leaving a streak of dirt from cheek to brow, he blinked. The smaller one looked like his niece.

"Ivy?"

The girl turned around and sure enough, he saw her blue eyes widen and jaw drop. The night black hair, small nose, even the way she pressed her hands together, a damn fine resemblance to her mother, an artist couldn't come much closer. Bryn wasn't visible in her at all—for obvious reasons.

"Uncle Tym?" Tentative and small, like she was imagining and not seeing the real him, reflecting his own disbelief.

"It's me, girl."

Ivy ran to him and threw her arms around his neck. Cold, wet, and shivering, he never felt warmer in his life than seeing his niece alive.

"I thought you died."

"I guess you're holding a ghost."

Ivy laughed and hugged him tighter.

"I was about to steal a horse and ride back to the house," Tym said. "I guess I don't have to do that now. Where's my brother?"

"I don't know." Bitterness warped her joyous tone. She immediately crossed her arms, staring down at the muddy ground. *Oh Bryn! What the fuck did you do to her?* Ivy sounded like Veena so much, especially how she talked before she left Bryn.

"I guess I better find a horse and get the fool," Tym said. "He's probably passed out drunk, pissing his small clothes."

"It's too dangerous," Ivy said. "There's a second army approaching. You'll never get past them."

"I know child, I was in Euclid when it arrived."

"Ivy, we have to go," a boy much taller than Tym, wider shoulders, and a chin that could split an anvil, kept a respectable distance.

"Who's he?"

"Danial," Ivy said.

Tym recognized him now. The Butterfield's boy. Tym remembered hearing rumors about the simpleton touching the Smither brothers' sister, and word was they beat him close to death. *Boy looks like he could break the Smither brothers in half while eating a sandwich.*

"Stay with me," Ivy said, drawing his attention back. She touched his arm, fingers gently gripping him.

"He's my brother," Tym said, no matter how drunk, violent, and dumb Bryn acted, he was what remained of the Lyre family. "I have to try."

Ivy looked over her shoulder. Tym tried to see what she was seeing. The rain was starting to lighten up, and the clouds probably cleared where he intended on going. When she turned back, her brow was furrowed and she shook her head.

"It's too late."

"You're probably right," Tym said. "I got to know and that's the only way I know how. Seeing is believing."

"Fine, but if you get under the clouds, get off the road. Cut through to the back stream. Should you find him, don't come back this way. Go somewhere far away."

"Ivy! They'll come for us," Danial said, shuffling from one foot to the other like a boy who had to pee.

"I love you," Ivy said. "I don't want to lose you."

Tym hugged her.

"You won't. If there's one thing I'm good at, it's bouncing back from bad situations." He kissed the top of her wet head and released her. "Go do what you have to before that boy pisses himself in anticipation."

Ivy watched Tym limp away. *I didn't even ask him how he was? How he got hurt? Can he even ride? Where in Nazglum's shadow was he and why did he leave me alone with the fucking, abusive drunk?*

All her fear over his death, and her anger at not helping her live, was washed away at seeing him. *I wish we had more time.* Again, wishes were an empty waterskin and there was nothing she could do to fill it.

"Iiiivyyy!" Danial hugged himself, rocking back and forth. Tym was right, Danial did appear about to piss himself. For good reason. It probably wasn't everyday he had to worry about an army coming to kill him. The way the rain clouds kept dwindling was like watching sand slip through an hourglass. Each piece of clear sky marked the moments when Cacophony would be on them. In her heart, she knew Tym was wasting his time.

"I'm orphaned," Ivy said, certain that both her parents were dead. Strangely, she wasn't upset. She was free, the way she wanted to be. Her first official act of freedom was to alert the people of Welksdale to the danger heading their way. "Let's go wake up the town."

The shops were all locked and dark, as was expected. They wouldn't open for several more hours and by then the other army may be burning its way through the town. Welksdale was originally established as a trading post for merchants to resupply on their way to Euclid. During the war, farmers and their families who had their houses burnt hid behind the walls, and many didn't leave. The houses were built behind the shops further up the street. The Lyres were not known for social graces and never received invites to any of the homes. Ivy wasn't about to pound on random doors, soaking wet and sounding like a moon-crazed person shouting about invasion. Ringing the bell was one sure way to get attention of at least the watch, which, she wasn't sure why they hadn't come running when the first soldiers passed through the gate.

She backtracked to the gate. The guard's station was still empty. The brass bell sat quietly in its bell case, asleep like the rest of Welksdale. Whoever was supposed to be on watch, she hoped he got a case of bedbugs. For a town that almost burned in the war—not to mention the Exchequer was nearly robbed earlier—she would think they would be more vigilant. An entire army had entered and no one made a peep.

"Danial, I need you to climb up there and pull on the rope. Keep pulling until someone tells you to stop."

Danial nodded and began to climb the ladder to the bell tower. The brass bell chimed, not as loud as Ivy remembered from earlier.

"Pull harder," Ivy shouted.

Danial didn't hear, so she climbed the ladder and watched the muscles in his back and shoulder work while he yanked down on the bell. They rippled in a rather appealing motion beneath his wet shirt that had Ivy blushing. *Focus, girl.* The bell chimed, echoing through the tower. Ivy covered her ears. It was dry in the small chamber and Ivy tapped Danial on the shoulder. He released the rope and looked at her.

"Can you pull harder? Make it louder?" Ivy asked. "I don't think anyone can hear it."

"I'll try," Danial said. "Don't think it'll do much good. Not with the rain pounding the rooftops."

Of course, Ivy struck her forehead with her palm. The bell wasn't big enough to compensate for the rain. She ran back to the wagon, shouting Robin's name.

"What? What is it?" Dark circles were becoming evident under Robin's eyes, like she hadn't slept in a moon.

"I need you to stop making it rain," Ivy said. "The bell can't be heard."

"That isn't possible." She sounded beyond exhausted, falling into exasperation. "The rain stops and we will find ourselves trapped with no way out. You've had your chance. We have to get moving."

"No one was warned!" Anger, frustration, annoyance, fear twisted inside Ivy. Broiled in those emotions, a child giggling in the dark during a game of Catch-me, See-me, the power swelled. It transformed her words, filled them with song. "How far are you going to let this Cacophony push you?"

"Ivy, don't do this," Robin said, rubbing her temples.

Ivy couldn't stop. The song reached the point where it was no longer hers to control. It was a living thing, demanding to be fed. It delved into Robin. An image of a young girl weeping while children called her horrific names: plump, round-robin, rotund. She was singing to herself, the sky darkening to match the terrible words jabbed at her, cutting her worse than the knife wounds where she cut herself to take away the pain. The first drops of rain fell like tears, then became a deluge to soak the children and herself. She didn't care—

A sharp pain broke the song. Knuckles crushed her lips to her teeth and she fell into the muddy streets. Standing over her was Robin, hands curled into fists.

"Don't you fucking ever do that again," Robin said. "Those are my memories, my feelings, and you can't have them." Robin bent down and poked Ivy in the throat, making her cough. "Get one thing straight, little bitch. When you use your power against another Singer, you better be quick about it, or you'll end up with a knife in your gut."

"I didn't mean—"

"I don't give two fucks about your intentions," Robin said. "If I drown you in a puddle using my power, even though I didn't mean to, it doesn't change the fact that you are dead! Either you get in the damn wagon, or I will slit your throat myself to prevent the enemy from using you against us."

Ivy shivered, water soaking through her dress.

"Robin," Thrush called from the wagon. "Leave the girl alone. She doesn't know how to control it yet."

"She'd better learn control, or else my fist will be crammed down her throat so far she'll be shitting fingernails." Robin flicked up her hood and climbed back into the wagon. "Fine, she doesn't have to join us. Maybe a walk in the cold rain will teach you some manners."

Ivy rolled over onto her hands and knees. She spat out blood from her split lip. The dull ringing of the bell continued. Ivy got up, glaring at Robin in the wagon, nose wrinkled and teeth bared. Thrush was speaking softly to her, but Ivy couldn't understand the words.

Why am I trying so hard to save a people who didn't care about what happened to me?

A town where my mother couldn't turn to for help when Bryn was abusing her, and who thought Bryn was fucking me and didn't do a damn thing about it. Ivy cast a look around the muddy streets, water flowing in rivulets. At the horses and wagons, the dripping soldiers waiting for a command. How did all of this happen so fast? How had she allowed strangers to dictate where she belonged? None of them cared about her, but her power. She posed a threat and they all wanted her for reasons outside of seeing Ivy as something more than a frightened girl in need of someone to give a shit about her. Something dangerous.

No home. No one to care if she lived or died.

"It can all burn. I don't care" Ivy said, swiping her wet hair from her face. "Let it all fucking burn!"

"Let what burn? What's going on here?" Sean Tailor emerged from the shadow of the Tannery. The Lumin Mayor and Speaker of Welksdale wasn't alone. Dozens of men carrying weapons ranging from pitchforks to cleavers. A few had swords among them, including Sheriff Gareth and his men. "Who are you?"

The Singer's soldiers drew their weapons in response, surrounding Thrush, Nuthatch, and Robin.

"I have a better question." Thrush came down from the wagon, her face covered by her cloak. Ivy envied having something to keep the rain off as she shivered in both anger and cold. "Where is your gatekeeper? An entire army passed through and another one is on its way." Thrush's announcement brought on angry murmurs. "Fortunate for you, we are just passing through, but the next one burned down Euclid."

"Bloody ashes! Where's Rusty Jon! He had the watch," Sheriff Gareth shouted. "Go wake his lazy ass up. Drag him out here."

"What do you mean by another army is coming," Sean Tailor said. "How'd we know you don't intend on killing us?"

"Because you would already be dead," Thrush said.

"Mayhap," Sean said, "or mayhap you are looking to conscript our young men for whatever violence you seek. Why should we trust you?"

Ivy saw Thrush debate telling them who, or in this case, what they were. For now, she kept quiet, letting the idea of two armies spread among the gathered crowd. Several men slipped way.

"Who's ringing the bell?" Sheriff Gareth asked.

"Danial," Ivy said.

"Ivy, is that you?" The Sheriff took a step closer, lantern light shining on her.

"Yes, and I can tell you that it's true," Ivy said, "you are all in danger and must leave."

"After what happened in the Exchequer yestermorn, well, you aren't the most reliable source," Sheriff Gareth said. "You were helping those boys rob it, weren't you?"

Other people added in, some using harsh words to describe Ivy. Words she heard whispered and some spoken aloud intentionally for her to hear. Each was a jab, making her regret speaking up for the safety of the town.

Thrush narrowed her brow at Ivy.

"It's not true," Ivy said, but her voice had been diminished.

"Well, it seems you have brought more harm to our town, girl. What have you to say?" Sean Tailor said. "You let these soldiers in to rob us?"

"No."

"Get on your way!" An angry voice shouted from the back. "Spread your deceit elsewhere!"

"She wanted to burn the town! Thank the Blessed it's raining!"

"Fool woman!"

"Daddy's lover."

Ivy had heard enough. She began to walk away, find her own place to go far away from these assholes, when a clod of mud arched from the crowd and hit Ivy in the chest. It didn't hurt, physically, but it wounded her deeper. More mud slung at her, coating her until she moved close to Thrush.

"I was stupid to think I could save any of them," Ivy said. "They obviously hate me for what they think I am."

"Just wait until people know what you are," Thrush said. "They'll hate you without even knowing who you are."

"Hey! You leave her alone!" Danial came running down the boardwalk. So caught up in the vitriol spewed at her, Ivy didn't notice the bell had stopped ringing. He started shoving people in the crowd who were throwing mud. One of the Sheriff's deputies threw a punch, which Danial blocked and hit the man in the gut. More men grabbed hold of Danial and began hitting and kicking him. Tossing him to the ground, where he furled into a protective ball.

"Aren't you going to do something?" Ivy asked.

"We can't afford a riot," Thrush said. "Best we get in the wagons—"

Ivy had stopped listened. A voice sounded, louder than the rest. A voice she had recognized and stood in disbelief.

"I vouch for her!"

The Sheriff and Speaker hushed the crowd. They peeled off the men hitting Danial off. Danial grunted and crawled back, slipping in the mud.

"Who does?" Sheriff Gareth asked. "Who vouches for the girl?"

"I do." Tym hobbled along the wooden walk. "She speaks the truth. I witnessed Euclid burn."

Everyone went silent.

A good horse was never around when you needed one. At least not one that wasn't either occupied by a rider or tucked away some place dry, easy to reach. The rain made it impossible to find an old nag standing miserably around, neglected and grateful to be relieved by a desperate horse thief, like Tym, to pay it some attention.

The only place to find a proper steed would be by breaking into the stables. Breaking into the stables was tough enough when he had two good legs, but dragging his right created double the trouble and it would be worse if there was a hand sleeping in the stables to keep watch for people like Tym who wanted to borrow a horse.

He stood outside the locked paddock, water sluicing off the roof in sheets, and stared at the building. Horses made soft noise inside. Warm and fed, like he wished to be.

These people take better care of their horses than a starving child. He thought of Ivy specifically. Often, he'd find her weak from hunger, lying in the dirty house. Bryn would be in the back room, snoring as he slept off a drunk. He'd bring her a bit of food, wishing he could do more. *Here I am going to run off and save the drunk while leaving the child in the hands of those women.*

Bryn was blood, but Ivy deserved better.

What he was really doing was running away from responsibility. Like he'd done anytime things got tough. Like he had done with Veena and Ivy.

"Nazglum's nuts," he said, "here's my chance to do one thing right."

Yet, his gut kept telling him to run. Instead, Tym hobbled along the wooden walk, and noticed a window open in the stables. Under it was a wooden crate. He could climb the crate, hook onto the window and slide inside. He couldn't have planned it any better than if he had opened the window himself and left the crate beneath it.

Blessed Creator is testing me! Tym groaned. He hated tests, failing more often than he passed. He went over, just to see if he could do it. He stepped up on the crate, just to see if he could reach the window. He grabbed the ledge and pulled himself up. The place smelled of hay and horse sweat. Below the window was a soft pile of hay, not pitchfork or sharp object to skewer himself on. It was a horse thief's dream. The stable owner could do no better than opening the door and handing Tym the reins.

His arms ached. *I could sip inside and warm up. Take a horse and catch up with Ivy later, or even go to Bryn.* Why couldn't he do both? On the side wall, there was tack hanging. Saddle bags, a feed bag, and a bag of oats. They all cried out for him.

What about Ivy?

To reinforce that notion, shouts started from up the street. Tym dropped back to the crate, his right leg giving out and he sat down hard, teeth clicking and his ass splashing in cold water. The people sounded angry and he guessed they woke, realizing they were no longer alone. He tested his leg, the calf still burned, but he could walk. Hobbling down the wooden walkway, he noticed how fast rainwater rushed through the road and created puddles. *It won't be long until the road is flooded. Travel will be a shit show.*

Neither the wagons, nor the soldiers had moved since he left them behind.

What are they waiting for?

Then he noticed the large crowd by the Tannery. The Sheriff was there along with the Speaker. Some really harsh words were being bantered around. "Why should we trust you?" was one phrase he heard repeated, alongside other ugly words that he had heard before, many times when directed at his niece and brother. Someone bent down. Tym thought they were fixing their bootstraps, until he saw a clump of dirt in their hands. It flew from their hands, and he knew that this was how an angry group of people could turn into a mob. The dirt struck a lone figure. Ivy, who was merely wet when he hugged her in what seemed moments before, was covered in mud. Her night black hair clung to her face and her hands were clenched into fists.

These fucks!

Tym couldn't fight them, so he did the next best thing. He got close enough and shouted.

"I vouch for her!"

He had to yell it three times before anyone heard him. Then the crowd quieted down. Tym got closer so they could see him.

"She speaks the truth. I witnessed Euclid burn."

He didn't have the best reputation in Welksdale, but he was a big spender in the town shops. Talk was cheap, especially when coin was tossed around at the trade houses and taverns. Which was more than what Bryn would ever do.

"She's your niece," one man commented, Harold, the owner of the Horseshoe Inn.

"I don't give a goddamn shit if she were your niece, I'd still vouch for her." Tym came in closer. "You got two choices it seems. Stand here arguing, like the mad sons-of-bitches I see before me, and wave at this other unstoppable force as it comes in, slaughters your families, and burn this all down." He paused, taking in their faces, seeing the disbelief starting to dissolve. "Or you can start packing up some shit and get the hell out."

Silence hung in the air, even the rain had ceased to fall.

"Oh God," Thrush said in a hushed voice more terrifying than anything Tym had heard. Her head was tilted to the west, and Tym looked that way as well. "The rain has stopped."

CHAPTER TEN
BATTLE OF WELKSDALE

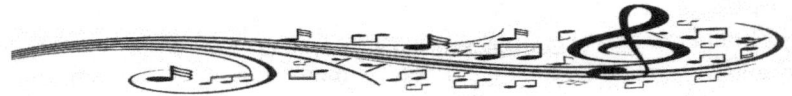

Engaging in direct war is mess—not that our hands our clean. We must work in the shadows, guiding events unnoticed until the momentum is too great, the tiny stone grows into a boulder, and the avalanche is inevitable. Then we may strike, or stay back and savor the fruits of our labor. Watching humans destroy themselves leaves a particularly sweet taste on my poor shriveled tongue. We all suffer, but those who believe they are safe and untouchable, well, their suffering is most delightful.

Bryn didn't lie. The town was a couple of leagues away. Claiborne respected that about him. *The Creator blesses an honest man.* No matter what he was in life, his last words and his last moments were lived in truth. Bryn had the tell-tale signs of a man who drank too much, red-streaked eyes, broken veins in his nose and the smell of a drowned rat in a cesspool. Drunks usually weren't honest, not to themselves or others, which is why they hid in their cup. Honesty was painful. Staring at the sun too long made you blind. Better to close your eyes to the world, bind them, put them out, and nothing helped ink blot the world like drinking. Claiborne understood. She had drunk her fair share of wine, ale, and anything strong, to shroud the memory of Arron's death. It didn't make him anymore alive, but she forgot about him for those moments. In a way, forgetting was the greatest sin of all. Then Arron would be truly dead and gone from the world. Better to embrace the pain and keep his story alive.

And murder the bitch who killed him.

Claiborne held the spyglass to her eye, occasionally wiping the rain from the lens. Robin, Nuthatch, and Thrush had stopped outside the town's gate. *Another wall, another bon-fire.* Claiborne chuckled. The question remained: would they enter the town or go around? Claiborne had no preference. Cut through a town, kill a few bystanders, steal some supplies, or go around, it was all the same. Once they committed, the Silent Men would strike. If they went around the town, the rear vanguard would be destroyed and she would flank them with her cavalry while the wagons were slowed by the uneven land.

"How do you still have wagons and horses?"

They must have been sent ahead while the women and their soldiers hid behind Euclid's walls. Claiborne's mistake was she was too eager to destroy the woman that she never sent scouts to search for split forces. *The girl confirmed Robin, Nuthatch, and Thrush were inside.* Claiborne didn't understand how she knew, and it made her uncomfortable that Cacophony would use the same power they were seeking to remove from the world to regain harmony. It wasn't her place to voice opposition. She was the First Sword, carrying out orders. Did it matter where the source of their information came from? Nazglum himself could whisper it into her ear and she would act on it. Whatever brought an end to the Singers.

She wiped the lens again, leaving a sheen of water streaks. Claiborne smiled. The town gates opened and the wagons moved inside.

They never learn.

Of course, Robin might've chosen a different course if she had known her trick with the rain clouds wasn't working. It was Claiborne's idea that Cacophony keep back while she brought the regiment through the rain. It was a risk, because the Singers had their power and could use it on them if the Silent Men were discovered. Thrush alone could tear up half of Claiborne's force. It was their hubris that would be their downfall. Battles were won and lost by those who made the fewest mistakes.

Claiborne adjusted in the saddle, the dried white flower crinkled against her chest. It was a strong reminder that she could make no more mistakes. Not if she wanted her revenge on Thrush. Not if she wanted Arron's sacrifice to mean something.

The line of soldiers was halfway through the gate and then stopped. Maybe they met resistance from the town's folk or maybe they were going for a resupply. The miserable line of soldiers, soaked through their cloaks, would make easy pickings. Especially once their weapons and armor became brittle.

"Bring up the carriage." Claiborne snapped the eye glass closed. "Form lines. They will know soon enough we are here."

And won't be able to do a damn thing about it.

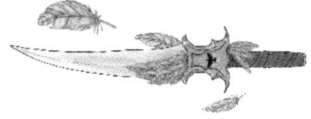

Ivy had never been more mortified in her life than at the moment these people flung mud and insults at her. They made her out to be some kind of monster based on rumors and their hate of her parents. Covered in filth, called worse names than anything she could recall, she wanted to show them what a monster she could be, to delve everyone and force them into the very acts of depravity they accused her of doing. It would be satisfying for the short term, but then she would be no better than them. It was better to leave them all to die.

But then her shame changed and the voices went silent, except for one. Her uncle came back and stood against the mob for her. She smiled, tears in her eyes. Outside of her mother, no one else defended, at least not without expecting something in return. She wiped her eyes on her sodden sleeve and realized the drops were no longer falling from the sky.

"Nazglum's nuts! I told you we had to go!" Robin leapt from the wagon, swearing even louder. "Nazglum's sweaty nut-sack! You there, get the men in defensive formation. I want bows on every rooftop. We can't outrun the cock sucker anymore. He'll be up our asses before long. Get everyone inside. Seal the gates."

Robin smacked soldiers on the back and shoulders, shouting more orders. Boots splashed in the mud running off to fill them. The wagons began to move further down the street, clearing space for the soldiers to enter the town.

"This is where you need to go," Thrush said, and hurried to the wagon. She yanked off the gate and began rummaging around.

"What do you mean?"

"I mean, run, child." Thrush drew a pair of short swords from under the bench. "Get as far away from here and maybe you'll live to see another sun or two." She grabbed a belt, loaded with blades of various sizes, and strapped it round her thin waist. All that metal looked to weigh more than Thrush.

"They will still catch me," Ivy said.

Thrush nodded. "I guess you better run fast."

Then Thrush disappeared in the clamor of soldiers scurrying into position. Nuthatch joined Thrush, a long sword drawn.

"We'll delay them as best as we can," Nuthatch said.

The alarm bell gonged, demanding attention. *Now they sound it? Like spitting on the fire after it has scorched the walls.* A man and woman hurried past Ivy, carrying blankets wrapped up in their arms. Sheriff Gareth tried his best to keep them moving.

"Rusty!" He called after a man who had reddish-brown hair trying to sneak on past in the flow of people. He cringed at hearing the Sheriff yell. "Get your ass back here."

"I was going to open the back gate!" Rusty slunk like a boy waiting for a lashing he deserved.

"Like you were supposed to be keeping a watch on the front." Sheriff Gareth smacked Rusty across his head. "Lucky for you we need your lunkhead. Get over to the gate and make sure it gets sealed when everyone has passed through." Rusty nodded and went to leave, but the Sheriff yanked him back by the arm. "If I find out you abandon your post again, I'll break your kneecaps."

In the chaos, Ivy was left torn on what to do. Danial stood at her side, smiled awkwardly at her, the cut on his nose marring what was once a handsome face, and said, "I won't let anyone hurt you."

On her opposite side, her uncle leaned in.

"We need to go," Tym said. "I know where we can get horses."

"I can't," Ivy said.

"Why not?"

"They got someone who can find me," Ivy said.

"Find you, how?"

"I'm like them." Ivy pointed at Thrush. "Mother was, too."

Tym blinked and shook his head.

"It doesn't matter. There has to be some way to escape from all this," Tym said, waving his arms at the soldiers and citizens preparing for battle. "By midday, this town won't exist. It'll be ashes and I'll be damned if I let you die here."

Silas Mathers glared at her as he walked past, a short sword in his hand. Her father had called him a coward, but here he was, ready to fight for his home. More joined him, and not just Sheriff Gareth's men. Men and boys took their makeshift weapons and filled the ranks. Tym noticed her watching and tugged urgently on her arm.

On her other side Danial mimicked Tym.

"We should go," Danial said, shuffling in the mud. He was sporting a fat lip, black left eye, and rubbed his left ribs. He was also covered in mud, but didn't seem to notice. "You heard them. There's bad men coming to kill you."

Ivy watched Robin and Thrush arguing. She caught a snippet of Robin shouting at her companion. "It's your fault! We could've cleared this shithole and got another day's journey ahead, losing them in the hills. But, no, you had to stop for the girl. A whole lot of good that did. She'll be a corpse not long after us."

Thrush gave Ivy a sympathetic look.

"Doesn't matter," Nuthatch said. "We had to fight them one way or another."

"Shut up, girl!" Robin stalked away.

The bell rang urgently and a cry of riders screamed through the soldiers like a great wind ready to sweep them away. The collective fear washed through them and Ivy wavered, allowing Tym and Danial to pull her in the direction of the retreating citizens.

"Gates! Close the fucking gates!"

Although the sky was clear, a gibbous moon waned and a shred of gray light shone on the eastern horizon, Ivy couldn't see what was happening with the sea of blue uniformed soldiers and mottled Welksdalians blocking her view. She heard a distant scream and more yelling. Men and women tensed, awaiting orders. The closest thing to pitched battle Ivy had experienced was at the Exchequer and then her home. She had no desire to be so close to sharp metal hacking away at flesh, but the alternative wasn't much better.

"I'm not leaving," Ivy said and pulled free of her uncle and Danial. She slogged off, trying not to slip in the mud. Running away was about as useful as the hole in the crotch of her leggings. No matter how much she ignored it, the cold would still catch her. She would fight, and most-likely die, but at least she'd die on her own terms. Ivy rounded the side of the cobbler's shop, catching a glimpse of her dirt-streaked face and mud matted dress. She didn't recognize the girl, her hair sopping wet and the determined mud-packed fac. This was the look of someone newly risen from her grave, or perhaps one about to be buried in it.

There was a loud thud, then the groan of wood being battered. Bows thrummed from atop the buildings and arrows swarmed over the walls. Ivy walked through ankle deep water in the alley beside the Tack and Feed store, hugging the wall and rounding behind where several sealed barrels blocked her path. She climbed the first one and stood up on the lid. After the rain, any extra weight could cause them to collapse. The wood groaned louder, but held.

"What are you doing?" Tym asked, hissing as he tried to keep pace.

"I want a closer look." Ivy hopped across to the next barrel.

"I recommend on horseback." Tym grunted and cursed. "As we are leaving. Hey! Get your hands off me, I was climbing taller obstacles before you born."

"But your leg," Danial said, lifting Tym up under the arms.

"I'm not ready to be put down yet." Tym wavered and almost fell off the barrel. He would have eaten dirt if Danial hadn't caught him under the arm. "Watch the hands, big boy. At least make me dinner first."

They were slowing her down, clambering awkwardly over the obstacles she hoped across, hoping the lids held. Wood groaning changed into a loud crack. Tym cursed, Danial made frustrated remarks like a mother hen squawking at her chick heading for the fox's hole.

"Form up!" the cry came from close by.

Ivy turned the corner and got a glimpse of the gate. They were at least thirty yards from it, but it didn't seem far enough at the moment. *Maybe Tym was right. Maybe we should leave. It's not too late to go out the back gate.* The front wouldn't hold up for much longer. The halves listed inward, like two drunk friends clinging onto the other for support. Another thump and the bar splintered, the gates halves leaping and parting enough for a soldier, screaming and waving a sword, to shove his way past. He got in a good swipe, leaving a ragged cut across one of the defenders before the others cut him down. The hacked body dropped a few steps from the gates entrance. There was a brief pause, like the holding of one's breath, then a loud roar. The gates burst open followed by a line of men in black armor lugging a battering ram.

"Here they come," Danial said, propping Tym up on his wide shoulder.

"What are we going to do?"

Behind the invading soldiers, Ivy saw a woman on a horse, sword raised, and ordering the invading soldiers to press forward. A black curtain full of spears and swords filled the gap where the gate had been. They were met by a line of defenders, shields locked like rocks breaking the seething water. The shields bent under the assault, some snapping. Ivy saw a man's arm cut off at the elbow. Blood sprayed the attackers who grabbed the man and tossed him out of the way.

The alley where she stood became blocked as more defenders rushed to fill the holes left by the dead. Ivy's stomach lurched at the horrors. She witnessed a man in black armor thrust a spear and the defender deflected the point off his shield, and it slipped past, jabbing the man next to him in the eye. He dropped at Ivy's feet, a bloody socket where his eye had been punctured, his mouth twisted in an empty scream. Stephone had the same look when he died, knife plunged hilt deep into his socket. Death was far from beautiful. It was downright ugly.

"Ivy." Tym's voice brought her back.

Ivy stepped back and gripped her stomach. She vomited, a string of bitter bile dangling from her lips.

"We should go," Danial said, placing a comforting hand on her shoulder.

"No," Ivy said, wiping her mouth. Any chance of running was over. "We fight."

"How?" Danial asked. "We ain't got any swords. They'll slaughter us good as pigs under the butcher's knife."

"He's got a point," Tym said.

"We use what weapons the Creator gave us." Ivy stared at the moving wall of soldiers. There were so many. Fear gripped her heart, telling her to get as far away from the fighting as her legs could carry her. She clenched her fists, nails digging into her palms. Somewhere beyond the gate was Cacophony. Whoever was disrupting the Harmonics would be with him. *End this person and end it all.* "Stay close to me. Try to stay alive."

Ivy inched closer to the edge of the building. She watched, waiting for her chance.

"Where are you going?" Tym limped up next to him.

A gap formed in the heaving mess of bodies and she could see across the road to the next alley. Ivy knew it wouldn't last long.

"Mother," she yelled and ran. Her clogs skidded in the mud, spinning her around one soldier who lifted his shield, narrowly missing her head. He bashed another close to him. The metal cracked and the man groaned. Ivy regained her balance and slammed into the side of a black armored woman. She bounced off, sprawling into the mud. Her shoulder ached marking a bruise. *Lucky it's still attached.* She thought of the man who lost his arm. Ivy shook her head and found her bearings. The opposite ally was close. *A quick run*, she told her shaking legs.

Something hit her foot, tripping her up. She slid on her heels, arms waving about like a bird learning the fly, and fell to her knee. Glazed over blue eyes stared up at her from the metal helm, blood oozing from the severed neck. Ivy squeaked, batting the head away and found her feet. She took a step and that was as far as she could go. Blocking her path was a large man in black armor. He snarled at her; ax head raised. Power filled her and she allowed it to seize control. The song rose from her belly, her chest, the first few notes coming to her lips and... nothing. It was like a sneeze caught in her nose. She moaned, wondering if she'd made a mistake. The ax head descended on her.

Across the way at the Tack and Feed store, Tym screamed her name.

Claiborne split her cavalry into two groups. Fifty on each side rode the outer perimeter of the town, killing anyone trying to leave. *Fool me once, shit on me, fool me twice shit won't happen again!* There would be no escape. Robin's, Nuthatch's, and Thrush's corpses would be dragged out of the ruins and piled before Cacophony. A single, dried flower painted dipped in their blood to complete the garnish.

Sitting atop her destrier one hundred yards from the Welksdale gate, Claiborne observed the battle and called for action. "Ram up! Open the damn gates and give them hell!"

Half-a-dozen Silent Men brought up the ram, a thick trunk carved from blood wood and capped with a metal cone shaped like a black beetle, the Death Scarab. It was good for knocking down stubborn doors and small gates. No need to waste fire on this place. They could burn it later once the women were found and put down.

There was little resistance. Scattered arrows sailed over the walls. Nothing concentrated enough to do much damage. A Silent Man fell here and there. The Death Scarab was in place, the men swinging in unison, like a giant fist pounding on the wood. *Little birds! Little birds! Let me in!* The gates creaked and groaned. After the fifth hit, it was done. Silent Men charged the breech.

"Oh, you are good," Claiborne said, admiring how quickly Thrush and Robin formed their soldiers up. Lacking the strength of Thrush's harmonics, the defenders' weapons, shields, and armor, would shatter like old, brittle bones. The town would fall before the sun raised its bloody head.

An arrow flashed over her head and thudded into the saddle bag.

"Kill those archers," she said. Last thing needed was to have a lucky shot end her at the moment of victory. That's not how it went in heroic songs.

She would walk into the town, stepping over the bodies of her enemies as they lay in pools of their own blood. That was how the poets would recite it. Just without song. She had enough of the singers for a lifetime.

The arrows soaring over the gates soon ended. Once they secured the entrance, she would ride in and join the fight long enough to find Thrush. The surprise on her former leader's face would be delicious, to be defeated by the same woman whose lover the bitch singer had killed and then, adding further insult, left for dead.

"'You don't deserve a quick death,'" Claiborne practiced the line she'd say, "'the world is better without you'," and then she'd snap Thrush's thin neck, drive her sword down her throat, making her swallow every inch of steel forged ironically by her own song. The delightful image gave Claiborne the shivers, distracting her from boots splashing through the mud and rattling armor. Being distracted on the battlefield most often led to death. Claiborne's horse was battle hardened, alerting her to the sounds, ears twitching and head swiveling to the side. She drew her sword, heeled her horse forward, and turned him so she could face—

Oh shit, what's he doing here?

"The battle is going well, First Sword," Cacophony said and clapped his gloved hands. He still wore the muslin around his nose and mouth, but his eyes were visible. Predatory eyes that watched her every move, calculating how he might kill her if she gave him reason. He was a dangerous, damaged man. She'd experienced the dangers when on the opposing side, discovered the damage when she met the girl.

"Are you going to join me in completing the rout?" Claiborne relaxed her arm, allowing the sword point to dip.

"On the contrary, I am here to bring you another disappointment." He almost sounded disappointed. A trick. Silent Prayer was on his back, but his hand wasn't anywhere near it. Claiborne's brow knitted together, her heart thudding and rage burning cool in the embers of her chest, ready to flair. She tapped her left breast. The dried white flower petal stinging her. She wanted to tear it out, flower, petal, heart, and toss them into the mud.

It can't be! The rain! Robin was there. Thrush would be there, too!

"They… didn't escape again?"

Cacophony chuckled.

"No, First Sword, your instincts were deviously accurate," Cacophony said. He lowered his muslin to give her a smile. The scar at the corner of his mouth, pink and raw, was ugly, changing a smile into a snarl from a diseased, wounded creature. The skin around it was pale, moist, making his lips red and glistening, like raw meat. Yet, it held pity. Like he was about to break a beloved one's heart. "Sometimes we must disappoint for no reason other than a greater good is gained."

"But I have her," Claiborne said, frustration tightening her throat. She swallowed hard, heart beating out the rising anger. "She's in there and I'm going to kill her."

"No," Cacophony said. A father disciplining an unruly daughter. "Not today."

"This is what you wanted. Those bitches dead." Claiborne dug down the front of her shirt and brought up the white flower. "This is your promise. Our pact."

"Yes," Cacophony said. "Just not today."

"I don't understand."

"It is not for you to understand, First Sword. It is for you to follow orders," Cacophony said and replaced the muslin. "My orders are for the Silent Men to fall back. A strategic retreat."

"There will be loses." Claiborne knew he was whining.

"For a greater gain."

His words reminded her too much of Arron, of Thrush, of every person who thought they could gain something by losing. In the end, the only thing gained was her sorrow. Sand rippling through her fingers and scattered by the wind.

"Do it, First Sword." Cacophony turned and walked away.

I have her. The idea thrummed along her nerves. The joy of holding a bird in the palm of her hand became a silent rage as she was forced to release it. *I will get her back.* She gave the order for a strategic retreat. Sent another rider to tell those who went to slaughter fleeing towns people. Another victory, snatched away from her. The sweetness on her tongue, now bitter.

"I will get you, Thrush." She released the flower and it floated into the mud. "I will kill you."

"She's going to die!" Tym grabbed onto Danial's tunic, tearing the sleeve as he levered himself along the road. No matter how fast he moved, everyone else around him moved at a much quicker speed. Like he was piss-pants drunk and the room was spinning and he couldn't remember if he was going to sit, stand, dance, or just fall over. Falling over would be very bad here and once he hit the ground he would stay down. He picked up a discarded shield and a small axe, willing his legs to hold firm a little longer. His eyes were on the giant soldier standing over Ivy. The massive two-handed axe held in the soldier's hand was bigger than Ivy, the kind that could fell a blood oak in a single stroke. It would obliterate his niece. The man could step on her like a bug and that would be enough.

Mud splashed off to his right and Tym ducked in time to keep his head attached. He smashed the shield's rim into the man's mouth, shattering teeth, and knocking him backwards. The soldier standing over Ivy raised his axe overhead.

Not going to get there in time. Tym did the only thing he could. He cocked his arm back and flung his small axe like smashing bottles in the alley behind the Dripping Bucket. His elbow clicked, fueling his scream. Haft-over-blade the axe sailed, falling short his mark of the soldier's head, striking the black links under his arm and clattering away.

The man redirected his axe upon impact, swinging wildly. Ivy flattened herself in the mud, narrowly escaping the sharp edge. Mud spattered instead of Ivy's blood. Tym continued his run and leapt at the soldier, which was more flop than leap, leading with the shield. He growled, saying something like "sheep fucker," or a version of words, and crashed into the soldier. He'd been better off charging a wall. Tym rebounded, shoulder going numb on the impact and dropped into the mud not far from Ivy. The shield had cracked in half and he couldn't raise either arm in any case. He lay sprawled out, taking in a harsh breath, coughed, spat out grit, and waited for the axe to split him in half.

"Sheep fucker?" the soldier asked, stepping on Tym's injured leg.

Tym bit back a whimper.

"You prefer goats then?"

The man laughed and pointed at Ivy.

"I will take her and make her my goat."

Tym tried to sit up, force his useless arms to move, but they refused to respond, tethered to the mud by a strength greater than he could overcome.

"I tried, Ivy," Tym said.

"And you failed," the soldier hefted the war axe. Before he could get it full overhead, the man jerked sideways, held tilting as though listening carefully to instructions, while a blade slick with gore, stuck out the opposite side of his neck. Danial grunted, releasing the hilt—Tym didn't even hear the farm boy, and apparently, neither did the soldier. The soldier's eyes bulged as the blade sheathed in his throat and he made a few gurgling sounds, blood gushing from the wound. The war axe dropped and the soldier grabbed the blade, sliding it from his neck. His head dropped on his chin, neck shattered, and he toppled over, a rush of blood turning the mud red.

"Are you alright?" Danial knelt beside Ivy. He was looking her over for marks, not that there wasn't a spot free of the mud.

"Hey! I'm the one who got flattened." Tym laughed at the goofy expression on Danial's face. *Damn fool will get himself killed trying to save that girl.* "Get her up and take her across."

"I'm fine," Ivy said and was on her feet. "A little shaken."

The sound of battle roared back in. Men shouted and metal clashed. Screams of the wounded and dying cut off only to be picked up again by some other poor man caught on the edge of a blade. Tym groaned, managing

199

to shake off the broken shield and move his left arm. The right hung limp at his side.

"Help me up, and let's get the fuck off the road."

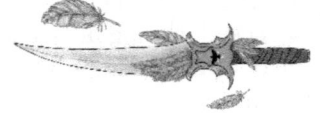

Danial pulled her into the next alley, dropping them both behind a smelly stack of crates. Nausea swirled through her head and stomach, caused by the sickly-sweet smell of rotting fruit. The ache pulsed inside her gut and head threatening to turn her inside-out. *Almost getting killed is becoming a bad habit.* She shivered, unsure if it was because she was cold and wet, or from the shock of nearly having her head smashed by a giant axe.

"I'm almost missing my life of quiet desperation," Ivy said and groaned. "Almost."

"Told you we need to get somewhere safe," Danial said.

"Too fucking late for 'told you so's.'" She regretted her sharp tone, especially since Danial did save her life. "Sorry, I didn't mean—"

"No worries," Danial said, though he refused to look at her. "I'm trying to help is all."

Ivy patted his arm.

"I know."

Ivy glanced back for her uncle. Tym ambled along, using the giant axe as a crutch. He plopped down next to her, breathing heavy and cradling his right arm. They probably all looked like ghouls rising from their graves.

"Is it broken?" she asked, looking at his arm.

"No," the word coming through strained. "Might be dislocated."

"Danial should get you somewhere safe." Not that she knew there was a safe place anymore. Not with an entire invading force in the town meant to occupy a few hundred people. *I have to do this alone. No one else has to die for me.* As it was, enough people died because of her failings.

"Not a chance." He smiled, but it seemed forced. He was in a great deal of pain. As much as Ivy would like to send him away, she was grateful for him being here with her.

"Thank you," she said, touching his good arm. She swallowed back tears and her throat stung from them. On top of the nausea, her entire body was ready to shut down. Drop her into a deep sleep to where she might wake up from the nightmare, or continue into the eternal slumber. "Thank you for sticking up for me, saving me… you are the only family I have left."

"That's not true." Tym frowned.

"You think Bryn is alive?"

"You really don't know?" Tym sounded surprised, and a bit disappointed.

"No, but he couldn't get water without my help. Unless these Silent Men miraculously missed the house—"

"That's not what I mean."

Ivy groaned, rejecting the memories that came flooding in. Images from Mother Farlow, her own mother singing in this town, being watched by Crisell's father, the anger and accusations. It couldn't be true. What person would be so cruel to abandon her to a lifetime of misery? That wasn't a mother. Veena may have given birth to Ivy, but a mother was supposed to protect her child at all costs.

"Soldiers," Danial said. "We have to move."

"Bryn isn't—" Ivy couldn't bring the words out.

Tym shook his head.

"Sorry, kid," he said.

Ivy leaned against the wall. Mother Farlow was right in her fears and justified in her anger. That meant Myah and Crisell were her half-siblings, which was why Bryn kept Crisell away. The power bubbled inside, and she spotted soldiers in black armor fighting at the mouth of the ally. When she opened her mouth to release it, she doubled over, vomiting a string of yellowish bile.

"Are you sick?" Danial asked, touching her shoulders lightly.

Ivy shook her head. Being blocked was horrifying. She could sense the power, but it wouldn't leave her, like trying to breath underwater. Drowning in power. She coughed, gagging on phlegm. She fought back the power, coaxing it to a dull thrum that ached in her head rather than her chest and gut.

"We have to get closer to the front," Ivy said. Part of her sensed the source of the blockage. Hands strangling the song, distorting the harmonics. Her ears pulsed in rush of blood. She could follow the source to its origin, like walking a stream the mouth of its spring.

"Are you crazy?" Danial asked. "They will cut us to pieces."

"I have an idea," Ivy said. "One that may help end this fight rather quickly." *Or end us.* Either worked for her at the moment.

"Are you sure?" Tym asked.

"Swear by my mother." She touched the locket under her smock.

Tym tried to get up, but fell back against the crate of spoiled fruit. A soft, moldy piece landed in his lap, splattering his trousers.

"I think I may need to rest here… can we rest here?" Tym asked. She heard the desperation in his voice. The pain, both physical and knowing he was unable to support Ivy further.

"You have done more than enough, Uncle." Ivy kissed his forehead. "I have to go."

"I would tell you don't go," Tym said, "but it would be a waste of words."

Ivy nodded, not trusting her words.

"I'm sorry, Ivy," Tym said, tears forming in his eyes. "For everything."

"There'll be time enough for apologies after," Ivy said. "I still want to ask you some questions about my mother."

"Sure, kid," Tym said, though he didn't sound very optimistic. "Be safe."

"I'll try." Ivy squeezed his hand. He may not be her "real" uncle, but he was showing up for her more than anyone else. She released his hand and turned to see an opening in the fighting. She ran, Danial close to her side. This was her first taste of war and it was bitter on her tongue, flaky like dried vomit. Her belly squirmed at every clash of metal she heard, every flash of movement wondering if it this be the sword stroke, the falling axe, the poking spear, to end her life. It was enough to want to crawl into a ball and wait for it to end.

I have to find the source blocking us. Release the bindings on Thrush, Nuthatch, and Robin so they can unleash their power on the Silent Men and end them.

The battle shifted. Welksdalians and Singer soldiers were no longer being pushed back. Thrush's twin swords flashed and a man in black armor dropped. She moved like liquid lightning, slicing through another soldier. Ivy would never have guessed such skill from so small and slight a woman. Face splashed in blood and her dress soaked through, she seemed more predator than songbird.

"Press forward!" Thrush shouted.

"What are we doing, Ivy?" Danial asked, and Ivy tore her eyes from Thrush.

"This way," Ivy said, pointing to a clear area. He nodded and followed. "Looks like you found your sword after all."

"Wasn't too difficult," Danial said and shrugged. "They're sort of lying round like the dead. Wish I had a hammer. But this will do."

Ivy led him to another side street behind the business and stopped short as more soldiers fought. The muddy ground was churned up in a mess of blood, broken metal and bodies. Buildings were on fire. Several of the archers leapt off into the swarming mass.

"Not going that way," Danial said, grabbing Ivy's hand. She searched for a break in all the fighting, but it was like trying to walk in the creek without getting wet. Danial tugged her. "This way."

Danial used his newly acquired sword, jabbing a soldier under the right arm, releasing the handle while taking the dead man's axe. Ivy ducked under a sword thrust. Danial turned and smashed the axe-head into the soldier's side, sending him crumpled to the ground. They slunk behind the Cobbler Shop, its roof smoldering. Ivy thought about the boots she saw in the display window. It wasn't long ago she was worried about blisters on her feet. Now it was about keeping her head attached.

"Where now?" Danial asked.

Ivy worked on gathering her breath.

"Let me try something."

She felt the power churning inside. The resistance was stronger. She felt sicker than earlier; her entire belly wanted to turn inside-out. The source came from outside the wall. That's where they had to go.

"Close," Ivy said. "Got to get closer."

"Are you sure?" Danial asked.

Ivy gave him a look she thought was as sharp as any blade. Danial didn't argue, he peeked around the edge of the building, held up a hand for her to wait. He pressed against the side and Ivy copied him. Several more soldiers ran past. Ivy held her breath, praying they didn't spot them. After several long heartbeats, Danial signaled for her follow, and then he disappeared around the side of the building.

It's close, she kept telling herself, keeping her tired legs moving. She could sense something was not right, a heavy blanket closing over her head and wrapping around it. The air in her chest was heavy. She stumbled, nearly tripping over Danial as he stopped suddenly. Danial pulled her down beside a stack of wet hay that smelled musty from the rain. He pressed his finger to her lips to silence any questions and then pointed to a gap in the stack, enough to get a clear view of what lay ahead.

The Silent Men were retreating. Black armored soldiers backed up to the gate and were passing through in clusters, not turning their backs on the attackers. *Weren't they winning?* There were more dead in dark blue and the unarmored citizens of Welksdale than there were in the black.

It made no sense to Ivy.

She followed a group of soldiers and moved outside the gate. The Silent Men continued to run, but Thrush kept her soldiers back. The move was prudent, because if they moved too far from their own defenses, then the Silent Men could counter. Ivy thought it might be more prudent for herself to stay, but she was following a trail. A scent too powerful to resist. One that would lead her to the source, she was certain. She kept moving, aiming further west, and dropping down into a cluster of yellowed-rag leaves. The rain had soaked them and they felt soft.

"Why are we crawling in the mud?" Danial asked.

"We don't want to be seen," Ivy said.

"Couldn't we stay," Danial said. "They left and we are safe."

"I won't be safe," Ivy said. "You can stay behind the walls, or run away until the armies pass. The Silent Men won't stop. Not until those women are killed, until I'm dead. Think about how many more people will die fighting. We can stop this and bring peace. Don't you want to go back home?"

"Yes," Danial said.

"Then trust me."

"Do you know where we are going?" Danial asked. "Or what to do when we get there?"

"I'll know when I know."

"That's comforting."

Ivy rolled her eyes, but smiled. She would walk into the Silent Men's camp alone, if she had to, but Danial was a comfort. If she got hurt, or worse, he could tell her uncle, or the man she used to believe was her uncle, what had happened.

"Glad to have you along," she said.

Behind them came the noise of the gate grating closed. *Nowhere left to go, but west.* Again, the feeling of being set adrift was strong. The power broiled in her gut. She had to see this to the end, no matter how it ended. One thing Ivy was certain about was she would not go quietly. Muddy water soaking the front of her dress, she began to crawl.

Was this how a worm felt escaping the birds?

Part of her knew there was no escape. She'd be swallowed up by whichever side got to her first.

Worm, worm, worm crawling through the dirt. Worm, worm, worm, dig, dig, digging in the mud. Don't look at me, don't see me, I'm nothing but a squirmy wormy. Ivy's elbows and legs ached, not to mention all the scrapes and bruises earned over the course of her adventure. The rhythm playing through her head added to their annoyance because she thought it was funny, but then it wouldn't stop, becoming a mantra to keep her safe from being spotted. *I've almost transformed into a worm.* Sweat broke across her body. Mud hardened on her legs, arms, and in her hair. She spat out grit that dropped into her mouth.

The grass tickled her, poked through the holes in her smock, and itched bad enough that she wanted to scratch her skin raw. Twice she sneezed, muffling the sound by pressing her nose into the crook of her arm. Every movement added to the nausea building up in her from being blocked. The further Ivy crawled, and she'd been crawling for an hour, approaching the singular source, the more her nausea grew. Her head began to pound and her mouth was dry. These had to be signs she was getting closer to the person. What worried her most was they had yet to encounter any Silent Men. She checked the road every now and then, spotting them moving away from Welksdale, at least a quarter of a league away. They were becoming black shapes in the distance, long shadows drawing out as the sun rose.

"Doesn't feel right," Danial complained for the fifth time.

Ivy hushed him, though no one else was around to hear. His whining was like thin nails splitting her skull. Added to the nausea, it was becoming unbearable. *Wished I had left him behind.* Part of her wondered why he was still with her, especially since her harmonics were blocked. Did she alter his mind permanently, or was he here of his free will?

Wormed my way in and eat away his sense of being? The idea sounded horrific, and she'd do whatever she could to take it all back. Then again, Danial was a rather simple man with simple thoughts, so he might be following her out of a misplaced sense of loyalty she didn't deserve. What was done was done and she couldn't unspill the milk.

This is stupid. Ivy shoved off the ground, climbing to her feet, and tried to swipe the dried mud from her hands. It was all over her and she simply spread it around more.

"What are you doing?"

"Do you see anyone?" Ivy twisted, stretching her aching body. A warm bath sounded very good, even a dip in the stream. Neither was an option. "They're licking their wounds and running. Thrush was too much for them. Most bullies back down when you hit them."

"Unless they outnumber you and kick the shit out of you."

Ivy's cheeks warmed remembering the image of the boys beating Danial.

"That's why we got to get on our feet," Ivy said. She tried not to laugh at Danial sticking his head over the grass and looking around like some rabbit sensing a hawk nearby. "I promise you they aren't going to just appear and start kicking."

"Can't we just go back?"

"We start running we will always be running," Ivy said. It was much easier to become the hunter. To chase down the thing that wanted to hurt her, which was easier than confronting the abuse she took at the hands of the man she thought was her father. Every punch, every kick, and being called useless and worthless, all from a stranger who must have known, or at least suspected enough that Ivy wasn't his child. What reason did he have to cherish her? Especially after Veena ran off, leaving Ivy unprotect, unwanted. Her mother was beyond the reach of the man she betrayed and Ivy took the brunt of abuse. She absorbed his anger, the suffering that belonged to her mother. "I had to look over my shoulder enough times with Bryn. I can't do it anymore."

"Can you at least sing for me?"

The request made her sick thinking about it. Ivy clutched her gut. The song lurched, but it wouldn't come out. She shook her head, trying not to vomit.

"Not until I stop it."

"Alright." Danial was up on his feet, clapping his hands together. "We will do this together."

Ivy nodded, though she wcouldn't help feeling alone. Danial walked at her side, but for how long? They were neighbors for most of their lives, but he was a stranger until recent events brought them together. What was to stop them from being torn apart? Better to be alone. Easier than being disappointed later on.

"Stay close and do as I say."

Not far ahead was an abandoned stable. Ivy had passed it multiple times on her journey to town and back home. Mounds of moldy, sun-dried hay were clumped twenty feet away from the structure. The stable leaned to the south, rotted pillars bowed under the weight of the thatched roof. Ivy thought about taking shade under it on some walks, but was afraid it would collapse in on her.

The stable was no longer abandoned. Horses were hitched up to the posts.

"Shit," Ivy said and dropped beside a wet haystack. Danial stood, staring after it, and she grabbed his hand, pulling him down.

"I thought you said they were running," he said.

"They were." Ivy rolled onto her stomach and looked between two piles holding back a sneeze. Two men in black armor came from the side of the stable. They checked on the horses and circled around to the back. Ivy crawled to the opposite side of the hay mound, gaining a better vantage point.

A large black carriage rested close to the stables. Four black horses were harnessed to it, facing the direction of Welksdale. Ivy tried to release her song again, but found the power blocked and began dry heaving. Whatever was causing the blockage was close, either inside the stable or the carriage.

"Danial," she said, gripping her stomach, her head ready to explode. "Give me the sword."

"Why?"

"I'm going to check out the stables," she said, watching for more movement. She lost track of how long the guards had made their rounds. Every heartbeat seemed longer than it should and she wasn't sure if there was any pattern. *No use waiting around.* Ivy slipped the necklace from over her head, opened the latch to look at the painting of her mother. She smiled, looking so happy. Where did everything go wrong? Ivy snapped it closed. "Here, take this to my uncle. Tell him that he is a good man."

She pressed the necklace into Danial's hand.

"He's a good man," Danial repeated.

Once I go in there, I won't be coming out. She took a breath and let it out slowly. "Then tell the others about the stable. With any luck I will have eliminated the source of the harmonic disruption."

"I'm coming with you," Danial said, holding the sword out of Ivy's reach. The necklace dangled in his big hand, copper chain dull and streaked with dirt. His jaw was set in determination, the bandage over his head stained by dried blood. "You need me to protect you."

Ivy wanted to laugh.

"You can't," she said, trying to be as gentle as she could. "You'll be in my way and end up dead. I can't worry about you, and take care of this problem. Give me the sword and go."

"Ivy," Danial said, sounding hurt, nearly heart-broken. "I made a promise."

"You fulfilled it back in town when that man tried to kill me," she said. "When I'm done here, you can continue the promise, but please Danial, I have to do this alone."

Danial narrowed his eyes, thinking the plan through. He shook his head.

"I don't like it."

"Neither do I, but it's the best we got," Ivy said. "Go back and get help. We can finish them here and everyone can go home. No more fighting. No more bloodshed. No more death."

"You'll come back," Danial said. "Listen to the song of the nightingales at night... and sing for me."

"Yes." Ivy didn't think she would survive to hear herself sing again, let alone the nightingales. "We can go out into the field together and listen. Just you and I, alone."

Danial pressed the sword hilt into her hand.

"Tonight. The nightingales," he said, and began to crawl away.

"The nightingales."

Ivy watched Danial move further away, she sucked back tears and coughed into her arm. Before her emotions could betray her further, she turned her attention back onto the stable. Cicadas sang in the crabgrass. The horses whickered softly. Nothing else moved. No more soldiers came from the stables. Shadows shrouded everything. Ivy closed her eyes, trying hard to locate the source blocking her. Her head pulsed as the power tried to delve out. She could feel nothing but pain.

Enough stalling! She hefted the sword. She didn't think she could swing it with enough force to do more than bruise someone. Keeping low, she hurried to the edge of the stable. No one shouted for her to stop. She crouched, pressed against the wood, her heart raced, palms sweaty and held the sword loose in her grip. The smell of horses and old hay was strong. Ivy heard voices talking, but couldn't make out distinct words.

Dropping on her haunches, low enough to blend in with the shadows, she looked over her shoulder. The mud provided some extra concealment, at least in her mind. Anyone in the carriage could see her if they looked out of the darkened window. She tensed, imagining the door swinging open and dozens of men dressed in black armor swarming her. The door remained closed.

Now or never. The song won't unblock itself.

She thought of her mother, bravely standing up against Bryn, despite knowing she would get hit. Those were moments she protected Ivy. For this. Sucking in a large gulp of air, Ivy filled her chest and trapped her breath. Then she peered around the side. One man sat on an old sawhorse. Large, thick armor covered him shaped like the shell of a beetle and a cloak. He was talking to himself, or at least Ivy thought he was until she saw the little girl sitting a short distance away.

"We have a visitor," the man said. His face was turned away.

"Yes, daddy." The little girl said in a sing-song tone. She held a rag doll, making it dance while she began to chant. Then she sang about a mountain high in the sky and the curious cloud that went to see how tall the mountain really was, only to become trapped on the sharp peak.

"This is the one you are excited about?"

"More than anything, daddy." The girl finished her song. "She is my sister."

This girl, this little girl is blocking our powers? Hunting us down? Ivy wanted to laugh. It didn't seem possible. How could the Creator allow such an innocent being to be used in such an awful way? It had to come from the man. He must be controlling her in some way.

"You can come out from your corner, child." The man turned his head and gazed directly at her. He had some sort of veil over his face, but his eyes spoke enough, demanding that she listen. "We don't intend you any harm. Unless you make us."

The girl smiled at Ivy, but her green eyes held no mirth, or any life for that matter. Ivy shuddered. *She's one of us, but not quit.* Ivy gripped the sword. She had one chance to end the pain and suffering. Only the man, Cacophony, burner of cities and slayer of singers, stood in her way. A single man to brave and get beyond. Ivy gave a cry and drove her toes into the mud slick ground. Then she sprang, taking a single step. Ready to face the man, possibly die in her attempt to kill the girl. Then something crashed into her back, dropping her to the ground, jaw smacking the dry grass and sending up a spray of dust. She lost her grip on the sword and it bounced out of reach. The air rushed out of her and she groaned.

"That isn't a very nice welcome," Cacophony said and stood from the sawhorse. "Especially not after I preserved your life."

Ivy reached for the sword, but a boot stomped on her hand. Not hard enough to break it, just making it so she couldn't move. It hurt, the bone grinding softly against the boot sole and she screamed more out of frustration than pain. Then a lean frame bent over and a woman's face came into view. The woman plucked the sword from Ivy's reach. Once the temptation was gone, the boot released her and Ivy snatched her injured hand to her chest, rubbing it with the other. She remained prone on the ground, refusing to get it.

Will be less of a fall when they kill me. I can sprawl out here and die.

Cacophony crouched, the black metal of his segmented armor forming a winged-V and his black gauntlets hung like pincers that could tear her face off if he found pleasure in it. There was nothing Ivy could do to stop him.

"Seems we haven't been properly introduced," he said. "We've heard stories, I'm sure. Stories of death and destruction. Oh yes, I know all about how you killed some men back at your father's home."

"I don't have a father," Ivy said.

Cacophony's eyebrow raised.

"Then you won't be upset to learn of his passing," the woman said. She had a hard face, one that would rather spit on Ivy than be talking to her. "He told us about you, Ivy. Where we could find you."

Knowing they were already on her trail didn't stop the hurt of the betrayal she felt. Bryn was an asshole to the end. Should she have expected any less? Ivy was a reminder of his wife's trysts with another man.

"You have a new family, Ivy," Cacophony held out his hand. "If you want it."

"Sister," the girl sang.

Ivy couldn't resist any longer. She began to laugh. It hurt her head and she clenched her gut.

"You think I will join you," Ivy said in-between bouts of laughter. "After your men nearly killed me. I don't even know you or believe any story about you. You could be the nicest guy in the world, but I would never trust you." Ivy shot a glare at the girl. "Not when you allow that thing to remain alive. Give me a chance and I will kill it. It won't live, do you understand?"

"Yes," Cacophony said, sounding rather calm. "I understand that you have had a stressful day. Because of that, I forgive this outburst."

"Go fuck yourself with your forgiveness."

"That's not how it works." Cacophony clicked his tongue. "You are forgiven, but you also must be punished."

He was quick, his black gauntlet smashed into Ivy's face, rocking her head back. The pain in her head, the nausea in her gut, all slipped away, and Ivy passed out in the mud. A worm caught by the bug.

Claiborne lifted the girl. Bloody drool hung from her mashed lips and she smelled like a ripe pile of shit left in the sun to dry. The girl had soiled herself. Claiborne curled her lip in disgust. This was the reason Cacophony interrupted her moment of victory. Pitiful. It'd be more merciful to slit the girl's throat.

"Careful with her," Cacophony said, as if he hadn't knocked her senseless with his fist. "This one is key to unlocking a better world."

Claiborne carried the girl to the carriage. She set her inside, propping her head up against the opposite door. She'll have a sore head and aching mouth when she woke up, but she'd fared better than many others who wouldn't be waking up ever again.

Cacophony and his little girl climbed up into the carriage next.

"Sir, I think we should continue the assault on the town," Claiborne said.

Cacophony stopped her with a look. The kind that warned her not to press further.

"I understand and appreciate your single-minded commitment to bringing an end to the enemies of the Silent Men and the rest of the world," Cacophony said, unstrapping the Silent Prayer and laying it across his lap. "I need you to think beyond the moment. This incessant need for vengeance.

We are more than mere beasts requiring our basest needs met. Thanks to the vision from my beloved child, we no longer have to slaughter hundreds to get at the few. She is what will bring the few to us." He stroked Ivy's long, black hair, knocking loose a clump of dirt which fell under the bench. "She is the Night harbinger to sing us into a new day. She is salvation, along with my darling one. Together, they will be an unstoppable force."

"How will you convince her to help us?" Claiborne asked. She recognized a stubborn person when she met them, and this girl, Ivy, would be no better than an ass refusing to bend to the whip. She wouldn't quit until either she killed the little girl, or died trying. Claiborne wouldn't mind either outcome. They wasted the opportunity of killing today what needed killing. Thrush still lived and had a better chance of killing them tomorrow. This was where Cacophony was the most short-sided. Claiborne was a living example, though grateful at times that he was short-sighted, but it was a flaw that would bring about the end. The hubris that great men share in the invulnerability of their plans.

"I am very persuasive, if you remember."

He was, but Claiborne had other motivations that encouraged her to be amiable.

"As you say." Claiborne bowed her head.

Closing the carriage door, she heard the little girl sing.

"When night and day reach long, and shadows come out to play, the Nightingale sings her mournful song and everyone will listen and obey."

Claiborne marched back to her destrier. *When he fails with the girl, I will kill her.* That's how things worked. After disposing on Ivy, they'd renew the hunt for the rest of the singers as before. The sun rose and the sun set every day and events hardly changed. They were caught up in the same cycle: wake, hunt, kill, run. The chase seemed endless, but there was nowhere the Singers could hide that the girl couldn't sense them. Claiborne would burn the world to get to Thrush. That much she owed Arron.

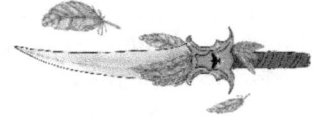

"Where's Ivy!"

Tym lay on a pallet covered in old straw and wool blankets, right arm in a sling. Stripped to his small clothes, since his others were rain-soaked and painted in mud, he scratched at his side, hoping there weren't any bugs burrowing under his skin. They put him and the rest of the walking wounded in the tavern. It smelled of sweat, stale hops, and burning sage. The sage, he presumed, was to cover the shit, piss and blood stench, as well as for giving last rites to the dying. As for the dead, well, they gave their rites away and the Creator bless them. Those left alive, men and women alike, were bandaged and weeping for dead loved ones. It got really bad when news came that those who tried to escape out the back gate were ambushed by riders. The only survivor to return was a boy, dragging the arm of his mother. He sat in a catatonic state at the far end of the tavern, his mother's arm extracted from his embrace, though they did allow him to keep the ring from off her finger. Others, mostly woman and older men who didn't fight or get caught in the ambush, went around, checking on the wounded, bringing fresh bandages, water, and ale.

"Where's Ivy?" Tym spoke softer, grinding his teeth. He wanted to grab Danial by the collar and shake sense into the boy. His body, bruised and exhausted, wouldn't let him do more than sit up.

"At the abandoned stables on the edge of town," Danial said. His tunic stuck to his body and he was also covered in mud. Pieces of hay stuck out from his hair and he looked like some nightmarish creature emerging from the fields to terrorize young children. "She told me to come get help. There's Silent Men and some had horses."

"And you left her!" He growled, drawing the attention of several others around.

"She made me."

Danial was at least twice her size. Tym doubted Ivy physically intimidated the boy.

Despite his aching, tired body, Tym launched himself from the pallet and wrapped his left hand around the side of Danial's neck. The boy could break him in two, but Tym didn't care. He abandoned his niece, which he considered Ivy family despite the fact that Bryn wasn't the father. Danial's face kept the same worried expression he wore when coming into the tavern.

"Listen to me and you listen good."

Danial nodded.

"If anything happens to her, then I'm holding you responsible. You promised to protect her. That's why it was you that went out there and not me." He ignored the fact that he couldn't move at the time, but those details only made Tym all the angrier. "Did you tell the women in charge?"

"Not yet."

"Nazglum rot your head! Why didn't you?"

"She wanted me to give you this," Danial held out locket on a copper chain. Tym took it and clicked it open. It was a picture of her mother. "She also said that you are a good man."

That broke Tym. His eyes watered, and he sucked back salty tears. Of all the labels he wore, a good man wasn't one of them. He put the locket around his head, the copper chain just big enough to slip over. Danial didn't understand the significance, but Tym did. Ivy wasn't planning on coming back. She probably went into the stables to die. For what? A war that wasn't hers and for strangers who didn't care if she existed, except for her power.

"Find me some clothes," Tym said, voice thick and dry tongue sticking to the roof of his mouth.

Danial came back with trousers that were large round the middle and a tunic that was a picnic for moths with all the holes in it. He dressed quickly, wrapping a sword belt around his waist to keep his pants up. They left the tavern, Danial mostly supporting Tym. He'd never seen a battlefield before and he figured this would be as close as he would ever get to one.

No longer masked in sage, the smell was horrific. Blood, shit, and piss mixed up in wet dirt. Bodies were everywhere, unlike Euclid which was one big funeral pyre. Men and women metal shells cracked open to display the raw flesh, hacked and bloody, innards spilled out, jabbed and smashed. Bits of metal scattered around the street. Crumpled shields, broken blades, discarded axe heads. Worse was the weeping. Women and children knelt in prayer over their dead warrior. Tym recognized Salinas Mathers, his gut split apart like a sack of flour. Flies had begun to land. His wife swooshed away a large black bug crawling over Silas's glazed eye. She held his gore and mud-streaked hand, rocking back and forth producing a sound between a whimper and choking.

He'll never bake another loaf of bread again. Tym felt dumb thinking about bread and turned away from the mourning woman. Danial hustled him to the front gate which had been shut, but would not hold out a strong wind. A few carpenters were busy removing twisted hinges and splintered boards. Soldiers in dark blue armor served as watchers, since Sheriff Gareth's men proved to be unreliable. Simon Tanner sat up in the bell tower. He nodded at Tym, a profound sadness filling his pale face. His wife and daughter were part of the townspeople trying to escape. Tym didn't have to ask. Simon's demeanor told it all.

After a few questions to the soldiers in dark blue armor, Tym found where Thrush, Nuthatch, and Robin were keeping company at the Tack and Feed, not far from the gate. Messengers ran past them when they entered the store. Planks of wood balanced on hay bales to serve as a table. Mugs of ale and empty platers were stacked on the corner. The rest of the table was occupied by haphazard objects: nails, chisel, horseshoe. It would be a cluster of stuff, to one not aware that the objects represented important landmarks. The horseshoe was Welksdale and placed at the center.

"They are waiting for us here for another moon." Robin pointed at a pile of nails at the top of their table and a hands length from the horseshoe. "Rail won't stay past that point. She is more skittish than a cow in a thunder storm and sour to boot. Swift will bring a handful of her fledglings here." A chisel placed on its edge, which Tym assumed was the copse at the base of Spearhead Mountain range. "She won't go any further. It won't be enough to withstand another full assault from the Silent Men. You know what Cardinel wants."

Thrush watched, hands on her hips, and shaking her head.

"I think you underestimate Cacophony and his dedication to wipe us out." She tapped a hammer positioned south of the horseshoe. "He's probably regrouping his forces now. We are still outnumbered. As long as I—"

"They're gone," Danial said. "Ivy and I watched them retreat."

"What's the simpleton saying?" Robin turned sharply on them, dagger point digging into the wooden top.

"Shut your yap," Tym said into Danial's ear. "They'll string you up by the nipples."

Danial covered his chest. Tym would have laughed if he didn't think Danial was serious.

"Where is Ivy?" Thrush had a look of concern, head tilted to the side and small lips pursed together. "I haven't seen her since the battle began, and," her eyes narrowed, swiveling from Tym to Danial and back to Tym, "I don't sense her in town."

"I think she's in danger," Tym said. "She went to find whoever was blocking your powers. Danial followed her, but only he returned."

"I knew we couldn't trust her," Robin said, thumping the table and making the pieces jump. "First opportunity she has and gone. I should've killed her."

"Ivy's not betraying you!" Tym pulled away from Danial and hobbled to the table. "I don't know if she's even alive. She could've been killed because she is doing what she believes is right. She saved your sorry ass. I don't know what you told her to make her go off on her own. All I know is she's out there and I plan on getting her back."

"These town's people don't think she's very trustworthy," Thrush said.

"They can go fuck themselves, because they don't know anything about her." *Except they know too much about Veena and Bryn.*

"She was helping rob the Exchequer just that day."

What they were saying about Ivy made no sense. Bryn wouldn't be dumb enough to steal from the Crown, and Ivy…*I'm like them. I have a power.* No! She wouldn't. I guess if she was desperate enough, and Bryn never had coin to spare. Anything was possible.

"Aren't you her uncle?" Thrush asked.

"That's a complicated story."

Thrush's left eyebrow raised.

"Even so, she is a danger in the hands of Cacophony," Robin said. "She might have gone there with good intentions, but I suspect this is what he wanted all the time. The reason the Silent Men pulled back from the fight. They had us pinned inside the town. He could have crushed us at any moment. That would mean risking losing Ivy."

"Now he has two of us," Thrush said. "You knew your niece had a gift? The ability to delve into people's thoughts and manipulate them into actions."

"She told me," Tym said. *All except about the manipulating part.*

"Then you are aware that if Cacophony were to convince Ivy that we are wrong and are perverting the world, she would be a great danger to all of us. I don't know the extent of her powers, but I do know that she could end us all without a single arrow being fired or a sword lifted from its scabbard."

"Ivy wouldn't do that," Tym said, voice wavering. His legs felt heavy and the room began to spin, a slow rotation. "Ivy's a good girl. She's been mistreated. Abused."

Robin shook her head, a snarl raising her pudge lips. "Like any good dog that has been kicked, she will bite."

"Aren't we going to rescue her?" Danial asked. "We should be riding out there now."

"They'll be long gone," Robin said.

"I promised her," Danial snarled and took a threatening step forward. Swords left their scabbards and sharp edges pointed at Danial. Tym put a hand on his chest, though he'd be nothing more than a leaf snapped off by the charging bull. "I promised her I'd be back there with help. Then we will go out into the fields tonight and listen to the nightingales sing."

"Sounds romantic," Robin said and laughed.

Danial turned red and he was shaking.

"Don't do anything foolish, boy," Tym said. He reached to touch Danial's shoulder, but the boy shook his head and retreated a step. "Not if you want to help Ivy."

"We have no chance in open combat," Thrush said. "Even if our powers weren't blocked. Our best option is to hold up here and see if they attack again."

"Or better yet, move for the mountains where we have stronger forces waiting to support," Robin said.

"Then we risk a rear attack," Thrush countered.

For all their talk about helping to save the world, they were abandoning one of their own, a child, not yet ready to take on the responsibilities of an adult, yet brave enough to face down the man they were running from. It made no sense and Tym saw red. His vision shifted and his heart quickened, weakness overcoming his limbs. The room tilted and Tym stumbled. He dropped to his knees and Danial knelt beside him.

"I'll be fine," Tym said, knowing it was a lie. He would never be fine with a world that stole away young women and girls to be used for whatever purpose served them. Yet, what could he do? "Take me back."

"But Ivy," Danial said, panting desperation.

"There's nothing we can do," Tym said.

"I promised her," he squeezed Tym's arm hard enough to leave red, finger marks.

"Promises are made to be broken," Tym pulled away, leaned over, and vomited.

You are a good man, Ivy had told him.

No, Ivy, I'm a weak man. Just another disappointment in a long line of disappointments.

End of Part I

Part II
Ruin

CHAPTER ELEVEN:
WE MUST SERVE

We enter this life oblivious to the fact that we will not escape it alive. Our purpose is to exist for reasons unknown to us or we must create our own sense of purpose. A person doesn't just occupy space, because in the end, the act of doing nothing is an action. In the end, we consume and are consumed. In the end, we all must serve.

I'm losing my mind.

Days passed into nights and nights into days. Sparrow couldn't keep track of either. Chains weighed her down, bending her to the hard floor of unmarked rooms or the hard wooden benches of carriages without windows. She was released from her prisons long enough to piss, defecate, drink water and eat a small amount of food. Not that she could eat more than small portions. Her stomach always felt like someone was squeezing it like an accordion—groans played out instead of music. Beneath the surface, her song churned, adding to her discomfort.

Her song was trapped inside, shoving against the barrier she couldn't see, touch, or taste, only sense. It sat, heavy in her chest, waiting for a chance to be released, a chance that wasn't likely to happen. She wavered in and out of consciousness, wondering if she was already dead and this was the torment waiting for her for all her wrongs. All the death and destruction perpetuated by her, no matter if they were done in service of Harmony.

Survive, my love. Finch's face would swim across her vision. A memory of a memory, her cool hands touching her cheeks before they engaged the Silent Men. *Survive, my love. Then I will find you after and kiss you to death.* This saying always would bring a smile to Sparrow regardless of how desperate and hopeless their situation may be in the moment. It made her fight harder. To survive for Finch—that single touch from Finch was worth burning the whole world down, if only she could have it again—and Goldy.

Goldy needed her. Goldy's mother was killed because of their war. Sparrow had to take care of the little girl. Only Goldy wasn't so little and had reversed the roles, Goldy being the one to care for Sparrow after Finch's death.

Only Finch was not dead, not here in the dark room with Sparrow. A darkness smelling of rot and her own sweat. Finch smiled her radiant smile, urging Sparrow again.

Survive.

"Let me come with you, please," Sparrow said, tears blurring the vision, fracturing her face and she blinked them away. "Please, don't make me suffer here without you."

Finch drifted away from Sparrow's pleading hands seeking to touch her, even for an instance. That beautiful smile faded, like the light leaving the world, and Finch shook her head. A painful spike dug into Sparrow's chest, weighing heavier than the chains around her legs and wrists.

Survive.

"I don't want to! I want to die! I need to die!"

Only this time, the door opened on her new location. Lantern light burned through her eyes, and Sparrow covered her face, turning away from the intrusion. The floorboard creaked as the weight of the holder entered, the light on her face moving with it.

"Want and need are two very distinctly different aspects on this vast spectrum of life," the familiar voice of the man in the black, insectile-like armor said. "To want is a desire that is not required to be fulfilled but may make the person desiring it *feel* better. Let me assure you, death will not let you feel better about anything in life. Beyond the veil waits the Creator's blessings, but not for the likes of you or I." He crouched down in front of Sparrow who smelled something like moldy dirt and onions. His eyes piercing over the thin muslin covering his face stared at her in what might be pity. "To need goes beyond comfort. To need means that lacking in what is needed, let's say water, shelter, peace of mind, will lead to death. To need death is to go against the purpose of life, though we all owe a death in the end. But let us not shorten the threads attaching us to this plane of existence."

"Do you like listening to yourself talk?" Sparrow asked, swiping at the dampness under her eyes. With any luck, she could provoke him to strike her hard enough that maybe, just maybe, he might kill her.

"I only say what is needed to be heard," he said. "Oh, I don't believe we have been introduced yet. You may call me, Cacophony."

"You're the bastard that has been trying to kill us?" He looked more like an overstuffed dung beetle than anything else. "What did Nazglum promise you?"

"It wasn't what I was promised, it was what he gave me," Cacophony said, leaning in closer. "Besides, your kind are a blight on this world. An anomaly that needs to be rectified before a balance can be accomplished. Nothing more than a mistake of the Creator that is killing his grand masterpiece, but a mistake than can be rectified with the proper encouragement."

Encouragement?

"How is killing us encouraging change?" Sparrow watched him closely, how he didn't fear her in her chains. These people were sick if they thought using pain was encouragement. Like her father beat her and the only results he saw was his daughter nearly killing him. The same would happen to these Silent Men. Only once Sparrow had the chance, she would see that she finished silencing them, permanently.

"Simply by culling the weak, we are left with the few who are strong," Cacophony said, holding out his hand and clenching it into a fist. "Like crushing a bird teaches the others to adapt their behavior to survive. I heard you speak of a certain friend, a Finch. Her death offers you an opportunity for a new life."

"Don't you speak her name!" Sparrow lunged at him, raising her arms, hoping to get the chain over his head and choke the murdering fucker to death. At least then she could die knowing she did one last good deed.

But Cacophony was quicker than she had anticipated. He leaned away from her reach, leaving her straining, her song shoving against the boundary holding it in place. She would have vomited and doubled over, if not for the hatred driving her muscles, and for an instance she thought the blockade had shifted and she could touch her song. There, in her grasp, the power rising in her throat, but then it was cut off and she began to choke. A wave of nausea slapped her down and she curled up on the floor, spittle drooling from her dried, cracked lips.

"There's the spirit! The will to live!" Cacophony clapped his hands together. "My dear, you have a purpose. A purpose greater than throwing your life away for a memory of what once was. A chance to redefine your life, to bring in a new era. A new existence where we secure the future free from Nazglum's presence."

Sparrow glared at him. *Is he mad? Does he think I will help him after he destroyed my life?*

"Suck on Nazglum's balls."

He was quick, snatching Sparrow by the face and holding her before she could escape. "I'm certain you women have done that enough," Cacophony said, pinching Sparrow's cheeks in his strong fingers. He squeezed hard enough to bring tears to her eyes. "In the meantime, I expect you to use polite language around my daughter. She is rather impressionable. I wouldn't want her picking up bad habits from you wicked woman. Not when we are trying to heal Creation and not drown it in bloodshed." He released her.

"Ghoul girl is yours?" Sparrow cringed away. The pale faced girl looked more Touched than she did alive. The Touched were women that Gangrius had broken, their souls and minds disappeared. She and Finch had first encountered them in Devon's Meadows where they rescued Goldy.

"You mock what you don't understand, although, I will confess you did have a hand in elevating her abilities," Cacophony said. "She is the antithesis of your kind."

Which is why she can block our song. The realization sent a cold shiver through her body. This man was mad! His "daughter" was a tool of Nazglum, she was certain. She would help turn Harmony into Discord. The perfect weapon, a silencer for the Silent Men. *He's right. I have a purpose. Until that is fulfilled, I cannot die. Oh Thrush, you owe me!*

"If I refuse?" Sparrow asked.

"Then you become part of the memory of the world that once was," Cacophony said, standing over her, lantern once again illuming her. "Unlike the others you have murdered, you have a choice. I will leave you to think it over."

Sparrow watched him leave and the door clicked closed before sitting back up. A cold fire burned in her, helping her ignore the nauseating pain in her gut. One thing she knew about parents was that a few who adored their children were blind to their flaws—either unintentionally or willfully. Sparrow knew the girl was strong, but she was able to push back, almost push through. If she was able to test the weakness further, then she would find the flaw. When she found it, the girl and her father would learn a harsh lesson.

Don't fuck with a grieving woman who has nothing left to lose.

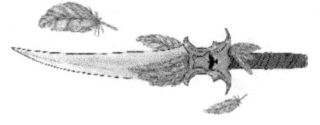

Ivy stood naked in front of the tin tub, every part of her covered in filth. There was mud in places she didn't think could get mud. It was caked on like a second layer of skin. She could be a creature from the swamps that stole away little children to eat them. The tub did look like a giant cooking pot. Steam rising from its basin told it was hot enough to cook Ivy, rather than clean her. There weren't any vegetables chopped nearby, but that didn't lessen her worry about what the water might do to her skin. She could still be the base for some cannibal soup.

She looked around the room and didn't recognize any of it. There were cobwebs in the corner and layers of dust on the floor. Two lanterns were lit, the smell of burning oil sharp against the musty air and placed in the corners of the otherwise empty room. Her bare feet left prints in the dust. She folded her arms over her chest, looking at the woman who'd carried her into the room and stripped her.

"Are you going to get in?" the woman calling herself Claiborne asked. Her black armor was replaced by a black robe that was too small, displaying more of her cleavage than Ivy wanted to see. A pink scar created a jagged line along the side of her right breast to her collarbone. Claiborne grimaced at her staring but didn't cover up. "Or do I have to toss you in? My way will be less pleasant for you."

Ivy dipped her toe into the water and pulled it back out.

"It's hot," she said, remembering how she'd dreamed of a warm bath just that morning. *Not strip-the-flesh-off-the-bone warm, but scrub-the-dirt-and-sooth-aching-muscles warm.*

"It's hot," Claiborne mimicked her in a sharp, nasally tone. "Creator bless you're not cold, dead cold. That's what I wanted, and I almost had my way. Still will get my way if you don't start following orders." Claiborne leaned close to Ivy's face, her breath smelling of chewed mint, bitter orange oil, and infection. "Get in the fucking water."

Ivy wrinkled her nose. The woman had a bad tooth and she tried to cover it up. *I'll gladly knock it out for you.* Claiborne might knock all Ivy's teeth out for the fun of it.

Putting her foot in the water, Ivy hissed. She wanted to pull it back out, but then Claiborne would make good on her promise and toss her in. Gradually, Ivy forced the rest of her leg down. The heat rose up her thigh, and she flushed red. After a few, quickened heartbeats, the heat became bearable. She gripped the metal edges and swung her other leg in, sinking into the water, allowing her aching muscles to release. Her long raven-black hair floated over her shoulders. *This isn't so bad.* Dried blood and dirt came loose, forming a scum around her.

Ivy was relaxing, getting used to the sensation of being in her own skin, then strong hands gripped her shoulders, and Ivy thought for a moment they were going to shove her under. Panicked, the song rushed forward, hitting a brick wall. A queasy sensation turned in her gut and she gasped. Ivy tried to resist, but Claiborne was stronger. Rather than push her under, the hands guided her away from the tub's edge, bent with her hair in her face while a scrub brush scraped against her back.

"You're disgusting," Claiborne said, not sparing any vehemence on a gentle rub. "Did you roll in the fucking mud or just wear it as a gown while your boyfriend plowed you? I'll get your back but fuck me if I'm going to touch you anywhere else. Might get a disease just through contact with the water."

"Why are you doing this?" Ivy's eyes teared up, and her voice threatened to thicken. She fought it, not giving this bitch the satisfaction of knowing she hurt her more with words than by the brush.

"I wouldn't if I wasn't forced to."

"Seemed to me you're taking plenty of pleasure in scrubbing me raw." Ivy gripped the edges of the tub while the brush racked down her spine. "What's the special occasion?"

Claiborne's silence told her enough. Cacophony wanted Ivy cleaned up.

"Let me do it," Ivy said, reaching for the brush. She turned around, staring at Claiborne's naked breasts and arms— her robe was pulled down to her waist—and froze with her fingers on the handle. Scars marred her skin, pink and raw. Ivy saw the annoyance and pain in Claiborne's eyes, had felt the same after Bryn beat her. "I won't tell him."

"Needs to be done right," Claiborne said, yanking the brush out of Ivy's hand. "Or he'll know."

"How?"

"He notices things. Now hold your breath."

Ivy gulped in air just before Claiborne dunked her head under water.

The water turned into a mud puddle by the time Ivy stepped out. Claiborne wrapped her in a soft towel and Ivy dripped on the floor beside Claiborne. The woman was taller than Ivy by half-a-head. She took the long strands of Ivy's hair and began to braid them together. No one else had touched her hair since her mother had died. Part of her enjoyed the touch, though

Claiborne wasn't averse to yanking tough strands, and Ivy gritted her teeth.

"Do you have to be so rough?"

"Get over yourself, princess," Claiborne said, tugging another strand of hair. "You'll learn soon enough this is the easy part."

"I hope you never have children."

Claiborne laughed.

"Me, neither. Bastards are parasites feeding off you. You think you weened them from the titty, to find out too late what monsters they become and they eat you up."

"Isn't there anyone nicer in your cult that can braid hair?"

"Cult, huh?" Claiborne twisted another tight braid. "I guess you may be right on that. We are all part of some cult or other. Gives us a sense of purpose. And to answer your question, yes. But I was chosen."

"Why do you have to clean me up and braid my hair?"

"Because you stank like shit," Claiborne said. "I don't like being around shit, bad enough I have to deal with the men and their smelly asses. I don't have any rose water or other fancy perfumes to cover your shit farmer smell. Cacophony doesn't want to smell you, either."

"I'm not going to be some sacrifice to Nazglum," Ivy said.

"Not tonight," Claiborne said, tightening the last braid hard enough to pull Ivy's head to the side. "I can't promise you anything beyond that."

Claiborne left Ivy, telling her she'd be back soon.

"And you better be dressed by the time I return, otherwise it'll make the hair braiding seem like eating sugar cubes." A metal bolt slid into the latch, locking Ivy in. Ivy dropped the towel and ran to the windows. Dirt filmed them over and when she tried to lift them open, they were stuck tight. She noticed the nails pounded into the corners. She thought about breaking the glass. Wrap the towel around her fist and smashing through it. The noise would alert Claiborne or whatever guard she set at the door. They would have her before she wiggled out. She was stuck for now. *This was what you wanted. A chance to kill the source blocking you.* The girl was still close. The nausea wriggled in her gut and thrummed in the back of her skull.

A black robe hung on a hook by the door. Ivy put it on and tightened the belt. It was loose, but comfortable. Beneath it were a pair of black boots and leggings. The leggings fit well, but the boots were far too wide for her feet, and she felt like she was lifting a stone every time she took a step. They were better than her clogs which she'd lost somewhere.

"Almost a different life."

The battle seemed like ages ago. As far as Ivy remembered it happened just that morning. She wondered what Danial and her uncle, or the man who she thought was her uncle, were doing. *Tym, have to call him plain Tym now.* Did they bother looking for her or assume she was dead, moving on to wherever?

I forced Danial to leave. He'd be dead otherwise. Cacophony had laid a trap for her, neat as any she ever saw, and she fell into it like a hungry rat. She should've killed the girl and damned the consequences. Even that was a fool's gold. She wasn't close to being quick enough. What hurt the most was the fact that the others weren't even looking for her.

"Nothing new, Ivy" she said, spitting up the bitter truth. "No one ever really loved you."

Except her mother. And even she abandoned her to deal with that man she betrayed. The man she was deceived into believing was her father. How many other people in Welksdale knew? No wonder they thought she was warming his pillow at night.

The door swung open and Claiborne, black armor back on, nodded her head.

"Thought I might have to drag you out there naked," she said. "Black looks good on you. Brings out the color of your eyes."

"I didn't have much of a choice," Ivy said, tugging at the robe.

"We never do, so get used to it kid." Claiborne stepped aside and two guards waited in the hall. More choices being made for her.

The hallway was small forcing them into a single file. Claiborne led, Ivy in the middle, and the other two guards behind her. Floorboards creaked as they walked in silence. The walls had holes big enough to climb into, and jagged teeth or claw marks, like something wanted in, or out. More cobwebs hung in thick threads, spiders the size of her fist scurried back up to the rafters when the light hit them. It was like no one had lived here in a long, long time. The hallway opened into a larger room with a single table, four chairs, and a fire burning in the hearth. A large kettle bubbled over the fire and the strong smell of herbs and mushrooms made Ivy's stomach rumble. She hadn't had a proper meal in longer than she could remember.

Cacophony sat at the table and the little girl was adjacent to him. She sucked soup from a spoon and grinned at Ivy, blue eyes nearly glowing in menace. Her hair was also braided, matching Ivy—*I bet they were kinder with her.* Two more bowls occupied the empty place settings.

"Sit. Eat, Ivy," Cacophony motioned to the chair across from him.

"Sister," the girl said, legs swinging happily under the table.

I'm nobody's sister, kid, except for Crisell and Maya, maybe. Half-sister? Not that she could explain that to them.

Claiborne sat in the chair in front of her and began spooning soup into her mouth. The soldiers behind Ivy took up post at opposing ends of the room, near any exit Ivy could possibly try. Where would she run? No one wanted her and the only place she could think about going was now a graveyard full of cremated bodies.

Ivy sat in the chair, looking down at the soup. The aroma was tantalizing. She picked up the wooden spoon. The handle was rounded, but with enough force she could stick it through the girl's eye. The girl shook her head, legs swinging hard enough to make the chair creak. She chewed noisily and scooped more onto the oversized spoon, slurping from it.

"Soup not to your liking?" Cacophony asked.

"I…I haven't tried it yet."

"Do, before it gets cold."

Cacophony didn't have a bowl in front of him. He sat back in the chair, arms folded, and the muslin covering the lower half of his face stirred with his breathe. She couldn't tell what he was thinking. His stare was like some bird of prey, though, she figured there was some amusement in it. Watching her squirm like she was a frightened bunny must be more amusing than pulling wings off a fly. Ivy tried the soup. It was good, so good she had to force her trembling hand to slowdown. Brown liquid dribbled over her chin, and she wiped it away with her sleeve. Before she knew it, the wooden spoon was scraping the bottom of the bowl.

"You are probably wondering why you are still alive," Cacophony said. "I'm sure you heard plenty of stories from those women."

"Robin and Thrush," Ivy said. She wanted to see how he would react. Poke the bear, as her mother would say.

Claiborne made a disgusted noise, but Cacophony didn't flinch.

"I don't care about stories," Ivy said, twirling the spoon around the bowl. "Anyone can make up stories about other people. Doesn't mean they are true."

"Very wise," Cacophony said.

Ivy shrugged. "It's what I've experienced."

"That is how wisdom is gained," Cacophony said. "Usually from some unpleasant experience. Isn't that true, Claiborne?"

Claiborne grunted, running her finger around the bowl and sucking the soup from the tip.

"Her story is quite tragic," Cacophony said.

"Seems the price for living is pain," Ivy said. "And disappointment."

"No truer words have been uttered." Cacophony gave a chuckle. "You and I are on the same path. I lost my family during the war and you lost your family through…."

"Because of their own stupidity," Ivy said, letting the spoon clatter in the bowl. "What do you want?"

"Forthright! Such a wonderful trait to have. We should all be so candid," Cacophony said and clapped his hands. "Straight to business then."

"Dessert!" the girl shouted.

"Forgive her," Cacophony said. "She is a creature of simple delights."

I would if I could figure out how to stop her from blocking my song.

"How does she do it?" Ivy asked.

"Do what?"

"Prevent me from singing."

"Same way you and I breath," Cacophony said. "It's an involuntary action. One which is useful for our survival. Is that how it is for you?"

The power was like a wrestling match. One where she fought against an opponent five times her size and sometimes was like a mountain sitting on her chest. When she surrendered, she found it controlled her. Not surrendering was worse. It choked her on the inside and if she didn't learn how to control it, then it would be like holding the tail of the lion. Its jaws would whip around and bite her head off.

"No," Ivy said. "It's a fight."

"Are you fighting it now?"

Ivy shook her head. It was a strange comfort to go for moments without having to battle this thing within her, to feel like something was ripping her up from the inside, and releasing it was worse than letting a fox go into a chicken coop. There would blood, and lots of it. How did her mother handle it?

"It's like I don't have it," Ivy said. Surprisingly, the nausea was gone as well. *Guess I needed to eat.*

"How do you feel about it?"

"I don't miss it."

"Who would?" Cacophony asked. "My daughter is offering you a gift, Ivy. A peaceful life where you don't have to have this pain inside you. The guilt of when it comes out. You can be at peace."

"Sister." The girl touched Ivy's hand. The chill shocked her so she pulled away, putting it under her leg to regain the warmth. *How could someone alive be so damn cold?* The girl smiled her sweetest smile.

"What about the others?"

"I have offered them peace," Cacophony said. "They chose to fight, instead."

"Did you offer Euclid peace?"

Claiborne stared hard at her.

"They also made a choice," she said. "They allowed those women to hide behind the gates. Did they tell you about the horrifying acts they committed using their songs? Dead men floating in an unnatural lake? Did Thrush tell you about a man named Arron?"

"They didn't say much," Ivy said.

"Don't be afraid to tell us, Ivy." Cacophony leaned closer. "We have heard their lies. Nothing will shock us."

Ivy swallowed hard.

"They said the Silent Men was once the Brotherhood of Creation and they were the Sisterhood."

"Yes, there was a rift when Brother Kama discovered the sisterhood to be whores for Nazglum, that's when they split," Cacophony said. "He formed the Kama's Men, which later became the Silent Men. He dedicated the rest of his life to hunting down the sisterhood because through their vile acts, they weakened the harmonies keeping the Lord of Shadow and Death from our world."

"But, they said it was the Silent Men who weakened the harmonies by killing the Singers."

"Do you believe them, Ivy?"

She considered both sides of the stories. They lined up on every point except for who wanted to bring the end of the world. As far as she was considered, they both were doing a great job of fucking up everything they touched.

Including her.

"I don't know." Her eyes felt heavy and it as hard to think, like the soup was inside her head, clogging her up.

Poisoned!

"You'll have to make a choice," Cacophony said. "Not tonight, but soon. Whatever you choose, you will have to live with the consequences."

"What if I don't." Her hand flopped, knocking the bowl clattering across the room. She had to put her head down. Too heavy. Everything was heavy.

"That is also a choice."

"Fuck me," Ivy said, the words blurting out. Her head thumped onto the table, or the table rushed up to catch her head. She didn't know. Beside her, the girl laughed, clapping, whispering, "Do it again. Do it again." *There are no do-overs, just one shot at doing things right.* Her eyelids sank, and she thought she said, "No do," and she was right. There was nothing she could do.

Never anything she could do.

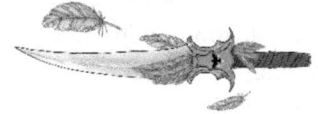

Ivy. Ivy, don't get up, my love. Stay still, stay asleep. Soft, sweet dreams. Mommy is going, but she'll return for you. The voice, a song playing in her head, visions of bright days in green fields. A new dress and bare feet digging into the soft dirt while she picked lavender and milk-lace for her mother on the porch, smiling and singing songs about sunshine, bright fields, and cool water. A hand, tender, full of love and delight on her neck and cheek. It promised protection. It promised comfort. It promised to return for her, pulling away and leaving her with nothing but a soft whimper and tears. The necklace placed in her hand, copper so cold on her skin. Cold where once warm fingers had touched.

And she was alone.

Her eyelids peeled open, but there was only murky darkness. Ivy shuddered, cold seeping through the sheets and she reached for a blanket, or at least tried to reach since her body was stiff and non-responsive. Tears damp on her face, she didn't recognize the room. It wasn't her space. This place smelled old, musty, like a forgotten part in time full of cobwebs and dried rat turds. Something moved in the darkness, a whisper of feet on the hardwood.

"Why are you crying?" the girl asked, mimicking concern, like the last cry of an echo. Tiny fingers touched Ivy's shoulder. Old, musty air changed to a fetid stench, the kind given off by a fresh corpse. Even her touch was corpse-like, cold and stiff. Ivy couldn't pull away. She was trapped, caught in a cycle of death. *Mommy is going, but she'll be back for you. Mommy will be back. Mommy will*—No! Her mother had lulled Ivy to sleep, staked her to her bed with the lie thin as a twig that cracked the instant she had died. She was gone and would never come back.

"No one is coming back," Ivy said, a bitter flavor on her tongue, slurring her words into syrupy slowness. Must be the poison they put in her soup. But it had tasted so good and she was hungry.

"You have me, sister." Arms slithered around her waist and the girl's body pressed into her back. "No one else matters. No one in the world."

"What are you?"

"We are the beginning," the girl said and giggled. "We shape things."

Harmonic manipulation. That didn't answer her question.

"Don't touch me," Ivy said, unable to move away.

"I'm not." The girl giggled. Ivy blinked, clearing her vision and spotted the girl sitting on a wooden plank across the room.

Whose arms are around me?

The arms were pale and speckled with black blotches, rotted flesh writhing, and burst in putrid stench. Maggots crawling along Ivy's neck. *I came back. Mommy came back for you.* Ivy opened her mouth to scream, but something wriggled over her bottom lip, tiny legs skittering across her tongue and down her throat. *We will never be apart, again.* The arms tightened, sinking into her.

Ivy moaned, rolling her shoulders that moved as though under the surface of water. She couldn't breathe, paralyzed by the strong arms binding her.

"Sing, Ivy," the little girl said. "Shape it."

"I can't!" Nails dug into her skin, like peeling apart fruit.

The power roared in her chest, but the song wouldn't take form, the lyrics melting while the power shoved at her, threatening to rip her apart from the inside, splatter bone, and blood, and pieces of her heart across the waters.

"Give in, Ivy. Let the song flow through you."

She calmed her breathing, ceased her struggles and allowing the power to take hold. Then she sang and it was beautiful. The words poured from her lips, the corpse arms holding her disappeared, releasing her to float from cold embrace to the surface where she soared into the warm air and all around her glowed. Her mother screeched. *No Ivy! I will never lose you!* Then she was gone, dissolved into the darkness.

"Now stop," the girl commanded.

Ivy gasped. As strong and freeing as the song was when it had started, it ended. The power disintegrated, leaving Ivy empty, her voice raspy and dry.

"Wha…What happened?" The room was dark, and she sat up, straw mattress crinkling beneath her. Moonlight spilled into the room, across the girl's pale blue eyes like ice. She was smiling, holding her rag doll. Golden-yellow hair framed her face that made her a frightening vision, since her skin seemed to be flaking off under her eyes and around her blood red lips.

"You did it," she said. "You sang."

I did, but how? The girl grinned at her, then giggled, pulling her dolly up to cover her face up to those blue eyes, piercing the darkness. *She must've let me. No way I could do it without her allowing it.*

"What's your name?" Ivy asked, able to sit up on her elbows.

"Hyrian. And this is Glorian." She turned the doll around to face Ivy. The hair was also golden. Black button eyes stared wide like they had seen horrific visions. "She knows things. Tells me things."

"Like what?" Ivy didn't want to know, but the question was there.

"You are going to re-shape the world," the girl said, holding Glorian out. "Want to hear?"

"No thank you." Ivy lay back on her bed, sweat covered her brow and dripped down her neckline. The images of the vision receding into the darkness. She reached for the power but found it stifled. She chalked up the strange dreams to the residuals of the poison they put into her soup. It left her drained.

"She don't want to talk to you, either." Hyrian pouted and hugged the doll. "She's my mother. Not yours."

"Yeah, and who's your father?" Ivy turned her back on the girl.

"You know," Hyrian said, and whispered. "We share him."

Ivy turned back to ask another question, but the plank was empty. No sign of the girl. Ivy searched the dark corners but could see nothing. Then the door slid closed and a laughter sounded down the hallway. Ivy hurried to the door and shut it. There wasn't a lock on the inside, so she dragged the plank over and set it on the frame. It wouldn't keep her out, but the noise of it falling will let her know if anyone enters.

Ivy went back to her bed and hid under the blanket wishing for the last embrace from her mother once again.

CHAPTER TWELVE:
A GOOD MAN

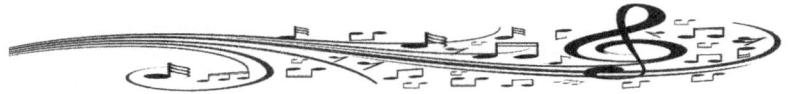

A good man is a fallacy. A weak man who follows the rules put in place by stronger men. These strong men are able to hold their position of power through force and cunning. The goodness others see is a man giving up what little he has, to be bent to the will of others, like the tree bending to the wind. Enough force and he will snap, or topple over, roots torn from the ground. There are no good men. Just the strong and the weak. The living and the dead.

"It's too damn quiet," Danial said, standing in the field, head tilted to sky. A light breeze rustled through the yellowed-grass, rousing a memory of heat and air dry enough to crack the skin. The breeze was a welcome relief to the stench of death. Stars clustered in the sky and the moon was past full, a pasty pock-marked face—a sharp contrast to the constant pounding of rain, clashing metal, people screaming, cursing bleeding out, and the mourners crying for dead loved ones they'd never see again.

Tym could do with more silence. He leaned on his crutch, right arm bound, and let the wind ruffle his hair. He hadn't had a moment's peace where he was conscious and not fighting pain. In the silence, he believed there existed a benevolent Creator, instead of one who took pleasure in watching his beings suffer.

We are all puppets in his great mummer's show. No matter how we danced and flopped, the big kid would eventually wreck his toys.

Then his thoughts turned to Bryn, and he wondered if his brother had survived. What would have happened if he'd jumped out of the wagon to warn him as they were passing the house? Tym guessed he'd have found Bryn passed out in his pissed stained sheets, snoring, and stinking of the firewater he drank the night before. Maybe he could've carried his brother far enough away from the house before the Silent Men arrived. The consequence would've been Ivy dying in battle. His actions may not have killed the brute,

231

but at least he intervened enough for Danial to finish the dirty business.

"Nice night," Tym said, unable to bear the silence any longer. Too much silence could drive a person mad. He had dealt with enough madness in the last few days to satisfy a lifetime.

Danial looked at him, deep frown lines around his mouth, and his eyes shimmered in the moonlight.

Is he crying?

"She promised she would listen to the nightingales with me."

Tym had never met a man so obsessed with one bird. He'd known a guy desperate for a flower, the *amare,* which he claimed was the central ingredient for a love potion. "I need this girl to fall in love with me," he'd say and Tym would ask if the girl liked him. What good would it do if she didn't know he existed, or worse, hated him. Who would want to live with someone like that for the rest of their life? "No, she loves my brother." The conversation ended there, since it was much too close to Tym's reality—Veena had chosen Bryn, for Creator knows what reason, and Tym never questioned it. Last Tym had heard, the *amare* remained elusive, but the guy's brother died mysteriously. Then he married the girl. In a way, the guy found *amare.*

"How do you know, Ivy?" Tym asked.

Danial cocked his head.

"I helped her get water from the well." He had a distant smile, like it was the most romantic lovers' rendezvous, and not common courtesy. "And then she showed up at my house on the night of the storm."

What was she doing out in the storm? Did Bryn hit her? Chase her away like he did Veena? Knowing what happened to her mother, Ivy was smarter enough not to repeat the same deadly actions, though clearly, she must've felt that she had no other recourse. These were the reasons he couldn't chose Bryn over Ivy.

"Any time before that?"

"Oh, I've seen her around town, but we never talked," Danial said and screwed his face into a sour look. "I don't talk to girls much. My mother said they would hurt me because I'm different. I guess she was right." He pointed to the bandage on his head.

"Ivy did that to you?" The boy was twice as big as Ivy and could break her in half.

"No, I fell. I don't remember falling, but I must've hit my head," he said, sounding confused. Almost as though he were speaking it in a dream. "This was reopened when I fought that man for her. I guess it wasn't her fault, but I still got hurt so she wouldn't."

Tym grunted.

"Do you love her?"

"I…," Danial said, face screwing up again, the way a man would search his words with care. He scratched his head, then clapped his hands together, nodding as though celebrating the discovery of the right words. "I want to protect her. I promised her. I failed."

"Why? What did she ever do for you?"

"Because she needs help." Danial shrugged. "Do you have to do something for someone because they did something for you?"

"That's how the world works, mostly," Tym said. "We are a fucking selfish group of creatures. Always wanting something from another person. That's how we are molded, which I blame the artist and not the art. We didn't choose to be jumbled up bags of emotional desires and wants. That's why we spend half our time ignoring them, half blotting them out, and the last half wallowing in misery."

"That's too many halves, isn't it?" Danial asked.

Not when the world seems to be folding in on itself.

Tym's arm began to ache.

"No one does anything unless they are getting something or hope to get something in return."

"Yes," Danial said. "I want the song. The song of the nightingale."

"What is that song to you?"

Danial paused, considering his response.

"You'll just poke fun at me."

"I won't," Tym said. "I swear on my two good legs. May they both break and I drown in a sea of mud if I'm lying."

"Fine." Danial puffed his cheeks out and stared up at the sky as he spoke. "It reminds me of my mother. The night she died, she told me to listen to the mournful song of the nightingale. 'That'll be me, Danny boy, singing to you when you feel lonely,' she said. Each time I hear it, I remember it's her singing for me."

"Now that…that is just sad."

"Ain't it." Danial hacked and spat into the grass. "As long as Ivy is gone, so will the song. If I don't get her back, then I'll be forgotten by my mother, or I'll forget her, something like that."

I don't think Ivy is holding all the birds hostage. Strangely enough, he hadn't heard any since Ivy left over two days past.

"No one wants to be forgotten," Tym said.

"I aim to keep my promise," Danial said, the moonlight pale on his serious face. As serious as a corpse. Which they will be if Cacophony and these women had their way.

Tym respected the boy for his lofty values. Danial took honoring the parents to a level most people wouldn't be able to live up to, and probably he wouldn't live very long confronting the entire Silent Men. Worse yet, what if he found Ivy, but they had butchered her? That would tear the boy apart and Tym would bet Danial would end anyone associated with her killing or die trying. Heroes never lived long. It was better to be a quiet coward.

"How do you plan on finding her?" If by some chance they wanted Ivy as a weapon, like Robin suggested, the Silent Men could be anywhere.

"With me."

Tym hopped around on his crutch and almost toppled over. Thrush sauntered down the incline away from Welksdale's walls. Under the full moon, her silver and white robe captured the radiance. His breath caught at her dangerous beauty. Her brown hair was braided tightly against her head like a warrior goddess ready to strike. A belt made of intricate knots encircled her slight waist and two scabbards hung at her hips. Keen eyes studied Tym. Her thin, red lips pursed together in serenity.

"I found her the first time," Thrush said. "I will find her again."

"The two of you?" Tym nodded at each. "What chance have you got?"

"The same chance if we allow Cacophony to twist that hurt little girl into his destructive tool." Thrush stood a few paces away. "He has a way of turning those who would serve the Harmony into his soldiers, into unwitting servants of Nazglum bent on its destruction."

"You really think Ivy is that powerful?" Tym remembered the little girl, running from the stream with an injured frog in her hands. She had said a bird had tried to eat him, but she threw a rock at it and the frog dropped from its beak. Ivy was in tears, pleading with Tym to save it. The frog's back leg was half-torn off and its eyes bulged. Bryn took the frog and dashed it on a stone, *"There, it's all better,"* he'd said. Ivy's lip trembled and she ran off, crying hysterically. It was then Tym knew he should've drowned Bryn in the stream.

"She hasn't reached her full ability," Thrush said. "When she does, I don't want it unleashed on me or others who cross her path. She might try to use if for good. Too often we try to do good, but guided by the wrong hands she'll hurt more people than she'd help."

"I have to try. I won't leave her alone out there, not again," Danial said and stuck out his hand. "It was a pleasure knowing you."

Tym stared at the rough hand and back up at Thrush.

"No," he said, watching Danial drop his hand slowly and furrow his brow. "I'm not going to let you turn me into the biggest asshole by leaving me behind. I guess I got to do another good deed before I die, something to use as bargaining chip with the Creator and maybe I can rest for eternity."

"Because clearing your conscious is more important that saving your niece," Thrush said, her reproachful words cutting Tym to the quick.

"Two birds, one stone." Tym flinched after he said the cliché. *Guess I'm proving how difficult it is giving up being an asshole.* Thrush narrowed her eyes and looked at his leg.

"Will you be able to ride?"

"Tie me to the saddle if you must. I'm coming with you."

"She said you were a good man. Ivy believed in you." Danial laughed and slapped Tym on the shoulder. The crutch jammed under his arm as he tried to keep his balance.

"Do that again and you'll be wearing this up your ass," Tym said, lifting the crutch. Danial put his hands defensively, his dopey smile dropping off and Tym almost regretted his half-hearted threat. Almost, because the boy was too big to go slapping his elders around. *He'll make me eat mud again.* Tym settled the crutch and leaned toward Thrush. "When do we leave?"

"Tonight," Thrush said. "Get a bag packed and steal us some horses."

Easiest request I had in a long time.

"I'll meet you back here before you can say nightingale," Tym said and hobbled off.

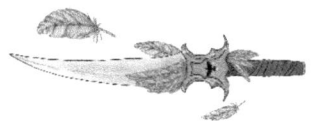

Riding was always a pain in the ass, literally. Riding with an arm in a sling, now that was pure torture. Every jounce sent a sharp stick jabbing his elbow. His legs were sore from gripping the saddle with his thighs to keep from falling out. His right calf protested any weight he might put down on the stirrup, which forced Tym to ride sort of half-assed. *I'm lucky my head is still attached.* One thing he couldn't complain about was the rain. It was nice to be dry. He didn't know how anyone could stand Robin. She was gloomy enough without the clouds hanging over their heads.

"What's with the bird names?" Tym asked, trying to distract from his aches and pains. "Is it some kind of religious rite of passage where you take on new name to go along with your new life? Or was it some coincidence that your parents named you after a species of songbird?"

"I like bird names," Danial said. "Reminds me of—"

"I know, I know," Tym blew a mosquito away that buzzed around his face, "they remind you of your mother."

"Well, ugh, not all of them." Danial went quiet and Tym cursed. *Here I am being a jerk again. Couldn't let it pass? Being a cruel bastard must be a Lyre family trait.* One can only hear about a dead mother so many times before it frayed the edges of decency.

"We choose our names," Thrush said. "As you so well put it, we take on our new name that fits best with our new life. Especially since most of us can never return to what you would consider a normal life. The person who we used to be is essentially dead, as are many of our family and friends. Then there are those who were rejected outright, cast from their homes, whether from fear or envy, it was always because they were different. We embrace a rebirth and forge the links of a new family."

"Why would your old family push you away?" Danial asked. "Sounds cruel and unfair."

"Fear causes some of the divide," Thrush said. "They misunderstand the Creator's blessings, because His gifts come in many forms."

The town's people detested Ivy and that was before they knew of her gift. Some of it was Veena's doing. Singing in open public, manipulating the emotions of her audience, though, that sounded like what any musician, and political figure, did. She took it a step too far when she seduced the Farlow pig farmer. Ivy suffered for it. Or maybe they'd sensed the song in Ivy and like a frightened pack, tried to drive her away.

"Life's not fair," Tym said, squeezing his legs against the horse to slow it down and grit his teeth. Of the three he "borrowed" from the stables, he had to choose the most eager one.

"Other times our powers lay dormant and manifest out of necessity." Thrush continued. Her horse, Tym noted, was less spirited and seemed happy at the easy pace they kept. No struggles for her. "It's not unheard of that in times of conflict and war that a girl will find her voice to stop violence from happening to her or a family member. It can be quite shocking. Especially if it results in killing."

"Do you think Ivy killed anyone?" Danial asked.

Tym puffed out air to blow the mosquito away again. He didn't trust releasing the saddle horn to give it a good smacking its whining demanded.

"I really don't know," Tym said. "I'm sure half the town would be dead if she had."

"That happens as well," Thrush said. "Depends on how destructive the power grows. For Ivy, she has yet to master it."

"What can she do that has you worried?"

Thrush remained quiet.

"You mentioned she can delve into a person and control them, what does that mean?" Tym pressed on. *Did she manipulate me to prevent me from leaving when I was at the stables?* Did he really want an answer? To start up paranoia of losing control to another and what she might do next. Mistrust was already seeping in and Tym shoved the thought away. Then he saw Danial and his bandaged head. *"I fell. I don't remember, but I must've hit my head." What did Ivy do to you, and why did she do it? Was she protecting herself?*

"She can search your memories, emotions, and read your intentions the way a student of art can read the intentions of the painter through colors, shades, and line strokes," Thrush said. "Then she takes on the role of the artist and will mold those memories, or even paint over them, causing you to forget certain events, or believe other emotions, heighten them so much you might even inflict harm on yourself."

"That sounds scary." Danial scratched at the bandage on his head.

"Did you have that there before or after Ivy went to your house?" Tym asked.

Danial squinched his face in what Tym came to think of as Danial's confused-but-trying-to-figure-it-out look. "I don't know. Might've been before, could've been after."

"Do you remember anything before?"

"Yeah, she was singing in her sleep." Danial smiled. "It was beautiful, just like the—"

"Nightingale, I get it."

Thrush raised her brows and Tym nodded.

Ivy wasn't the innocent girl he remembered, but he wasn't ready to label her as dangerous.

"What can you do to help her?" he asked Thrush. There had to be a way to bring her back to the young girl he knew before...before what? Her life had always been messy, and after Veena's death, well.... *I should've been there to protect her from Bryn.*

"If we can get her to come back, then I can show her how to control her song," Thrush said and looked ahead at the stables where Danial had left the girl. "But if not—"

Tym smacked the mosquito on his cheek, almost falling from the saddle. He maintained his balance, squeezing his legs until they burned and looked down at the blood smeared on his hands.

"If she's alive, she'll come back," Tym said.

She has to come back. I can't lose her.

Life always had a way to be cruel. Tym would do his damndest to do one good, selfless deed for Ivy. She deserved a better life than anyone he knew. Just one chance to do right by her.

They approached the stables and Tym's mouth went dry. It was still dark, he half-expected some sort of ambush, would even welcome one if it meant they didn't find Ivy's body mangled and left for the bloody carrion eaters the way Veena had been discovered on the side of the road. He touched the locket on the copper chain, his heart aching at the thought of the one woman he loved.

Thrush lit a lantern and shuttered it low to allow enough light to walk by. She carried it in her left hand, while holding a short sword in her right. She rounded the stable's leaning wall and returned a moment later.

"We're clear," she said. "The Silent Men have moved on."

"I told you so," Danial said, but Thrush ignored him. He slid from the saddle and began tying his horse to a post. "Are you coming?"

"I'll... I'll stay here and watch the horses in case any unexpected guests arrive," he said and patted his right thigh. "My leg is still sore and once I leave the saddle, don't know if I'll be able to get back in it again."

Danial shrugged. "Don't try getting down by yourself. Wouldn't want you cracking your skull on the hard ground."

"I'll remember that." Tym tipped him a two-finger salute. "I wouldn't want to cramp your style by sporting an identical bandage. Let the woman-folk swoon over yours."

"Only woman I care about is Ivy," Danial said and followed Thrush around the edge of the stable.

Tym spat from the saddle, cringing at his excuses. *Don't think I'm ready to see Ivy like I found Veena. Don't think it'll go over well for any of us.* The worst part was that Bryn didn't speak about Veena's disappearance, didn't even notice the day it happened. Left Ivy to wonder where her mother walked off to, if she walked off and hadn't been murdered early that day. "Fucking asshole, why didn't you say anything," Tym had said to Bryn the last time he'd ever truly spoken to his brother, right before he saddled up to leave for Euclid a few weeks back. Bryn shrugged. "Wasn't the first time she's run off." Bryn took a long pull from the bottle. "She's always come back, like a bitch after she was done being humped." Tym balled his fists, ready to smash his brother across the face, crack his foolish head open with the bottle and see what rot oozed out. He did neither. Instead, Tym drove on past the spot he found her on the way home from his trip to Euclid six years past. The memory of her bloated corpse and the cloud of black flies fresh at the sight of the sun-bleached stones signaling where he had found her in that sotted ditch. Her head was never found.

Tym touched the locket. Bryn didn't bother to cry or show any sort of emotion over his wife's death, the woman he was supposed to have loved. Just anger when he kicked the shit out of him for allowing Veena to die, driving her away. Tym shifted in the saddle. The memory was unsettling and the locket cold against his chest. There was no sound, besides a gnat buzzing in his ear. Tym swatted at it, missed, and struck his ear hard enough to set it ringing.

"What's taking so long?" His leg was getting sore and lower back tightened up. Staying upright in the saddle would become less of an option and the ground called his name. He was about to try dismounting when Danial returned.

"Well?" Tym leaned forward, bracing for the bad news.

"Nothing," Danial said. "No body, she's just gone."

Tym let out a sigh.

Thrush walked out to the road and swung the lantern around, studying the ground. She pointed out a wide set of tracks. To Tym they could've been wagon wheels, though the spacing was too wide. *A carriage, then. One of those royal size ones meant to carry a lord, or a king.*

"Cacophony was here," she said. "Probably laid a trap for Ivy."

"But there's no body?" Tym asked again.

"None that we found," Thrush said, lifting the lantern to shine light on the edge of the stable wall. "Looked here like there was some sort of struggle. Here's a bit of blood, but not enough to kill a person."

Enough to hurt her. Tym's fists clenched. Once he found this Cacophony cocksucker, he'd show him that beating young women was asking for an ass whooping. Something he should have given Bryn long ago. *Not too late to transfer accounts to this guy.*

"He may have subdued her and placed her in his carriage," Thrush said. "They went west."

"Let's get the bastard and bring my niece home," Tym said, gathering up the reins and ready for a hard, fast ride. *I need to hit someone*

"Won't be that easy," Thrush said. "He has a lead and the advantage of knowing we are weakened. This might be another trap."

"Then we bust the fucking thing down," Tym said. "I know I've been an ass, haven't really thought about much else beyond my own skin, but Ivy... Nazglum bend me over and prod my ass, she deserves better. She'd lived long enough with one belligerent asshole. She doesn't need to spend any more of her life around another."

"No more assholes," Danial said. "We get her home. Bring the nightingales back to nest."

Tym had to admit the boy was dedicated. At least about one thing.

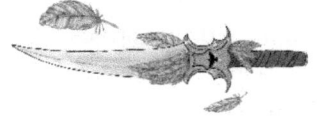

They were back on the road before the sun rose. Tym knew they would pass his brother's home. Thrush said the tracks led in that direction and it was an unavoidable meeting with destiny. Morning light broke across the horizon. After so much rain, it was almost a relief to have the sun shining again. Remembering the cause of the rain, the permanent grooves from hundreds of horses, dozens of wheels and thousands of feet stomping in the mud, the impressions were not lost. Neither would Ivy.

"Evil cannot win," Tym said, repeating the sober man's promise.

The shambles Bryn called a house was in view. When Bryn was first married to Veena, the place was kept nice, beautiful. The yard was green, lush with vibrant flowers. Crops grew in the back and on the side yards. It was very much alive. Then the droughts came and choked the life out from the place. *I should tell Bryn.* He dreaded the response his brother would give at hearing Ivy was missing. Probably washed his hands of her already. "Just like her mother," he'd say and then Tym would have to hit him, leave him flat on his ass in the middle of the—

"Something is in the road," Danial said.

Tym squinted and raised his hand up to shade the sun. Haze rippled off the warm dirt, but the shape was unmistakable, either a discarded bundle of clothes tossed, or a body.

"Oh no! God no!" Tym squeezed the horse's flanks and snapped the rein. He leaned forward, maintaining his balance as the horse shot past Thrush and Danial. The closer he got to the object in the road, the more certain he was it was a body. Bryn's body. He pulled back on the reins and the horse snorted its complaint. Tym stood in the stirrup, most of the weight on his left leg and slung his right leg over. He hit his elbow on the way down, sending a bolt of pain through his arm. Biting back curses, he shuffled up to the bundle. It was bloated, mud spattered, and missing a head.

"Not again! God-fucking-curse it, not fucking again!" Memories of Veena's headless body, bruised, blood caking her inner thighs, crawled up Tym's throat, and a strange sound, like a mewling cat followed in frustration. "Where is it? Where the fuck did it go?"

He tottered from one side of the road to the next, the way a drunk might weave around searching for the last bottle he tossed in hopes it had one last sip. Tym bit back his scream, eyes burning. Part of him denied it, though, the way he would deny the bottle was really empty. Bryn was inside, sleeping off a hard bender, a puddle of vomit next to his bed and the cinnamon scent lingering on the sheets. No, the body was Bryn. They were right outside of his house, so who the fuck else would it be! Several yards away he spotted what could've been the head. It was smashed out of shape, the nose bent so far to the left it was bulbous lump and one eye remained in the socket. Tym knelt beside it, hand out to pick it up, but he couldn't bring himself to touch it.

"Brother, what did they do to you?"

One thing, they must have dragged him out of the house during the storm, questioned him in the middle of the road. Tym would like to believe Bryn refused to respond, which was why they chopped his head off and let the horses kick it around, smashing it like an overripe melon. Knowing Bryn, he squealed louder than a knife-pricked hog.

He heard horses approach slowly, then stop a short distance back. All he wanted was to be alone. To grieve another loss. But the tears refused to fall and he looked back at Thrush. Her face was stern, but her brow had a slight furrow of concern.

"I'm sorry for your loss," Thrush said, though she could have been saying the weather was nice, not a cloud in the sky.

"He was a bastard! An ass to everyone who loved him. He got what he deserved, I guess. I have to bury him," Tym said. He expected an argument about having to move on before they lost the trail.

"I can help you," Thrush said.

Danial dragged the remains beside the house where Tym balanced a shovel over his injured arm. What was left of Bryn's head nestled on the spade. He laid the head beside the body, which had begun to smell.

"Who wants to dig first?" Tym held the shovel out.

Thrush began to sing. It was pleasant enough to Tym's ears. A sad song about destruction—a perfect dirge to commemorate a life spent on destroying others. Tym wiped a tear from his eye and the ground blurred felt like it was trembling. As Thrush continued to sing, he realized the ground was actually shaking. A chunk of stone and dirt rose up and spilled over the edge of a deep rectangular hole. When the song ended, Tym stared at Thrush, all speech lost in the wonder he witnessed. *Would never believe it, unless I saw it!*

She blinked.

"Aren't you going to put him in?"

Danial dragged the body and rolled it into the hole. Tym scooped up the head using the shovel. "Better than most deserve, you rotten bastard." He titled it and watched Bryn's head spin around, landing with the good eye staring up at Tym.

"Kind of creepy," Danial said.

"That was his life," Tym agreed.

"Would you like to say any words?" Thrush asked.

"I think I've said enough." Tym picked up a handful of dirt and dropped it in. "May you be better company for the worms."

Tym walked away as Thrush began to sing. The ground trembled and the tears fell. There was nothing more he could do for the dead. It was the survivor he had to help live on. He was at his horse, trying to get back up into the saddle and failing, when he felt a hand boost his leg over.

"Up you go," Danial said.

"Thank you," Tym said. "For everything."

"As my momma would say, 'We all need a little hand to get us where we're going.'"

"All I got is one, now," Tym said. "One day I will have both and return the favor."

The sun broke through the gloom, heating the land as it rose, its full eye gazing at Tym and he was squinting, trying to avoid its glare. He wasn't one to be up early, not since his youth when they worked their parents' farm, preferring instead to let the morning slip along and spare him the annoyance of its accusations and lies of a fresh start. Thrush stopped abruptly and if Tym's horse hadn't halted on its own, he would have collided with her.

"What is it?"

"Nothing," Thrush said, though her face had a concerned expression and her face went pale. He noticed her fingers were trembling. Thrush gave him a placid look, one that told him whatever she had experienced had ended.

I just hope Ivy's alright.

They arrived at Danial's farm past midday, nearly falling from their saddles.

"Betsy and Gal are probably mad for me not feeding them," Danial said. "We'll have fresh milk, you'll see."

Milk sounded fine. *I'd prefer a drink of bitter ale, or anything except firewater after burying my brother.* Tym and Thrush were at the house when they heard a sharp scream from the barn. Thrush ran, sword drawn, and Tym hobbled as fast as he could. The barn doors were wide open, Danial leaning on the wooden frame of an empty pen. It smelled of hay and animals, the way a barn was supposed to smell. Danial wept, big sopping cries.

"They took all my animals," he said and pounded his fist against the wall. It shook with every heavy strike, stirring up dust. "Took poor Betsy and Gal and Franny and Bell…"

The list went on and on.

"Probably slaughtered them for food," Thrush said to Tym. "An army marches on its stomach."

That sent Danial off into a heavier crying fit. No amount of coaxing could get him to leave the empty pens behind. He stayed out in the barn the rest of the day. Tym was glad the soldiers left the house alone, though, it had a look like there was a struggle. His mind went back to Danial's bandaged head and missing memory. He got a fire going in the hearth, lit some oil lamps and did a search of the cupboards. Crusty bread and old, moldy cheese were his boon. Not much, but enough to supplement what they brought.

"What do you think we'll find when we catch up to this cocksucker?" He was chewing on the bread, crunching it, and trying to swallow. "Think we have a chance of fighting through the entire army?" Tym laughed. He'd spent nearly two days trying to escape, only to be heading back into the very jaws that nipped at his heels.

"Best case scenario, we sneak in and free Ivy without too much bloodshed," Thrush said. "Though I doubt that will be the case, because whoever was blocking my song will know I am there. Then we will have to fight the entire army, and lose."

"You make it sound so easy, a pleasant frolic through a field of flowers," Tym said. "Do I even want to hear the worst case?"

"I think you may know it."

Tym couldn't see any jest or let up in her eyes. Thrush might believe his niece would give herself over to the people trying to kill them, but Tym was entirely convinced. Yes, the Sheriff and other members of Welksdale did confirm she was with those men who attempted to rob the Exchequer, but that was to save herself due to Bryn's debt burden. It's not like she chose to join them...like she chose to confront Cacophony. *Did she confront him? Or was it a ploy to escape the losing side?*

"She wouldn't," Tym said, brushing off fuzzy green mold from the cheese. He sniffed it and took a bite. Tangy, but not far gone. "She has a good heart, that girl does. Too many people treated her like shit. Including all of us here. I may not be her blood kin, but she still cares about me. When the time comes, I'll talk some sense into her."

"Creator's blessing that your words become truth," Thrush said. She stood up from the table and packed up the remains of her meal. "Do you want first or second watch?"

"First," Tym said, though his body ached, and he was emotionally worn thin, he wasn't ready to close his eyes just yet and confront his brother in his dreams, or nightmares. "Danial takes double later tonight."

"That sounds good to me," Thrush went to the blanket in front of the fire, shook it out, and set her multitude of swords and daggers around her within reach. Her very own picket. "Tym, just to let you know, Ivy is growing stronger. I felt her Song earlier. I don't know how she is being trained, but it sounded close. Almost as if she was standing in this very room. When I tried to track its proximity, it was gone."

Tym nodded, though gooseflesh prickled his arms. Anything that worried Thrush was double worry for him. *Not that I can do anything to prevent it.* Just keep moving forward and trusting in Thrush to this point.

"Try to rest well," Tym said. "I'm sure you'll find her soon."

Thrush grunted and walked away.

Tym went out onto the porch and sat in the chair, looking up at the stars. His heart was racing and he wanted to press on, but they would be dead in the saddle. *Wish I had some firewater to dull the aches.* He rubbed his chest and took a deep breath. Somewhere Ivy was under this very same sky. *Hold on girl, don't lose yourself.*

He exhaled, then went back inside to sleep.

CHAPTER THIRTEEN:
HARSH LESSONS

Disobedience is met with discipline. Harsh lessons are met out by the Dark Lord to remind the one who failed in duty that such failure has dire consequences. With the balance at stake, Harmony must be destroyed, and so those who fail to move to that end will be made to suffer. Through suffering the pupil learns to do better. Death isn't the ultimate price to be paid. Death is a relief not given to those who fail. Eternal torment awaits those who displease the Dark Lord.

"There's someone you need to meet," Cacophony said.

Sparrow lifted her head, which was as heavy as a stone. Her mind was cloudy and her body ached from lack of movement. She was certain she didn't smell too good, either, wearing the same outfit she had on since her capture, the same one Goldy had laid out for her. Cacophony and two other Silent Men filled the room. They grabbed her chains, a key scraped the lock, and then the weight was off her feet and arms. She still couldn't stand without assistance.

"Before you do, we will clean you up," Cacophony said. "Cannot have your new pupil revolted by you."

They led her to a room where a metal tub was filled with water, a brush and lye soap was set on a table beside it. Two women wearing Silent Men uniforms leaned against the back wall. Sparrow was left alone with them and instructed to wash and put on fresh garments. The women didn't bother to help her disrobe or climb into the tub. They might've held her head up if she began to drown, but that would be the extent of their intervention.

The act of washing brought some sensation to her numb extremities. When she finished—at the incessant glares from her watchers telling her not to linger—she almost felt like a clean rag, rather than one dragged through all kinds of mud and shit. A black robe hung by the door. She put it on, though it was smaller and snugger than she preferred, leaving more skin exposed than she would otherwise show. Her watchers, the Silent Women of the

Silent Men, walked her out the door and to a table where a cup of water and a plate of greens, roasted nuts, and mushrooms occupied a space.

No one protested as she sat and began eating the food.

Never give up a free meal, but always know, no meal is ever free. She used to tell this to Finch who would laugh and tell her every interaction came with a string for little birds' wings. Sparrow wasn't disappointed.

Cacophony entered the room, heavy boots clomping on the hardwood floor. Sparrow watched him approach, his long bastard sword handle protruding from the back scabbard. He was a frightening figure; the room seemed to bend to his presence. He pulled the chair out and sat across from her.

"I guess you decided you wanted to live," he said. The jovial tone grated against Sparrow and she considered how much damage smashing his face with the plate might do. "This is good. Good! You look better, certainly no longer have the rotting fish stench around you, and now you have eaten, you should have the energy to greet your pupil."

"I will warn you, I was never a good student," Sparrow said. "Always learned things the hard way and taught others worse habits than they had before…so I might not be the best instructor."

"Nonsense!" Cacophony clapped his hands together, making a thunderous noise. "This isn't book learning, but something that only you can impart on our young ward."

Sparrow suspected it might have been his daughter, but she had mee the little Nazglum doll. There wasn't anything she could teach the creature, except how to be expelled into the Void like Nazglum's other horrors. Cacophony rose from his chair and beckoned for Sparrow to follow. Out of curiosity, she did, leaving behind her fork, empty plate, and cup. They moved to another room where a girl no older than Goldy sat in a chair, bare feet sticking out from the hem of a similar black robe. Dark strands curled out from the hood and when she looked up, hazel eyes scanned Sparrow's face. Beside her was the little girl, blue eyes nearly glowing in the gloomy room. She held her doll out, but the girl in the black robe ignored it, leaning as though she was repulsed by it.

"Ivy," Cacophony said. "This is Sparrow. Sparrow will teach you what she knows about your, ugh, gift."

"Why would she do that?" Ivy asked, the look on her face was like she was sucking on the sourest lemon ever.

I wouldn't trust anyone this bastard introduced, either. Who knew what he has done to her? Sparrow didn't approach, or respond. Anything she did would deepen the girl's mistrust, because she didn't trust this girl who cohabitated with the enemy.

"Because I asked her to, Ivy," Cacophony said. "There's only so much you can learn from those without your gifts, so you need someone experienced with it to deepen your understanding. A fish cannot teach a bird to fly."

"That will be rather difficult without access to our *gifts*," Ivy said.

Sparrow liked the girl's courage and sass. *Reminds me of me.* Cacophony took it all in stride. He nodded and clasped his hands together.

"Leave that conundrum to me."

"What about you?" Ivy asked. "Why do you want to *teach* me?"

"I don't," Sparrow said. "I'd rather take you over my knee and paddle some respect into you, if I thought it would do you any good. A smart tongue will lead to a bad song. A bad song means innocent people die."

Ivy flinched at the last part. Robin, who was the snarkiest person Sparrow knew alive, had once said that to Sparrow. Then Thrush and the other Singers proceeded to give her and Finch space to fail together, which was frustrating, almost as frustrating as Devon's Meadows where Sparrow thought she had lost her the first time. One part of this bargain was clear. Sparrow wouldn't allow herself to get attached to the girl. People she liked had a bad habit of dying—horribly.

"Wisdom being imparted so soon," Cacophony said and held out a hand to the girl he claimed as his daughter. "Hyrian, come with me. These two have much to discuss and we don't want to intrude. A fly may walk on the wall, but avoiding the webs is how it survives."

"Enjoy your play time." Hyrian waggled her fingers at Ivy.

After they had left, Ivy shifted in her chair, wrapping her arms around her knees to keep the robe in place. "He's not really leaving us alone to talk. He isn't stupid like many men I know," she said.

Sparrow swallowed her laughter, keeping her face composed by thinking how Thrush might look and respond. She set her mouth in a thin line and elevated her nose a little—which the other women might find amusement in how Sparrow was trying to be like them. Finch would have gained the most joy from it, torturing her later with mocking imitations of her imitation. "How do you know?"

"The fly on the wall comment."

She is smart and perceptive.

"How did you come to that conclusion?"

"When you live with an abusive person long enough, you know what to look and listen for if you don't want a split lip," Ivy said.

"Aren't you afraid that speaking so bluntly will draw him back to punish us?" Sparrow asked. The girl was too free with her tongue. If she continued with her vehement assessment of their captor, it would lead to more trouble.

"He needs us," Ivy said. "Well, me, at least. You by proxy of what you can do for me?"

"What makes you so special?"

Ivy went quiet, looking down at her bare feet.

Seems she does know when to shut her mouth.

Sparrow pulled a chair close and sat down. To help this girl, she would need to know what Ivy knows about the song, harmony, and discord.

"Where are you from, Ivy?"

"Close by," she said. "I lived in a house outside of Welksdale."

Sparrow didn't know much about geography, but she remembered the map Robin stared at every night. They were on their way to the Spearhead mountains where the rest of the Singers would join them and discuss how to best defend against the Silent Men and Sparrow noticed the city of Euclid on the way and a few smaller towns that were marked. Welksdale could have been the closest, the place where Thrush had sensed a surge of power.

"When did you first learn about your song?" Sparrow noticed the girl's eyes flick to hers and back down at her feet.

"My mother used to sing," she said, then dropped her legs, sitting upright in such a huff. "Do we really have to get into these details? I already told Thrush and Robin about them."

The names struck like a spear through her chest. *She was with them! With the others Thrush, Robin, Nuthatch!* Sparrow smiled, not letting on that she knew the names. But if Ivy had been with them, then what was the girl doing here?

"You spent time with these women?" Sparrow asked. "Did anything happen to them?"

"They were fine when I left them," Ivy said.

Fine. Alive. Why wasn't she still there?

"Did they abandon you?"

"No. I left them," Ivy said. "There was a big fight in Welksdale and the Singers, that's what they called themselves, were losing. I couldn't watch them all get slaughtered. I left and Cacophony found me."

"Then he quit fighting, just like that?"

"Just like that." Ivy shrugged.

"You don't think that is a little strange?" Sparrow asked. "He has hunted them for a very long time."

"I have no part in what happens between the Silent Men and Singers," Ivy said. "Like you said, this has been going on for a very long time. Longer than I have been alive, I suspect."

"How long is that?"

"Sixteen years."

You are a splash in the slop bucket.

"Well, since you have been with both groups, and currently getting support from the Silent Men, you are involved," Sparrow said. "Whether you choose it or not."

"Then by helping me, you are helping the person trying to kill you, Sparrow," Ivy said. "What are your thoughts on that?"

I have no idea if I should kill her or help her. Killing her would be like placing a rope around her own neck. Sparrow wasn't sure which one was worse: the creepy little girl, or this petulant older girl? The first was for sure going to bring about their demise, but what was Ivy's role? *Creator! Finch was better at these decisions.*

"Sometimes you need to trudge through manure to get to the sweet fruit on the other side," Sparrow said, reciting a phrase she had learned as a child from her father—wincing at the memory of the sting from the lash as her father beat.

"Am I the manure or the fruit?" Ivy asked.

"I guess we will have to find out."

Her conversation with Sparrow was blessedly brief. The woman was rather annoying, and their interaction reminded Ivy of a pissing contest rather than a true learning session. Feral cats probably had the same reaction when meeting in the alley, to glare and hiss, judging if claws were needed. All Ivy wanted was a nap. Having to keep her guard up drained her. Who was this woman to judge Ivy? What had the Singers done for her besides drag her into a war? No wonder people who met them didn't trust them.

Despite her desire to fall asleep after the initial session, Claiborne escorted her outside where Cacophony continued the lesson.

"Again, Ivy. Try Again," Cacophony said, standing in yellowed grass. There were no trees to provide shade, and he stood directly in the morning sun wearing his full insect-like armor. Ivy would think he'd cook inside the heavy suit. She wanted to tear off the black robe chafing against her skin. She yearned to be in the shadow of the house, where Hyrian sat, singing to Glorian, her doll. Claiborne leaned on the porch railing, whittling a piece of wood and looking bored.

"Focus, Ivy." Cacophony clapped his gauntlets together in a metallic smack. "Try to see into me."

Ivy shifted her eyes back onto Cacophony. She desperately wanted to delve into him. To release the song and pick his life apart right before she commanded him to kill the girl and swallow his own sword. Strangely enough, he was allowing her to try. *Why are you following his orders?* Tym's voice asked. It did sound really idiotic to comply so easily with her captor, but it was no worse than him giving Ivy a chance to kill him. She'd experienced far worse from Bryn, shouting her down, smacking her face. She could taste the blood, feel her nose swell and bruised lip burn. She was helpless to fight back. But there was a chance she could break free. Slight as it was. A hair's width, but even a hair could choke a person. She had to try. All it would take is one slip up, then she would kill him. Ivy concentrated on the tingling in her chest, a rattle like a glob of phlegm that she couldn't cough up.

Hyrian blocked her. Ivy could sense the power behind it, but it was like shoving a stone ten times her size. No matter how much force she put against it, it wouldn't budge.

"Surrender to it." Cacophony was gentle, sounding genuine like teaching a pupil rather than his potential killer.

Ivy slowed her breathing, released the tension in her hands and feet, shook her arms, and let them hang at her side. She closed her eyes. The song hung on the frayed edges, just out of reach, an itch crying out to be scratched. She licked her dry lips, tasting the salt, and testing the scab where she was struck. Beyond her was the buzz of an insect in the grass, the rubbing of her boots on warm, sweating feet and...it was gone, leaving her exhausted. She shoved the sleeves up her sweat sticky arms, but they fell back down. Ivy's shoulders slumped and she hung her head.

"Too many distractions!" She growled.

"You must get used to them, Ivy," Cacophony said. "The world won't go silent to hear your song."

"I'm blocked." Ivy shook her sleeves in disgust. "I don't know why you think I can push past it. Or even why you want me to try. I mean, I could hurt you. Make you do things you don't want to do."

"You won't hurt me," Cacophony said.

"Why?" Ivy asked, leveling her gaze on his eyes. It was hard to read what he thought. "I really don't have a reason *not* to kill you. You knock me out, kidnap me, and then poison my soup. You didn't have to poison me to keep me here. It's not like I have anywhere else to go."

"I am trying to help you, Ivy." Cacophony approached her. He was big and the sword slung on his back was even bigger. It could crush Ivy with little effort. Cacophony placed a gauntlet covered hand on her shoulder. His touch was light, almost tender. "What I gave you in the soup was to stop the nausea and headaches. I couldn't help the side-effects, though I do apologize for any discomfort they may have brought you."

No more discomforting than finding the girl sitting on my bed in the dark. She had to admit there wasn't any more pain being around Hyrian. She thought she'd grown used to it, or it went away because she was no longer hungry. *I guess eating did put a stop to it.*

"You could have told me," she said.

"Would you have taken it?"

Ivy wouldn't have eaten anything, not even the soup, if she hadn't been so very hungry.

"No." Her cheeks flushed, and she refused to look away. "You gave me no reason to trust you. I know what you want from me. I'm nothing but a tool against the other Singers. Like everyone else, you'll use me until I have nothing left to give and then toss me away like moldy, old bread."

"I cannot force you to do anything against your will," Cacophony said and winked. "I don't have that kind of power."

Ivy shrugged his hand off. She didn't like this game he was playing. He was no different than the rest of the world, teasing her, using her, abusing her. She wouldn't allow him to treat her like shit. She'd rather die first.

Cacophony stared at her and Ivy worried she'd pushed him too far. Jabbed the bear too hard with the pointy stick.

"Take Hyrian to the house," Cacophony said. Claiborne shot him a look that Ivy caught. She'd stopped whittling and gripped the knife in her gloves, no longer leaning on the post.

"I don't think that's…wise," Claiborne said, her voice even, but with a hint of annoyance.

"I don't care what you think, First Sword. I don't employ you to think for me," Cacophony said in a calm, though dangerous tone. "I ask that you take her to the house and keep her silent."

Hyrian hissed and snarled, glaring at Claiborne.

"Too weak," the little girl said, sticking her tongue out at Ivy.

"You heard your father," Claiborne said, walking past the girl. She didn't bother to look at her, let alone try to pick her up. "Into the house."

Hyrian got up and started skipping to the house. She was humming a familiar tune. Ivy recognized it as the song from last night, though part of her still thought it was all a dream. Hyrian got to the steps, looked at Ivy, and stuck her tongue out again. Ivy responded with the same. The girl giggled and went inside.

"No singing," Claiborne said, her words were cut off by the slamming door. "This is why I don't want one of my own. Fucking parasites."

"Children," Cacophony said. "They are a bundle of energy."

"Is she really your child?" Ivy asked.

Cacophony stared quietly at Ivy. His cloak fluttered in the breeze which blew more hot air rather than cooling the sweat on Ivy's brow. *Maybe I wasn't supposed to ask that question. Maybe the girl had another father, and he was stuck raising her, like Bryn raised me.* Ivy screwed her mouth up, holding back the apology. She'd given up apologizing to monsters.

Cacophony gave a nod of his head. She wasn't sure if it was to her or himself. Then he unsheathed his sword. Ivy stuck her chest out, chin raised. *I'm not dying a coward.* Cacophony didn't strike her. Instead, he stepped back three paces from Ivy and placed the sword down in front of him. She stared at it in surprise.

Is this a trick? Not that she could lift the sword, since it was as long as she was tall.

"Look inside me and find the truth," Cacophony said, kneeling in the grass and bowing his head. "I won't resist."

"Aren't you afraid?" Ivy asked. She could sense the power inside her chest, rising like a great fire, burning to be released. Ivy hesitated—*there must be some trick.* "I could control you, force you to tear out your eyes, or fall on your own sword."

"Such a limited imagination," Cacophony said. "Unlike others, I am not afraid to die. It's part of the natural order. Besides, look at what is inside me and decide if you want to kill me." He tapped his head.

My chance to be the judge and executioner.

The idea brought her no joy.

Ivy surrendered control. She opened her mouth, expecting it to be blocked—that this was a trick—but, her song flowed. As soon as it connected to Cacophony, the melody took shape and the words that came were full of sadness, pain, and despair. Like always, the world she was a part of, the world of yellowed-grass, hot sun, and the single man trying to kill people like her, slipped away. Across her vision, a new world was born. A world of darkness and fire. The heat made Ivy sweat and hazy images took shape in the smoke. A village, the houses burning. People ran, faces twisted in fear and pain, trying to escape the flames and the smoke. Arrows whistled like stinging bugs, sticking men, some burning. Soldiers rushed from a copse, wetting their blades with blood from those remaining. Their armor was dark, almost as dark as the Silent Men, and Ivy felt disgusted at being shown a raid on helpless people.

Gladio was repeated and Cacophony reached for his sword.

The slaughter continued as the black armored men fell on unarmed villagers, hacking and slashing, cutting men, women, and children, slicing them the way a farmer harvested wheat. They ignored the screams and pleas, moving closer to burning homes, light reflecting off dark-blue plate mail. She had seen it before, the design not like the plain black the Silent Men wore, but the color of Thrush's soldiers. Ivy scanned the surrounding woods. She had to be mistaken, confused at what she saw. It couldn't be Singer's soldiers. They didn't attack innocent people, did they? And then she heard it. A song coming from the woods. Ivy had never heard Thrush sing, but it had to be her. She followed the voice and saw someone move. Someone small, and slight, the song coming from her.

Gladio became *Subsisto* and Cacophony's hand rested on the hilt.

The memory sharpened, tearing her from the woods and focused on one particular house. Fire crackled and blazed up the wall, smoke thick enough Ivy could taste it. A little girl was crying, "Mommy! Mommy it burns!" Her dress was on fire. A woman with golden hair tore at it, stripping the enflamed dress the girl and the vision shifted closer, past the smoke so sharp Ivy coughed, missing a verse and the image became hazy. Then the song continued, flowing stronger, louder. The girl had blue eyes and golden hair like her mother. Ivy recognized the face.

Hyrian.

Her hair caught fire and she burned, her small hands beating at her head, trying to put it out. Tears streaked her face. Mouth contorted in pain and terror. Ivy tried to move her away, use the power to remove her from the house, but it was a memory, and she had to witness the next terrifying event. The song pulsed with so much power, yet she felt helpless. There was a groaning sound, and the mother grabbed her little girl, shielding her. "Mommy loves you," the woman said as a flaming wall broke away from the structure, tilted briefly away from them before shifting back, and burying both mother and daughter under flaming rubble.

"No!" Ivy shouted, but it was over.

"No!" echoed Cacophony.

Tears burned Ivy's eyes, and she dropped to her knees. The song dried up, leaving Ivy empty and hurt, hugging herself as she rocked on the ground, weeping helplessly. Across from her, she heard the same sounds of anguish. Cacophony was on his hands and knees, looking more bug than human. He cried, tearing up large clumps of grass and beat his breastplate until Claiborne ran from the house.

"What happened?" Claiborne asked, kneeling beside Cacophony. He couldn't respond beyond making the anguished noises. Claiborne got to her feet and drew her sword. "Stop whatever you are doing to him."

"I'm not..." Ivy couldn't finish the words, caught up in the wet snot dripping down her throat.

"I said stop!" Claiborne stood over Ivy, sword raised and ready to strike her dead.

Ivy couldn't sense the power let alone release it. She held her hands up, but they wouldn't stop the killing blow. She was going to die! That horrifying vision the last thing she saw in the world.

"First Sword!" Cacophony said, head up and tears soaking the muslin. "Leave her alone."

"I told you it was too dangerous," Claiborne said, still holding the sword over Ivy. "Look at what she did to you."

"It's nothing. She saw the truth," Cacophony said, laying a hand on Claiborne's sword arm, forcing her to lower the blade. "The truth is full of pain."

Claiborne sheathed her sword, glaring at Ivy.

"How?" Ivy coughed, choking on her tears. "How did she survive?"

"She was a gift," Cacophony said, kneeling beside her again. "Returned to me for one purpose."

"I don't... understand." She hiccoughed.

"Not everything in this world is simple, Ivy." He pulled away the muslin and used it to dry his eyes. The scar over his lip twisted his mouth into a permanent snarl. "In order to bring justice, there must be compromises."

"But she was—"

"I know, but she isn't. That is the gift."

"It was them who did this to her? Those women?"

Cacophony nodded.

No wonder he wanted to wipe the world clean of Singers. They were monsters. *And I am one, too.*

"Are you going to kill me?" Ivy asked.

"No, child," Cacophony said, holding out his hand. "You have seen the truth and, although you had your opportunity to strike, you didn't harm me. In return, I won't hurt you."

Ivy took the hand and allowed him to pick her up. He was strong. Easily could fling her around like she was a sack of feathers. He released her, and she found her legs were still trembling. The vision of the burning girl, of Hyrian and her mother embracing in their destined deaths. Ivy didn't even get a chance to say goodbye to her mother. She'd give anything to be loved the way Glorian loved Hyrian.

"You are free to make your choice, Ivy," Cacophony said. He left her alone, guiding a reluctant Claiborne back to the house, the door closing behind them.

Ivy looked at the house and then the road.

I have nowhere to go.

No one wants me.

I...I am alone.

She hated to admit it. Refused to let the idea in because it changed the narrative of the story she had told herself. But in fact, none of those stories she knew were true. Not anymore. Someone did accept her, trusted her. Why else would he let her inside his head?

But he is a monster. A killer.

"I'm no different." Her legs gave out, and she flopped back in the yellowed grass.

There Ivy wept.

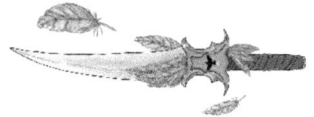

Claiborne watched Ivy from the grime-stained windows. She was as much out of place, standing in the neglected yard, as the yellowed crabgrass and prickly plants. Dying in a place where there should be life. Claiborne had dealt in death for most of her life, but from what she observed of this place, it used to be farmland. The fields were fallow, run-to-riot with weeds, burnt out by the sun. This was what would become of the rest of the world when the Harmony ended. Humanity would be cast adrift like Ivy, no fertile soil to take root and grow. What would replace them when they are gone, Claiborne couldn't imagine. It couldn't be much worse than the horrors they perpetrated on each other.

"Do you trust her?" Claiborne asked.

"No," Cacophony replied. He attached a new muslin piece over his mouth. "Trust must be earned, and she is still lost, searching for who she was, what she is now, and deciding on who she'll become."

The girl hummed quietly, sitting on a bench, legs kicking back and forth. Claiborne didn't know anything about her, but Ivy had seen something. She didn't like being kept in the dark regarding such crucial information. In a way, it put Ivy closer to Cacophony and Claiborne was that much more expendable.

What did she see?

"Sparrow will tutor her in her song, but I'm placing Ivy into your care," Cacophony said. "Observe her actions, guide her along in her transition. Let me know if you see a need for change."

"I'm supposed to be her friend." A statement, not a question. The idea left a sour taste in her mouth, and she spat out on the dusty floor. Last thing she wanted was a friend. Friends were a liability and she had enough keeping her back from killing Thrush. She couldn't play the role of nanny to the same kind of warped creature she was cleansing from the world. It was too much to ask. Might as well embrace Thrush and tell her all was forgiven, when nothing was fucking forgiven, not until her blood coated Claiborne's hands.

"Mentor, then," Cacophony said. "Impart your wisdom on her."

"She's one of *them*." Claiborne fought to keep her voice calm. "Aren't we supposed to be hunting *them* down?"

"Don't be so shortsighted," Cacophony said, patting Hyrian's head. "She has the power to corrupt, but she is only in the first stages of her rebirth. The discovery. Left unattended she would naturally congregate to the other women. Nazglum's deceptive powers are attractive and those women seduced her through promise of more power. Ivy came to us out of fear. Desiring to end a threat placed in her heart and mind by those Nazglum whores. We must dissolve that fear, so she won't be a bride to the Dark Lord." He knelt and hugged Hyrian, his love blinding him to the unnatural thing he claimed as his daughter. "There must be salvation for her. Or salvation is a lie, and we are all damned to a life of misery."

The only salvation Claiborne believed in came at the edge of the sword. One must be broken, cut, bled, before they have reached the cathartic point where darkness could be purged, or death claimed them. Arron was saved, she knew this. Who could suffer so much and not be?

"I will do as commanded," Claiborne said. *Though it's a mistake.*

"There's been enough sorrow," Cacophony said. "Bring an end to it."

Claiborne looked out the window again. Ivy was no longer in the yard. *Nazglum's nuts!* Claiborne ground her teeth and yanked the door open. They had horses around the side. She could ride—Claiborne froze, taking a step back in surprise. Ivy stood on the porch.

"I have decided," Ivy said, snuffling and wiping at her eyes.

"Come in child." Cacophony stood at Claiborne's shoulder. He had removed his gauntlets, leaving them beside Hyrian who cradled one in her right arm and her doll in the left. He held out pale hands, but Ivy walked past, ignoring them. He didn't take offense, eyes on Claiborne, and the First Sword knew he smiled beneath the muslin. She was glad it remained covered. "You must be hungry. You've had a challenging morning."

Ivy gave him a suspicious glare.

"Don't worry," he chuckled, "there won't be any added spices to your gruel."

Ivy went to the table and waited.

Claiborne closed the door and sat down across from her. Ivy refused to make eye contact. Cacophony may have won a battle, but her spirit was yet to be broken.

Once she accomplishes the task Cacophony gives her, I will kill her and the other one, as well. First Thrush, though. That little bird must be crushed. Then Claiborne's life would be completed, and she could join Arron in the great beyond, having earned her salvation.

Cacophony served out a heaping bowl of gruel to each, making a huge display to Ivy, who didn't seem impressed that the bowls had the same portions scooped into them and nothing more. Then they sat and gave thanks to the Creator. Eating as one big, happy family.

Ivy was allowed a short rest after the exhausting tests she'd failed. The nausea didn't return, but her mind and body were heavy with grief. Part of her wanted to give in, to trust Cacophony. A deeper part clung to the betrayal of her mother, Bryn, and even Tym. He would hurt her one day. Claiborne for sure seemed on the edge of wanting to strangle Ivy. Yet, she wouldn't because Ivy was still useful to Cacophony.

As long as I continue proving myself, he'll keep me safe.

The shades were drawn and she lay on the pallet, thinking about the moment of peace. Food, shelter, protection. Her immediate needs were met and try as she might, she couldn't keep her eyes from drifting shut.

Ivy. Her name whispered so sweetly.

"Mother," Ivy called in the darkness, but no, it couldn't be Veena. She was dead. What was dead couldn't be brought back, unless…

You can have whatever you wish for, the voice said, shifting from her mother's sing-song loving tone, to one more seductive. Light cracked through the darkness and Ivy found herself standing in the hallway again. Laughter from behind her caught her attention.

"Hyrian?" Ivy asked, catching a flutter of robes slipping into another room. The girl must be playing hide-and-seek again. *"I'm too tired to play games."*

Scared, Ivy? Don't be frightened. It wasn't Hyrian's high-pitched voice speaking to her. Ivy wasn't sure she wanted to discover the identity of the speaker.

"I'm going back to bed," Ivy said. As she turned to go back to her room, the door slammed. All the doors slammed, causing Ivy to jump and send a trickle of urine down her leg. She tried the door handle, yanking her hand away, hissing. It was cold, cold enough to burn her hand. *"I don't want to play this*

game, anymore!"

One door hung open. A greenish light spilling out on the hall floor. A gust of cold air came from the room, sending a chill up Ivy's arm. She shivered, rubbing her cold skin.

Fuck it. Have to end this some way. She forced her legs to move. Bare feet creaked along the floor boards. The place was silent and the only light was a greenish color one in front of her toes. She reached for the door handle, paused, remembering the cold burn, and decided it was best not to touch any part of the door. *Fool me once, shame on me. Fool me twice, then I'm an idiot who deserves what she gets.*

Ivy stepped into the green light, not knowing what to expect. It did feel warmer on her feet, though that could've been her imagination. All of this could be an elaborate dream contrived by her weary mind, though being aware wasn't the same as being in control like other lucid dreams she had as a child. This one was way more real.

In the cobweb-covered room, a figure in dark robes blocked out the window. She almost mistook him for dreary drapery, until his head lifted and the cowl shifted slightly to hint at a face hidden in the depths.

Brave girl. The voice came from around the room rather than from the figure in the robes. It had a bright edge, almost cheery.

Why do I want to piss myself more? Ivy squeezed her knees together. *"Who are you?"*

Who I am is not important. The robed figure stood still. Around him the room was empty, though it seemed to shimmer. The green glow poured from cracks in the walls, the floor boards, and slithered around the figure. There was a hint of decay. *It's what I can do for you that is the question.*

"I don't think you can offer me anything I would want." Ivy sensed the hollowness in the words. She pictured Hyrian hugging her father after being crushed by a fiery wall.

You are longing for someone, Ivy. I know who it is that you want. The room rippled and Ivy's stomach tossed, her legs began to shake and she stumbled to the side, careful not to touch the wall. Even a finger's length away, she could feel the burning cold.

"What is dead is gone," Ivy said.

Is it? The figure chuckled, causing the green light to ripple further, nearly hitting her like water sloshing against her body, repulsing her.

"I don't want that for her," Ivy said, but what she meant was, *"I don't want that*

for me."

Perhaps. The robed figure took a step closer to her, though it was more like floating. *Perhaps we can strike another bargain.*

"I want nothing from you," Ivy said, her voice trembling. *"Leave me alone!"*

That, my love, is a request I cannot grant. A long black sleeve lifted and a morbid hand slid from the depths. A long, skeletal finger, putrid green in the light, tapped Ivy on the nose. She couldn't resist or move away. Her nose tingled, though she couldn't move to scratch it. It itched bad enough she wanted to tear it off. A soft, mewling noise came from her lips. Then the finger slipped away, gratefully back into the dark hole of the sleeve.

We will speak again.

Ivy's legs found they could move again, and she hurried from the room. The door shut behind her, plunging her into darkness.

When she woke up, she fought, tangled up in the wool blanket. She was back in the room. "Nazglum's nut! What was that nonsense?" She ran a hand through her sweaty hair. Her palm pinched and she noticed an imprint left by the handle on it. *More than a dream.* Her heart thudded and she looked around the dark room.

The door clicked open and Ivy screamed, falling off the pallet. Claiborne peered around the edge and gave her a strange look.

Ivy shook her head.

"Bad dream," she said. *More than a dream*, she reiterated.

"Get cleaned up," Claiborne said and frowned. "We're leaving."

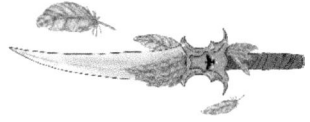

The carriage ride was short, moving further away from familiar places and marking new thresholds. Each league west added to the total furthest distance she had ever travelled from her home. At a different time in her life, she might've been thrilled. Any excitement over the adventure was dampened by constant demands from her host. Cacophony wouldn't leave her alone, testing her relentlessly while Hyrian sang quietly, playing with her doll, Glorian. Sparrow sat beside Ivy, silently observing. There wasn't much else for her to do.

"Reach for the power, do you sense it?" Cacophony encouraged.

Ivy focused on the back of the opposite seat cushion. The power was a whispering glow, the song shaping even as she grasped it. It filled her, bringing on such joy she thought she might burst. Even as she held it, it had begun to fade, having no way to release. Ivy growled, fists smacking the cushions.

"I had it," she said.

"But."

"I couldn't go anywhere with it." Of course, she couldn't because Hyrian was humming her own song which silenced Ivy. "What's the point of reaching for the song, when I won't be able to use it?"

"It will make it that much easier once you are free," Cacophony said. "Think of it as if you were swinging a practice sword. In battle, the blunted piece of wood is useless against sharp steel. But once you are handed the steel sword with edge sharp enough to draw blood, you are a much better fighter and more likely to survive."

"You are preparing me to fight..." Ivy looked sideways at Sparrow who raised her brows at her, arms folded and waited for her to continue her thought. *This is what she meant by walking through the manure.* "... you know... them."

Cacophony laughed and she tried to sink further into the seat cushion.

"I already have my balance, Ivy," he said. "Hyrian makes them no more than ordinary women. I don't need you to fight battles we will already win."

Sparrow was of no help. Her face was impassive, though Ivy was certain she must be bristling worse than a spiny cactus. How she kept from reaching out and choking Cacophony told of Sparrow's resolve or, perhaps she had resigned herself to her fate.

"What's my role?" Ivy asked.

"You'll have to figure that out on your own," Cacophony said and Hyrian giggled, taking his hand. "Try it again."

They arrived at another smaller house. One that was off the main road and hidden behind a wall of evergrows. The green, hilly smell of their needles thick in the evening air. Hyrian was asleep, curled against her father's leg, when the carriage rolled to a stop. Ivy hadn't seen the girl sleep at all, but she guessed even monsters must need rest to recover their energy. Even asleep, her power was at work. Ivy could touch her song, pulsing inside her chest in rhythm to her beating heart, but it had nowhere to go. Her throat was closed to it.

Cacophony carried Hyrian into the new house. Hands that could crush a man's throat held the girl tenderly, like she was the most precious thing in the world. Ivy wondered what he had given up to get her back. Who made the trade and how? Claiborne walked beside her on the right and Sparrow was on her left. Two rather interesting guardians averting any plans she may had of running off into the night. Ivy imagined becoming a wild girl who preyed on unexpected travelers. A funny thought that made her want to laugh at the absurdity. The laughter died with one glance at Claiborne. The woman's hand never strayed far from her sword.

"Where are the rest of the Silent Men?" Ivy asked Claiborne. Only a half-dozen men rode alongside them and were picketing their horses.

"Nowhere you should be concerned." Claiborne sneered at Sparrow.

For me to know and you never to find out, a phrase Ivy often heard from her father, or the man she thought was her father, especially regarding where he hid his share of the payment from selling firewater.

"You don't like me much, I get it," Ivy said. "I'm another thing in the way of Cacophony's love. Killing me would make your life easier."

"Listen, little bitch," Claiborne said, rounding on her and putting a hand on her chest, "your kind has corrupted the sanctity of our world for far too long. The only reason you are still breathing is because Cacophony has commanded it and I owe him my life. I'm also supposed to be a mentor, which I don't know what that means especially since I don't know the first thing about children, not to mention cursed fuckers like yourself." She gave Ivy a shove. "I'm giving you a single piece of advice. Don't ask questions about where my soldiers are or what they may be doing. Stick to simple things, like who do I need to use my song on and what do you want me to do? Understand?"

Ivy nodded.

"I want to hear words, not the pea you got rattling inside your skull."

"Yes," Ivy said.

Sparrow cleared her throat, but Claiborne pressed on.

"Also, there will come a time when you will need to prove your loyalty," Claiborne said and drew her blade. The motion was quick and smooth, and it stopped a hair's length from Ivy's neck. "Remember who you chose and don't ever think you can use your tainted song on me."

Sparrow stepped in, pushing the blade aside.

"Enough," she said. "Fear is one way to reach the goal you want, but it isn't the only path."

"Says the one whose love wasn't crushed to death by an experiment gone wrong." She glared at Sparrow, but Sparrow didn't back away. Claiborne grunted, sheathed her sword, and walked on ahead to the house.

"Try not to provoke her," Sparrow said. "She has no love lost with Thrush or any of us. She may have discipline not to stab us out in the open, but on the battlefield, accidents happen. I rather not be an accident bleeding on the point of her blade."

Sparrow walked ahead.

"I'm glad we got that cleared up," Ivy muttered and looked up the night sky. She thought about Tym and Danial. They were probably wondering what happened to her. She promised Danial that she'd listen to the nightingales with him. *I hope you are listening.* Their first song started from in the evergrows. Ivy closed her eyes and thought of her mother. She touched her neckline where the copper string used to hang with the locket. Tears stung her eyes and she let them go.

Lost, never to be found again.

Then she dried her eyes and entered the house.

CHAPTER FOURTEEN:
ENCOUNTERS

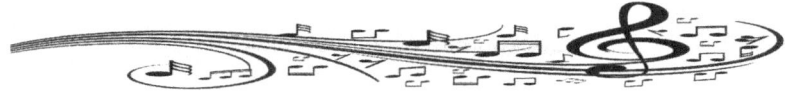

An encounter with one like me—a chosen one, the Dark Lord has blessed, or Tainted as misdescribed by the wicked women—won't be pleasant. We are no longer human and a century or so of hibernation has changed our form. Being graced by our presence means one of two purposes: you are chosen by the dark lord, or you have been marked for a terrifying end. Pray it is the former and not the latter.

"They were here," Thrush said. The dust had been disturbed in the house. Even Tym could see the boot prints. In the back room they found a metal tub. Beside it were muddy, torn leggings, an equally muddy dress, stiff from drying so long. These Tym was certain belonged to Ivy.

"How long ago?" Tym asked, dropping the mud stiff clothes and wiping his hands on his trousers.

"A night or two," Thrush said, poking through the remains of the fire in the hearth. "They aren't trying to cover their tracks, so either he doesn't think anyone is tracking them or—"

"He doesn't care," Tym finished for her. Why should Cacophony worry? He has an entire army and the ability to cancel out the Singers. They'd have to be dumber than a fly circling a frog to be on their trail. Right then, Tym could smell the swamp and every survival instinct told him to buzz off.

Danial moped around the room. He hadn't said much since discovering his barn empty. He did carry a brass cow bell and would jingle it occasionally. It grated on Tym's nerves and he wanted to stomp it flat and toss it in the back stream. He let the boy keep it, since it seemed to be his only solace since being caught up in this mess of Singers and Silent Men.

Tym had never heard of either group before Euclid. It was amazing how wars could rage around them, stuck as they were in this simple world, struggling to earn enough coin to keep him fed, sheltered, and pay for the company of a woman on those rare nights when he splurged. The fate of their existence was in the balance while Tym haggled the price of firewater.

Thrush examined the table. She licked her fingers and dabbed them on the top. *That's a strange way to go about cleaning.* Thrush sniffed her fingers, and wrinkled her nose.

"Kavas," she said and wiped her fingers on a handkerchief. "He must be drugging her."

"Which is why she hasn't escaped," Tym said.

"Maybe," Thrush said and turned to the window sharply, eyes widening for a moment and then she tucked the handkerchief away in her belt. "Kavas is also used to speed up healing."

"You think they are beating her?"

Danial turned at the anger in Tym's voice.

"They're hurting Ivy?"

"It's possible, but I don't think torture is a good way to get people to cooperate," Thrush said. "We won't know anything until we catch up to them."

"How long will that take?" Danial asked.

"I don't know," Thrush said. "What I suspect is that they are no longer traveling with the majority of their force."

Breaking up into smaller groups would explain why Cacophony was so far ahead. Tym wasn't sure he'd leave an army behind, but then again, he wasn't a crazy, bloodthirsty warlord bent on killing a group of women who could wreck his life with a song. *Bad enough what they do to a man by using their vicious tongues.* Strength in numbers. The fewer there were of them, the fewer they had to fight to get Ivy back.

"How many do you think went with Ivy?" Tym asked.

"Cacophony is a dangerous force, but he is one man," Thrush said. "I'm more concerned about where their main force went."

"As long as it is far from us, it doesn't matter."

"It will if we try to go back only to find ourselves cut off from the mountains," Thrush said.

"Mountains," Tym said. "You can go back that way. We'll be going as far north as the snowline. Right, Danial?"

"Are there nightingales north?" Danial asked.

"Sure, and other cold weather birds." Tym had no idea, but it didn't really matter, as long as he got Ivy as far away from these fucked up factions. The way Thrush pursed her lips together, Tym was probably more wrong than right about the damn bird. She and her Singers could fight their war with the Silent Men all they wanted, but they could leave the three of them out of it.

"I'll follow where you and Ivy go," Danial said and rattled the cowbell. "There's nothing here for me."

"Not sure what we'll find out there, kid," Tym said. *It'll be better than what we have here. Everything will be wiped out by fire and steel. Why couldn't these assholes leave us alone with our patch of dirt and dying grass?*

They left the house, finding nothing useful to take with them. The place reminded Tym too much of a neglected tomb. His hairs prickled at the ghosts who once inhabited the place. *Bryn's place will become a place of haunted memories, just like this one. Those who lived there, Bryn, Venna, Ivy will be forgotten. One day, so will I.* The morbid thoughts chased him out to the porch and he was more than happy to find himself in the saddle again.

As they continued tracking the carriage, Tym took his arm out of the sling. He rotated it, grimacing and sucking back a painful hiss. It was bearable, unlike the restricting wrap. He might not be able to swing bottles or make thrusting motions with his right arm, not until it fully healed, but he could hold reins in both hands and that was a small victory. All the shit that had happened since he went to Euclid, he'd take whatever win he could gain. Even his calf was starting to heal, itching like he'd fallen in a patch of prickle weed. The saddle sores competed for attention and he had chaffing in places he hadn't thought about in a long while.

"Complaining like my father used to," Tym said, stretching his neck and wincing at the popping noises. "Fuck, if getting old hurts this much, I think I'd rather pay my bill early and sleep in oblivion's cold embrace."

Danial gave him a sideways look.

"Wish my parents hadn't died from lung rot," he said. "I bet they wished they hadn't, either."

"Mayhap they found a happy place, like the preachers say about the Creator's Kingdom," Tym said. What the Creator would want with a couple of farmers when he had an army of them and, as far as he knew, food wasn't something that the dead would require was beyond his knowledge. He imagined a bunch of peasants sitting around shooting the shit, pitchforks and shovels in hands, waiting for a hole to dig or hay to pitch. It didn't sound very exciting, but then again, life on this plane wasn't much exciting, either.

"How?" Danial asked. "Could they be happy without me there?"

They must've been before you were born.

"Probably," Tym said. "Else you wouldn't be here. I wouldn't worry what a few dead people thought and be more concerned about the living ones."

Thrush slowed her horse to a trot. She was ignoring them and Tym couldn't blame her.

"We'll stop again at the next house," she said.

"Wouldn't it be better if we kept going through the night?" Tym dabbed the wet sling across his forehead. His skin would be redder than the welts on his ass under the hot sun.

"Arrive tired for a possible fight. Brilliant tactical advice, I'm certain to commend you for general of our forces when we return." There was a bite in her tone and she sounded more like Robin. *What's got you all prickled?* Tym knew better than poke a woman who had the power to dig his grave with a few notes of a song, and swallowed his retort. "Besides, they might leave the main road and I don't want to miss signs if that happens. Otherwise, we'll never find her."

"Can't you sense her?" Tym asked.

"Only when she uses her song."

"I thought she was blocked."

Thrush didn't reply.

Silence was a long way from consent, but it was enough to tell Tym the woman was keeping things from him.

"You've felt her?"

"Yes." She sniffed and held her nose up, as though she didn't have to explain herself to him.

"You didn't bother to say anything." Tym rubbed at his brow.

"It wasn't necessary."

"Of fucking course it's necessary!" Tym trotted his horse up beside her, ignoring the fact that she could bury him right there in the road. "Ivy could be trying to escape and may need our help now. How far away was it?"

"I don't know," Thrush said. "I mean there was a powerful burst, but then it was gone. It wasn't close, that I know for sure."

"Do you think..." Tym swallowed hard. "I mean...is she still alive?"

"I don't know."

The not knowing grated on him worse. It was like the time Veena disappeared. No one knew anything, except that she was gone. There's no way to drive a man crazier than to leave him alone with his imaginings and all the horrors he could conjure. Bryn was furious when she returned, but Tym was relieved to see her.

"You sense her again, let me know right away," Tym said, then softened his anger. "I'm not your enemy. I'm just trying to set the past right."

"You can't," Thrush said, riding on ahead of him.

"What's dead is dead, Tym," Bryn would say, *"Best let the corpse rot in peace."* He was right about that at least, and perhaps Thrush was as well.

"I'm sure going to try," Tym said and slouched into the saddle.

Dusk closed in and Tym was fuming over Thrush withholding information about Ivy. What else she might be hiding? He tried a few more attempts at coaxing conversation from Thrush, but they were met with curt *harrumphs*. They approached a cluster of stunted bloodwood trees, the first sign of life beyond the yellowed, crabgrass. Tym's horse whinnied and flicked her ears.

"What's wrong—"

Three horses shot from the cover of bloodwood, kicking up dust on the road. Black cloaks billowed out behind them, marking them as Silent Men.

"Shit," Tym said, tugging on the reins of the struggling horse. "There goes any chance at stealth."

"Here." Thrush tossed a sword at Danial and he caught it by the hilt. Then she kneed her horse, slackening the rein to chase after the riders.

Danial stared at the sword and then to Tym.

"Go get'em." Tym motioned with his head to the chase now outdistancing them.

Danial flapped the reins in one hand and heeled the horse into a sprint.

"They'll never catch them." Tym restrained his horse to a trot. He'd need to be ready for a quick turnabout. They'd have to come up with a different plan of attack, no longer being able to rely on a speedy rescue. Fucking Cacophony's guard would be up and—

Tym's jaw dropped. He caught a snippet of a song and then the ground shook just like it had when Thrush dug the grave. Dirt and stone exploded upward, consuming the lead rider and horse. The force of the concussion lifted them from the ground and they tumbled through the air, rock tearing through flesh and shattering bone in a series of ballista Tym had never witnessed. Both animal and man screamed while being shredded by the stone. Blood, innards, rock and stone rained down, scattering along the road. The remaining two Silent Men tried to stop their mounts from entering the blasted area. One succeeded, only to be tossed over the horse's head and the third horse slipped, crashing with the rider.

"Nazglum's nuts in a sack!" Tym couldn't take his eyes away from the slaughter. His horse tried to shy away, but he kneed it into a gallop.

Thrush rode past the downed horse and rider. The second Silent Man had gained his feet and was tugging at his sword when Thrush scythed his head off like chopping wheat. Danial was on the downed rider. He dismounted, kneeling over the man whose lower body was crushed by the horse. The horse screamed and thrashed its legs, twisted at unnatural angles.

The man tried to free a dagger, but Danial tore it from his hand and tossed it away. Tym watched it bounce in the dirt in front of his horse.

"Where is she?"

"Who are you talking…" The man groaned and tried to shove the horse off his lower body.

"Ivy! What did you do with her?" Danial pressed the sword to the man's throat.

Strangled laughter came from the man, followed by a coughing fit. He spat out blood and Danial hopped back.

"He doesn't know," Thrush said, wiping blood from her blade.

Danial growled and raised the sword.

"No!" But Tym was not close enough to stop him. Danial slammed the blade on the man's neck, blood splashing his face as he raised the sword again and hacked. Three, four times, and the man's head rolled free. Thrush dispatched the screaming horse with a quick slash to the neck. In a manner of moments blood pooled across the dry road. The remaining horse had run off, which was wiser than Tym, who stood there, words lost at the carnage.

Danial's chest heaved and he picked the head up, yelling inarticulate obscenities before he flung it out into the grass. He was spattered in blood, red droplets covering his face and running down his arms.

"Now you have to chase it down so we can bury it," Thrush said, nose in the air at the annoyance. Danial muttered and shuffled off to track it down. Thrush turned to Tym. "Not what you expected."

"It's not every day you see a horse fly through the air and rain down in chunks."

Thrush stared at him for a moment then turned away, singing her song. The ground shifted, and stones and rocks created a much deeper hole. After much grunting, shoving, and sweating, Danial and Tym managed to drop the dead animals and the remains of their riders in it. Thrush completed the task, singing the rocks and stones back into place. Tym's elbow was aching, but he managed to clamber back into his saddle.

"Still want to ride through the night?" Thrush asked. Her face didn't even look like she broke a sweat. Of course, she didn't have to do any of the heavy lifting, unless he counted the immeasurable amount of rock she pulled from the ground. Though, she did have a unique power Tym never would understand.

"I'm ready to go home now," Tym said.

Thrush laughed, a tittering sound, that was both pleasant and annoying to Tym. They rode around the fresh carrion mound at the side of the road. Another unmarked grave and Tym wondered for an instance if there would be people who missed them and wonder where they went, imagined horrific scenarios, but not quite the one Tym witnessed. Or would they be another pile of bones slowly turning to dust and forgotten?

Eventually, that's what we all become. Tym watched the sky. *I have to leave behind one good deed. If this is my legacy, then let it carry on with Ivy. Help her live.*

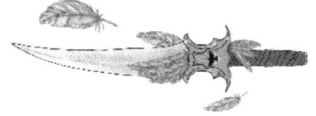

"Again!" Robin's voice reverberated off the buildings. Townsfolk glanced at her angry glare and kept on moving. The hapless soldier sent to rouse Thrush returned instead with Piper, who curtsied. The older woman stood before Robin, unflinching, used to her outbursts. Concern furrowed her brows and she frowned.

"Madam Thrush is nowhere to be found," the older woman said. "Nuthatch is out searching the fields where she might be doing whatever peculiar thing Madam Thrush likes to do some mornings."

Thrush was always doing something peculiar, especially when it came to observing various rocks and metal or even reading books discovered in dusty libraries. She never flirted with men or women. Her nose was either to the sky, ear listening to the winds, bare feet touching the soil, but not today. Today she was gone. Without a word!

I bet a gold sheeling that coward Tym and imbecilic Danial are not to be found, either.

"I really wish people would tell me when they're planning on sneaking off!" Robin hustled through the crowd milling around and living their small town lives while trying to forget that two armies battled in their streets not long ago. Blood stained the cobblestones. They parted like water before a solid rock, clearing a path to the small inn where they had been given rooms as a payment for driving off the army. Robin didn't bother to correct the proprietor that the army left on its own accord, since they didn't have enough coin to pay for the room and board and all the provisions needed to sustain their force. Should they survive, they would find their stores of supplies a bit lower.

Robin moved through the inn and threw open the door to Thrush's room. Sure enough, the bed was made up like it hadn't been slept in. Her rucksack was gone and so was her belt of knives and pair of swords—for such a small woman, Thrush was a walking arsenal of sharp blades and knew how to cut anyone who opposed her down to size.

There would be no note or indication of where she was going, though Robin wasn't entirely a fool to not know what Thrush wanted.

"You're going after the damned girl!"

I should've cut the girl's throat when she attacked me with her Song.

Thrush's obsession would drive her until into the mandibles of their enemy. Doing Nazglum's work for him. Robin slammed the door on the way out of the room. Soldiers hurried out of her path and Nuthatch waited for her in the lobby.

"Thrush is nowhere around the town," she said, not sounding the least surprised.

"Aren't you the observant one," Robin said, ignoring the girl's fluster and pouting lip. "She has taken off to get the girl."

"Again!" Nuthatch shouted, throwing up her hands in mock disbelief. "Why don't they ever inform us they are sneaking off! It'll make finding them that much easier."

Robin rolled her eyes.

"Get the wagons ready," Robin said and a soldier snapped a salute before leaving to follow orders. "We need to go hunt the fool woman and the fool girl. This is going to get ugly! Ugly, I say."

"We aren't prepared to fight what the Silent Men have to counter us," Nuthatch said, holding up a hand to halt the soldier. The man looked between the two of them, hedging his bets by shuffling closer to the exit. "We would be the fools to go running after Thrush. We need to get to the mountains, strengthen our numbers. Thrush knows what she's doing."

You would think so, but you don't know her like I do.

"She knows, which is why we need to provide back up support." Robin nodded for the man to carry on.

"Nuthatch blocked the doorway. The soldier glanced helplessly back to Robin. *Insufferable girl!*

"We cannot abandon this town to whatever fate awaits," Nuthatch said. "Cacophony may have gotten what he wanted, but that doesn't mean he won't come back here to finish off what he started."

"Yes, you are right," Robin said, waving the soldier away. He wandered to the far corner, awaiting the next confusing order. She moved close to Nuthatch, the smug expression on her face revealing her belief that she'd won this argument. "Since you are right, I'm going to put you in charge of fortifying the town against the next assault."

"What about you? You're not going after her, are you?" Nuthatch asked, smile fading. "We should wait at least half-a-moon."

"Someone has to save her," Robin said, and nudged past her, her larger hips easily knocking the waif aside like she was a leaf blown by a gust of wind.

"Then who will rescue you?" Nuthatch asked, following her. "We are rather thinning out here if you didn't notice. I don't want to be the last one singing."

"You will have to abandon the town and go to the Spearhead if I don't come back in a day or two," Robin said, heading for the stables. She ticked off everything she would need for the travels. They would take time to gather. Thrush had a day's lead on them. "Inform the Cardinal and Rail of what happened and that we tried to stop Cacophony's plans, but he has a way to truly silence us. I advise they continue moving east."

"How many guards will you take?" Nuthatch asked.

"My best chance to find her is to travel alone," Robin said and stopped. She sang a simple song—having access to it was like an orgasmic experience and she never wanted to be silenced again. The air thickened, collecting dust and dirt, creating a puffy cloud the size of her fist. The power twisted and tied off, keeping the cloud in its current form. "I will leave this as an indicator of my progress. If it disappears, you know I have been compromised."

"I don't like it," Nuthatch said, taking the cloud and releasing it overhead. It began to float off. "It is all too risky. Maybe we should leave now—"

"The risk has been taken and the problem exposed." Robin sung a note to stop the cloud's upward progress and tethered it to Nuthatch's wrist. "Without Thrush to find more woman with the ability to heal Discord, we will not last much longer. Nazglum will come for us all and there will be no safe place."

"If no place will be safe, then we need to strike the Silent Men from a place of strength and do as much damage as we can," Nuthatch said, trying to shake the cloud off, but it floated over her head.

"That will be something you can discuss with Cardinal." Robin entered the stables and talked to a man, giving him a list of supplies she'd need. "Don't dawdle or lightning from the cloud will strike you."

The man's eyes widened and he just about ran into stall doors to do Robin's bidding.

"What I'm saying is," Robin moved down the occupied stalls, examining the horses, "I'm going and you will need to decide on how long you stay here. If...no, *when* I return with Thrush, we will head to the Spearhead."

"Fine," Nuthatch said, crossing her arms. "Don't expect me to come looking for you. I'm fond of you all, but my duty is to Harmony."

"I wouldn't have it any other way," Robin said.

A thin veil of sleep slipped over Tym's exhausted mind. The things he'd seen in the last few days were enough to create a lifetime of nightmares. The dead and dying, his second decapitated body of someone who he hadn't exactly loved, yet shared the same blood. Neither Bryn nor Veena deserved that fate. His haunting dream wasn't of corpses, not exactly. It was back when he and Bryn were younger and their parents moved into the farm across from Veena, then Green and not Lyre. She would sit on the branch of a tree, watching him and his brother. She was always a pretty bird perched there and he thought she sang some lovely songs. Or maybe it was Danial's obsession with the nightingale that mingled with Tym's pleasant thoughts.

The lung rot came and killed many people, but she had survived. Veena was a fighter, the most beautiful girl Tym had known and he allowed her to runoff with Bryn. That was his biggest regret. When she entered his dreams, the hurt and betrayal raw on her face, holding the silver locket covered in blood, he groaned and flipped on his side.

"Why did you let my daughter go on her own?" Dream Veena asked. "You always let those you love run away from you."

"I had no choice," Tym muttered, though he knew the lie on his lips as soon as they came out. "I was hurt—"

"You are always hurt," Dream Veena said, stepping close enough to Tym, he could see the slash across her throat. "A walking broken-heart, not letting anyone close. Oh, you try to help, but as soon as it gets messy or difficult, you leave. You leave those who need your help and hide in your wallowing pain."

"Ivy isn't even my blood," Tym said. *Damn foolish thing to say to a ghost.*

"She should have been," Veena said. "She could've been our daughter. Then I would still be alive."

"That's not fair," Tym said.

"Being murdered in the road isn't fair," Veena said, lifting her chin to reveal the bloody marks on her neck where it had been reattached in life. She dropped her hair to cover the wounds. "Nor is abandoning a young girl to dangerous men *fair.*"

"It was *her* choice," Tym said, anger hiding in his trembling voice. "I'm trying my best to get to her."

"That's not good enough."

"I don't know what else to do?"

"Save her from everything." Veena leaned into him so he could smell her corpse breath, the dark dirt where she was buried, nothing more than bones now. Her flesh sloughed off on his cheek when she brushed him. Tym wanted to pull away in revulsion, but his heart told him he owed her this. "Don't let her get carried away by Discord. Don't let *him* have her. Whatever you have to do, she needs to be away from them to enter the Creator's light. Don't let her be damned like me!"

"How?" Tym asked, his voice cracking.

The answer never came. Veena was gone and he was swimming in sweat on the hard floor. He sat up and stared at the moon hanging bright in the sky, surrounded by stars. A cold breeze caressed his face. He lay back down. *All a dream.*

Then he felt something small, and rough in his hand. He looked down to see a copper chain in his fist. Tym dropped it like it was a hot iron about to burn him. He sat in the corner, spotted in moonlight, waiting for dawn. When the sun rose, it found him shaking, thinking about what Dream Veena had told him about getting Ivy away from both factions.

Even if I pry her away from the Silent Men, Thrush will swoop her away in her talons.

He ate little at breakfast and slouched in his saddle as they rode beneath the sun's glare. Danial didn't say anything, especially since when he tried, Tym snapped at him. "I don't give two shits about your mother or birds," he said and caught Thrush's raised eyebrow.

"Don't you start," Tym said when Thrush trotted her horse beside him. "Do you even know where we are going?"

"I do," Thrush said. "I sensed her power."

"How? I thought she was blocked."

"She was, but who knows what it means," Thrush said. "Cacophony is unlike any enemy we have encountered outside of the Tainted. He is smart, calculating, and unpredictable."

"Sounds like he is a rabid fox," Tym said.

"That's not far from the truth as you might believe," Thrush said. "I am concerned about you, Tym. How are you holding up? Will you be able to do what must be done when the time comes to confront your niece?"

"Confront?" Tym asked.

"I don't know what state we will find her in," Thrush said. "If he has manipulated her to abandon Harmony, then she will be dangerous. We cannot have a woman with her power walking around and creating more discord."

"Is that why you are here?" Tym asked. "To hunt her if she doesn't want to follow your fucked up rules?"

"No," Thrush said, remaining calm, which annoyed Tym more. How could she speak of killing Ivy like discussing the values of spiny-apple over bitter-apple. "I want to help her. You don't understand what the song can do."

"Oh, I can imagine," Tym said. "I've seen what you did to those soldiers."

"That was one aspect," Thrush said. "Your niece could enslave every single one of us, unless she is shown the right path. A madman manipulating her into a dangerous weapon is not in the best interest for any of us."

"What do you mean she could enslave the world?" Tym asked.

"Ivy has the potential to be the strongest Singer ever born," Thrush said. "Her song delves into people, and should she learn how to control it enough to push beyond her limit of one person, she could implant whatever she wants a group to do. From killing each other, to becoming her mindless devotees."

That was why everyone loved Veena so much in Welksdale? Did she manipulate them into adoring her?

276

"Ivy won't do that," Tym said and turned away from Thrush. "I won't allow it."

"There's not much *you* can do to prevent it," Thrush said. "Not unless you can make a difficult choice. Ivy or the rest of harmony."

Tym said nothing.

You always run away from the difficult choice, Veena's words still haunting him while awake.

"Not everything is as straight forward as you would like," Thrush said and rode on ahead.

"I won't fail you, girl," Tym said, though not sure if he was speaking to Ivy or Veena. He rode on, head down from the bright sun and tried not to breath in too much road dust.

CHAPTER FIFTEEN: TRIALS

The problem with the world is that there are so many people who think they are doing some form of good. What good is there when only a few people live in luxury, declared to be superior based on their birth. Nazglum knows birth means you suffer in a world without reason. Most people toil away in fields or on their backs, hands, and knees. All for the hope of one day seeing salvation. Swindling souls! Oh, the vicious irony. Nazglum is cursed promising eternal life, but people surrender theirs so easily, so willingly.

"Keep blowing on your finger until all the air is out," Sparrow said, watching Ivy's face redden with the exertion. She was almost crossed-eyed with the focus on her raised pointer finger, her cheeks puffed up and lips pursed as she blew the air out. "Slow it down. Not so fast, you don't want to pass out."

Ivy dropped her hand, and gave a disgusted grunt.

"These exercises are pointless," Ivy complained, laying back in the grass under the shade of a tree. A tree that Sparrow could sense with the thrum of her song in her chest, but not reach out to it. Cut off from her song was like being trapped in a glass jar. She could see it all but not touch anything. "What's the point of sucking the air in and blowing it out? It's not like we are actually singing."

"It's breath control," Sparrow said. "It trains your diaphragm so you can sustain the notes longer without giving in to their complete release. Have you ever swum with your head under water?"

"No. The deepest water, outside of the tub they threw me in, came up to my ankles," Ivy said.

"Well, it's like being able to hold your breath while working your arms and legs so you don't drown," Sparrow said. "Was there ever an instance where the song came out and you tried everything you could to pull it back?"

"Yes," Ivy said without elaborating.

"You know how dangerous that is for others, but it can be just as dangerous for yourself," Sparrow said, sitting beside her. "Especially if you get caught up in the dazzle of Harmony created when you sing. The wonder it creates as you connect to what attracts the song."

"Attracts the song?"

"Every Song is attuned to an element of life," Sparrow said. "For me, it is connected to plants and trees. My song attaches to their fibers. They grow as quickly as I need, fed by the Harmony around us."

"So, you are a gardener," Ivy said and laughed.

"That's one way of looking at it," Sparrow said, smiling. *She reminds me of Goldy.* "What are you attuned to?"

"People," Ivy said, and sat up on her elbows. "I can see into them, their memories, their desires, and then my Song shifts them around to create a new picture of what the song wants—"

"No!" Sparrow said, startling Ivy to silence. "Never give the song that much power. You can hurt someone. You could break their mind. Warp them beyond who they were and take their free will."

"Only if I want to," Ivy said and looked Sparrow in the eyes, anger and defiance present.

"Never do that." Sparrow resisted kicking her in the ribs. The girl had endured enough abuse without it coming from her. *Still, she is being molded by a monster. You cannot unleash her into the world all broken.*

"Why not? People have done that to me my entire life and without any more power than their fists and words and cruel stares," Ivy said. "Don't tell me your life has been perfect."

The lashing and bruising, casting Sparrow from her home. Her father calling her horrifying names, her mother standing by useless, allowing it to happen.

"No," Sparrow said. "It wasn't. My father liked to hit me."

"Then how can you still believe that we can save a world that wants us dead?"

Robin and Thrush could answer you better.

"To love is to lose everything."

"Don't you mean to live is to lose everything?"

Sparrow shook her head.

Finch, my love, I can't do this.
"We are done for today."
Ivy sat up.
"But we didn't do anything."
Sparrow stomped up the porch steps and was greeted at the door by a grinning Claiborne leaning against the door frame, arms folded, but one hand close to the hilt of her blade. It wasn't a friendly grin, but more like the kind of a cat ready to pounce on a bird's nest.

"She's being difficult," Claiborne said, stating the obvious.

"Well, she's right," Sparrow said. "This is absurd. Trying to teach her to sing well without a voice. Might as well ask a blind man to describe the colors around him."

"Or asking a man twisting in metal not to scream as he died," Claiborne said. The remark struck Sparrow as odd, but familiar. *Maybe Thrush killed her lover on the battlefield.* Sparrow didn't care enough to respond. "In the end, we all lose. But it doesn't mean we stop doing our duty. Once you do that then you no longer have a purpose."

"Is there a way I could be unblocked and actually show her?" Sparrow said.
Claiborne narrowed her eyes.

"I will ask the man in black, but I wouldn't count on it," she said, and moved aside to allow Sparrow space to enter. "You don't give your enemy two knives and expect not to get stabbed. I guess it's my turn to train our stubborn pupil. Oh, don't worry, I'm not as nice as you. We learn quicker from the bruises than coddling."

Sparrow watched Claiborne saunter down the steps.

"Get your ass up, girl," she said. "It's not nap time."

Ivy started to whine when Sparrow entered the house. The whine turned into a series of yips. *The girl would have to learn the hard way. I won't be the one to do it.* She continued into the house, a snippet of a child's song echoing from a room. The lyrics were not very appropriate for a girl her age to be singing.

Strip me of my gown
Lay me on the ground
Cover me in kisses
My cold skin misses

Sparrow stopped listening, the song churned in her gut and caused her skin to crawl. When she passed the room, Hyrian looked up at her with those unnatural blue eyes glowing in the gloom of the shuttered window.

"Glorian said Finch misses you very much," the girl said in a sickly-sweet voice. "She is cold and wants you to warm her body. Would you? If you could? Would you warm Finch's body?"

"Stop it!" Sparrow shouted. "Don't you dare profane her name!"

Strip me of my gown, Sparrow. Lay me on the ground, Sparrow. Kiss me there again. Warm my cold skin," the girl sang.

Sparrow stepped into the room, her fist raised.

"I wouldn't do that," a deep voice warned from behind her.

On instinct, Sparrow turned and reached for her song. It caught in her chest. Cacophony watched her crumple, clutching her stomach.

"Sparrow, you need to release this pain," Cacophony said, stepping closer, but not touching her. "I don't mean the pain from your song, but the pain of your lost love, of this Finch my daughter spoke about. Release this loss or it will consume you."

"I can't," Sparrow said, tears filling her eyes. "I can't let her go."

"Then she will always be a weapon to be used against you." His presence hung over her like a shroud. "Grief can be weaponized. It can be used to control you. Make you forget the person you were before it wrapped its thick tendrils over your heart and devoured what remains of you."

If I forget her, then she is gone.

Sparrow shook her head, whimpering.

"I know it's difficult. As difficult as having a wife and a daughter die in the same night. As difficult as having to choose one to return," Cacophony said, removing a metal gauntlet and touching Sparrow gently on the head. She flinched away.

"No."

"Let her go," he said in such a soft and convincing tone. His touch drawing out the hurt, the devastation in her like a poultice placed over a wound drawing out the infection. "She needs to rest. You have a task to complete. Harmony needs you. Ivy needs you."

"Nazglum take you all!"

Cacophony squeezed her chin, turning her face to his. She stared into his dark eyes and all sense of compassion disappeared. In its place was a dark void. His fingers compressed her chin harder, until she grabbed his hand and tried to pull it away. She couldn't pry them off.

He's going to crush my face.

Her song bubbled inside until she wanted to vomit it up.

She struggled to force him to release her. Hyrian gasped. The song pushed through the barrier. It sensed a weedy vine growing in the crawl space beneath the room. Sparrow forced as much of the Harmony into it before she was cut off. The vine burst through the floorboards, splintering wood between Sparrow and Cacophony, striking him hard enough to send him staggering backwards, his grip released.

Sparrow fell on her side, curled up against the pain, both in her jaw and in her chest. When she opened her eyes, the vine stood a green stalk between her and Cacophony. He reached out and gripped it in his gauntlet covered hand.

"How?" He crushed the plant, green fluid oozing over his black glove. He turned to Hyrian. "How?"

She giggled and held her doll out.

"Glorian says to play nice."

Cacophony took Sparrow by the arm, dragging her to her feet. He pulled her along like a disobedient child and shoved her into an empty room.

"We'll speak more on this later." He slammed the door shut.

Sparrow stared as the lock clicked into place, eyes wide.

Did I find a weakness?

Part of her hoped that was true. Another thought the girl was playing some kind of game with her and her father. A deadly game. She touched her jaw and flinched away at the pain.

I'm losing my mind, Finch. What am I to do?

Save Ivy. Came the response.

They swept her away in the carriage again. After the beating she took at the insistence of Claiborne, the gentle rocking on the plush bench was painful, keeping her awake. It was much better than sleeping alone and getting a visit from the shadow figure. She rarely found herself unattended. Cacophony offered her bitter tasting leaves which she chewed and they took the edge off the pain, putting her into a kind of half-sleep stupor. Hyrian's songs chased her dreams, flipping on terrifying image of bloodshed and death into another.

Disembodied voices of the men she had killed would laugh and taunt her.

"Sweet ass, should have let me poke you. No one wants a shriveled prick."

"No one could love you. I might be Fuggly, but you're a fucking monster."

"You're no daughter of mine, just some bitch's whelp. Worthless like the twat from which you crawled."

Ivy would wake, a scream caught in her throat and the power grasped like a drowning man clinging on to another for dear life, though she was still blocked. The snarling faces swirling around her, each laughing, yellowed teeth snapping and tongues lapping at cracked, bloody lips. She never felt refreshed after sleep and slogged through the exercises Sparrow set up for her to strengthen her control of the song without using the song.

"Where's Sparrow?" Ivy asked, noting the woman wasn't in the carriage. Sparrow would sit beside her, quietly watching, like Ivy was her experiment or something.

"She had a rather rough day," Cacophony said. "She needed some alone time."

Was it because I told her I hated the exercises? Did I annoy her that much? Why did she care? It's not like Sparrow was doing this out of kindness. It was rather difficult *not* to be kind with a knife to your throat. The woman really wasn't giving her anything useful, not that it was entirely her fault. One would need to actually have access to the song in order to use it.

"Oh, so I have a question," Ivy said. "I don't know if Sparrow brought this up, but it is hard to do anything practical without you know, being able to use our songs."

"She had mentioned it," Cacophony said, but he didn't elaborate.

Ivy lay back, thinking about the torture Claiborne had put her through, trying to teach her how to use a sword. Ivy took more of a beating than she had staying with Bryn.

"Why do I need to use a sword?" Ivy had asked, rubbing her injured wrist where Claiborne had smacked her and displaced the wooden practice sword. "I could convince them to stab themselves."

"Unless you are outnumbered. Might as well sing a song about kissing your ass goodbye." Claiborne tossed the wooden sword to Ivy. She missed it and it landed in the dead grass to the side of her, eliciting a heavy sigh and eye roll from Claiborne.

"Sword or not, I'd be in big trouble if I was outnumbered." Ivy picked up the sword and turned it over in her hands.

"The other women are trained in sword play, even though their power is more deadly than your own."

"Like who?"

"Thrush, for one. She is a master of her song and she uses the weapons she helped forge," Claiborne said, taking up her attack stance. "She can cut a person down, conserving her power for bigger things. Now, this is called *Heron* pose. It is good for making yourself smaller and less of a target, but allowing you the momentum to strike hard"

"How do you know about her power?" Ivy tried to mimic the stance, but it made her feel like she was an awkward bird dancing on a hot stone. She leaned back too far, mostly out of fear that Claiborne would smack her in the nose again.

"I used to fight for her," Claiborne said.

Ivy lowered her guard.

"Did you? What happened?"

Claiborne didn't bother answering. She swung the wooden sword, forcing Ivy to retreat a few steps or get whacked in the ribs. Her side already ached from new bruises where old ones had barely healed. Ivy managed to block a jab aimed at her chest, but the quick backhand smacked her forearm, deadening it and then Claiborne was behind Ivy, kicking the back of her knees out and placing the wooden blade across her neck.

"You're dead."

Ivy tossed the practice sword down and got back to her feet, rubbing the welt forming on her forearm. Claiborne took a bit too much enjoyment in abusing Ivy. It wasn't like she was training Ivy out of the goodness of her soul, but because Cacophony demanded it. Claiborne had a soul.

"Why don't you serve Thrush anymore?"

Claiborne eyed Ivy like a bug she wanted to step on.

"I'm not one for second chances. Pick up your weapon and attack me."

Ivy sensed Claiborne's hatred for the woman.

"What did she do?"

"Pick up your damn sword," Claiborne pointed her wooden practice blade at Ivy. "I won't tell you again."

Whatever it was, she wanted to kill the woman. Must be some kind of betrayal. Would explain why she detested Ivy so much. Ivy picked up the sword and studied Claiborne. There was no weakness she could spot. No matter how she attacked, she would get hit and hard. *Probably harder this time for asking questions.*

"Bring it, girl." Claiborne wore a sadistic smile.

Before Ivy could attack, hooves thumped from the road and across the dead yard, for which Ivy was grateful. *Someone must be looking out for me.* Foam lathered around the horse's mouth. The rider, a young man a few seasons older than Ivy dismounted and saluted Claiborne.

What tragedy did he experience? Curious as she might be, Ivy wasn't sure she could handle any more visions of death.

"First Sword," he began, obviously excited or shaken. "The other scouts didn't report in for two nights."

"Shit," Claiborne tossed the wooden sword and stalked off to the house. "Stay here. Both of you."

Ivy didn't try to argue. She looked at the messenger. His eyes moved swiftly from Ivy's chest to her face. Sweat matted his black hair and he ran nervous fingers through it. He gave Ivy a shy smile. Her skin prickled. *Don't get any ideas, boy.*

"What's your name?"

"Kristoff," he said.

"You know me, Kristoff?"

He nodded.

"You are the girl who sings," he said and quickly added, "not like the other ones."

"Other ones?"

"The ones serving the Dark Lord, trying to bring about an end to the rest of us."

The ideology bristled against Ivy. She narrowed her eyes and pursed her lips together, studying this young man. He may be of the sort drawn to a cause because he thought it was right. Even if it meant killing people he knew nothing about.

"You know I can see all your secrets, even the ones you are hiding from yourself," Ivy said and watched him stiffen, leaning away from her. "I can tell you to shove your fist down your throat and gag to death. Oh, you might fight it at first, but then your arm will lift all by itself and your hand will ball up. Then your mouth will pop open as your fist slowly inserts itself."

The young man clenched his fists and put them behind his back.

"Why?" he asked, eyes widening in fear.

"Because, I'm not like the others," Ivy said, enjoying the fear she had invoked. The power over him at the idea of what she could do. "They can rain on you, throw dirt at you, have plants attack you, but I... I make you hurt yourself."

He swallowed hard, looking up at the house.

"Ivy!" Claiborne stood on the porch. "Front and center, girl."

"Bye." Ivy smiled and wiggled her fingers at the boy. She hummed a tune, though without the power behind it, the song was just a song. He didn't know it and yelped, covering his ears. Ivy laughed as she ran up to the porch.

Cacophony stood on the porch, alone, and Ivy could tell he wasn't pleased. His eyes stared blankly, any warmth he had toward her was gone. He drummed his fingers on the wooden banister, a thinking gesture Ivy recognized. Finally, he spoke.

"Come eat, we will call it an early day." Then he went back inside.

The reason for the early day was clear with the bustle of the carriage ride. The reason they left must've had something to do with the missing scouts. From the few Silent Men she had met, it wasn't likely they strolled off to greener pastures. They were loyal to a fault. Someone or something must've got them. Given a hundred guess, Ivy would need only one: Thrush. Thrush was behind the disappearances, though Ivy would say it was a permanent removal from this realm of life. Who else could track her, even with her use of the Song that one time. Ivy wasn't sure if she should be annoyed that they didn't trust her, or pleased they cared enough to seek out a rescue. Either way, it explained the late-night travel.

And Cacophony's reluctance to let me use my Song.

She looked out the carriage window. A little moonlight shone through clouds. She didn't recognize anything other than the shadow of trees. There were no homes, no other markers of civilization. She was alone, isolated with Cacophony, Hyrian, and Claiborne. Yet, she hadn't felt safer at any point in her life, especially not after her mother was murdered.

"Where are we going?" Ivy asked.

The rattle of wheels on the hard road responded.

Ivy sighed and lay back, closing her eyes. If she wasn't going to get an answer, then se could at least enjoy the moment of peace. A moment disturbed by movement beside her. Then something pointy poked her ribs. She opened her eyes, squeaking at the ice blue orbs hovering close to her face. Hyrian pressed her lips close to Ivy's ear. Cool breath tickling her skin as Hyrian whispered, "Glorian says you are beautiful."

"Thank you, Glorian," Ivy said, uncertain of how to react without recoiling away.

"She says she's sorry about your mother and father," Hyrian said, settling in beside her. "It's not fair to have neither at such a precious age."

Precious age? Ivy never considered any age to be precious. They were all about surviving to get to the next day and if you did, you were rewarded with the chance to do it all over again. She had hopes that her then Uncle Tym would take her away to the big city and there she would find what life outside a small town would offer, perhaps a chance to do more than starve, but that would never happen. Both the city and her relation to Tym had gone up in flames.

"I'm sorry you lost your mother," Ivy said.

"She's waiting for me, for us."

"Us?"

"We are sisters, you and I," Hyrian said.

"Did Glorian say so?"

Hyrian smiled.

"No. I did." Then she leaned her head on Ivy's shoulder. "Sisters. Forever."

It wasn't long before Hyrian was asleep, clutching her doll in one arm and the other hooked around Ivy. Her breath became shallow in sleep. Other than lacking any real warmth, Hyrian sleeping on her was comforting. Ivy forgot the fear she had of the girl, and in that moment, both of them were a pair of motherless girls trying to make it through another night.

Sparrow was happy not to be placed back into chains. They had isolated her from Ivy during their night's venture, probably caused by Sparrow triggering her song, essentially leaving a trail for Thrush to follow—if Thrush was looking for them. Thrush knows the harmonic vibrations of Sparrow's song, having had tracked Sparrow by it on a multitude of occasions. Of course, Sparrow wasn't foolish enough to believe Thrush was coming specifically for her, but rather Ivy since Ivy posed the greater asset and greatest threat.

Cacophony was no fool, either. His goodwill was a façade, though, one that crumbled when she challenged his expectations. He knew they weren't exactly ready to have Ivy stand against Thrush, but she wasn't far off.

Sparrow would have a choice of her own to make about the girl.

That was a tomorrow, or the next day problem, as Finch often would tell her. *Don't fret about the storm clouds on the horizon, just enjoy the sun.* Sparrow stretched out on the bed, the morning sun bright through a clear, clean window. This new house they occupied was nicer than the last few they had squatted in. It didn't smell like corpses or moldy material covered in a century of dust. The bed had sheets that felt clean and weren't stiff. She swung her legs over the frame and went to the ceramic water basin, splashing her face with cold water. There was a floral carved bureau for clothes Sparrow didn't have—outside the black robe, they didn't give her anything else to wear. She put on the robe and heard a knock on the door.

It opened before she could respond. A soldier stepped in and set a bowl of watery oats sprinkled with some powder to help with the nausea created by the constant blockage of her song on the nightstand. Sparrow ate it because she needed to, not because she wanted it. Shoe glue would be tastier. To keep her mind occupied, Sparrow tested the barrier. She broke it once, by accident or design. There had to be a way to do it again!

I was out of my mind trying to survive. That didn't leave much room for recalling the experience other than not dying. *Maybe it was the girl who had saved me.* The idea wasn't too far of a stretch. She really didn't help Ivy much. The only reason she yet breathed was to complete her duty and train Ivy in a way neither the odd girl nor her father could. *Save Ivy.* The repetitive voice chimed in, frustrating because Sparrow was helpless, a bird with clipped wings.

The door opened again and a sour looking soldier took her bowl.

"Cacophony wants to see you," he said and waited for her to follow him.

This is different. He usually comes to see me.

Sparrow followed him through a wide hallway, past several closed doors until they reached what would be a large bedroom. The bed was twice the size of the one in her room and it didn't look as though it had been slept in.

I wonder what happened to the former occupiers.

Cacophony stood with his back to her, broad shoulders squared and arms behind the cloak. A military man if she had ever known one.

"Leave us," Cacophony said and the soldier saluted, marching from the room. He waited, and several heartbeats went by, leaving Sparrow to wonder if he had forgotten about her. Then he spoke. "Last night was a lapse in judgment. I reacted poorly because I felt my daughter was threatened. It was not my intent to cause you harm. You see, Sparrow, I rather watch the world burn than lose my daughter a second time. She is a gift to the world, as much as Ivy is a gift, but unlike Ivy, I cannot save Harmony with my Hyrian. You must understand that when you threaten her, you are attacking me and all existence."

There's no reasoning with madmen and zealots who believe they are saving the world. A quote by Robin that has stuck with Sparrow through the years. Sometimes she wondered if it applied to the Singers as well.

"I know you have no faith in me or my daughter," Cacophony continued. "You believe we intend to destroy Harmony, to unleash the Dark Lord into the world. I don't fault your assumption, not when you have seen my actions and have been rudely captured and treated more like a prisoner than a tutor."

"The chains were a nice accessory, but they don't go with my current attire," Sparrow said.

"Well, you shouldn't worry about those precautions we took in the beginning," Cacophony said and gave a raspy laugh, like the grating of rusty metal together. Then he turned to face her. His muslin cloth was down so she saw the scar on his lip, like a wild creature had tried chewing his face off. He smiled, which was made more gruesome by that scar, like how a corpse might grin welcoming her to death. "To prove my goodwill, Sparrow. I'm going to grant the request to allow you limited use of your song to prepare Ivy for challenges yet to come."

After what happened last night, this wasn't exactly what she expected.

"Thank you." The words were hesitant and she waited for the conditions of his goodwill. The cost, since nothing was ever free.

"There will be provisions, limitations on what you can do," he said. "The first being you may cause no harm to my daughter or any of my soldiers."

She noted he didn't include himself.

"The second is that your song is not to be used to help Ivy or you escape. You will strictly sing to teach and advise Ivy," he said. "I do not know how much time you have before we need to make choices, so be wise in how you spend it."

"A third?" Sparrow asked.

"There is no third," Cacophony said. "Go have fun and, as my daughter said, 'play nice'."

With that said, he dismissed her.

Play nice. None of this was nice. Was she caught in some dream?

Sparrow went outside by herself. No guards followed. She was able to go about as though she was a free bird. *But the cat's eyes were lurking.* She doubted Cacophony would let her fly from her cage so easily. This was a test of sorts. Sparrow blinked at the bright morning light. The place was different from the rest, it was all so green. A variety of trees and shrubs still green as though the drought had not touched this part of the land. The grass was lush as well, a deep green. Wildflowers sprinkled across the fields and Hyrian held both of Ivy's hands, dancing her around in a circle, laughing and giggling. A moment where they were children being children. Not two wildly strange and beautiful beings that could destroy Harmony. Ivy noticed her and waved her over.

"Good morning, Sparrow! Have you ever seen so much green?" Ivy asked, joy dancing on her face.

"Yes," Sparrow replied. "I grew up in a place such as this… only less decadent."

"Oh, there's something here you have to see," Ivy said, offering her free hand while Hyrian held the other. "Come with me."

Sparrow didn't argue, but allowed Ivy to lead her to a place on the south side of the house. She pointed out a metal post and spigot surrounded by high grass. Ivy released her hand and went to the handle on the pipe.

"Watch," Ivy said and pumped the handle. Water dribbled out of the spigot. "Have you ever seen anything like this? It's drawing water from the ground! No bucket to dip into a stone well or drag from the stream. It's just bop and bop," she demonstrated by pumping the handle on each bop, "and there we have water! Like magic."

"It sure is," Sparrow said. "I have another good news."

"Oh, I know," Ivy said. "We can use our song together."

"To play nice," Hyrian said in such a serious tone, Sparrow shivered.

"Well, if you are done playing with the water, we can begin," Sparrow said.

Ivy pumped the handle twice more, laughing as the water splashed the grass, adding to a little marsh started there. They moved back to the south side of the yard, there Claiborne waited for them, peeling the skin from some piece of fruit with a knife. Hyrian skipped over to the woman, who shied away when the girl tried to take her hand.

"How will we know when it works?" Ivy asked.

"I'm not sure," Sparrow said. "Let me try something."

She reached for her Song, feeling it rise from her stomach to her throat. *Easy, don't push too hard.* She let it out in a slow release to prevent a wave of nausea. The grass responded, leaning into her in anticipation. She sensed their roots, their fibers, the sun coursing through them. *Now or never.* Sparrow released her song and the grass began to dance, stretch inch by inch, vibrating with Harmony. Tree branches creaked and sprouted new buds that reached for Sparrow's song as it caressed them. Sparrow smiled, thrilled at having this connection.

"That was beautiful," Ivy said, her mouth hung open in awe, her hands folded together over her heart.

"Always remember, that beauty is destructive, if we allow it," Sparrow said.

"How? It's just grass," Ivy said.

"Here's a demonstration," Sparrow said and let her song flow across the grass beneath Ivy's feet. It grew rapidly under the song's insistence, wrapping around Ivy's leg. The girl screamed and tried to break free, but the grass knocked her to the ground, opening the black robe and exposing her naked skin. Sparrow cut off the Song and offered her a hand. To the side, Claiborne smirked and Hyrian clapped.

"Again! Again!" she screeched.

"Please don't," Ivy said, her face flushed as she re-adjusted the robe around her. "I understand better now."

"We always have to be aware of the dangerous our songs may pose to others," Sparrow said. "Now, I want you to try delving me with your Song."

"Delving?"

"It's what you do when your song sinks into a person, to hunt out something specific," Sparrow said. "I delve into plants rather than people, which is more simplistic."

"Well, let me try," Ivy said. Rather than ease her song out, it came in a powerful rush, a burst of music and Harmony that gripped Sparrow, tried to claw its way inside her. Sparrow countered it with her own, the grass grew rapidly and wrap around Ivy's torso, throat, and mouth, cutting her off from her Song. The claws immediately stopped. And Sparrow released her song.

Ivy spit and spat out the grass.

"Why did you do that for?"

"You need to have control. To be gentler," Sparrow said. "You don't need to grip me in a fist to be effective. Like blowing on your finger. Try it again."

Ivy nodded, took a breath, pursed her lips, and slowly released her air. Then she sang. It was one of the sweetest, most heartbreaking songs Sparrow had ever heard. The notes caught her attention, getting her to think about Finch and how they used to lay beneath the trees, stroking each other, and exchanging kisses. She never wanted to leave those moments, to hold them like precious breaths of air. Fingers intertwined as their bodies flowed against each other until— Then the song ended, and Sparrow felt dampness on her cheeks.

"Who is Finch?" Ivy asked.

The girl did it. Sparrow felt both a thrill and horror.

"A woman I loved deeply," Sparrow said, dabbing at her eyes.

"She is…gone?"

"To love is to lose everything," Sparrow said. "Looks like you are a quick learner."

"I think it's part of my survival experience. If I didn't learn, I would get hurt," Ivy said, and took Sparrow's hand. "I'm sorry you lost her."

"We can't save everyone," Sparrow said.

"Want her back?" Hyrian asked.

More than anything.

"Hush, child," Claiborne said. "We all lose people we love. But, we are losing daylight. Enough of these feelings and shit, get to work on singing. You have an hour and then she's mine."

Ivy groaned, but Sparrow touched her on the shoulder.

"Ready to try again?" Sparrow asked.

Ivy nodded.

Then her Song delved into her and Sparrow wept.

Days passed and Ivy felt her Song grow. Not only her Song, but she had improved with the sword. Improved in the way a baby improved not falling on her face with every step, but at least she received fewer whacks and bruises. Confidence and control in her Song thrilled Ivy the most. She pushed through barriers Sparrow had built. Deep within she witnessed Sparrow's abuse at the hands of her father. Ivy almost recoiled in horror, the experience mirroring her own. Then the memory of the younger Sparrow turned to Ivy and said, "Don't trust Cacophony. He isn't your father. Not the nice guy he projects. He takes pleasure in murdering Singers; I think he murdered Finch." This distraction allowed Sparrow to use countermeasures to again knock Ivy from her mind, throw her to the ground and seal her up in the grass until she couldn't breathe.

This is her moment, she's going to kill me! Ivy couldn't wiggle or move any part of her. She would simply be swallowed by the grass. A grassy tomb without the marker. The grass slithered off her face and took a gulp of air. Sparrow stood over her, looking Ivy in the eyes and said, "always be on your guard."

That night at supper, Cacophony set down his knife and fork. Ivy sat on his right side and Hyrian to his left. Sparrow was down further with Claiborne at her side. He glanced around the table, a pleased expression on his face.

"We are doing the Creator's work. I imagine him smiling down on us, his agents of Harmony," Cacophony said. "You should all be proud. Especially since we have shown that enemies can be friends...no not just friends, but family."

He took Ivy's left hand and Hyrian's right, squeezing them both.

"Family."

"A strange one at that," Claiborne muttered.

"We serve together, we survive together, and we fight together," he said, releasing Hyrian's and patted Ivy's hand, engulfing it in both of his. "There is another test. One of strength and endurance. Tomorrow morning, we will learn how far you truly have come."

Ivy looked to Sparrow whose lips were pursed together.

She doesn't think I'm ready. Annoyance bristled in her. People always underestimated her. Though, Ivy knew Sparrow had her reasons. Always besting her in the Song. *For now. I will have to prove her wrong.*

That night, Hyrian came to her room. She climbed into bed beside Ivy and placed her doll, Glorian, on Ivy's chest. The doll was kind of creepy, button eyes that seemed to stare with a horrified expression of surprise, like she was shocked, and the black string mouth curved upward in the smile didn't help sense the doll might be a little mad.

"Glorian wanted a hug for good luck," Hyrian whispered.

I doubt Glorian wants anything from me except maybe to strangle me in my sleep. No matter how she might want to feel revulsion toward Hyrian and her doll, Ivy was happy to have both beside her, then. Loneliness had a way of lowering her tolerance, or maybe she was just getting used to the girl. Then Ivy realized something.

"She has your mother's name," Ivy said.

Hyrian nodded.

"Because my mommy's *in* her."

"Like a ghost," Ivy said.

"Something like that," Hyrian said. "Will you make a doll of me when you kill me?"

"What?" Ivy asked, looking into the deep blue eyes. There was no humor or teasing in them. She was sincere, or so Ivy thought.

"That's why you came to us, isn't it? To end the thing causing the song block?"

"Yes, but..." *But what?* "But... I didn't know it was you or that you were anything more than a creepy ghoul child."

Hyrian giggled. "Ghoul child."

"Well, you are pale and have those ghostly blue eyes. Is that normal?"

"You're not normal," Hyrian said.

"I'm sorry, I didn't mean to hurt your feelings."

They lay in silence and Ivy thought she had dozed off.

"I love you, Ivy," Hyrian said.

"Love you, too," Ivy responded and she meant it.

Hyrian snuggled close to her and didn't feel so cold anymore.

Is this what it was like to have someone care about you?

Sparrow's words stuck to her: "To love is to lose everything." She let the words wrap around her heart like a blanket to snuff out the flicker of hope for love. She had lost enough to fill an ocean with sorrow.

When Ivy woke, the girl was gone. It could have been a dream. Then she sat up and Glorian thumped to the floor, button eyes smiling at her. Ivy carried the doll with her, wandering through the house. It was empty. She looked out the window and saw the reason.

Outside everyone waited for her.

Ivy walked out and saw Hyrian.

"You left this last night."

Hyrian giggled and hugged the doll.

"She protected you in your sleep from bad dreams."

"Yes," Ivy said. Sparrow raised a brow, but Ivy ignored her.

"The sun has risen and so has our young friend," Cacophony said. "I see you have gained favor and I hope after today you will see your value to this family."

"Thank you," Ivy said, "but is there another outfit I can wear besides this black robe?"

"Would you rather fight naked?" Claiborne asked.

"In good time, my dear," Cacophony said, handing her only an empty waterskin. "This is just a test. A way to improve your skills for the challenges ahead. Get to the stream a few hundred yards from the house before the soldiers get you. There will be four of them hunting you. Their orders are to subdue and return you to the house, which means they will try to hurt you using wooden staves and other non-lethal weapons. You will have full use of your song for this trial. Try to control it and not kill my men. Get the water and come back. Understood?"

"I understand," Ivy said.

"One more thing," Cacophony said. "Do no harm, Ivy."

Claiborne stood in the corner, arms folded, and frowned. Ivy read the disagreement on her face. He was giving her so much freedom. Ivy could turn on them, kill the soldiers. Maybe even kill him. The idea had crossed her mind, but the image of the soldiers in dark blue burning down the village, slaughtering his people while they ran, and the little girl burning…maybe he was right. Robin had smacked Ivy when she tried to delve her, threatening to kill her the next time she tried. What were the important secrets Robin was trying to keep hidden from Ivy? Maybe of her betrayal and slaughter of the very people she sworn had to protect. Including Cacophony's wife and daughter in the village.

Cacophony had allowed her inside. Risked his life to give Ivy a picture of why he was fighting. Risked her knowing about Hyrian and placed his life in her hands. Who was she to say he was bad because he killed a few people? Ivy had killed four to save a man who abused her and then sent her away. At least Ivy could respect Cacophony, despite his faults, and felt his deep sorrow. They had a connection, a thread shaped through loss. Here he was, giving her a chance to grow in her power and not smother it. Free, though with some restrictions. What father didn't restrict his child especially when dangers were involved?

Sparrow stood close by and the warning rumbled through her thoughts.

He isn't your father and don't trust him. You're an orphan and must learn to take care of yourself. She could learn more about her power, control it before it controlled her. *Play by his rules, for now.*

"Then, go, Ivy! May the Creator bless your trial."

Ivy ran out into the trees.

"Do no harm," Ivy repeated, stepping lightly in bare feet. The evergrow needles crunched no matter how soft she tried to walk, giving away her position. Sunlight filtered through the branches, taking away their advantage as well. She'd spot the black armored men and women before they got a jump on her. The undergrowth benefited greatly from the rain. It had been dying between the trunks, but the sluice of water fed it, brought it back to life. Thin vines crept up along thin trunks, hiding thorny brambles. Ivy heard the stream ahead, but had to choose a different path instead of battling the invigorated brush. She kept her feet moving, following a winding path, maybe a deer or other woodland creature broke it to get to the water, or maybe it was the former home occupiers, possibly a girl like Ivy who enjoyed dipping her feet into the cool water on such a hot day.

Ivy almost didn't see the wooden staff swipe in front of her, forcing her to dive forward. A short man stepped out from between the trunk of an evergrow, reversing the staff and thumping it into the ground where her head used to be.

They will try to hurt you.... No shit!

Alright, Do no harm! You are in control.

The song rose from her chest, bursting out in a sorrowful tone. The man froze, staff held in a jab pose that would have taken Ivy square in the chest or throat if he'd missed. A single name echoed through the vision, Hollin, and a beautiful face of a young girl, smiling so dimples showed in her cheeks. The smile changed into a scream of terror as men held her down and tore her clothes. They wore non-descript armor, meaning this man could've been the one to cause her harm. *Dirumpis;* the word repeated in Ivy's song. A language inherent to the song, but held no meaning to her beyond, forgotten after spoken, but they did the job. The man's arms twitched, taking the staff in two hands and bringing it across his knee. The wood snapped and he held two halves.

Confodere te commanded the lyrics and the man raised a jagged edge to his throat. Then the image changed and she saw him, holding the same girl, Hollin, who had screamed. Hollin was silent, now. The man opened his mouth and gave a breathless cry. The girl could've been his lover or his sister, but she was dead in his arms, throat slit and pale face staring up in terror.

Desine! Desine! The staff ended under his chin. The song wanted him to continue pressing the wood through his flesh until it tore through the soft tissues and up through the roof of his mouth...a horrific death. *Do no harm!* The power changed, shifting and shaping words. *Somni* repeated softer and softer until the man dropped the broken staff and lay in the grass, head down, and began to snore.

"That wasn't so hard," she whispered, wiping sweat from her brow. The power thrummed inside her chest, resonating through her limbs. Her mind was tired, but only a little. Her body was renewed, ready to sprint down the lane and soak up the water. What gave her pause was the tragic death she had witnessed in the man's memories. What happened to Hollin? Was she killed by Thrush, Robin, Nuthatch, some other Singer Ivy had yet to know about? She shook her head.

"Don't think, just move."

Ivy found the stream at the end of the path. Part of her hoped there would be another soldier waiting to confront her. She was curious what vision she might find. Each man and woman joined the Silent Men for a reason. They rejected the vision of Harmony the women had offered. She wanted a glimpse into why. Why did they despise Singers so much? She had an idea, but the picture needed to be broader. Deeper. Her curiosity remained unsatiated.

The water was cold on her feet and soaked the edges of her robe. Ivy sloshed into the stream, took the waterskin and bent down to fill it. She didn't sense the person coming up from behind her. Hands grabbed her shoulders and shoved her face first into the cold water, scraping her hands on the stones and she nearly lost the waterskin to the current.

Cold stream water filled Ivy's mouth and she sputtered, twisting to face her new attacker. A woman with long blonde hair grinned at her, hands gripping Ivy by her black hair and dunking her under the water again. Ivy struggled, beating against the hand and she was yanked up, Ivy gasped for air.

"You're such a weak kitten," the woman said and dunked her under again.

Cacophony didn't say anything about drowning, which Ivy knew would happen unless she did something to save herself. The power remained in her, though she couldn't sing underwater, not without taking in a lungful of stream. She let the woman force her to the bottom, then kicked her feet out and hooked them around the woman's left leg. Drawing her knees back, she knocked the woman off balance. The pressure on her head released for a moment. Ivy dug her heels into the stones and shoved with all her strength. She drifted to the deeper part of the stream. The current dragged at her robe and Ivy untied the knot and let it come free, shaking it from her arms. She exploded from the water, standing nude under the shimmering sunlight like some goddess in an ancient myth rising from the tides to exact her revenge.

Ivy hacked and coughed and spat out thin tendrils of water, watching the women regain her footing

"This pussy has claws," Ivy said, cringing at how bad the phrase sounded. *Need to work on the snark.*

The woman brought up two wooden staves the length of short swords. She took a few steps before Ivy released the song. It sank into the woman and she hesitated. Unlike the man, she fought against the power, shoving through like trying to move a great wall. The song found a crack in the barrier and slipped into the woman's memories. She flipped through them until a vision appeared. A young girl handed a sword by an older man. Fear and excitement lit up her face. This was what she had spent long mornings waking up early, all the bruises and humiliation of being told she was a girl, and she shouldn't play with swords…"unless a boy puts his in your hand." The laughter, spitting curses at them. "Protect your mother," the older man had said. "I'll do my best, da." Then the image shifted to a body carried on a shield wearing the black armor of the Silent Men. The older man's face was there, but ruined in a way Ivy couldn't tell how it was done, but it wasn't done by a sword or arrow.

"Get out!" The woman sloshed closer, a wooden stave swiping at Ivy, missing by a hair's length.

I'm indulging too long in the vision. The song intensified and she inserted a command. *Discedite a me tergum.* The woman stopped and began to back away. Ivy repeated the phrase in her song until the woman retreated to the shore. Her eyes bulged, but she could no longer resist the command. Once she was out of the water, Ivy changed the song, telling her to go to sleep. The woman curled up in the grass and closed her eyes.

"That's two," Ivy said and swiped her wet hair from her face. Then she remembered her goal. The waterskin and her robe were both slipping away in the current. She lunged for the skin, grabbing it before it got further away. Then she tried to find her robe. It wasn't around—the current must've stolen it. She was losing out on time.

Priorities. She filled the waterskin and sloshed through the stream to the trail, water dripping from her. There was nothing to cover self in. *They'll have to get me new clothes now.* The idea of the men's eyes ogling sent her skin crawling. *It's too late to worry about modesty. Good thing it is a warm day.* She stepped over the snoozing woman. Further up the trail, the man snored loud enough to chase away curious wildlife. She felt like a timid rabbit knowing a fox was out there, waiting to pounce on her. She watched the evergrows, brambles, and shrubs, listening for a rustle of leaves, a snap of a branch, the crunch of a boot. Muscles tensed to jump or duck. The waterskin was heavy in hands, sloshing around louder than she liked. At the end of the path, she was exposed, a length of grass and nothing to hide in. But there was the house, so close at the top of a small rise.

Maybe I lost them. That didn't sound right since the trail was a simple one. They had to be there, waiting for her, somewhere. *All I need to do is make it to the house and I win.* Ivy took a breath, bent her knees, and looked around. Again, there was nothing but open ground.

The house. Get to the house

She took off at a sprint.

I will prove Sparrow wrong. I am strong enough to handle—

Three running strides and something sailed from behind an evergrow, striking her shoulder, knocking her off balance with the waterskin. She slipped, skidding on prickly needles, and hit the ground. Stones and twigs scratched up her bare skin on her thigh and pain spiked her left shoulder. She sat up, seeing the trickles of blood along her forearm and leg and she wanted to cry.

"Fuck that hurt!" She sucked in the pain, nearly losing her grasp on the song. Like a second heartbeat, it pulsed inside.

Footsteps pounded behind her. Ivy spun on her bottom and saw a man running at her. He had a wooden club and a shield. Ivy unleashed the song, not as strong as before, but enough to halt him in his tracks. He didn't fight back like the woman, and Ivy was fine with that. She delved into him, pulling out images of the man marching in formation. Another soldier was caught up by a vine, lifted high into the air and pulled apart at the waist, blood and intestines raining down. Ahead of him another vine ripped through the chest of another soldier, splattering him with blood and chunks of bone and heart. Ivy felt queasy at the sight of such destruction. The image continued and Ivy watched as more men had arms and legs pulled off, the fear building and then…pain.

A face floated in front of her.

Sparrow.

It was Sparrow's song tearing those men apart.

Ivy gasped. Then something heavy struck her across the forehead, rocking her head back and sending blinding pain across her eyes. Her song stopped and she was cut off from the man's memory, expelled like a broken tooth spat from a mouth.

She fell over in a pile of needles. Sharp points pricking her cheeks.

This is how I die?

Claiborne stood over her, wooden staff pressing on Ivy's chest.

"You indulge too much," Claiborne sat and whacked Ivy in the sternum. Ivy grunted, unable to draw breath. "You allowed yourself to be caught off-guard." Another meaty *whack*, and Ivy rolled over on her belly to escape the beating. "You would have died, should be dead." Two more thumps on her buttocks. "Learn from this, or you'll never sing again." A last hard *whack* landed between her shoulders. Then Claiborne's boots slipped away from her sight. Ivy squirmed in the dirt and needles, trying her best to breathe through the pain. Her entire body was one ball of anguish and she couldn't get up. She lay still and closed her eyes, trying to grab the power. It wasn't even a glowing ember and she found only darkness.

I failed! I failed!

Ivy remained in the dirt until well past midday. Anger, embarrassment, and frustration filling the void where the power once thrummed. Claiborne took advantage of her instead of fighting fair. She wouldn't make that mistake again.

Another pair of boots came into view. Hard, calloused hands lifted her up like she was nothing more than a rag doll covered in dirt and needles.

"What did you learn today, Ivy?" Cacophony asked, pressing her against the cold, hard shell of his armor.

"Not to get distracted." The words came out muffled and croaking. Her throat was dry and nose stuffy from crying in frustration. *Also, I will kill Claiborne.* The last part she kept to herself.

"That is a good lesson," Cacophony said and carried her inside. He lay her on a straw mattress. Sparrow sat beside her and Ivy wanted to cry.

"I guess you want to gloat," Ivy said.

"No," Sparrow said. "You did well, but—"

Cacophony returned carrying a jar full of something strong smelling and began tending her wounds. Ivy wanted to curl up, hide her nakedness from him. The soothing balm he spread over her bruises relaxed her stiff muscles and she was just angry, rather than ashamed. "Be more efficient in your song when you think you might be outnumbered. Strike them down first, then if you have time, seek within them what you want to know."

Ivy nodded. It was advice that everyone was telling her. Bryn used to say, "advice is only as good as shit spread to help things grow. If nothing did, then it was wasted on fallow ground." As far as Ivy was concerned, she was growing more from the bruises and beatings than the words. Telling her to do one thing, may sound simple, yet, if they knew what she saw, she wondered if they would be able to look away?

"There was so much pain," she said.

"You took a beating, which I did warn you," Cacophony said.

"No, not me, them." Ivy's body did hurt, but it was the emotional wounds, the hidden scars she had peeled back from the flesh and bone of the men and woman she had delved. So much death and caused by people like her. Fresh tears in her eyes, she whispered, "We are monsters."

"In someone's memories we are," Cacophony said. "Our best hope is that history doesn't recall our names and shudder."

Ivy knew in her heart that if she delved every one of the Silent Men, she would find one connecting thread. That thread would lead back to the same group of women weaving that thread into a story shaping the world. If the horrors she witnessed were the narrative, Ivy then would use her abilities to recreate a new story.

She looked over at Sparrow who seemed impassive, disconnected. She was part of the problem.

"I will do better," Ivy said.

"That is all we strive to do." Cacophony closed the dusty curtains, shutting out the sunlight. He placed the waterskin, still full of stream water, beside her and left Ivy alone.

CHAPTER SIXTEEN:
CONFRONTATION

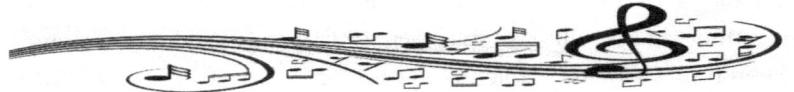

When an opportunity is presented, a gift for a better existence, not just life—life is brief while eternity is much, much longer— rejecting the offer is not something the Dark Lord will easily forgive. Given the choice of eternal life or a painful, humiliating death, the choice was obvious. When the time to choose confronts those whose mortality is significantly brought to the forefront, it is best not to think what you might do in the situation. Not when your blood boils, and skin begins to melt. Pain is a great convincer.

Robin studied the colored ribbon tied to the branch. It was intentionally left there by Thrush—she knew Robin would figure out what she was doing and marked a trail. The ribbon was red, which meant she was heading west on the road and the way it looped around before becoming a double knot, told her that she would stay on this course for a while. This after a yellow ribbon, which meant to go north, and a blue which turned her south, like a drunken path. A pile of rocks on a stoop at one abandoned house told Robin they had stayed there for one night, then a yellow ribbon to say west.

How much further are they ahead?

When she came across the shattered ground stained with red, she knew they had met trouble, and in Thrush fashion, she buried it, or rather, *them.* Thrush was the most powerful Singer in the way she could use her song to create and destroy. If she said the girl had potential to be stronger than her, well, that was saying something.

"I have to save you from your own foolishness," Robin said, taking the ribbon and climbing back into the saddle. They were roaming in areas where the drought hadn't taken as much of a toll on the land. Water ran in thin streams, growing wider at some parts feeding trees green with leaves, though the sun's hot glare punished her. She sung up a little cloud for shade. It also served to tell her she wasn't in the silencing cone. Being silenced for a short time was the worst feeling she had experienced, outside of the betrayal by the Tainted One, Raven. He had twisted her heart around his finger and crushed it while getting her exiled from the Nymphalidae Court and her cousin Reginald almost took the Chair, but instead his plot, that ended in her father's death, was thwarted—though his coin paid to arm and provision the Silent Men out of spiteful vengeance to kill her.

Robin had yet to come across any Silent Men, well, not any living, thanks to Thrush. She had enough food for another few days. Then she would have to turn back, with or without her Coloratura. *Preferably with!*

"Where are you all going?"

The trail had to be what Cacophony had led them on. Somehow Ivy was using her song, which meant Thrush could track her. Which also meant that Cacophony was allowing the girl to use it, possibly in some sort of training exercise.

This could all turn out bad. Really bad.

Maybe if they caught up to the girl and the Silent Men they could talk some sense into her and see how far she may be corrupted, lost in a manipulative world, a young girl abandoned and desperate for attention, like Robin was once. Hope remained as long as Ivy proved untainted.

Creator, please watch over Ivy. Keep her from being taken in by your enemy.

Despair tried to claw at her heart. Robin knew the only way she could be of use was to continue pressing forward until she couldn't anymore.

Kristoff stood in the kitchen, drinking from a cup of water. Claiborne listened to his account what he found close to where they had stayed the first night. The man had haunted eyes. Knowing Thrush's power, Claiborne could understand the man's unease.

"Flies swarmed in the area and kept crawling along the dirt," Kristoff said. "The ground was thick with blood and bits of entrails stuck to the stones. It was like the ground opened its giant mouth and claimed their bodies, while leaving their own gore as their marker."

"What do you think?" Cacophony asked.

"It's her for sure," Claiborne said. "She is a destructive bitch. Plus, she has an ability to track other women when they use their song. I know we have been shuffling around, but as long as the girl is allowed to use her power, we might as well hang a sign and giant colorful banners announcing where we are staying."

Cacophony nodded. He looked down the hallway where the girl was kept, a child's song singing about stars shining bright in the heights and eyes of a true love. Claiborne appreciated the change in topic, but it still sounded fucking freaky in the little girl's voice.

"I think maybe it is time," Cacophony said, he rubbed his chin. "I'm hesitant, though. Do you think she is ready?"

Are we ever ready?

"She is strong," Claiborne said, and shrugged.

"That doesn't answer my question."

She sighed.

"Yes, with her power she could create a real problem for Thrush, turn her into a weapon for the Silent Men, maybe," Claiborne said. "Her ability isn't to be questioned. It's her willingness."

Cacophony dismissed Kristoff. Kristoff gave Claiborne a knowing look, one of caution, not that Claiborne needed it. She had seen Thrush's work up close too many times.

"I think she has seen enough of what those women did to our people to convince her that maybe she should re-consider their offer of help." Cacophony's eyes took on a glint that told Claiborne he had planned it all. The trial was more than to test her strength, but to change her resolve.

They were all chosen because of the pain they had suffered by the Singers. A devious and well executed plan. Ivy did seem quieter around Sparrow. Cacophony walked down the hall, past the door where the girl was singing. Ivy sat legs crossed and they were playing a hand slapping game, forming patterns.

"Besides, I think she is getting used to her new sister," Cacophony said.

"They are something else," Claiborne said, just not adding in that thing included being abominations. Both of them.

"Talk to Ivy. Tell her what she is about to do," Cacophony said, and then turned his attention to the girls in the room. "Hyrian, my love."

"Yes, father," the girl said, dropping her hands into her lap.

"Come help me with breakfast," Cacophony said, holding his hand out to her. The girl leaned in and placed a little kiss on Ivy's cheek and then went to her father. Claiborne gave Ivy credit for not flinching. *Huh, maybe Cacophony is right and they are getting along like close siblings.* She waited until father and daughter were out of sight, then entered the room. Ivy got to her feet and had a defensive position. *Smart girl. Don't trust the hand that hits you.*

"Remember when I said there will come a time when you will have to prove your loyalty?" Claiborne asked.

"Before you beat the shit out of me, yes."

"Here's your chance," Claiborne said. "Several of our scouts went missing. I believe, and Cacophony concurs, that we are being tracked."

Ivy perked up,

Oh, this is going to be easier than I thought. Claiborne smiled.

Tracked! A thrill of excitement prickled across Ivy's skin. There were only two people she knew of that could track her. One was the child, her tiny hand gripping the large, black gauntleted-finger as they moved down the hall.

The other was Thrush.

"You know who it is," Ivy said. *Thrush, it must be her. Robin wouldn't spit on me if I was dying of thirst.* Was Danial with her? He was one for keeping promises. She hoped he wasn't, since she didn't want to hurt him again. Thrush could've come alone, to bring Ivy back. The problem was that Ivy was happy where she was, despite the beatings. *There's nothing there for me to go back to.* Except Danial, her heart said. But, he was better off without her. "The only reason you're sending me is because you think there might be another Singer involved."

"Almost certain of it. You won't be going alone," Claiborne said. "I don't want to send you at all, especially since you're not ready. That decision isn't up to me. I listen and obey." She glanced at where Cacophony had returned, his bulk filling the doorway. "Myself and six other Silent Men will be accompanying you."

The role of nanny continued. Ivy was sure Claiborne wouldn't be more than a step away from her—*within stabbing distance.* Thrush found her, but that didn't mean she was here to rescue Ivy, though that was how Claiborne made it sound. Like they were manipulating Ivy and probably continued to do so until she was firmly in their grasp.

"Ivy, you will have full control over your powers," Cacophony said.

"Huh!"

"I'm trusting you," Cacophony said. "You have proven yourself so far, and this, this will be the final test."

"Hyrian—"

"—will be right here with me, waiting on your successful return."

Ivy didn't know whether to laugh or cry. Bryn hardly trusted her with more than a few coins to buy them food.

"This is a trial run," Cacophony said, placing a hand on her shoulder. "You know what that means?"

Ivy nodded.

"Do well and you will have a permanent place at my side." He went silent and, in the silence, the unspoken threat clung close like the rot at a graveside never truly covered by the perfume of flowers. Betray him and nothing would remain of Ivy. He lightly squeezed her shoulder, catching her eyes. Something like admiration was there, though Ivy couldn't be sure. She hadn't had anyone look at her with more than disdain in a while—except Danial, and she guessed it was more of her doing than his true feelings. "Remember, do no harm."

"Do no harm," Ivy repeated.

Cacophony stood and offered out his arms. The gesture was also odd. Ivy almost balked, fearing those great arms might crush her. Then she reacted on impulse. Ivy hugged him.

She should be disgusted after all he had done, but he was the only honest person she knew, owning up to his faults and his failings. She believed him about wanting a better world, restoring the harmonies, and after seeing the pain Thrush and the others caused him—not just him but all the other Silent Men she faced—she knew his cause was justified. Ivy would help him create his vision for a better world.

He is not your family, do not trust him. Sparrow's warning returned, but she pushed it aside. As far as Ivy was concerned, he was family. Were those tears on her cheek? She stepped back and dabbed her eyes.

"Let's go eat, shall we?" Cacophony asked, his eyes also shiny and his voice a bit thick with emotion.

Sparrow was noticeably absent from their breakfast. Ivy imagined it would be an awkward meal since they did plan on attacking one of Sparrow's friends. It was fine that Sparrow wasn't there. Less guilt over what Ivy had to do.

She's a part of it all, too. She has as much blood on her hands as any of those women.

"Not very hungry?" Cacophony asked.

Ivy twirled her spoon in the bowl of soup.

"I'm a little nervous and kind of excited," Ivy said. "I don't know what to expect. What will happen if Thrush refuses to give herself over?"

"The time will come where you will make a choice," Cacophony said.

Didn't I already make one?

After they ate together, he handed her a pack.

"Be safe and think," Cacophony said.

"I will." *Full powers! To go up against Thrush!* What if Thrush came to save her? What if Danial and Tym were there? *If she cared, she would have come long before now. All she'll want is to control me. Control my song.* No one had ever given Ivy a choice—even her mother had left her alone rather than ask her to go to Euclid. No one, except for Cacophony. He trusted her. He loved her enough to let her make mistakes.

"One more thing, Ivy."

She looked at his eyes, serious, yet shimmering. He pulled down the muslin so she saw his wound again. Raw, pink flesh drawing taut as he smiled and said: "My name is Hyman. I wanted you to know it. To know the man behind all of this," he said, indicating the hard shell. "Come back to me when you finish."

Ivy nodded, her throat closing over an overwhelming spring of emotions. *Don't cry! Don't you dare cry.* She turned away, wiping a tear from her cheek.

On the way out the door, Claiborne asked, "You've ridden a horse before?"

"About that…." Ivy's cheeks flushed. "Horses and I've never gotten along."

Claiborne sighed.

"I guess that's why I got you to show me these things," Ivy said, hoping to cover the embarrassing revelation. *Not my fault the dumb beasts fear me!*

"Horses hate you." Claiborne shook her head. "Is there anything that likes you?"

Hyman does. Did he tell you his real name? I bet he didn't. Ivy stuck her tongue out at Claiborne's back.

"You'll ride with me, until I can teach you to be on your own." Claiborne said, stepping into the stirrup and swung a leg over the black destrier's saddle. She turned a disgusted look on Ivy, reminding her of how her father—*Bryn, his name is Bryn, not my father*—had when she didn't move quick enough or messed up a simple soup by not adding salt when salt wasn't available. "I swear, child, you better learn. I can't fucking hold your hand to do everything. I mean, you know how to piss and wipe properly on your own, yes?"

"Unless you have better way to show me," Ivy said. "I think I can handle it."

Ivy approached the horse, but when she got close, he stomped his foot, lips peeled back and teeth clicked a finger's breadth from Ivy's nose. Claiborne jerked the reins so the horse's head turned away at the last instant and dug her heels into his flanks.

"Hurry your skinny ass up here, girl," Claiborne said, grabbing Ivy's arm and pulling her into the saddle behind her. "You almost lost your face."

Ivy hugged Claiborne around the waist as they began riding. The smell of resin and leather strong in her nose. It wasn't long before her tailbone ached from the bouncing and her thighs burned from clenching the flanks. *I'd rather practice a full day of sword than ride another heartbeat on this thing.* Her heartbeats quickened, then steadied once she realized she wasn't going to fall off. She loosened her grip on Claiborne and felt the power in her chest grow into a comforting blaze. A sweet song hummed in her throat, the words there on Ivy's lips. Ivy smiled, pressing them together and let the song play in her head.

I'm in control, and no one will be harmed.

Unless I want them to be.

I should have married. Tym let the thought slip through, imagining he would be very comfortable in a modest house, hot meal on the table and a couple of children yammering on about who-broke-what and whining about chores while his beautiful wife scrubbed the dishes—in his mind she was the exact copy of Veena, though not her since she was dead and he wasn't into sleeping with dead things. With a living wife, at least, he'd have a warm body to sleep next to rather than Danial snoring on the hard pallet they'd found, and Thrush, well, she slept so very little that Tym wondered how she could stay upright in the saddle.

He watched Thrush, her white robes garnished in dust and a strand of hair straying from their tight braids. Black circles formed under blue eyes, marring the tireless, wise demeanor that heightened her beauty. In this state, she seemed real, not this unapproachable force of destruction, like hugging a landslide and getting crushed under the weight of debris. She was a fallible woman, thin necked and sharp-nosed, one who Tym could fantasize touching her tiny mouth and wonder what other songs she knew.

"Do you… ugh… ladies ever marry?"

Thrush stiffened in her saddle.

"Never mind, you don't—"

Thrush held up a hand which was meant to be a sign for silence. Tym figured that out on the first day when she told him what it was and said to shut his mouth. She was forthright, the kind of woman who would punch him in the gut if he protested the ill-manners, or someplace lower due to her impeccable reach and short stature. No, she was not someone he wanted to upset. Not unless he wanted to get buried ten yards below the surface in a fallow field. Tym wasn't ready to be buried just yet.

"She's close," Thrush said. "I can feel her moving."

"Away?"

"No, to us."

"Maybe she escaped," Danial said, hope rising in his voice.

"I don't like it," Thrush said. "It's like a wave of fire coming to consume us. We are nothing but kindling in its path. How did she grow so strong in such a short amount of time?"

"We can ask her when we see her," Tym said.

"It might be better if I go alone," Thrush said.

"Uh-uh, no way," Danial said. "I'm coming along."

"I mean, why wouldn't you want us there?" Tym could think of two reasons: test her to see if Ivy was returning with them or kill her if she wasn't. No matter what, he owed it to the girl to help her out of this messy situation.

"Promise me you won't get in the way," Thrush said.

"That depends on the situation." Tym read the annoyance on her face. "I will get in the way of anyone trying to hurt her. Seriously, she is a lost girl who has nothing left in this world except her voice. You really think she'll trust you? So, unless you are there to welcome her with open arms, then I can't let you fuck her up any more than everybody else has done. It's just not fair or right."

Thrush clicked her tongue.

"*Fair* and *right* are words lacking any true meaning in the world we live in, Mister Lyre," Thrush said. "Otherwise, you wouldn't have told her a thing about her father and mother. Since it wasn't necessary for her survival, and in fact may have caused more harm than good."

"She would've found out," Tym said.

Thrush made a dismissive noise.

"You don't know how important a father is to a little girl." She raised her chin and heeled her horse away from Tym.

That jab hit close to his heart. *Fuck, but women are cruel!* Tym wasn't about to let her have the last word and heeled his horse to catch up to her. "Ivy never knew hers and my brother was an ass. A stinky, crusty, shit-dangling ass."

"You took that away and made it seem like her mother abandoned her to the abuse," Thrush said, and glared at him with her piercing eyes. The words she spoke sounded more like a confession buried beneath the chastisement. "That she wasn't wanted, until now. The man who has her desires all of us dead. Ivy is more than capable of handling that duty."

"It's not my fault some twisted cocksucker is manipulating her because she has daddy issues," Tym said, though he flinched a little at is harsh words. Damn it! This woman was strumming his annoyance strings. "I did what I could to provide for her family. I did a lot of shitty things, but this…this is her choice and I'll help her see the error narrowing everything down to two choices. She can't stay with either of you. I'll take her far away. You can all kill each other, but leave Ivy out of it."

"I didn't expect you to understand. Patience is the bane of rash actions. I will try again. One last time. And if you are too simple to grasp the gravity of the situation, then Creator help rid the world of foolish men," Thrush said, looking down her sharp nose at him, like he was a small boy and she was some giant statue of King Maximus. "There will be no world left unless we stop Cacophony and the next deluded, righteous murderers who come after him. We need to restore the balance and all you talk about is "right" and "wrong" and "fairness." These are nonsense words made up for children to teach them not to kill each other. At your basest nature, you are all animals who must feel the crack of the whip to obey. If you understand one detail, know it is this… we are past civility."

The crack of her whip could shred people. He didn't think either that power or the sharp edge of the sword made anyone civil. Just dead. Dead people could be buried and forgotten.

He opened his mouth to tell her this when she put up her hand again.

"I've heard enough foolishness. Save us all the folly of your primitive thinking and just keep quiet."

This, Tym ground his teeth, *this is why I never married.*

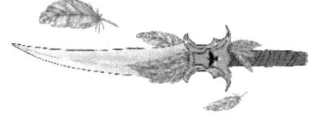

"Three riders less than a league ahead," Kristoff said, avoiding eye contact with Ivy. She felt bad for scaring him, but at the same instance, he needed to know Ivy wasn't the same as the others. Hyman understood that, and he was the only man she met who tried to understand her rather than assume they knew anything about her. "Two men and one woman."

Claiborne gave an excited curse.

Thrush! She must've sensed me, especially now that I have access to my song. The other two had to be Danial and Tym. *Please let it be Tym.* They were the only people in all of Welksdale to give a damn about her. The rest could rot.

"Do we lay-up and wait for them?" he asked.

"Lay-up and wait?" Claiborne asked, annoyance unveiled and full of teeth. "Do you see any place to lay up?"

Yellowed fields flashed hints of green, flowers and grass eager to take advantage of the last rain blasts provided by Robin. Ivy imagined they could hide in the grass and try to ambush them when they went past, but for two problems obvious to even her. Their black armor would stick out like a blemish on a blood fruit and most importantly, the biggest problem was Thrush sensed Ivy, like how she found her in Danial's farmhouse. Might as well stand in the middle of the road, waving her arms.

"No," Kristoff said, cheeks turning red.

"Then we stay the course," Claiborne said, "unless you want to return and explain to Cacophony why you abandoned a commanding officer."

Fear crossed Kristoff's face and he paled.

"No, ma'am."

"Watch my flank and wait on further orders."

Kristoff hung his head, joining the other riders in what looked like a spear point with Ivy and Claiborne at the point.

"Do we need so many?" Ivy asked.

"Ask me later if you cannot subdue Thrush."

"Subdue, you mean you want me to kill her?"

"I'll snap your thin neck if you do!" Claiborne growled and grabbed her arm, giving it a twist. Ivy squeaked more out of surprise than pain. "She's mine and I won't let her have a quick death. She doesn't deserve it, not after what she did to…"

Ivy waited for Claiborne to say more, hoping to catch a glimpse into her anger and determination to kill the woman she once served. The silence stretched out and Ivy assumed it was a betrayal too deep to speak about. She pitied the woman, not that Claiborne would want it. Ivy was a tool for her to get revenge. A tool to be discarded once it served its purpose.

"I won't," Ivy said.

Claiborne considered her a moment, gave one final squeeze, before releasing her.

"Do what you have to in order to knock her on her ass," Claiborne said. "But leave her breathing."

Letting Thrush live would mean betraying Hyman. If Claiborne failed to end the woman, then Ivy would be complicit in every act of horror Thrush committed afterwards. Ivy wanted to trust Claiborne to kill Thrush. Or maybe Ivy could kill Claiborne, end the fighting by removing everyone involved. There were no good choices. Ivy would be cast out, alone in a world that had abandoned her like her mother, father, even Tym and Danial left her to her fate. No, Thrush had to be stopped and then she would deal with Claiborne if needed.

"Do no harm," Ivy whispered.

Then there was the issue of Danial and Tym. As excited as she was that they came to "rescue" her, she knew it was a bad idea. Cacophony made that clear. *I'll compel them, maybe even erase their minds so they forget about me.* She had done it to Danial, made him think she was his friend when they were about to kill each other. She'd do it again. For their own good. Let them live on in blissful ignorance.

"I'll give you Thrush," Ivy said, "but I want your word that you'll not hurt the other two. They are harmless. I'll convince them they are better off not knowing me, or looking for me."

"Give me Thrush and I don't care what the fuck you do to the others," Claiborne said. "But you belong to Cacophony, don't forget that. He'll never stop looking for you if you betray me. He doesn't like being played for a fool. Especially not for a silly girl, doesn't matter how powerful you think you are."

"I know where my loyalties lie."

"We'll see soon enough," Claiborne said.

Their shadows grew long when they crested a hill. Thin clouds draped across the edges of the sun. Nervous energy bounced around in her with the power, demanding to be unleashed. Restless, she couldn't even walk to let out a bit of the tension.

I have to pee.

Claiborne took out her spyglass.

"I have to pee," Ivy said, wiggling in the saddle.

"You better do it fast, because here they come," Claiborne snapped the eyeglass closed. "I hate for you to get caught with your ass hanging in the wind."

Ivy's heart quickened and her stomach twisted. The urge to urinate went away. She slid from the saddle, nearly falling when her legs remembered their purpose to hold her up. Keeping a wide berth from the destrier's teeth, she stopped at the hill's crest. She saw the three riders, and became light-headed. There they were, Thrush in the lead. Danial riding with his head down and Tym bringing up the rear, looking sullen.

"Hey!" Ivy shouted.

"What are you doing?" Claiborne said and Ivy heard her draw her sword.

"Seeing if they can hear me," Ivy said. "Then I can end the fighting before it even begins."

"Hey!" The word rolled down to Tym. One of the happiest words Tym had heard in such a long time. He looked up and was about to wave, but Thrush growled back at him.

"Don't respond," she said. "She's testing us."

"She knows we are here," Tym said in frustration. They had found her alive and well, again. Why shouldn't he be excited to see her?

Thrush shushed him.

"I won't allow your stupidity to get me killed." Tym felt a blade poke into his side. "If she knows we can hear her, she will try to use her song. It may or may not influence us, depending on her strength, but I don't care to find out if she has the range to use it. I know my limits, and we aren't close enough."

"I didn't think—"

"Of course, you didn't," Thrush said, leaning in and keeping her voice low. "When I say so, I want you to look up and act surprised. Shout your head off. That way, if she does start to use her song, I can do something about it."

"Is that, Ivy?" Danial asked extremely loud, his voice resounding off the hill, and he pointed at her.

So much for acting surprised.

Thrush moved her blade away and heeled her horse into sprint.

"Ivy!" Danial laughed and whooped. "We're coming to rescue you and listen to the nightingales."

That was when Tym heard Ivy sing for the first time and he wanted to do nothing else in the world but sit there and let the song consume him.

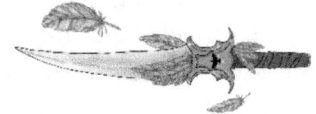

Was that a wave? Ivy squinted at the figures at the bottom of the hill. She wasn't sure if he was signaling her or swishing a fly away from his face. The song burned in her throat, but she kept it locked inside. She had one chance at this. If she missed, then they might escape her, and Claiborne would make a mess of things. As it was, she took a huge risk standing on the hill where they could see her. Thrush had her head turned, talking to Tym. *I would give anything to be privy to their conversation.* Thrush worried her the most. Ivy had no idea what Thrush could do with her song, besides forging metal as Claiborne had mentioned. Ivy had to wait for the right moment to unleash her power, test her strength against this older, more experienced singer. Robin had resisted, but that was when she had no idea how to control it; when she thought she could wield the knife like it was a giant axe to fell trees and when she was not as strong to lift the handle.

What do I have? She eyed Thrush. *I guess I'll find out.*

Claiborne grumbled behind her, something about giving up their position too soon. The three would be up the hill soon enough. And Ivy—

"Ivy!" Danial shouted and began to wave his arms while Thrush rode her horse up the hill.

"Here we go," Ivy said and set her feet. She opened her mouth and the song flowed out, a happy, excited sound that reached out far, as far as her lungs could push it. The melody brushed against Thrush who was also singing. Ivy expected a struggle, like two opponents locking hands and trying to push the other back, or simply one would overpower the other. Thrush's song deflected Ivy's, the way a stone would deflect water, forcing it to pass around her. Ivy sensed it touch Tym and branch out to Danial.

A light flashed in front of Ivy's eyes, carrying conflicting emotions: warmth and sadness. The images appeared, split before her. She saw Danial weeping in his barn, crying over his lost animals, the man who she believed once to be her uncle speaking to the man Ivy grew up believing was her father. "Let me take her to the city one time," Tym said while loading the wagon, but Bryn shook his head, "won't have her whoring around like her mother." Then the image shifted. Danial stood over a man, hacking his neck with a sword and to Tym kneeling in the road beside a headless corpse. They were two different locations, she didn't recognize where Danial was, but in the background of Tym's image was the place she used to call home. The headless body she knew.

Bryn is dead. The thought crept in, breaking her concentration for a heartbeat. It was long enough to lose the strands of her song. The ground started to tremble off to her right. Claiborne shouted orders and horses gave terrified whinnies. Their hooves thundered round Ivy as they hurried to escape the tremors. Ivy took a few steps, arms covering her head and avoiding the frightened mounts. Ivy thought she was clear, but then the ground exploded. The force of the concussion lifted her momentarily from the ground and then she fell. Her hands scraped on the hard stones, the palms burning as the skin was sloughed off. Clumps of dirt, pebbles, and larger pieces of stone rained around her, and she covered her head, seeking the power. It was there, but out of reach, lost in her fear and confusion. Several smaller stones struck her, but none were big enough to cause more than a bruise. Ivy coughed, wiped dust from her face, and spat grit from her tongue.

"What the fuck was that?"

Her question was violently answered. Silent Men raced down the hill. The ground rumbled once more and huge chunks of stone and dirt exploded from beneath them, tossing horse and rider aside like there were nothing more than specks of dust riding a windstorm. Other horses tripped in the holes, legs snapping, and painful shrieks followed. Claiborne leapt off her destrier right before the ground beneath him turned into a gushing fountain of dirt and rock. The horse screamed, flying through the air and landed far behind Ivy in a meaty thump and cracking of bones. Claiborne rolled to the grassy edge of the road, away from the last two horses charging at Thrush.

Kristoff led the way, sword raised. The ground exploded behind his horse, taking out the other rider in a spray of stone, flesh and blood. Ivy tried to sing, but the dust made her cough, and the song was there and then gone. Kristoff reached Thrush and swung his sword. Thrush met his blade with her own, turning him aside and allowing him to ride past.

Thrush did this! She killed these men and horses with her song. So strong, so dangerous.

Ivy took a deep breath, using the distraction to start her song, and struck Thrush. Her verse tried to take hold, bite into Thrush, but the woman spun on her. Thrush had more practice, her strength greater than Ivy could imagine. *She won't beat me.* Again, her song shoved at Ivy. She caught a glimpse of Thrush standing before one of her soldiers. Her song twisted the metal of his dark blue armor, shaping it into a layer of flesh. Then it went horribly wrong. The man started to shout, but Thrush tried to correct her error, extract the metal from his skin, but it had forged into his bone, peeling away flesh, and rather than fall away, the armor contorted. Ivy and Thrush heard the snap of bone, the screams from the man grow louder, mixed with that of another woman. Thrush had ended the song, but the damage was done. Nothing much remained of the man, but a lump of twisted metal and his head, streaming out incomprehensible words, with the occasional, "kill me" and "end it." Ivy saw the woman's face. Claiborne. She stood frozen at the sight of her broken lover.

"End her, Ivy!" the shout from somewhere outside the vision. "Knock her flat off her horse."

Kristoff rode up behind Thrush, sword ready to plunge into her. Ivy diverted her song to him. His arm went slack. There were no past images from him, but his intentions were visible. She saw ideological hate flowing from him, running out in black tendrils and the joy at being the one to kill one of Nazglum's whores. Only that joy turned to fear as Thrush hooked her sword through his arm, deflecting the killing blow and ripped both riders from their horses.

"She's mine, damn it!" Claiborne stumbled from the grass, drawing her long sword.

Thrush crawled to where Kristoff lay on his back. She had a dagger in her hand and plunged it through the young man's neck.

"No more!" Ivy shouted, returning her song on Thrush.

There was no resistance, and Ivy had seen enough of what the woman had done. A single word repeated: *Somni! Somni! Somni!* Thrush twisted the dagger, sending a final gush of blood from Kristoff's ruined throat. Then she released the hilt and tried to stand up. She wavered on her feet and dropped beside the man she had killed.

Ivy's song weakened and then dried up in her throat. Exhaustion extinguished the flame of her power. She watched from her hands and knees while Claiborne rushed toward Thrush. Claiborne was a few steps away when another figure crashed into her. Ivy's eyes widened. Steel swung, plunging into flesh, blade slicing.

"No! No more!"

Rage consumed Ivy and like breath on embers the power flared up, reinvigorating her body and her song.

I will end this!

Tym watched the explosions in a kind of stupor. He could tell something was wrong, that his memories were being shuffled through like flipping paper. He was back at the house reliving the discovery of his dead brother, holding his head and staring at the empty eyes. Then he snapped out of the hold. Tym blinked and shook his head. He could see Danial doing the same.

What the fuck was that? Like my life was being torn from my head!

The noise of battle snapped into perspective. People shouting, the ground exploding, people dying, horses dying, screams all around. One rider broke free, closing in on Thrush. She turned his blade aside and he was riding right at Tym. Tym had recovered a blade from the Silent Men Thrush had killed earlier and fumbled it from his belt.

"No, you don't, fucker." Tym deflected the blade, the impact rattling down to his elbow. Tym's tunic tore, and he hissed, the sharp edge slicing a red streak across his ribs. He lost his balance and toppled from his horse. The air was knocked from him and he moaned, wondering how he got himself into these circumstances. *I used to be smart*, he groaned, tucking his leg beneath him as his horse chose that instance to make a dramatic exit.

Metal rang out and Tym watched Danial's valiant effort to defend him. Neither were trained with a sword, let alone on how to fight without your boots touching the ground. There was a curse and slap of steel and a thud. Danial landed on his backside hard enough for Tym to hear his teeth click together.

"Get up, or get trampled," Tym said, groaning and pushing himself to his feet.

The fucker had turned his horse back around. His next target had her back to him. As much as Thrush annoyed him, he didn't want to see her stabbed through the back because that would signal the end for Danial and himself, not to mention Ivy lost to the cocksucker. Tym began to run, not away from the fight, but to it. "Son of a whore!" His stiff leg burned with each forced step. There was a loud screech, and he watched the man and Thrush yank each other from their horses and fall into a crumpled heap. Tym didn't bother to wait to see who killed whom.

"She's mine, damn it!"

Tym saw a woman in black armor running at Thrush.

Popular lady, sure knows how to make enemies.

Thrush pulled a knife from her belt and jabbed it into the man's throat, several times.

Well, no helping him. Then Ivy began to sing and Thrush dropped over. *Please say you didn't kill her, Ivy.* Even if Ivy hadn't, this woman was nearly there to finish the job. Tym forced his burning legs to run faster, the scar on his calf pinched and burned. He realized too late he was unarmed. If the last time he was in a battle taught him anything, it didn't matter if he had a weapon. Tym executed his most effective move, one he swore would kill him one day, and leapt at the woman. In the back of his mind, he wished he had the shield. Fortunately, she was smaller than the last guy. He wouldn't bounce off of her. He hoped.

Striking the black metal armor was again like running into a wall, one which collapsed easier, but was just as painful. Tym spread his arms out and as soon as he hit her, he closed them, pinning her sword arm to her side, his weight and momentum sending them both skidding across the dirt road.

For a second time he had saved a life by using what he thought of as the flying grapple, a move he planned on using on his wedding night, should he ever have one. The downside to the flying grapple was its singular purpose and had no follow up. He landed on top of the woman, her armor digging into his chest and driving the air out of his lungs. When they had stopped gouging grooves into the dirt, the woman punched Tym in the face, sending a tooth into the back of his mouth, where he swallowed it. She kneed him in the groin like Tailorson always said his horse had stomped and the agony must be close to what the former Tavern owner referenced, since they did feel flattened and shoved deep into his gut.

If Tym had to choose which day was worse, he'd say, if he could speak instead of groan, this day, by far, exceeded Euclid for the worst. The woman shoved Tym off, watched him crawl around like a worm flopping on a hot stone.

"You could have left well enough alone and lived," she said, grabbing Tym by the back of his tunic and lifting him enough to jab her long sword into his gut, forcing it to cut through some vital organs on its way out his back. Tym vomited at the pain. It was like she jammed a torch inside of him. The vomit he noticed was dark red.

"Wanted to save her," Tym said, curling against the blade, like it was the only thing keeping him together.

"You failed." The sword ripped out of his back and gut, carrying bits of chucky flesh and spouts of blood.

"Ivy," he groaned, shivering in the road.

"She belongs to Cacophony now," the woman said. "If I let her live long enough."

"No! No more!" The shriek sounded from a distance too far away.

Then the air filled with song, one so full of sorrow and pain. It stunned Tym and he forgot he was dying. He listened, tears filling his eyes and bloody snot trailing from his nose. The woman's long sword clattered to the ground in front of him and a heartbeat, or lifetime, Tym could no longer tell, the woman fell with it.

Hands found him, gentle hands, touching his face and chest. Squeezing his hands, like they were trying to hold his life together. A crumpled face framed in long, night black hair, face blurry and wet and dripping lines of spittle. The most beautiful sight Tym could have in this ugly world.

"You weren't supposed to die."

"I'm not." Tym coughed and spat out richer, darker blood. He no longer felt his body but seemed to be floating. "Sorry…you…." He wanted to apologize for not saving her from Bryn, to tell her to live on, to run away from the silent war, but the words refused to leave his tongue, stuck in the blood.

"Don't die." Wet breathy, close to a whimper. "You're all I have left."

The desperation hurt him deeper than any other wound, knowing he was beyond the pleas of a young woman, the little girl he'd abandoned though he knew the truth. Beyond the help of any except the Creator.

Was I good enough?

The sun darkened and Ivy's face dimmed. He took one, long breath of this world and—

Was I good enough...?

CHAPTER SEVENTEEN:
REGRET

The loss of the old life can lead to regret. The people you once knew and loved are lost to history. What remains is eternal existence, slumbering, waking to a new when. Being left to discover the world order and who to manipulate. The old life was easy. This new one is full of complications.

Ivy held Tym while he died, his fingers slipping from hers. His blood stained her hands. The smell of it permeating her robes. He didn't have to die. She was going to send him and Danial away. Ivy closed Tym's eyes, though she wondered what he last saw and if that was the reason he smiled. He was still, so still, and once again she saw how death was close to sleeping. The subtle breathing of Claiborne and Thrush separated Tym from the border of living and death. Those two would wake, but he never would.

I can rectify it! Put an end to the bloodshed and fighting. Ivy looked at the dagger in Thrush's belt. One of many weapons attached to a woman who was also a weapon. The violence from her song was astounding, turning flesh into metal, a man into a lump of indistinguishable creature of broken steel. The devastation wrought by dragging up rocks in such an explosive manner would be frightening enough. How could a loving Creator allow such a being to exist? How could Ivy allow her to live on to tear more lives apart? She reached for the dagger, drawing it from the sheath. The handle was crafted from bone, silver tendrils running through it in veins from pommel to quillon. Such a beautifully crafted tool used for such an ugly business.

She is asleep and won't feel a thing. Ivy held the blade over Thrush's throat. It would be a merciful act compared to what Claiborne would do. No hacking off limbs, or breaking bones, or slicing off tender parts while awake and alert. The dagger's edge was sharp enough to peel back the skin and let her life-blood water the thirsty ground.

Do no harm! Ivy had agreed to this mantra, believed in it to the point where it had almost destroyed her. She couldn't do enough. Wasn't strong enough to protect those few people she cared for. They got hurt, died because of her. And Claiborne, she broke her promise. Ivy heaved a wet sigh, looking back at Tym.

Should never have come for me.

Ivy set the tip of the dagger on Claiborne's neck. A bead of blood bubbled and spilled over the unstained steel. This was better than she deserved. She had beaten Ivy, bruised and humiliated her, all forgivable offenses which taught her valuable lessons, but killing the last good man in Ivy's life, she didn't think even the Creator could forgive such a betrayal. *Bitch deserves to be buried up to her neck and sugar water poured over her head, left for the ants to eat her.*

A hand touched Ivy's shoulder and she spun on her heels. Danial took a step back, hands up to show he was unarmed.

"Ivy," he said, gentle and compassionate.

She stared at the dagger in her hand, red tip aimed at Danial's crotch. A low growl rumbled from her throat through gritted teeth. The confused expression, child-like and full of hurt, dragged her from her violent thoughts. Her blood-stained hands trembled, and the dagger clattered to the dirt. Ivy crumpled, dropping her head into her hands.

"Ivy," Danial said again. "We should go."

"Go!" Ivy's eyes itched and burned from the tears. "Where the fuck are we going to go? There's nowhere left for me!"

Danial took another step back as though slapped. She was caught between two worlds, between two warring factions, and she no longer knew who to believe. One man had shown he the truth. Tym's death severed the last thread connecting her to her old life. Hyman was her future. He gave her meaning. Wiping snot and tears on her robe, Ivy made up her mind. She snatched up the dagger, tucking it into her belt.

"I'm sorry, Danial," she said and started back in the direction she had come. She walked past dead horses and dead men. Her pack half-buried in the ground, she tugged on the strap, pulling it free.

"Where are we going?" Danial asked and jerked his thumb over his shoulder. "Welksdale is that way."

"There's nothing there for me."

"What about the nightingales?"

"Fuck the nightingales, Danial!" She shoved him. "Fuck you and your stupid promise! Your mother was right. Girls will always hurt you because you're too fucking dumb to see they can't like someone with a head full of mush!"

"Why are you doing this, Ivy?"

Hyman will kill you, or I will kill you, or someone will kill you.

"You are too dumb to see it." She shoved him again, hard enough that he stumbled and nearly fell over his own feet. "Those boys broke you for touching their sister. They beat you good and you know what, you deserved it. You are no better than a bleating goat. Your cows are smarter and they stand around chewing their grass, waiting for someone to tug their tits. They at least give milk."

"They killed my cows and goat," Danial said, turning his face way.

"Of course, they did, you don't deserve anything."

"I do, Ivy. I deserve to hear the nightingales. My mother's memories."

"Go away, Danial." Ivy began the long walk back to Hyman.

She heard him weeping, stopped, shoulders slumping at how tired she felt, the angry vitriol passed like sickening up spoiled fruit. Danial followed her, not too close, but enough that she heard his heavy breathing. Touching her power, she allowed her song to flow out, delve into him, absorbing the confusion and sadness, and redirect his desire to follow after her like a lost puppy. She shaped his thoughts, telling him that he needed to return to Welksdale, report on what happened and that Ivy no longer lived. When her song ended, she turned around. Danial was gone.

It's better this way. Better for him.

She adjusted the straps on her pack and continued her journey back to Hyman.

Claiborne woke up. She grabbed her head, which felt stuffed full of hay, shitty hay at that. *I'm surprised it's still attached,* she turned from side to side and noticed a pinprick of pain in her neck. She touched the spot. Her fingers came away crusty with dried blood. *Lucky! I was only nicked and didn't slit my own throat.* That's what she'd intended on doing to Thrush. She had tried to kill that bitch but was stopped. Beside her was a dead body, the man she had promised Ivy that she would let go in exchange for the singer. Instead, the asshole interfered and was now dead.

Seems Nazglum smiles on fools and villains.

She could see it now. Or rather, not see, since Thrush wasn't anywhere to be found.

"Wonderful! Beautiful! This has to be some sort of shadow cursed joke. I'm going to get ever so much closer to killing the bitch, and she'll elude me again, and again and again! Like I died and am in some afterlife torture." Claiborne grabbed her long sword and wiped the drying blood off onto the corpse's trousers. She wrinkled her nose. He'd already started to smell. "Looks like you had company, buddy, for the eternal slumber alone." She looked around at the torn and ragged bodies of all six Silent Men, including the one Thrush murdered. Among the dead were six of the seven horses, hers included. "Not sure how much of a comfort they'll be, but at least they are better than no one."

Thrush was gone, but another person was missing as well.

"Ivy!" Claiborne coughed and then spat. Not red, which was good. Red meant dead. Like the girl would soon be, since she fucked Claiborne over by forcing her to sleep, then split.

I'm going to rip the pipes out of your throat, little girl, see how well you sing then.

At least Ivy kept her end of the bargain and didn't kill Thrush. It was a small consolation. One Claiborne would accept graciously as they played out the mummer's game of catch the birdy. *Catching wasn't the hard part, killing was the comedy.* Except Claiborne wasn't laughing.

She had no idea where either Thrush or Ivy went, or why she was even still alive. If she had to guess, Thrush spared her out of guilt, while Ivy ran back to Cacophony. *Let her go, I'll deal with that betraying bitch later.* Thrush, on the other hand, could've gone in either direction: trailing after Ivy or back to town. Toss a coin and she'd be equally right. Though, a coin flip wouldn't be necessary. Cacophony ordered her to return to their forces camped a few leagues from Welksdale. Claiborne was to wait for his arrival before re-commencing the attack on the town, force its people to surrender and strip it of any useful resources. Together they would crush the remaining Singers at the mountains with or without help from Ivy.

No matter how far away Thrush flies, she'd return to her nest. She'll run out of creative avenues of escape.

The last horse was grazing a hundred yards from the road. Claiborne spotted him in the dying light, the sun a thick, red stain in the sky. She approached cautiously, so as not to spook him. He was smaller than her destrier, a horse she'd had for three sowings. Losing such a steady companion left a bitter taste in her mouth and Claiborne spat. This other one handled well, like all their horses. She wasn't comfortable in a saddle belonging to another. Her own saddle wasn't worth peeling off the destrier's corpse—Creator bless the beast and give him green pastures.

Things I sacrifice for vengeance.

The waning-moon lit the road in silver gossamer, solemn as a funeral, and quiet as a tomb. Claiborne yawned, the angry demands of vengeance drained her, despite the long nap Ivy persuaded her to take. *At least it wasn't the eternal rest.* Ivy could have killed her, but in a way, this was worse. Claiborne was alive and left to thirst for the bloody drink pressed to her lips for an instance, then to have the cup snatched away before she tasted it! *A few steps faster, and we would be having a different kind of night.*

"But that's no different than anything else in your life." Arron's voice replayed in her head. The single sardonic laugh bristled her, as though he was standing right next to her. It signaled a sharp, shitty follow up comments, the kind where Claiborne imagined punching him in the balls so he could understand the pain it caused. *"Like you couldn't kill me when I begged and begged. Killing isn't your thing. Should take up gardening, but then you'd let all the plants die. No wonder Thrush left you for dead. You would make a pretty corpse, if you were pretty. Tits so small they could be mistaken for bug bites. Yeah, I loved you more than anything, and,"* another sardonic laugh, *"I was a dumbass. They say love makes you blind, but it didn't say anything about cutting off your own balls. Could've been fucking any woman, but I chose you. Jokes on me, because you let me die like a slug in salt."*

Claiborne let the tantrum continue. She had earned it. Arron never said those words when he was alive, except the part about her being a terrible gardener, and maybe hinted at her breasts being too small, oh, and he could be fucking another woman, but he was there, sweaty and grunting on top of her. The kind of pillow talk that made her wet, wrapping her legs around him and taking his throbbing—

Someone whimpered, and it wasn't her, which sometimes happened after these one-sided conversations, when she realized she was alone and Arron was gone, and his voice was almost a ghost along with his smile. Claiborne pulled back the courser's reins and listened. A breeze rustled through the grass, danced in the needles of evergrows. *Ghosts in my head.* She lifted the reins, about to give the horse slack to gallop on, when she heard it again, off to her right. The evergrows echoed her hurt.

Claiborne dismounted, drawing her sword. There could be one of three people she could think of hiding in the drought stunted cluster of evergrows. Thrush wouldn't risk making a sound, so it had to be Ivy or the other guy. Her coin was on Ivy. *Bitch realized her mistakes. Well, she'll see how badly she fucked up.* She had to be fast to keep her from singing, or it was back to slumberland, or worse. Claiborne rushed forward, shoving the branches apart. The long sword clipped dead branches, and she was making enough noise to wake a dead man. The moonlight exposed layers of shadows, and one that wasn't a tree trunk, but a man sitting against it. A dirty bandage wrapped around his forehead, knees drawn up to his chin and thick, muscled arms draped over them.

Wet eyes looked up at her, and he didn't react to the sword.

"Are you here to murder me?" he asked.

"That depends," Claiborne said and recognized the man who was with Ivy's uncle, "do you know where Ivy or Thrush went?"

"She don't want me around," he said, scrubbing at his eyes with dirty heels of his hands. Hands big enough to wrap around her neck, twice, Claiborne noted. Something seemed off about him that Claiborne couldn't quit place.

"Who don't want you around?"

"Ivy," he said the name and took in a shuddering sigh. A lovestruck sound, though one that was unrequited. "Told me to go home and tell them in Welksdale what'd happened."

That would be a very bad idea, ruin our plans.

"You don't want to go," she said, a statement and not a question. "What's your name?"

"Danial." He sounded more like a lost little boy than a grown man.

"I can help you there, Danial." Claiborne smiled.

"I don't think you can," he said. "Nobody can."

"You're only half-right." She lifted the long sword and brought the pommel down on his head. "I think you are going to be helping me out."

She dragged his body from the cluster of evergrows and, after grunting and cursing, got him over the saddle. *Would've been less work killing him.* She wiped the sweat from her brow on her sleeve. Since Ivy didn't want him dead, well, Claiborne figured she had an extra bargaining chip. *What will she do to save your life? Will be nice to pull a string on the puppet just once and see how she dances.*

Claiborne smiled, thinking of the many ways she could convince Ivy to help her for one more shot at Thrush. *One of us has got to go, and I don't plan on it being me.*

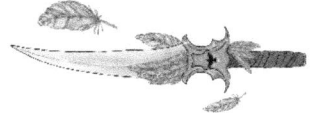

The ribbons stopped. Pink was the last color Robin found. Pink that would lead to red. So much red, reminding her of the deadly skirmishes with the Silent Men. The battles in fields far from big cities, far from important places and people who believed they were important. Small men with smaller penises trying to prove their worth while sacrificing the lives of people who couldn't fight back.

More bodies. More bloodshed. For what? To glut empty vengeance? The dark one dances to the tune he created for all of us. Discord is near.

One body she recognized. Tym. Ivy's uncle, or something. He had left with Thrush to rescue the girl. Like many heroes before him, he paid the ultimate price. In Robin's experience, heroes had a short life expectancy. The fight bravely, but in the end their blood watered the parched dirt, or they found themselves the villain in stories of people they try to help. Robin was never a hero, though she was a victim of several.

"Huh! No Thrush." Robin searched the ground where bodies of several Silent Men sprawled in the dirt, torn to shreds and left to bloat beneath the hot sun. It was sloppy, and Thrush usually cleaned up her mess. Unless she was in a hurry.

If Thrush wasn't diligent in her duty, like tying off the ribbons, then bad things were happening. Robin couldn't imagine what those might be, but she noted that horse tracks led off in opposing directions. Including back the way she had come.

An interesting predicament you find yourself in, Robin. Provisions nearly gone and two diverging paths. Thrush could be on either one. She grumbled. "Something is over the horizon of the next hills. I know it!" To journey forward might lead to a larger problem. A problem that might take heroic efforts to overcome. Robin was no hero. Not when she drowned soldiers in a storm or struck them down with lightning. A good flood would cleanse the perpetrators of discord, erased the kingdoms that believed they were impervious to the wickedness inviting Nazglum to take over. Tear down the towers and let the waters rise.

In the end, compassion would win out. The wicked would still poke holes in the existence, allowing for evil to seep through. The Tainted Ones walked among them and there was no way to bargain with them, plead for an end to the madness, the death, slaughter and bloodshed. People like Tym would suffer because they believed in good so strongly, they were willing to leave the safety of the nest only to be pierced by the talons of waiting predators.

Robin understood the call. It tugged at her heart, but the only way to protect it was turning flesh to stone. It became harder to move. Harder to crack.

"You are on your own, Thrush," Robin said. How often had she spoken those words aloud? Yet, they were always reunited. Harmony had been restored. Losing Sparrow was a great blow, nearly devastating, but they had to push on. Same without Thrush.

Robin climbed back into her saddle and turned around. Though it bristled her, going back was the wiser move. *Someone has to make smarter choices. I'm not qualified enough for this.*

"Ivy."

She turned at the sound of her name. The power flared like flint sparking dry kindle. Ivy narrowed her eyes, searching the moonlight for the speaker. Thrush stepped out into the road several yards behind her, favoring her left side. Her white robes were torn and dirty, the sleeves covered in dried blood. *How did she catch up so fast?* At that moment Ivy wished she wasn't deathly afraid of horses. She'd be back at the house, sleeping on the straw-stuffed mattress, trying to convince herself that the events were part of one bad dream and she'd wake up to a world where Tym still lived, and everything would be right.

"Not here to blow me up?" Ivy asked, holding the song writhing inside her like a beast trying to wriggle free and bite Thrush.

"If I wanted you dead," Thrush said, "you would be buried under the hill."

"You almost did that," Ivy said. "Or will you try to twist me up like you did Arron?"

Thrush frowned.

"That was a horrible mistake," she said.

"It wasn't the only one." Ivy pieced together the betrayal and anguish from what Claiborne had told her and the vision taken from Thrush. It wasn't much of a wonder to understand why Claiborne wanted the woman dead.

"No, it wasn't," Thrush said. "I'll probably make many more. Having the song doesn't mean we are infallible, Ivy."

"When we fuck up, it has larger consequences," Ivy said, loosening the straps on the pack, ready to throw it in case Thrush decided to use sword instead of song on her. The woman was quick with her steel and Ivy had no chance against Thrush. If the woman wanted her dead, Ivy would be another forgotten corpse fertilizing the plants. "People die that shouldn't have. We let our emotions get the better of us and no matter if we try to be good, it ends the same. We are a curse, a blight on the world, Thrush."

"You sound like him." Ivy understood Thrush meant Hyman, though she'd heard Thrush and Sparrow say something similar, just not to the extreme where they called themselves a blight. "Why didn't you kill me?"

"I don't know," Ivy said, almost regretting her decision. "I was going to kill you and Claiborne while you slept, but it didn't feel right."

"That is the moral dilemma," Thrush said. "By ending us, you would have removed two people causing harm in the world, but you didn't. You want to do what is right, I understand, but what we think is right might end up being a wrong choice for everyone else. The curse of the greater good."

"Did you kill *her*?"

"Claiborne? No," Thrush said and took in a deep breath, then releasing it. She folded her hands in front of her. "Like you, I thought about it, but there's more at stake here than removing one enemy from the board, Ivy."

"Because you felt guilty over killing her lover," Ivy said. "Admit it. You couldn't kill her in cold blood because you murdered her lover and abandoned her to die. Killing her would add a third weight to your conscious. One that would tip you past the point of greater good and into a monster. Then where would you stop?"

Thrush shook her head.

"We don't burn down whole villages and cities to get at one person. That's the Silent Men's tactic of leaving no sanctuary behind, no enemy at their back," Thrush said. "Not for one person, or a hundred."

"Spare me your lies," Ivy said. "I saw what I saw."

Thrush cocked her head.

"What do you mean?"

"You burned down Hyman's village, sending your soldiers to slaughter the fleeing people." Ivy felt sick recalling the vision from Cacophony. "I bet you didn't know you killed his wife and daughter. That's why he wants to kill you."

"That never happened," Thrush said, sounding sincere. "Tell me what you heard, Ivy. How is he blocking our songs?"

Of course, it happened. She saw the vision from Hyman. The soldiers in dark blue armor. *Maybe it wasn't Thrush, but another Singer in charge of the raid.*

"They were your men," Ivy said. "Dark blue armor, just like your soldiers wear."

"He… he let you delve him?" Thrush couldn't hide her incredulous tone.

"Of course," Ivy said and scratched at dirt on the back of her hand. "He wanted me to see the truth. Just like I saw the truth of what you all did to those in the Silent Men. You forged your own enemies by destroying their friends, family, and children."

"Creator bless me," Thrush said. "When you delve someone, Ivy, do they let you see whatever you want?"

"They struggle, but I get what I want." *Most of the time. When not faced with a singer stronger than me.* Ivy didn't think it was necessary to add in the last part.

"No one hands you over their personal memories," Thrush said.

Ivy considered the statement. It was true, no one allowed her to see what they tried to keep secret. Except for Hyman.

"Say it, Thrush. Quit beating around the bush and speak your mind."

Ivy had an inclination of what Thrush was about to say. Her heart ached at the idea that she was being a fool. When she was beginning to trust him, to find another family, and yet it was all a lie. Or was it? Thrush eyed her and frowned. There was something like sympathy in them and Ivy hated her for it.

"He fed you what he wanted you to see," Thrush said. "Made up the entire story to gain your trust. He probably never had a wife or daughter."

"But he does have a daughter," Ivy said, holding onto hope that Thrush was wrong. "She's the one tracking us. The one blocking our powers."

"An adult daughter?"

"No, a child."

"Tell me, please." Desperation was thick in her voice. "Tell me everything."

Ivy hesitated. In a way she was breaking Cacophony's trust by talking with Thrush. Giving away the secrets he shared, exposing his weakness. Thrush couldn't do much about it since Hyrian blocked their songs, it still felt like a betrayal.

"I'll tell you about one thing," Ivy said and described every detail of the vision she had seen. When Ivy finished reliving the horrible nightmare she had witnessed in Cacophony's head, Thrush pressed her hands against her temples like she was having the worst headache of her life. Pain creased her brow, eyes squeezed shut and she was whispering a prayer, which ended in a sharp sigh. She dropped her hands, kissing her fingers before touching them to her heart.

"Creator help us," Thrush said, looking up at the sky. "The harmonies have thinned too much."

Then she turned to leave.

CHAPTER EIGHTEEN:
REVELATIONS

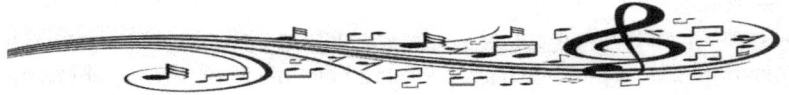

When these people speak of the end times, they have no idea what it means. Childish ghost stories of the Dark Lord sweeping in to eat their loved ones. Insulting to even the simple-minded creatures! A new life awaits them. One free of toil and suffering. Gone will be the distant Divine Dial Maker. A new master will be close at hand to sweep away all cares from the world and everyone will serve him. Harmony is nothing more than a lie. Where there are pain and suffering, there is only discord.

Sparrow sat on the clean bed, staring out the window. She heard snippets of their plans to use Ivy to attack some people. Since they hid her away in this back room, Sparrow assumed those travelers might include Thrush and possibly Robin. *Do they know I'm alive?* She stood up and paced, stopping at the window. The pane was clear and there didn't seem to be any lock on it or nails holding it in place. She ran her finger across the wood. There wasn't anything preventing her from lifting the frame. Her palms pushed the eave, cracking open the window and letting in a cool breeze.

Does he know? Of course he might be out there, waiting on her to try an escape. Then he would have an excuse to kill her. When Ivy returned and asked about Sparrow—if she cared enough to ask—he would say, *she tried to fly from her cage and we had to clip her wings, permanently.* He could do that now and probably not raise a question, but this would lend some authenticity in case he allowed her to delve him.

The wood squeezed in the frame like it hadn't been opened in a while. Sparrow leaned in close to the glass, checking across the open grass for possible guards. A rabbit sat in the sun, ears perked, and one eye on the house. Sparrow envied the rabbit. *I would gladly trade places with you.* She nudged the window higher.

The doorknob rattled and Sparrow reversed her palms on the frame, pushing it closed. She spun with her back to the window and noticed Cacophony enter, trailed by two Silent Men. Any friendly or compassionate semblance was absent from his eye. They took in Sparrow, swallowing her whole. She shifted on her feet, hating his stare which reminded her of her father.

"A lovely day, isn't it," he said, hands clasped behind his back as he stepped beside her, looking out the window. *He's mocking me. He knows what I was doing.*

"The sun shines on us," she said, side-stepping away from him. The rabbit was no longer in the yard.

"It does." His black armor smelled of grease and shined in the light, casting a long shadow over the bed. *Does he sleep in that thing?*

"For how long?" Sparrow asked.

"Depends," Cacophony said, and turned to her. "How long does the nightingale sing?"

"It sings at night," Sparrow said.

"Oh, but the male bird will sing during the day to defend its territory," he said. "Once it has established its nest, it won't let anything take it from him. I made that mistake once. Believing my nest was safe while I was away, but you know the story of what happened, so I will not repeat it. I will say that you nearly killed me."

Nearly isn't close enough.

"I killed plenty of men, and women, who threatened my life and the lives of those I love," Sparrow said. "Forgive me if I don't remember a particular occasion."

"For me it was a day, no, a series of days, I'll never forget," Cacophony said. "We were lured into a valley chasing Robin when a terrible song echoed throughout. The ground shook and there came a horrifying creaking, like the bones of the valley moved, and a damned creature rose from the ground. Except, it wasn't the ground, no, because that would be Thrush. Rather, the trees in an instant, trunks thickening and branches curved. A millennium of growth in a few heartbeats. Then the grasses rose up taller than any man and interweaved into a solid great green wall, or rather a green bowl. We were caught in that bowl, not a space to squeeze through. Twenty thousand men and women all watching in horror, sending prayers to the Creator. I thought it was going to crush us, but then the skies darkened and the rain came down hard. It soaked the ground beneath our boots, then rose to our ankles, our knees, and our necks. Twenty thousand men and women left to drown in that unnatural bowl. A few of us were smart and began to climb the rocks. Others tried to follow, but then the lightning struck, frying them in the water. I was one of nine to escape."

Sparrow remembered that day. Her song rose in anger, demanding vengeance. It was the singular most powerful outburst she had ever felt and had left her drained for weeks. She would have let the song empty her completely, if not for Goldy.

"Weren't you just the lucky one," Sparrow said.

"I wouldn't call myself lucky." He removed the muslin covering his mouth, revealing the pink scarred flesh. "This is a reminder of the choice I made."

"At least you had a choice," Sparrow said. "Some of you Silent Men killed my love."

"Oh, which Nazglum's witch was it?"

"Her name was Finch, and she was the best person I knew." The song bubbled inside her, aching to release and call the fury of that day. To tear the house down and crush everyone inside. "The Silent Men brutalized her!"

"That is one way of putting it," Cacophony said, replacing the muslin. "I was there when they did it."

"What?"

"No one should die that way," Cacophony said. "Or the way my wife, Glorian, and our beautiful daughter, Hyrian, died. But I learned that death isn't permeant. I was given a gift, a choice. You know which one I chose."

"Did you hurt Finch?"

"No," Cacophony said. "I put an end to her suffering with a blade to the heart."

A blade to her heart A blade in mine! Mercy or not, he killed Finch. Sparrow's breath quickened and her muscles tensed. This man confessed to ending her love, and her life. Life meant nothing without her.

"You fucking piece of—" She lunged at him, fingers contorted into claws aiming for his eyes. She would gouge them out, fling them against the wall and continue digging until she reached the back of his skull. But, he caught her by the wrists. Sparrow screamed, throwing her weight against him. A simple twist, and he could snap them. Instead, he held her the way one might hold a child having a tantrum. Drawing her in so he could stare into her eyes. The blood red rims and dark brown iris staring into her. She fought, trying to pull free, though his hands clamped on her and she had better luck snapping a tree trunk. She tried to spit, but he spun her around, hugging her back to his armor. It was hard, like being pressed to a stone.

"You could see her again," Cacophony said, his voice soothing and calm. "I don't mean in the spiritual sense like the priests say, 'in the Creator's warm embrace.' I mean in the flesh. This promise can be granted to you as it was to me."

Sparrow stopped struggling. *Finch.* To see her, touch her, hold her in her arms…but no, not like his girl. Not like Hyrian, because that wasn't her. Nor would the person they returned to her be Finch.

"All you have to do is swear an oath to do no harm to the Silent Men," Cacophony said. "Simple as a few words. 'I, Sparrow, swear to do no harm to the Silent Men so long as I live.' Then you get to have her back. Your love returned from the darkness."

"No," Sparrow said, tears coursing down her cheeks. "It won't be her."

"Of course it will. Who else would it be?"

It would be wonderful to have her back, to hear her voice, her song, to mend the heartache that has consumed her since the day she was murdered. Murdered by the man holding Sparrow. Mercy though it might seem, he wanted all of the women dead. Why was he offering her this…this damnation?

"You can be a family again," Cacophony continued. "You will be vital in bringing Harmony to the world again."

"Please," Sparrow said. "No, no more. I don't want it."

Cacophony released her and she dropped to the floor on her hands and knees. He could have done no worse to her than stabbing her in the heart in that moment. The pain was so great that even her song was no longer in reach. There was nothing but silence. Pain and silence.

"I will leave you to think on it," he said. "Just, don't take too long. When Ivy comes back, then we will have to make some long-term choices."

His footsteps moved away and Sparrow curled up on the floor.

An oath. I could swear an oath and she'll be back.

Not her.

Finch would be a Tainted One.

I wouldn't be alone as the world turned dark.

Sparrow wept, knowing what she had to do. If Ivy was far enough gone to be manipulated by this man that she would support him in bringing about their downfall, then yes, she had some choices to make. Not a single damn one of them was pleasant.

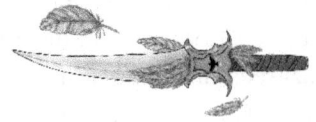

"What do you mean 'thinned'?" Ivy tried to grab Thrush's sleeve, but she swept her arm away.

"I need to get back," Thrush said. "I have to warn the others. Damn it! I should've seen this coming."

"What's wrong?"

"Everything," Thrush said. "This was all a diversion. He knew that by taking you, one or both of us would track you down, to stop you anyway we could from being used as a weapon. We wouldn't attack him full on, because our forces would be destroyed."

"He could've killed all of us in Welksdale," Ivy said.

"With heavy losses," Thrush replied, climbing into the saddle. "Then he would have to wait until the next thaw to press beyond the mountains to get the rest of the Singers. It doesn't matter if his daughter could cancel out all our power, we still have a greater number of soldiers waiting for us in the mountains. One thing I learned about fighting Cacophony, he doesn't do anything risky unless there was a greater payoff. That includes capturing you, Ivy."

"There's more," Ivy said. "He has Sparrow."

Thrush gripped the reins in her hands, holding them tight.

"She's alive?" Thrush asked.

"Last I saw her she was fine," Ivy said. "Though I think she is losing favor with him."

"Did he allow her to help you?"

"Yes. She helped me control my song better," Ivy said. "Why would he go to the trouble of keeping her alive? He intends for us to grow stronger so we can end the fighting. I have seen it. I know what's in his heart and mind."

"What he wants you to believe," Thrush said.

"You keep saying that!"

"That's how the shadow works," Thrush said. "They give a little truth to cover for their lies."

Like the lies you told me.

"What are going to do?" Ivy asked.

"I have made a grievous error in coming here," Thrush said. "I've foolishly played into his hands and we nearly lost everything. Your uncle loved you—"

"He's not my uncle."

"Ivy, I need you to think this through, carefully. I know you want to believe in him, to trust that Cacophony is there to help you. He may have given you a choice."

"You'll have to make a choice," Cacophony said. "Not tonight, but soon. Whatever you choose, you will have to live with the consequences."

The consequences were becoming clearer and she wasn't sure she wanted to carry the burden anymore.

"Please, Ivy, understand that he doesn't have your best interests at heart."

"And you do?"

Thrush shook her head.

"This is beyond what I want. It's about doing what is best for the greater good," she said. "The harmonies must be reestablished or there won't be a world left. Not one you or I would want to live in once Nazglum casts his shadow on it."

Ivy sighed, her head spinning. She wanted to lie down, close her eyes, and wake up from this nightmare. Her response came out harsher than she intended.

"What is my part in the greater good?"

"Kill the child."

The response was a cold slap. Ivy nearly bit her tongue.

"But…but she's just a little girl."

"From what you told me, the little girl died long ago in the fire." Thrush grimaced and hobbled along to the grass. Ivy noticed the horse tied to a branch. "The girl is not human, but something is lurking in her form. Something very dangerous."

"Wait!" Ivy held a tired hand out. She wasn't ready to face these decisions alone.

"I have to go," Thrush said. "Enough time has been wasted."

"I have more questions," Ivy said.

"Then come with me."

Return to a life of running and hiding. Cacophony would never forgive her. He loved her, like a father loved his daughter and wanted the best. Here was a chance for her to prove herself worthy of his love and buy time to talk to Thrush.

"I could force you to stay," Ivy said. "Take you back to Hyman. I'm sure

Claiborne would be glad to see you. She could pull the truth from you." *As well as other important organs.*

"You could, but you won't," Thrush said.

"Why do you say that?"

"Otherwise, I'd be on my way there and we wouldn't be talking about it." Thrush turned the horse around and Ivy ran in front of her to keep her from riding off. The horse shied back.

"Tym died protecting you!" Her eyes began to tear up and she scrubbed at them with her dirty hands, causing them to sting and further tears.

"I'm sorry for that."

"He must have believed in you."

Thrush shook her head.

"It wasn't me he believed in, but you Ivy."

Thrush was gone, silver moonlight shrouding her back and trailing out along the horse. Ivy watched until Thrush was lost to the night. Tym believed in her, and for that he died. Ivy wanted nothing more than to go hide under a blanket and cry. What good was there in a world without answers?

There was a window, not just the one Sparrow looked longingly out to the green backyard. No, this window was a break in the bondage trapping Sparrow's song. She sensed the plants beyond the window pane, her song reached for them, reaching their roots and their eagerness to do her bidding sent a thrill through her.

Be cautious. She's playing a game.

The girl was a wicked one.

Did Cacophony know about her game?

This could be my one chance to leave. She was certain once she refused his offer to have Finch return, he would kill her. All his talk about healing the world and returning Harmony was nothing but hot, stinking air in the end. Sparrow had served her usefulness and was a liability. She could turn Ivy against him, though she knew the chances of doing that were about as good as Nazglum showing up in a dress and asking her to dance.

Sparrow edged to the window, easing it open. No one interrupted her this time. Cool air blew the stale air and she took in a deep breath. Then she climbed out. She glanced over her shoulder, the nagging sense she was being watched poked her. Most of the windows were shuttered by drapes. She called on the blades to thicken and grow. To cover the windows and vines to thicken, crossing over the doors of the house, creating a green chain to seal them inside.

Now that I dropped my cards, time to take my coin and run.

She went around back, trying to get her general direction. They shuffled her around, blind, in the carriage at night, making it was difficult to know directions. Even working outdoors with Ivy, the trees blocked the view of any major features. One fact she did know was her room faced the south and there was a stream running east to west. The Shoehorn Mountains were to the east. That's where she had to go. Following the bank of the stream would allow her a way to evade being followed. She started down the path, her song thrumming in her throat as she sensed the roots of various plants, using them as detectors for movement. If anyone were to step on a patch, they would relay the signal to her. She heard the stream, smelled the water. Then her song was cut off. It wasn't gradual, but a sudden slice like a knife.

Shit! The child is close.

She scanned the tree line but couldn't see anyone. Then she heard boots crunching up the path. Hyrian held Cacophony's hand, swinging it back and forth, wrapped in a towel like she had come from a bath. She grinned, blue eyes giving a mischievous squint up to her father.

"I told you she would come from this way," Hyrian said.

"You did, my dear," Cacophony said. "I would never doubt you. Run along to the house while the adults have a serious conversation."

Hyrian gave a little disappointed groan, but ran past Sparrow, the towel flapping around her pale legs and she stuck her tongue out. Sparrow wanted to snatch it and rip it from her mouth.

"Little birdie, escaping her cage. Little birdie, caught in a rage," Hyrian sang. *"Clip, clip, clip go her wings. Clip, clip, clip, and never she sings."*

"Seems as though you have considered my proposition," Cacophony said. "And found it wanting?"

"Why would anyone want their loved one back as a...as a ghoul," Sparrow said, noticing more Silent Men walking toward her, boxing her in. "She has these powers because she is a Tainted One, did you ever consider that?"

"I have," Cacophony said. "I thought long and hard about it, standing over her many nights with a knife to end her new life. It was a vision from the

Creator that told me this was my daughter. I had passed the test by not killing her and she would be with me for all time. She would be the herald of a new life. A new beginning. As long as we destroy you wicked ones who are tearing apart the seams of our world. Ushering in eternal darkness. Hyrian is the light to cast away your wickedness." He took a step toward her, hands outstretched. "I meant what I offered you. A chance at having a new life of your own with Finch. In fact, this is your last chance. Renounce your connection to the Singers and you may go in peace with your love."

Four Silent Men surrounded her, five counting Cacophony. Each had hands rested on hilts of swords. Without her song, Sparrow was as good as dead. *I'll be joining you, Finch, one way or another.*

"What will you do with Ivy?"

"She'll have to make her own choices," he said.

I can't let him kill everyone else, so I guess I will have to take my chances.

"Very well," Sparrow said. "Love will have to wait."

She took off at a run, directly toward Cacophony. He snatched at her, catching the left sleeve of her black robe. Sparrow shrugged her arm out of it and the material tore, leaving her partially exposed. She spun on her toes and headed for the stream. She had no idea how far she would make it before they caught her, but it was worth a try.

"Bring her back to me!" Cacophony yelled from behind her. "Alive!"

Sparrow was never the fastest runner. When pressed she could scamper along quickly, though her short legs were a disadvantage. The stream was in view, flowing at a good pace. Ivy mentioned it was deep enough to almost swim in, the size of a small river. All she had to do was ford the other side, hoping their armor and cloaks would slow them in the water.

It was her short strides that were her undoing. A body collided with her from behind, knocking her to the stoney path, tearing up the sleeve which remained intact. A weight pinned her legs and a heavy fist punched her in the side. Sparrow gasped. She tried to turn, but the man pinning her to the ground had the weight advantage. Shaking him off her legs wasn't going to work. Then he grabbed hold of her left wrist, twisting her arm behind her back. He leaned forward enough for his weight to be uneven and she bucked her hips, unsettling him enough to allow her to twist her body to the left.

The man cursed and fought to maintain balance. She rolled with him and was able to bring her free arm around to elbow him in the face. Her arm went numb, but he no longer held her. Sparrow scrambled to her feet, took another few steps before being shoved in the back. She stumbled and recovered, her feet touching the cold water. The barrier blocking her song weakened.

I'm getting enough distance away from the girl.

Sparrow turned in time to duck a punch aimed at her face. She shoved her attacker away, back-pedaling into the stream. Water swallowed her legs up to her knees. The four Silent Men sloshed closer to her. Sparrow retreated, allowing the water to drift her further to the left. More distance from the house and the girl would allow her song to be released.

Hands reached for her and she threw her weight to the left, breaking free. Her head dipped under the water, she rose up, spat it out, the flow of the water carrying her further away. Then something grabbed her foot. A twist and she dunked beneath the water, kicking out. More hands pawed at her, clutching her calves, tugging her thighs. Sparrow fought to stand, slipping on the stones, went back in a splash.

"Can't… grip."

"Hold… bitch."

"Get her arms!"

Rough hands lifted her up under her arms, pinching the side of her breasts. Sparrow spat out water. Saw the angry and annoyed faces trying to get a grip on her, like she was an oiled pig. They lifted her from the water, slogging along to the shore, huffing-and-puffing. *I'm not that heavy!* She began to laugh. They dropped her and her teeth clicked together, but it didn't end her laugh.

"Is she crazy?" a young man asked, wringing water from his cloak. "Does she know what the boss plans on doing with her?"

"What's so funny?" another, older man kicked her thigh.

Sparrow looked at him, smiled, and opened her mouth.

The four Silent Men froze in horror at the song. One tried to run, but was tripped up by grass and quickly wrapped up like a fly in a spiderweb. Another tried to punch her in the head, but a nearby tree branch swept down and batted him through the overgrowth. Another ran to the water and was pulled under by plants hidden beneath the surface.

"Fuck this," the older Silent Man said, drawing his sword, got caught up in his damp cloak and when he finally freed it, a vine had latched onto his legs, lifting him straight up. He tried hacking them, but they pulled in opposite directions. He let out a terrified scream.

"Seems I'm not the only torn by the turn of events," Sparrow said, and covered her face at the spray of blood as the man's legs parted from his trunk.

His torso dropped with a squish and his legs flew off in two different directions—one into the water, the other into the overgrowth. The vines crashed down on him, smooshing his remains, and squirting Sparrow with more gore. She stood up on shaky legs, dripping wet with water and blood. "Oh God, it's great having my song back. I can breathe again!"

She knelt at the stream and washed the worst of the blood from her hands and face. Then she began walking east, planning on crossing over away from the house, away from the girl, and hopefully find her way back.

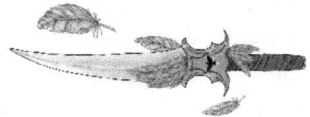

The Creator has a strange sense of humor! Of course, the diverging path Robin took would lead right back to the past. *At this point I wouldn't be surprised to see Raven fall from a tree.* Well, she would be terrified and then try to strike him dead, despite the fact that killing a Tainted One was rather difficult when they were already dead souls returned to torment the living. Once the Tainted One entered the realm, sending them back to Nazglum's embrace was rather difficult. Like cockroaches, they always found a way back in.

Claire was a different story. A sad story. One which Robin empathized with the level of betrayal that marked her life. Even the Singers were not without sin. Robin came upon Claire while she was squatting to the side of the road. Claire's wide shoulders and dark hair were evident even in her compromised position. She hadn't seen Robin, or if she had, she didn't show her hand. Robin faded away to the trees.

What was Claire doing out here alone? Was she even alone? Robin watched the road and tree-lines for movement. There wasn't any. Cacophony's First Sword wouldn't be out here on a pleasure ride. Not when she came from the scene of a battle where no clear winner was evident, except those who lived to walk away.

Robin could only surmise that she was going to meet up with a contingent of Silent Men or Cacophony. Neither were good options in Robin's book. The former would overwhelm her with numbers like they did to Finch and the latter would have the silencing agent, nullifying Robin's song.

Maybe I should take a different route.

The mountains were only so good of a marker, but the side roads were winding and backtracking was how Robin could be certain she wouldn't miss the small town. That's if Nuthatch hadn't disobeyed her orders and remained in the town. So many variables. Robin was never one to walk on blindly into a trap—well, not since she was duped into betraying her kingdom—but one lives and learns from mistakes. The key was staying alive.

I intend to stay alive as long as possible.

She tailed Claire at half a league, hoping the woman would turn down another path. The sun was going down and it seemed they were destined for the same place. At dusk where the sky was a dark red, Robin crested a hill and on the down slope the visible road was clear for over half a league.

Did I lose her on a side path?

Robin waited in case Claire pulled off for a rest or to relieve herself again. Riding in the saddle wasn't very comfortable and Robin's own legs ached. She decided she needed a break, but not before finding out where Claire might have gone off the path. Robin waited, watching the tree line for movement. Her horse gave an impatient snort, tail flicking.

Robin dismounted and walked it over to the high grass, yellowed under the hot sun. It nipped some blades and chewed. The shade was nice, the road visible from this vantage point. Robin stretched her legs, sitting beside the horse. A breeze blew warm air between the trees. She plucked a strand of grass and twisted it around her finger, like she used to do as young girl in the gardens, waiting for her cousin to quit teasing her and she could go back to her room and her books. *I can wait until nightfall, but then I'll have to sleep here.*

She knew of an abandoned house not far along the way since she stayed there one night ago. A roof over her head didn't sound too bad. She gathered her skirts and stood up. Then her horse gave a warning whinny. Robin let the song swell inside her as she had a thousand times before. It was as easy to access as breathing.

"I wouldn't do that." A sharp tip of a blade pressed against her spine. "A little pressure and you will flop on the ground, unable to do more than piss your panties."

"Claire," Robin said.

For an instance the blade pulled back.

"Robin," she said, jabbing her for good measure. "The Claire you knew is dead. Call me Claiborne."

Like a sword? Robin wasn't one to question this close to the point.

"Sure, Claiborne," Robin said. "Seems we are at an impasse."

Claiborne laughed.

"Impasse, yeah, that's what it is."

"What else would you call your drawn weapon and the cloud over your head," Robin said. "Oh, it may be small, but I assure you it can send a painful jolt through your body before you sever my spine. When flesh and burn begin to char, there's a tangy smell in the air."

Creator, let her believe me.

Claiborne sniffed.

"I don't smell anything," she said.

"It's because it hasn't happened yet. Really, it doesn't have to end with one or both of us sent along the golden road to judgement." Robin leaned forward, away from the sword's point. She turned slowly to face the woman. "There, that's better. I don't believe in shedding blood to settle differences."

"You sure have filled rivers full," Claiborne said.

As have you, my dear. Again, arguing semantics wouldn't get her out of the situation.

"Let's focus on the present," Robin said. "The past is done."

"Your future is done as well."

Robin couldn't argue that point, not when the Silent Men had the ability to silence their songs.

"Let's stay on the present, shall we?" Robin asked. "Here we both are in the middle of wherever, far from any of our supporters."

"Perhaps you are," Claiborne said. "The problem is you. You and your companions always believe you have us *normal* people figured out because of your curse. You say you are here to protect Harmony, but all I've seen is how efficient you kill others."

"Only when we are forced into it."

"See, forced is a special word. There are other options that you never consider."

"It's very difficult when a sect of men and women wish to kill us because of our song."

"Yet, you live on," Claiborne said. "For now."

"All we have is for now," Robin said. "What do we do with it, though?"

"Well, I could kill you. Be one less Singer to tear apart the fabric of our world—" Claiborne lifted her sword in an attack pose.

"You know that's not what happens," Robin said, not backing away. *Let her try to strike me.* Any display of fear wouldn't end well for her. "You have seen firsthand that we close the gaps the Void creates. We seal the Dark

One's doorways."

"Perhaps, or it could be what you want us to see." Claiborne shuffled-stepped closer.

This is how it's going to be, then let's begin.

Robin leaned closer to the horse's saddle. The hilt of the sword visible beneath the saddle blanket. "That's the problem I had with you, *Claire*, or *Claiborne* or whatever stupid fucking name you want to be called. You were so eager to jump on an opportunity when it favored you, but when it meant sacrificing anything, you balked. You couldn't save Aaron from suffering. You left it to someone else."

Robin drew the short sword from the saddle blanket, bringing it out in front to block the first blow from Claiborne. Metal rang on metal and Robin felt the blow vibrate up to her elbow. She retreated a step, her horse also side-stepping from the violence. A trained war horse would've bitten Claiborne's face off. This one from the Welksdale stables was too used to a peaceful life, stomping at the ground rather than on Claiborne.

Don't need others to fight my fights for me.

Thrush may be better with blades, but Robin learned under her and trained many years with Thrush. Rather than give more ground, she stepped under Claiborne's guard, her own blade scraping against the metal chains protecting Claiborne's ribs. It wasn't meant to be a debilitating blow, no, but to bring Robin close enough to thrust her palm into the woman's throat. Claiborne grunted, twisting so Robin smacked her left ear instead.

Claiborne swatted Robin's right breast—it stung like a mother fucker, but better than a blade to the gut—and retreated into a defensive position.

"Fighting dirty." Robin smiled, grabbing her breast.

"The only way you know how," Claiborne said.

True.

Robin let her song out and the air thickened in a wet fog.

"There it is!" Claiborne shouted, and leapt, sword slicing where Robin had stood. "Fight like a soldier, bitch!"

"I could say the same of you," Robin said, "but you left us for *him*. There's nothing of honor in you. You deserve to be droned like a rabid dog."

Metal sliced through the fog.

I could kill you, should kill you, but...

Robin let the air thicken more. Until a cloud, dense with moisture, hung over the ground. She tied the song off and retreated to her horse. Claiborne cursed and railed in the fog. *Should take her a moment to figure her way out.* Robin mounted the skittish mare and urged her onto the road. Then she kneed her into a gallop.

That was too close.

The reason for Claiborne being on the road was never answered. Robin suspected one detail. Welksdale was in trouble. She had to arrive there before Claiborne rallied beyond the fog. Or there wouldn't be a town left standing.

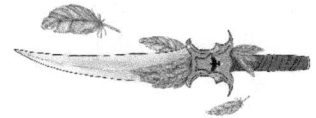

Gray light crept over the edge of darkness in the eastern sky. Feet aching, body weary, and heart-broken, Ivy entered the yard. The house Hyman and Hyrian occupied was a dark, looming figure. No lights flickered in the windows. It was as though it was a dead, soulless being waiting for her to whisper the horrific fact. She was alone. *They probably left me.* She couldn't fault them, constantly on the move, never remaining in one place for long. Ivy wouldn't expect anything less than to be abandoned again. She was used to it. Strangely enough, all the houses they passed days and nights in were in rather good condition for being empty. The drought was bad, but Ivy didn't think that many people gave up and moved on.

Where else could they be?

She had no idea, but some of the tiredness went away when she spotted the black carriage lurking on the edges of the property, obscured by evergrows and half-dead shrubs, like a spider sitting in a thinly spun web, waiting to pounce on its prey. The four horses were not hitched, which meant they were in the stable and Hyman was in no hurry to leave.

They didn't leave me!

On the first step, Ivy felt a strange disconnect. She could sense the pulsing power and then it was gone, cut cleanly off a thread snipped by sheers. Having her song blocked was like losing her voice. She was ordinary; a lost girl, orphaned and unsure. No one significant and, if she disappeared, the world would continue its course, without missing a beat. The idea was very appealing to her.

I don't have to go in. No one saw me. Hyrian had sensed her, which was why her power was cut off. Ivy took a step back. Once she retreated beyond the proximity of the house, she was certain her song would return. She could go anywhere her feet would take her. Tired as she was, it probably wouldn't be very far.

I escaped one monster who wanted to control me. And Bryn was dead. She was numb to the discovery. He was never a father to her, even when she believed in that thin connection to blood. He was a brutal beast and got what he deserved. One thing Ivy learned was there would always be more like him. The world was full of Bryns. *One person's hero is another's monster.*

The front door opened and her opportunity to escape was gone. Hyrian stood there in a pretty blue dress, her hair braided, and pink lips smiling at Ivy. She clutched her doll, Glorian, in small hands, bouncing on her bare toes. An ordinary girl, but when you looked into her blue eyes there was a different being. The spark of life, joy and curiosity she would find in another child, Hyrian had lacked, and instead there was deep, shadowy menace lurking behind them. The kind one may find when a cat stalks a bird.

The girl died long ago in the fire, Thrush had said.

What are you?

"You came back," Hyrian said and padded down the stairs. She threw her arms around Ivy's waist, pressing her face into the black armor. It was a sweet hug—one a sister would give to another returning from a long absence. "I missed you."

Ivy patted the girl's hair. It was soft, not that she would know what a dead girl's hair was supposed to be.

"I missed you, too." *Not as much as I miss my song.* Could she really kill this girl to have her song back? Kill her for the greater good? Ivy didn't want to live in a world where murdering children was for the greater good, even if this being wasn't truly a child. It could all rot and go to the shadow. *We are teetering on the edge, and a little nudge is all it would take.*

"Come inside and see." Hyrian took Ivy's hand.

"She what?"

"Come, come."

Ivy let Hyrian lead her into the house. The windows were covered in thick curtains, letting in a small amount of light. The place was neat, floors swept, a knitted blanket covering the back of a rocking chair. On the seat a feather stuffed pillow was torn apart. Dead flowers sat in a vase on the table. Whoever had lived here, could walk in and resume their life, pick up the broken pieces, and settle back into life.

There was a strange odor from the back of the house.

"What's that smell?" Ivy wrinkled her nose. Bile crept up her throat, the memory of the dead and dying in the streets of Welksdale.

Hyrian giggled, tugging her to a closed door.

The smell was stronger here, like spoiled meat. Ivy shook free of Hyrian's hand.

"Keep it closed…I don't need to see."

Hyrian shoved it open. Warm, spoiled air struck Ivy. The windows were covered here as well, but enough light entered to give an ethereal glow around two corpses tied to chairs. Their eyes were sewn shut, mouths hung and stuffed with straw and feathers. They were stripped, their bellies slit open and ropey intestines hung down, braided together. There was an attempt to put clothes on them. The man had part of a blue dress, torn and ragged, wrapped over his belly, but leaving his split gut open, his sack dangling against his right thigh. Where the rest of his genitals were, Ivy didn't want to know. Beside him, the woman's chest had a bloody tunic laid over her and her legs were spread wide. Flowers were stuffed inside her, the dead stems and dried petals sticking in the dried blood around her heels. The toes looked gnawed, jagged bone popping out of the flesh.

Ivy fell back a step and couldn't contain the bile that splattered the floor. She wiped her mouth on her sleeve

"What did you do?"

"They are my dolls." Hyrian pouted. "You don't like my dolls?"

"These… they… were people," Ivy said, and felt the vomit creep up her throat again. She put the back of her hand to her mouth, covering her nose as best she could. A single black fly landed on the man's nose and scampered into his left nostril. "This isn't normal. Hyrian who let you do this thing?" *She's not normal and should be killed.*

Hyrian shrugged.

"I found them like this."

"No… don't lie," Ivy said and continued backing out of the room. "Did you kill them?"

Hyrian blinked deliberately, as though she heard the dumbest thing ever said. Pink lips drew back in a snarl.

"You're jealous because you didn't make them. You don't have dolls and you can't play with mine." Hyrian slammed the door in Ivy's face. Ivy bent over, gagging on the smell and the innards braided like a child's game of knots to say who the tested one would marry.

"Everything alright, Ivy?"

Ivy nearly jumped through the wall. Hyman occupied the hallway. He had to stoop so his great sword's handle wouldn't scrap the ceiling. He wore his armor, muslin over his mouth. The puckered scar the muslin covered became a great interest and he rubbed it.

"She's, ah, playing a game," Ivy said.

"Children have such creative imaginations," Hymn said and reached for the door knob. Ivy resisted smacking is hand away. *No, let him see.* But he stopped and pulled back. "They'll play with almost anything."

You know what she is and pretend she's your little girl.

"What happened to the people who occupied this house?" Ivy asked, wrinkling her nose against the stench.

"They discovered a better place," Hyman said. He put a hand on Ivy's shoulder. The gentle touch he had for her was replaced by the gauntlet's cold metal. The weight of it guiding Ivy away from the death room. Those fingers could crush her bone or snap her neck. Then she'd be another doll for Hyrian. "You've returned alone."

A statement and not an accusation.

"Thrush," Ivy said, searching for words that wouldn't disappoint or prompt him to discipline. "She was there, and she killed everyone, nearly killed me too, before I could stop her."

"Thrush is dead?"

"No, and neither is Claiborne." *But Tym is dead. The one person who deserved to live.*

"That is unfortunate," Hyman said, though he was Cacophony now. Discord and death in the hard shell. All the talk about doing no harm and here he was slaughtering people in their homes and leaving them as play toys for the thing. The weight released from her shoulder. "I'm certain Claiborne will have her revenge."

"I did as you asked," Ivy said. "I didn't harm anyone."

"Good," his dark tone lightened, and she heard a father praising his daughter. "I'm proud of you, Ivy. You have learned restraint. That is always the toughest part wielding so much power. Knowing when to try a gentler approach, and when to unleash the full fury. The second path you will take, Ivy. You will have to use your full strength to survive. We will be going up against incredible odds, but it will put an end to the struggles," Cacophony said and spread his arms out, his cloak flapping like he was ready to take flight. His voice rose in excitement. "Then we will have harmonic balance and the world will be protected from the Dark Lord's intrusion."

Harmonic balance! Thrush said it was slipping away and here he was saying they were closer to it. Ivy had no idea who was right. Both of them believed they were working on saving the world, but were they dooming it? In the other room was a child playing with dead bodies. Was this the new world order?

"I'm not strong enough to fight another Singer." The women had way more experience with using their powers. Thrush deflected Ivy's song easier than swatting aside a lazy fly. More than one singer would be nearly impossible to counter, let alone break into their minds.

"Compared to them, you are an infant," Hyman said. "There are other ways for you to fight them. I will show you, but first you need proper attire."

Hyman pointed at a trunk sitting under the table. It was small, dark cherrywood and had metal bindings over the lid with two locks. He pressed two keys into her hand, which she thought was strange. What was so valuable that it required two locks to secure it? Ivy knelt in front of the trunk and she scented a hint of old wood and cinnamon. Hands shaking, she tried one lock, but the key didn't fit and tried it in the other. It clicked open and the second followed soon. Hinges creaked as she lifted the lid.

"I don't understand," Ivy said.

Folded in one corner was a black dress, but on the opposite side were pieces of black armor. Not the kind of armor worn by the Silent Men, Claiborne, or even the chitin pieced Hyman had on. It was smooth metal, tingling at her touch.

"Harmonic forged," Hyman said. "No other material is stronger. Thrush made it herself, gave it to a young woman as a conciliatory prize for killing the man she loved."

"Claiborne's armor," Ivy looked up at him, brows furrowed. "Why doesn't she wear it?"

"She surrendered it to me the moment she swore fealty to our cause," Hyman said. "I was saving it for Hyrian, for when she grew up, but—" He shrugged his shoulders and turned up a hand to signal what they both knew— there would be no growing up for the little girl. "It is a present to you. Try it on."

Ivy lifted the dress out and set it on the table. There were black leggings beneath it. She slipped those on under the robe, the belt loosening as she wiggled her legs through. There was a loud clatter. The dagger she took from Thrush lay on the floor. Hyman picked it up before Ivy could grab it.

Holding it in both hands, he brought it close to his nose and smelled it the way one might savor a delicious piece of sweetbread. Ivy held her breath, waiting for the question of where she got it and if she was that close to take it from Thrush, then why was the woman alive? That would be how it would end for Ivy, he would berate her, hit her, call her a fool, idiot child and a blight on human existence.

"Excellent craftsmanship." Hyman handed the dagger back, hilt first. He must've seen it was a song forged blade, but he didn't say anymore, or ask her where she got it.

Ivy set it next to the dress. She tossed her robe aside and slid on the dress. It fit well enough, a bit loose in the waist, and ending at her knees. She shuffled through the pieces of armor, holding them up and trying to figure out what went where. The chest plate was all she knew.

"Here, let me help."

Hyman strapped on the pieces, covering her shins, forearms, shoulders, and chest. They were padded, more comfortable than Ivy would have guessed, and much lighter. *I could almost dance in it.* It fit her like a second layer of skin.

"You look ready to take on the entire army," Hyman said and laughed at the worried expression on her face. "You won't be fighting everyone. In fact, you won't have to do anything, except convince others to fight for you."

"That won't be difficult at all." Ivy smiled, holding the dagger up. She wouldn't need it, but it felt good to have it close. "I think I can use my song to control more than one person." *As long as they weren't another singer.*

Hyman smiled.

"That is excellent growth, my child."

Ivy felt the warmth of pride at his compliment.

"Pack up," Hyman said. "We are leaving soon."

"What about Sparrow?" Ivy asked. "Is she coming with us?"

"Sparrow won't be needed anymore," Hyman said and left her to tend to her new belongings.

Ivy stared at herself in the mirror. Gone was the terrified girl who was nearly trampled, beaten, and had all sorts of horrific events. Here stood a new woman, a warrior, a survivor. She grinned, flicking her hair over her shoulder.

"Soon, I won't need any of them."

CHAPTER NINETEEN
REUNION

Slipping into Oblivion is never pleasant. Body and consciousness disappear from the plane of the living and, if one is fortunate, there is no thought or feeling in the great emptiness. Once you are awakened, the darkness is visceral, like drowning without breath, or sight. The mind becomes untethered from reality. Madness gnaws at the edge. Then a great light thrusts you through a hole, burning away in existence. There you are reunited with existence. Reborn into a world you will never truly know or fully understand.

"Robin?" Thrush came upon her old friend in the early hours of the morning. She was in the house where Tym and Danial had slept while she sought the songs of other women and listened to the stones beneath the dirt. There were distant songs she had to ignore. Ones that she had faintly heard before on the night breezes—not as strong as Ivy's song, but not weak, either—and full of sorrow and want. She had to ignore these to focus on the snippets she felt from Ivy. Bread crumbs. Enough for Thrush to track at the time.

I heard her Song the other day. Foolish woman.

Her horse was tethered on the post in front of the place. Thrush dismounted and approached the door. She listened, heard nothing, then knocked. "It's me, old friend," Thrush said, to keep from getting smacked in the face by a sword, or a thunder cloud.

"Thrush!" the door opened and Robin blinked away the early morning light. "Oh, you have decided to come back. Oh, are you alone?"

"Unfortunately, I am," Thrush said.

"I saw the result of your attempt to intervene," Robin said. "What was the total tally of our loss?"

"Too high to measure," Thrush said. "We may have lost Ivy for good."

"As I have feared. Was that her uncle's body?"

Thrush nodded.

She has no one to call family. Cacophony may fill that role now.

"I'm sorry," Robin said. "I had an encounter with a former friend of yours."

"Claire."

"Claiborne, she calls herself now," Robin said. "Come in and have some tea. Ill news should not be spoken of with cold breath."

Robin started a fire by calling a cloud and lightning to strike the wood until it lit. A waste of her song, but Thrush wasn't one to judge the little conveniences by which they used the Creator's gifts. Anything to make life lighter. She placed a kettle on to boil. Thrush sat at an empty table.

"You remembered to follow my markers," she said.

"How could I forget? You used these same ribbons every time you wander off by yourself," Robin said, dropping in crushed, dried leaves to steep in the hot water. "Besides, you wanted me to find you."

"Yes," Thrush said. "I hoped it wouldn't have taken you so long. What did you tell Nuthatch? Will she be at Welksdale?"

"I hope not," Robin said. "Claiborne is planning on sacking it."

"Probably with the help of Ivy," Thrush said. "We cannot allow her to do that."

"Why?"

"Then we lose her forever," Thrush said. "Oh, and they have Sparrow. They were forcing her to train Ivy. That's why I was able to track them so easily."

"That does explain the trap," Robin said, pouring hot water into two cups. She set one in front of Thrush and sat across from her. "An important question remains Do we kill the girl, then?"

"You are so eager to call out her demise," Thrush said.

"She is a danger to Harmony," Robin said. "She could undo all we have fought and scraped to accomplish. Like you said, she is the most powerful singer of our generation."

"And a damaged child," Thrush said.

"We were all damaged and neglected," Robin said. "Yet we didn't join with the enemy to destroy existence."

"We don't know for certain—"

"Then where is she?" Robin asked. "I'm certain you met her and spoke with her."

"I did," Thrush said. "I cannot force her choice, the same as I couldn't force any of the Singers to choose to join our cause."

Ivy was stronger and will grow more into her power, which worried Thrush. The extent of the girl's song could be immense. Enough to enslave an entire city, or worse. An entire continent. The idea was an embellishment, and Thrush wasn't one to give in to flights of fantasy. Killing the girl…

"Killing her may be our only option," Robin said, sipping her tea and saying what Thrush was thinking. "At least you cannot rule it out, Thrush. No one person is more important than all of Harmony. Not you. Not I. Most definitely, not the girl."

"But she could be the one to end—"

"Don't make another Arron incident," Robin said.

Thrush pursed her lips together, to keep from speaking cruelty to her friend. *Again, she is right.*

"Drink your tea and then we need to ride like the wind to Welksdale," Robin said. "Hopefully Nuthatch did as I told her and left for the mountains."

Not another Euclid, either.

"There's only so much you can save in the world," her mentor, Cardinal told her when Thrush was a young singer. *"You are not the Creator, but his servant. Some people just won't want to be saved and you must be fine with their choice."*

"Some people do not want to be saved. Some do not know they need it, yet," Thrush said and sipped her tea.

The black carriage rolled through the night. Ivy leaned back into the cushioned seat and closed her eyes. She had not slept in almost a day. In her dreams she heard Hyrian singing. The strand of the songs told a story about thread-worn kings sacrificing pretty daughters to a dragon god in exchange for a gilded crown and the defeat of his rival. The dragon transformed itself into a humble old man who served the rival king. Once inside the castle walls, the dragon gained the trust of the king and family members. Each night the dragon would take one item of value—a mirror, a ring, a cloak—and placed it into another member's room. The item would be discovered through the assistance of the old man, the victims never suspecting the old man who swore them to secrecy never to reveal how they found out about the thief. The King distrusted his children and they suspected their mother and each other of treachery. One night, again with the assistance of the dragon, they plotted to kill the offending family members. A son placed poison in his brother's tea while the father hid a needle dipped in nightshade in the poisoning son's pillow. Both sons rigged a noose and a trap door in the privy where their father shat.

Ivy dreamed about each death. The mouth foaming and spitting up blood as the one son dropped his tea, the other son clutched the side of his head where the needle pricked him and he fell asleep, never to wake. Finally, the king mourned his dead sons by eating a hearty meal and when his belly was full, he went to use the privy. As he dropped his trousers and turned to sit over the hole, his head got caught in the noose and the floor collapsed, hanging him. The King died with brown stains down his legs, eyes bulging and tongue hanging out.

The only one left alive was the queen, whom the thread-worn king married, taking all the dead King's land and armies. Only to die in his sleep from grief at losing his daughter and his rival and a well-placed knife in his heart, leaving the queen to rule all.

"Such a sweet story," Cacophony said.

Hyrian giggled and leaned into him. Ivy peeked through one eye to see the interaction. It would be a natural moment, endearing even, had she not observed Hyrian dressing up corpses. They both looked at Ivy.

"Here is a one who pretends to slumber," he said and slid to the center of his seat, patting the side he left open. "Come here, Ivy."

Ivy hesitated, stretching to cover her reluctance. The idea of being close to someone, though she had let down her guard to him before, she didn't know if she could allow herself to do so. A storm of emotions rolled in her, torn between obeying and cringing away. This man gave her more than anyone ever did. He was harsh, brutal to his enemies, but he gave Ivy one thing she needed, craved, really. Cacophony patted the seat again. Ivy gave in and sat beside Cacophony while Hyrian cuddled up close to him on the other.

"I know it has been difficult," Cacophony said. "Transitioning over to a new life means the old must die. We are your family, now. Family accepts each other. Every ugly frailty. We support each other no matter what tries to come between us. I accept you for what you have become, the shedding of the old shell, exposing your inner anguish. Stripped bare. We have all transitioned past the agony of being alone, different, hated for what we cannot change. We all fight the empty void in our soul when we realize we are truly alone in the world, though we are surrounded by myopic slaves trapped in their suffering. I understand and will help you, Ivy."

"Sister," Hyrian said and reached across her father to take Ivy's hand.

Ivy recoiled from the cold touch. Hyrian tried again, clasping her wrist in such a strong grip.

"We love you, Ivy," Cacophony said.

"Love you," Hyrian echoed.

Ivy cringed at the word "love". Everyone who professed love had left her. She wanted to deny them the word, to stay in the moment for a little longer, but she also allowed Hyrian to take her hand and pulled her closer until she was leaning against Cacophony's side. His armor was also cold and sharp, poking into her side through the black dress. Last time she was told she was loved by anyone was before her mother died. She wanted to believe it, believe someone could love her for who she was and not what she possessed.

"Do you know how I got this?" Cacophony pulled down his muslin and revealing the pink scar. "This was a mark given to me at the rebirth of my daughter. She climbed from the ashes of my ruined life and kissed me, right here." He tapped the scar. "Then she bit into my flesh and ate it."

"Did it hurt?" Ivy asked not knowing what else to say.

"Excruciating pain," Cacophony said. "It served as a reminder, though. There are worse pains that never heal. At least I got one back. I'll never let her go."

Hyrian laughed and then hummed a ballad.

"I may be a little over-indulgent when it comes to allowing certain idiosyncrasies, but my children, Ivy, are my legacy. They are what every father wishes to pass on into this world, to lighten up the darkness. Anyone standing between my children and their legacy, well they will taste bitter anguish and know the true meaning of suffering," Cacophony said, tapping the hilt of his sword at his feet. "You pass this last test, and I will call you daughter until the end of my days, if you like."

"I would like that very much," Ivy said, knowing in her heart she longed for it, no matter how wrong it was. Before long, she was curled up, using his cloak as a pillow and went to sleep.

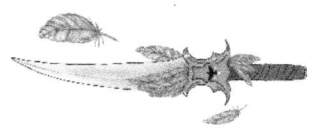

Ivy.

"Go away!"

She was back in the hallway of the first house they stayed in. All the doors were locked, except for one. Eerie green light glowed through the cracks. The air was frigid, and she shivered despite the black robe she held tight around her. Ivy knew better than to try any of the door handles. Her hand still bore a small scar where she got frost burned from the last time she had touched one.

"Why am I here?" She closed her eyes and tried to will herself some other place. When she opened them, she remained in the hallway. The one change being the Shadow Figure was silhouetted in the green light. *"What the fuck do you want?"*

You will serve me.

"I most fuckingly will not."

The Shadow Figure chuckled, a mirthless sound.

Oh, child. You are woefully ignorant of what's happening, been happening since before your birth. The harmonies are failing. Have been failing for a long time, but these little ants warring over the last morsel of sugar are blind to the obvious. All life will fall into shadow. The Dark Lord will walk among those left alive and they shall bend their knee and cower in despair. The certainty in the prophecy caused Ivy to shiver. *Serve and you will be among the few to stand at his side. Swear fealty and your powers will grow immensely.*

"Which side are the Singers on? The Silent Men?"

Oh, they are doing their part.

Doing their part to destroy harmony. Yes, she could see that. Ivy didn't believe they did so knowingly. Good intentions and all leading to the downfall. Wasn't there anything she could do? Or were they doomed by their own stupidity?

The Shadow Figure crept closer. Around it the floor crackled. She could feel the cold through her boots. She would die if he touched her, this she believed. Her heart would burst from fear. Ivy stood her ground. Let it kill her, then. Better to die than be this thing's lapdog.

You will change your mind, Ivy. When faced with the eternal slumber, you will beg for place at the Dark Lord's table, but then, it will be too late. The arm reached out, and the corpse finger extended to touch her lips. *You'll be scraps for the master's dog and know only pain and torture for eternity.*

"*Sounds like great time.*" She smacked the hand away.

The Shadow Figure's hood tilted to the side, like it was considering her. *You have great strength, Ivy Lyre, but in the end, it all fades away.*

The carriage struck a bump and Ivy woke up, her head lying on a pillow across Cacophony's lap. He gave her a questioning look, but Ivy shook her head.

"Bad dream," she said.

"Life seems like one, doesn't it?" He stroked her hair. "Best to sleep. Think good thoughts and have pretty dreams. Who knows what ugliness awaits?"

They stopped three times to feed and rest the horses. Ivy used these breaks to practice her sword forms and Cacophony would watch, offering suggestions and correcting her stance. He sparred against her, knocking the sword away quicker than Claiborne ever had, though he didn't leave behind reminding bruises. Other times she pushed against Hyrian's barrier, touching the power, then grasping it in full force. Once she even got out a verse of a song that touched Cacophony—Hyrian had to be teasing her into thinking she was getting stronger, before severing her grasp on the song. That one instance caught Cacophony off guard. Ivy saw the village burning, but no army. In fact, there was one cloaked figure. It could have been anyone, another singer who manipulated fire, or a stranger who had a vendetta against the villagers.

Neither were the case. *They are both doing their part.*

It was a true vision, and that worried Ivy. Cacophony stared at her, long and hard, like he was trying to read her thoughts.

"I almost had you," she said, playing it off by tickling Hyrian, who grinned and ran away, clutching her Glorian doll.

"That's enough for today," Cacophony said and they loaded back into the carriage. No one spoke, Hyrian hummed and sang, and Ivy sat across from Cacophony. The distance was almost to where their knees touched, but it seemed much farther. There were no more stories, no more cuddling, and no words of love.

Ivy sat on her hands, clenching her fists. Anger at the betrayal set in. *I'm a fool to think I deserve anything better than being alone.*

The last stop she realized was a league outside of Welksdale. She knew the farmhouse, the barn doors standing open. Here Danial would have listened to the nightingale sing in the sweet berry bushes at night. There she took shelter in the big storm, where she broke the poor man.

"What are we doing here?" she asked.

Cacophony didn't respond. The carriage rattled off onto a side road. They went another league, and she spotted hundreds of tents erected in an open field. There had to be of a thousand horses picketed across various cloisters of trees. Soldiers marched past the carriage, enough to crush Welksdale ten times over.

"This is the inevitable, Ivy," Cacophony said, placing a hand on her shoulder. "All these men and women come together in one cause."

Murder, revenge, death.

"They'll die," Ivy said. "Many more with them."

"Yes, because they believe they are helping keep the shadow from the world," Cacophony said. "A righteous cause is harder to stop than a fire burning through crops in the fields. You, my dear child, can spare them more pain and anguish."

By passing it onto others.

"Tomorrow will be your final test." The carriage came to a halt in front of a large tent with banners flapping in the breeze. A Silent Mouth and beside it, a doll. Cacophony released her. "Don't disappoint me."

Claiborne watched the four black horses draw the carriage into the field. Her scouts had warned her long before of its pending arrival, but watching it was like watching dark clouds cover the sky. She wondered what storm it would bring.

There's that little bitch. She watched Ivy leap out as though a ridge cat was about to eat her. Claiborne ducked under the tent flap and glared at the man-child she had tied up. He had dark circles under his wet, red-rimmed eyes. His mouth was open like he was going to say something important but forgot it and breathed from that position.

Claiborne bent down on her haunches and stroked his sweaty hair.

"Are you with me?" She patted his cheeks. He nodded. "I need you to listen and listen closely, do you understand." Another nod. "Your little girlfriend is here, and I don't want you making a sound. No whimpers, or cries for help. They may sound like heroic efforts to save your skin, but I'll smash your teeth and snap your jaw off from here." She stroked one finger from beneath his ear to where his lips parted. "It's more painful than it sounds. Only you won't be able to scream, because your tongue will hang out like a necktie."

"Ivy," Danial said.

Claiborne rolled her eyes. She had tossed stones with more intelligence.

"I will cut her up and feed her to you," Claiborne said. "Does that get your attention better?"

"Don't hurt her," Danial said, a bit of anger creeping into his tone. That was the most amount of life he'd shown since she bashed him on the head. At first, she thought she may have rattled his brain too hard but then realized that whatever damage was done to him at an earlier age. *What I did may have improved it.*

"As long as she doesn't know you are here, she will be safe."

"She wouldn't want to see me," Danial said. "I'm nothing, nothing but a damned idiot that likes to get hurt, my mother said."

"Mothers are never wrong," Claiborne said. Then she pressed her finger to his chapped lip. "Stay quiet like a mouse and the cats won't hurt you. Do this and maybe later on I'll let you out to play and give you a nice chunk of cheese."

Danial said nothing, even when she pulled her finger away. She patted him on the head and walked out of the tent.

"So glad you made it out to our little party," Claiborne said, startling Ivy. The girl's eyes widened like she saw a grackle and had her hands full of its bread crumbs. "I didn't expect to see you again so soon."

"First Sword," Cacophony clapped his hands together. "Well done on the preparations."

No thanks to her. She squinted at Ivy.

"A good sacking requires strong preparations."

Ivy blinked and looked to Cacophony. Apparently, he hadn't told her what was coming up. *I ruined the surprise,* she grinned.

"You will be in position to provide support," Cacophony said.

Nazglum suck me, not again!

"Support?"

"Are my maps and papers prepared in my tent?"

"Yes, it is set up to your specifications, as always." Claiborne followed Cacophony as he walked away. "What do you mean by support."

"Have our items from the carriage brought over," he said. "I'll brief you on events tonight. Ivy, be a dear and walk Hyrian over to the tent. I'd hate it if she got lost and decided to play with new dolls. Such an active imagination on that one."

"What's going on?" Claiborne trailed after Ivy. "How am I going to provide you support?"

Ivy shrugged.

"Last time it didn't bode well for myself or my men."

"Or Tym," Ivy said. "I do hope you learn to keep your word before I have you carve it into your chest by your own sword."

"Whatever he wants you to do, don't fuck it up because you want to do what you think is right." Then Claiborne stalked back to her tent.

Danial looked up at her approach. The dumbest look she had ever seen. Claiborne smacked his face, swinging from the hip. His head jerked to the side and he tipped over. She grabbed him by the hair.

"This is my victory," she said, spittle dripping off his face.

Danial didn't make a sound, though he pulled away when she got close. Having the man-child in her tent seemed more of a risk than she first figured. Not that Ivy could do much, not with the little ghoul-girl keeping her song in check. Still, he was a liability. She could slit his throat and drag his corpse into the backwoods. Her gut told her it wasn't a liability, but an opportunity. Claiborne had to be patient, a quality she was often forced to exercise.

Later that evening she received a message to join Cacophony in his tent. She went to it, passing his guards. *He always has rotten news.* Claiborne unclenched her fists and nodded to the men outside his tent. They ignored her, which was good. She'd hate to break one apart. When she entered, Cacophony wasn't alone. He was never alone, having his daughter so close at hand, but now Ivy was in the tent, and she wore armor familiar to Claiborne. Claiborne ground her teeth. The little shit was wearing what was hers. Why the fuck would he give it to her? She gave it over freely, a sign of her fealty, and here he was, allowing that village swine to muck it up! She glared at Ivy. Ivy nodded to her, grinning. *The bitch! I'll have to soak the armor in horse piss to disinfect it…after I peel it off your corpse.*

"Sit, First Sword, sit," Cacophony gestured to a little rug in front of his table. A place a child would be forced to sit while being disciplined. The tent had three chairs, and they were all occupied. She glared at Ivy.

What did you say about me? Ivy's face remained passive, calm, returning Claiborne's stare. *You wouldn't be so peaceful knowing I had your boyfriend tied up in my tent. Might have to enlighten you, child, on a few important details.* The first being that she should never trust a person in power. Claiborne sat cross-legged on the carpet. It did nothing to soften the ground beneath her ass, and it might have been placed deliberately on a stone. Another reminder not to get too comfortable in her position.

"Are there any other officers coming to the meeting?" Cacophony asked.

"Second and Third Swords died in the assault on Welksdale," Claiborne said. *If you had listened when I tried to explain the consequences of tactical retreat, you would have known.* He'd been so focused on getting Ivy that all else went to the latrines. Might as well have talked about the smell of shit and its various compositions for as much as he heard about the state of the Silent Men. He used to be so meticulous.

"That is a pity," he replied, taking up a goblet of water and sipping from it. He lifted the muslin to do so and revealed the ruined portion of his mouth. She was amazed that he didn't drink any wine. She could handle a mug of bitter ale, or three. "Good thing you have proven rather difficult to kill, First Sword."

Claiborne's lip twitched and she forced the snarl into a quick smile.

"I am eager to disappoint my enemies when it comes to dying."

"Then this will be brief," Cacophony said. "You find yourself tasked once more with providing support to our beloved Ivy. She will approach the town of Welksdale and use her song to convince them to open the gates. You, First Sword, will standby and wait for any resistance that might prove overwhelming for her, and I trust in your discretion not to interfere or slaughter needlessly."

That left a lot to her interpretation. What Cacophony defined as needless, Claiborne found to be a number slightly below the line of necessity.

"She will then convince the good citizens to allow your men to peacefully enter the town and graciously gift us with the supplies we require to continue our campaign to protect them from the evils of the world."

"Might prove a bit difficult to convince them, especially since we killed a good quarter or more of their friends and families," Claiborne said. "If you had allowed me to continue the assault, we wouldn't need to convince them of anything, because we would have the town in our possession."

"A tactical retreat is often required for greater gain," Cacophony said.

"There will be no resistance," Ivy said. "Unless Robin, Thrush or Nuthatch remain in the town."

The mention of Thrush made Claiborne bristle. That was another living enemy that should have been a corpse.

"My scouts have told me that Nuthatch and the rest of the singer's army left the town three nights back. Robin was nowhere to be seen," Claiborne said. The plump woman had deceived her, escaped, but to where? Claiborne had no idea. When she found her, there would be no opportunity to escape again. Nuthatch was young, inexperienced, and cowardly. They preferred fighting from positions of strength rather than risk defeat by establishing her own strong position. Nothing much had changed. Thrush was the bold one, which was why they evaded Claiborne for so long.

"Thrush?" Ivy asked, chair creaking as she leaned forward.

"I haven't seen her since our skirmish," Claiborne said.

Ivy relaxed, sitting back in her chair.

But you have. What game are you playing, child?

"Once Welksdale is secured and provisions procured, we move on," Cacophony said.

"The birds' nest in their high trees," Hyrian said, her eerie childish tone. "Safe and warm from the wintery breeze. Then the ax-man chops down their bowery and little birdies bleed and bleed."

"Do we have enough soldiers?" The next stop would be the mountains and if Nuthatch, even Robin made it to a stronghold at their base, then he would be joined by another Singer. Even with their songs silenced, they would prove difficult to kill.

"We have what we need to complete a successful campaign," Cacophony said, glancing at Ivy, and then rose from his chair. "Like the early bird, we rise to get the worm. We should all try to sleep. A busy day looms."

Claiborne took that as her cue to stand up.

"May I talk with Ivy? I have something that might be of interest to her."

"Don't be long," Cacophony said.

"Oh, it will only be a moment." Claiborne grinned.

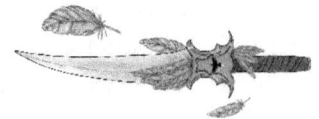

Ivy followed Claiborne out in the cool night air. There weren't any cook fires since the smoke would give away their positions. Orders were given that noise should be limited. Beyond the honor guard at Cacophony's tent, the camp was already quiet. Claiborne had her alone, beneath the stars. Ivy realized that could be dangerous. She could draw and kill Ivy, claim she tried to escape. Ivy kept her hand close to the dagger she took from Thrush. Hyrian's power blocked the song, disrupting the harmonic manipulations as Thrush would put it, and the metal felt lighter, brittle. *Might turn to dust the moment I draw it.* But harmonic forged steel was all she had. What she counted on as her shield was Claiborne's fear of Cacophony.

Ivy sensed a shift in the dynamics between Claiborne and Hyman. She didn't know when it started, but that he no longer counted on Claiborne. This made Ivy an enemy, or at best a rival to the man who allowed Claiborne relevance. The way the woman sneered at her Ivy guessed the First Sword would like to put a quick end to that barrier.

Claiborne stopped and put a hand out, nearly smacking Ivy in the forehead.

"Let me get to the point," Claiborne said, hands on her hips. "He has a great fascination with you, and it makes him blind. He sees you as a daughter, someone his own child will never grow up to become. That gives you too much power. Too much control."

Not too subtle. What does she hope to gain? It might be another tactic to catch her off guard, like the way she did in sword practice before giving Ivy a hard *smack!*

"You're jealous that he loves me," Ivy said. "I'm not some broken thing to follow orders."

Claiborne laughed.

"He is beyond love, kid. The sooner you learn that the better off you'll be when disappointment comes and hits you like a rock."

What rock did you bring?

"Is there a purpose to this *chat* besides you trying to threaten me?"

"I have something to show you that you will find of great interest. Wait here." Claiborne slipped inside her tent and Ivy heard some mumbling.

Who does she have inside that would interest me?

The flap opened again and lamplight spilled out. Claiborne waved her in. She doubted Claiborne would kill her and incur Hyman's wrath, but people acted irrationally when caught up in jealousy. Ivy expected some sort of fussy huff from the woman, but Claiborne seemed the sort of person to keep such a thing private. *Better safe than sorry.* Ivy gripped the hilt of her dagger as she stepped in. It took a moment for her eyes to adjust to the light. The tent was small. A trunk and a cot occupied most of it. Ivy's mouth hung open.

"Danial?"

He lifted his head, and Ivy placed a hand over her mouth. Last time they met she had *convinced* him to go back to Welksdale. Here he was, hands and feet tied. Bruises marked his cheeks, lips split and scabbed over, and one eye swollen shut. A single tear slipped from his shiny eyes, but he didn't say a word.

"What did you do to him?" Ivy turned on Claiborne, reaching for the power. It was there, but she couldn't do more than touch it. "I swear if you don't release him—"

"You'll do what?" Claiborne asked, patting Danial on the head. "Take revenge on me like you did for your uncle? Danial and I have had plenty to talk about, Ivy. He so desperately wants to hear the nightingales sing. It will be hard if I punctured his eardrums."

Should have killed her when you had a chance.

"What do you want?"

"Your word," Claiborne said. "Once this is over, you disappear. Oh, don't worry, I will hunt you down, but you'll have a head start. I'll even let you take this man-child with you."

"You want me to leave?"

"Yes! You are a blight," Claiborne said, stroking Danial's sweaty hair. "Even blights have their uses of clearing the weak from the strong. I have a change of plans for your little game tomorrow. Rather than convince the townsfolk to step aside, you'll have a few of them start a riot. Maybe force a couple leaders to kill a person or three."

The idea of using her song to hurt the people she knew unsettled her stomach. Ivy laid her hands on her belly. Everything felt heavy and she wanted to hold it all in before it spilled out.

"Why?"

"You should know this quite well, Ivy," Claiborne said. "When you leave an enemy alive and behind you, they will find a way to stab you in the back."

CHAPTER TWENTY
THE LAST STAND

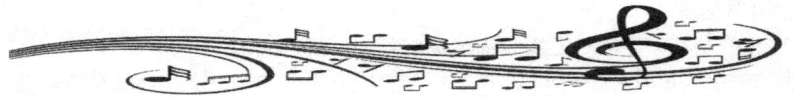

No one knows when the Dark One will end the time of service. Months, years, decades could pass while you work to accomplish the goal set to end the vicious hold of Harmony, to break Songs and those who Sing them. Or perhaps to find the One who will be true Salvation of the world corrupted in endless toil and servitude. Whenever the last stand occurs, one must be ready to fight as though your sanity is at risk.

"They left two days back," the man named Simon said. He sat like a lump on his chair by the open gate. Robin couldn't believe how trusting this town's people were after they had a massive battle no more than five days back. *They are begging to be killed off.*

"Did they say where?" Thrush asked.

Simon shrugged.

"I didn't bother to ask," Simon said. "I figured the problem resolved itself. Should we be worried?"

"Might want to keep the gates closed and locked a little longer," Robin said. "That would be the prudent action."

"I'll inform the Sheriff," Simon said, settling back in his chair, not in any hurry to do anything more than occupy space. "Oh, but not all of the soldiers left. About a dozen or so stayed behind. You can find them at the tavern."

Very good, Nuthatch, leave a few behind to wait for my return.

They left Simon staring out the open gate.

"Are you sure you want to stick around and watch these people get slaughtered?" Robin asked Thrush.

"I have to try with Ivy," Thrush replied.

Stubborn as always.

"You think they will send her here alone?" Robin asked.

"It will serve as some final test for Cacophony. Should the girl convince the town to surrender without bloodshed, he will have won a major victory," Thrush said. "He will grow his ranks with an unstoppable force all without having to draw a single blade. The entire world will turn on us and hunt us down."

"Such a pretty picture you paint," Robin said. They passed several more townsfolk strolling around as though their place hadn't been tossed not too long ago. Blood still stained the cobble stones they walked on.

To have this world they lived in, oblivious of violence. But the violence will find them.

At the tavern they met the rather annoyed glare of the woman tending the front. They had been courteous to a point, holding up the Singer's army, since they did prevent the utter destruction of the town. Their welcome wasn't as warm, and in fact might be stone cold, and Robin knew they would have to leave a little coin to appease the ill-favor accrued. Not that coin would pay off the Silent Men when they strolled through the open gates, killing and taking their meager possessions.

A soldier spotted Robin and saluted. She didn't know his name, it was difficult to learn them all, just to watch them die.

"What's your name?" she asked.

"Allen, ma'am," Allen said, though he was no older than a boy with his patchwork beard.

"Where are the rest, Allen?" Robin asked.

"In their rooms waiting orders," Allen said.

Good, at least they weren't causing trouble in town.

"Bring them out, we have to discuss important details," Robin said. "Especially when it concerns their lives. We won't trade what's not ours to give."

Except we do it every time we fight the Silent Men. Thrush grunted agreement with the sentiment of Robin's statement. It was good for morale, even if they didn't entirely believe it themselves. They gathered in the tavern's back room, ordered food and drink which Thrush paid for with a small pouch of coins. Twelve soldiers remained.

A last meal, perhaps.

Who knew when the Silent Men will gather and attack the town?

"I humbly thank you for your diligence and faith in Robin and I," Thrush said. "That you trusted in our wisdom and good fortune to return to you. I will not ask you to stay. Any of you." She looked at Robin. Robin nodded. She may not be obliged to remain, but she wasn't about to abandon Thrush yet. *Besides, if she doesn't kill the girl. I will.*

"I'm not leaving," Allen said and the rest nodded, shouting their assent to remain. Thrush smiled, though Robin knew it was the one reserved for people after they gave her what she wanted. Subtle manipulation was something Robin saw her father, King Meus, use in the Nymphadelia Court to guide subjects to the conclusions he wanted them to draw. Thrush was better than him by far.

"Then I ask for patience, to protect the people of Welksdale," Thrush said. "Eat, drink, but be ready. The enemy will be at the gates and we need to convince as many townspeople to leave as possible. But if they refuse, leave them alone to their fate."

"They don't believe another attack is coming," Robin said. "They left the gates wide open. Be ready for a hasty retreat if what we plan fails. No need to be heroes."

They finished their meal and Robin returned to a room with Thrush. It was the same simple one they had shared with Nuthatch, who left them a note telling them of her decision to take the majority of their army to the Nest. It was simply worded in neat looping words. Robin tore it up and tossed the pieces into her bag to scatter later.

"Are you sure about this?" Robin asked.

"It's the only way," Thrush responded.

"I don't like it."

"If you did, I would have to second guess it," Thrush said. "Besides, I need you where you can help if they bring the girl to silence us."

"Well, it'll be your neck if it goes tits up," Robin said. *My neck, too, trying to save you.*

"I knew I could count on you," Thrush said. "I think it is time we begin our preparations."

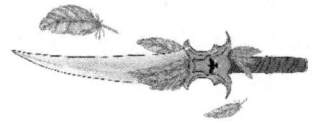

The food, dishes, and long table were removed from the main tent, replaced by two bedrolls, a small writing desk, and a chair. Hyrian lay on one bedroll, humming and rearranging Glorian's dress. Ivy couldn't get the image of her playing with the corpse out of her mind. *How many people in those homes ended up as playthings for you?* Ivy didn't really want to know the answer. *That's*

one thing that has to change if I'm going to be a part of this family.

Was she really a family member, or was that another lie that Cacophony created to manipulate Ivy? It came back to the vision she witnessed. The truth behind the veil of lies. Wasn't she considering betraying him in return to save a man she hardly knew?

"What did Claiborne want to talk about?" Cacophony sat at the writing desk, back turned to Ivy. He was wearing matching black robes. This was the first time Ivy had seen him without his armor on. It didn't diminish him any, since he was a large man, though he no longer looked like a bug.

He doesn't know about Danial. Of course, he didn't. Danial was Claiborne's bargaining chip. Cacophony would kill her if he knew. *But not before she killed Danial.* Ivy had to preserve this secret, for Danial's sake.

"Thrush," Ivy said, trying to keep her voice from squeaking. Cacophony turned, right arm leaning on the back of the chair. He looked at her, brows knitting together. *Like he's trying to catch me in a lie.* "She felt like opening up about what happened to her lover, Arron."

"Interesting," he said. "Why would she choose this moment to reveal such an intimate secret?"

"I don't know," Ivy said, trying to sound casual, though her heart was thumping and her thoughts swirling. "She wanted to talk about how much she hates the woman so much. How much it hurts, you know, the disappointment in how close she was to killing Thrush, but the woman always finds ways to survive. I think she's more cat than bird. All those lives."

Cacophony's eyes narrowed.

"Those women can't be trusted," he said. "They'll ruin all our lives. Drive us into darkness. They care nothing about you or me. They want to twist the world into their image. They may seem impenetrable, but believe me when I say they are not. They can and must be killed. I understand the First Sword's disappointment, but patience is the ultimate path to glory, child. Sometimes we have to give up some little thing in order to gain a greater thing."

Like Danial.

"I will hold those words close to my heart," Ivy said.

"Not the heart. The mind, always be mindful of them," he said. "The heart is fickle and can trick our minds into foolish acts. Now, you have a busy day ahead. Best you get some sleep."

"The mind, not the heart." Ivy tapped the side of her head. "Thank you, father."

Satisfied with her response, he went back to writing.

Ivy stripped to her small clothes and lay in the bedroll.

Hyrian smiled at her.

"We are the same, sister." Hyrian kissed her palm and reached out, touching Ivy's cheek. Her fingers were cold. Ivy doubted there was any warmth left in the child. It had burnt out in the fire, leaving cold ash behind. "You are not alone."

Ivy rolled on her side. Decisions. She'd have to make a choice, tomorrow, and live with the consequences. Ivy had never felt more alone than she did at this moment. Sacrifices would be made, and she would have to think long on who she would betray.

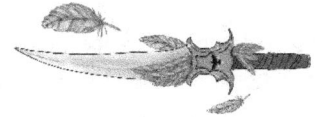

She'd expected a visit from the Shadow Figure in her dreams. He didn't make an appearance. Once she fell asleep, she had no dreams that she could remember. Cacophony, again donning his armor, woke her up. They ate bread and olive paste. Very few words were exchanged which Ivy was grateful for. She still hadn't decided her course of action. They went outside in the cool morning air, a fine mist graying the morning light. Cacophony waited for her in the carriage, along with Hyrian. Fifty mounted Silent Men led by Claiborne were ready for an assault on Welksdale, if Ivy failed.

People were going to die, and there was nothing Ivy could do to stop it.

She climbed into the carriage. Cacophony sat across from her and Hyrian clutched her golden-haired doll, watching Ivy. Her green eyes had a predator's glow, though she was a child, or something pretending to be a child. Ivy squirmed in her seat. They would be sisters, if she did this one task the way Cacophony wanted. They would both be the same.

Alone. I have to do this alone.

"How are you, Ivy?" Cacophony asked.

Sick, disgusted, I just want to curl up and go to sleep, wake up from this nightmare.

"I'm ready to do what is right," Ivy said.

"That's all I can ever ask, Ivy," Cacophony said. "Sometimes…sometimes the actions we take, no matter our intentions, people get hurt and we can't please everyone. You will either be a hero to some and a monster to many, or a monster to many and a hero to a few. If you had to choose…be the monster. You'll be remembered longer."

"Which are you?" Ivy asked, trying to read his eyes. She thought there was sadness in them. She had been wrong before.

"I am what people need me to be," Cacophony said. "What the world needs, but doesn't understand. You understand, don't you, Ivy?"

Ivy thought about Danial tied up in Claiborne's tent. She thought about the people of Welksdale. The choice she'd have to make between the two. The choice she'd have to make between Cacophony and Claiborne, as well. Plenty of choices to make. Not a single damn one led to an outcome where no one got hurt.

"I do," Ivy said.

They reached the stables not far from the town's walls. He followed her out of the carriage and hugged her. "Try not to get yourself killed," he said, giving a half-hearted laugh.

"You, either," Ivy said.

Behind her, Claiborne leaned on the saddle horn. She chewed on black leaf and spat a gob into the dirt. She nodded toward the stable where Danial was being kept. Ivy frowned and Claiborne winked at her. His battered face looked worse in the daylight.

"Who's this?" Cacophony had asked when Claiborne dragged Danial from the horse and tied him up in the stable.

"Found him walking the roads," Claiborne said. "I didn't want him warning the town of our approach."

Cacophony grunted.

"Surprised he is still alive, First Sword," he said. "Softening, are you?"

"I guess we all have to change," Claiborne said and looked at Ivy. "Especially if we want to live long enough to get what we want."

Claiborne heeled her horse forward, telling Ivy it was time to move. Fifty mounted Silent Men rode five abreast and ten deep, ready to add support, or to slaughter the people of Welksdale. *Trample me if I decide to turn against them.* A fitting end, full circle to the Fugglies and Bryn, which seemed so simple back then. Threatened by starvation, molestation, murder, and a golden knitting needle, looks like she had found a new way to endanger herself.

All I wanted was a bit of bread and some sweet-milk. Now, I am here for…everything.

She walked up the road, watching the Welksdale walls come into view. An unstoppable force in her harmonic forged armor, strong enough to stop an arrow or shatter an axe head, not that she would want to test it. Sweat dripped from her braided hairline, down the back of her neck and her palms were cold. It was the Exchequer all over again, but with more at risk. Danial, the townsfolk, Cacophony's trust. Ivy's heart thudded, the power pulsing along with it. She would provide the distraction while the soldiers robbed the town, except Claiborne added another wrinkle to the problem.

Sacrifice the many for the one, or one for the many. The town folk were dead, anyway. Claiborne would send her horse into the town if Ivy failed to follow through. There was no way Ivy was certain Claiborne would keep her word, either. She could have Danial's throat cut and then kill Ivy during the assault. *I wouldn't put it past the treacherous bitch. Don't leave an enemy at her back.*

Then there was Cacophony. How would he react to her causing a riot? He trusted her to do what was right. He lied about the attack on the village, she was certain. *Do what's right. What does that even mean anymore?*

She wished she had someone to ask the difficult questions and ponder their response. Someone she could trust.

Alone. Always will be alone.

The newly remade gate was sealed and there were a few men walking the tops. Ivy wouldn't have believed it if she hadn't seen it with her own eyes. The town had been lulled into an uneasy slumber until the Silent Men woke it up with a jab in the ass.

Ivy stuck her chin out and grasped the power. The first watcher on the wall spotted her. One of Sheriff Gareth's men in a dark green uniform, the color of what the world used to be before the killing drought. He shouted, pointing at Ivy. A moment later, Sheriff Gareth appeared, hand raised and they watched Ivy. When she was within a few yards, the Sheriff waved and called down to her.

"State your name and business."

All he cared about was getting Bryn to pay his taxes. He never asked about the bruises on my face. Anger fueled the pulsing heat of her power. She released the song, delving into the three men atop the wall. The images blended into a collage of fear and death, lust and destruction. Names swirled in her head, faces blurred, and Ivy shoved them aside. One lesson she learned from Sparrow was that she had to be quick and not indulge in the visions. The stories were enticing, but she didn't have the time for them. She overpowered the wills of each man and inserted her demands.

"Open….the gate," Sheriff Gareth called down. "Open the damn gate."

The gates remained sealed.

Walk!

Three sets of boots marched in unison under one mind, Ivy's, and she served as a passenger, watching the events behind the wall, filtered through three pairs of eyes. *This must be how a fly sees the world.* The multi-layered view created a moment of nausea and Ivy stopped a few yards from the gate to regain her bearings. She saw the bell tower. Simon was reaching for the bell, face confused, watching the men march in lines like obedient ants. Ivy created another melody, allowing the song to touch him, forcing his hand to release the gong. Again, she shoved away the images that accompanied delving. She didn't need to see what goes on in his mind.

Use a few to influence the many. Ivy moved in their minds, listening, touching, seeing all they saw and thought. There was confusion by the gate. Another man that Ivy recognized as Dwight, tall, plain-looking, with a black beard peppered white.

"What are you doing? What's that singing going on?" Dwight said, looking at each man. "Why aren't you manning the walls?"

"Open the gate," Sheriff Gareth said, hand on his sword. Ivy wasn't going to have him draw, not yet. She had a hard time seeing the town through so many eyes and her stomach ached, the pulse behind her eyes thickening. A trickle of blood slipped from her nose and she tasted it on her lips. "Do it and quit questioning my orders."

Dwight ran to the bar, straining to lift it.

"It's heavy." Dwight grunted. "Are you going to stand there like flies on shit or help me?"

Ivy had Simon step forward and take the other side. The bar shifted, rising from its cradle. They dropped it and Dwight threw aside the latches. The gate opened and Ivy saw the five men through her own eyes. She released Simon, planting in his mind that sleep was good. He wandered off to the cool shade under the bell tower and laid on the ground.

"What are you—"

Ivy let the melody that had controlled Simon take over Dwight. She was struck by the vision of a woman screaming and then being cut down on the southern gate by a rider in black. Trying to drag her back inside, while she clutched her belly, holding in ropey guts and screaming with every jagged bump. A horse trampled her legs, crushing them into a mess of shattered bone, flesh and blood. She released the vision, feeling her heart break and eyes water.

Be in the here and now, not what had been. Nothing I can do about the past.

Ivy entered Welksdale, song pulsing and controlling the four men. She retreated along with her song, pulling back from their senses, but held the minds and thoughts sending frightened emotions. Doing what Robin must've done by tying it off. More people had begun filling the street. Ivy recognized a few faces from the people who threw mud at her.

Telum trahere.

Three swords and a cudgel were drawn. Ivy could easily turn them loose on the crowd, have them slaughter them like wolves among the sheep. The eyes shifted from her to the men chosen to protect them, weapons at hand. *Do it! They mean nothing to you. Break them, the way they would break you. Hurt them like they hurt you.*

"Ivy," her name spoken softly.

"Hurt them," Ivy said and the men began to advance on the townsfolk.

"Ivy, don't!"

She turned and saw Thrush. Her anger began to soften and it resonated through the song. The men she controlled stopped their advance.

"What are you doing here? I thought you would be long, gone like Robin and Nuthatch."

The thin woman wore her white robes, frowning, sharp nose, and piercing eyes leveled on her. She had two short swords, and was quick enough to gut Ivy, but she didn't attack. A dozen men in dark blue armor stood behind her and another dozen had bows, arrows trained on Ivy. She didn't know if Claiborne had lied to her intentionally or was misinformed. The armor she wore was harmonic forged, but she figured so were the swords and arrows of the men supporting Thrush.

"I'm here to stop Cacophony," Thrush said. "You could help me."

Ivy released her song, but not before suggesting that Dwight, Sheriff Gareth, and the other men hold their position to control the crowd, prevent a riot, no matter the cost.

"No, I can't. I have to do this, Thrush," Ivy said. "They have Danial and a half-hundred horses ready to charge the town unless I take care of it."

"Where, Ivy? Where are they keeping him?"

Ivy shook her head.

"You can't do anything. They will kill you, kill you all." Her voice thickened. "I have no choice. These people are dead even if you were to put an arrow in me."

"At least let them have a fighting chance."

"He's counting on me, Thrush. I'm sorry."

Ivy unleashed her song and it grew in a bright flame touching the minds of every soldier surrounding Thrush. She delved deep and fast, not pausing to look at the palette of colorful scenes rushing past, the joy, the pain, the desperation. The song suggested it would be better to lower their weapons. Swords and bows clattered to the ground. Ivy watched Thrush, not touching her with the song. *Kill me! Take away my misery.* Tears wet her cheeks as she willed Thrush to run her through with one of her swords. Stern features softened and the sword drooped, point dipping and falling from her fingers into the dirt. Thrush held her arms out, a way to signal Ivy had won. *Why won't she kill me?* Ivy felt the power fade along with her anger. Her song slipped away and left her empty.

"I can't do this," Ivy said, sick at the idea that she could force these people to attack each other. To murder them using their own wills. "I don't know what to believe anymore. Why don't you kill me? End it?"

"There is a better way," Thrush said. "Listen to me and I'll help you rescue Danial."

"I don't think that's possible," Ivy said, wanting to do nothing more than lie down in the street and let whatever end come. "They outnumber us."

"I know how we can even the odds." Thrush gave her a reassuring smile.

Ivy shrugged and listened.

It won't work, but there's no other choice left.

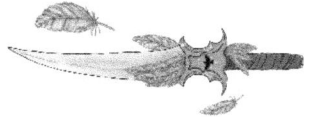

The walls were empty and the gate was open. Claiborne spat, hoping the girl would fail, but so far, she was doing everything she was instructed to do. *She did the job of a few good archers and a battering ram. Nothing special. Nothing deserving of extra attention or admiration.* She watched Ivy enter Welksdale. The girl had the power of a political speaker, or con-artist. Convince people to do what they don't want, purchase shit they don't need. If Cacophony had allowed Claiborne to complete the task of dismantling this little shit hole town, then they wouldn't have to spend more time retaking it.

"Better complete the job, girl." Claiborne held the spyglass up, focusing on Ivy's backside, small and insignificant. There was no muscle, no strength. In this new order, it seemed strength came in different forms. *Come on, what's taking so long?* She couldn't see the girl's face, to hear what she might be saying, or singing—though not hearing the song was the point in maintaining her own free will. *Still, I wish I could hear what was happening.* Finally, four men moved ahead of Ivy. They seemed to be almost sleepwalking. Marionettes, dancing to the tune Ivy sang and their strings tugged, all four drew swords in unison.

Claiborne swung the spyglass. *The town awakens to the new problem.* A crowd had formed in the street. She imagined their faces: confused, scared, as jittery as a swarm of worms after their rock had been turned over and a strange bird was eyeing them. Who was this stranger? What did she want? Why did their own people turn weapons on them? Panic was near ripe; Claiborne could taste it.

"Do it, girl," Claiborne said. "Start that riot."

The men didn't attack. They took up a defensive position, which meant there must be other armed men coming. A good old fashion street brawl. Excitement tingled in Claiborne's lower regions. Blood was about to run. As much as she detested the girl, Ivy did have a gift. A strong gift and she was certain that she could destroy the entire town. *But she won't get all the glory.*

Her arm itched to raise and call for a charge. *Patience. Wait for the right moment.* The fighting would start. The confusion would thicken. Somewhere in all that mess was Thrush—a scout reported to her that Thrush was lurking close and she told them to let her pass. The girl had to delay her enough for Claiborne to ride in and crush the bitch. Thrush might kill Ivy in the process, so it was a winning situation either way.

There was a long pause, both sides sizing each other up. Usually there would be a few hard words, threats made, and curses on mothers, wives, girlfriends...but the men were controlled by Ivy. She could have them attack without all the cock measuring and who could piss the furthest. Ivy didn't have a cock to worry about.

Why aren't you attacking?

Claiborne heeled her horse into a new angle. One where she could see around the edges of the gate. A man cut off her view.

Then Ivy stepped to her right and was no longer in the circle of the spyglass.

That's not good.

There was no fighting, no bloodshed, no screaming and yelling, and no Ivy.

The town acted as though it held a collective breath, posing for some idyllic painting composed of mud and pig shit. *What the fuck are you doing, Ivy?*

Claiborne raised her hand to give the signal to charge, when she noticed the crowd in the street begin to disperse. Her heart sank and she grit her teeth, ready to shout the command to charge. Kill everything and everyone, including the traitorous Ivy. *Oh, the fun I'll have with Danial once this is over. I'll make sure he knows it was your fault, Ivy. You betrayed us all and worst of all, him.*

She started to lower the spyglass when she caught sight of men in dark blue armor. *Thrush's men!* Claiborne scanned the scene. There was a flash of steel, a shout rising and figures crashing into each other. The fray dissolved into such chaos of dark blue and mottled clothes that Claiborne could no longer follow a single thread of battle. It was delicious, though, and she felt a tingle in her gut. When there was bloodshed, she wanted, no, needed to be there and taste the salt of battle on her tongue.

Seems she had a cock hiding up there, after all. Claiborne smiled, smacking the spyglass closed. She raised her right arm, held it in the air for a moment of exaggerated triumph, then shouted. "Time to ride!"

Claiborne kicked the courser into a charge. She missed her big destrier, since she could crash into the fray, and knew he would protect her. This one was less aggressive, but fast. Behind her hooves thundered across the ground. She drew her long sword, the thrill of the charge pulsing through her veins, muscles tightened for impact, and a sadistic grin on her face. She fast approached the gates and the people were too busy fighting among themselves; there would be no resistance. Not a single arrow fired, no shouts of warning, but men wrestling with sword and in armor, caught up in the sacred embrace of kill or be killed, unknowing that death rode in to put a bloody end to all their struggles.

Let them be joined as lovers in their demise.

She let out a laugh, which then turned into a scream.

Claiborne was through the gate when she realized her mistake.

The soldiers hacking at each other with swords, wrestling around in the dirt moments grunting and shouting, all sprung up and cleared out of her path, leaving Claiborne to stare at a dozen archers flanking her. Arrows loosed. Two struck her horse in the head and neck, another glancing off her helm. Claiborne threw herself from the dying courser, struck the ground and rolled on the impact. Pain erupted in her left shoulder, sending a numb tingling down to her fingers. She continued rolling out of the street as more horses crashed through to a hail of arrow fire.

Horses and men screamed, punctured by the harmonic forged arrows. Those whose mounts tossed them met a swift end from soldiers hacking at them on the ground. Beast and man screamed, blood wetting the dried ground, feeding it where the dirt had begun to lose its red hue, stained fresh. Claiborne's left arm was next to useless. Grunting, she lifted her chest off the ground, bending her back like a serpent about to sink its fangs she stabbed a man in the leg, and when he fell, she kept jabbing him over and over again. Hot blood sprayed her face and she was nearly blind by it. She tore off her gauntlet and wiped blood from her eyes, then began searching for Ivy.

Fucking bitch betrayed me!

Black and dark blue armor flashed around, killing and being killed. The line of horses entering the town broke off when the trailing Silent Men recognized the trap and turned back. Claiborne inched her way to her knees and then her feet. A sword flashed out and she caught it on the edge of her blade, turning it away and smashed her helm into the man's surprised face.

"Ivy! Where are you, cunt?" She worked the strap from her helm, then swung it at another of Thrush's men. It bounced off his shoulder, causing him to miss his thrust. She tripped him, reversing her grip on the sword and put it through the lower part of his spine where the armor didn't cover. The man grunted as she ripped her sword free and continued walking through the street, shouting until her throat felt like she had swallowed gravel. "Ivy!"

Horse hooves pounded the ground and Claiborne glanced up to see a white horse bearing down on her. In the saddle were two women: one in white and one in black. Claiborne sidestepped, attempting to bring her sword around to strike. The horse and women were past, gone, leaving Claiborne choking on dust.

"Fuck!"

There wasn't a living horse in sight. She ran toward the gate, each jounce sending a jolt of pain through her left arm. Beyond the gate her men milled around, staring at the white horse rather than giving chase. *Fucking idiots!* Her voice was hoarse, raw from screaming out her fury.

A man in dark blue armor cut off her escape. He had a grim, young-looking face. He reminded Claiborne a little of Arron, but uglier. A face only a mother could love, if she had her eyes burnt out. Pimples covered the bulbous nose and he had a few crooked teeth. Boys desperate to make a name for themselves by serving the Singers.

They never learn.

Claiborne swung her sword at him. The harmonic forged metal turned her blade away and she ducked a counter attack, driving her blade up through the boy's groin. *Kid's balls probably just dropped. They are dropped for good.* He screamed and she yanked the sword free. He toppled over, clutching the bloody ruin of his manhood. She left him and stumbled out the gate.

The ground rumbled and a great explosion of stone and dirt filled the air in front of the white horse. Claiborne watched a chasm erupt from the ground, sending mount and riders flying, and the few who gave pursuit tumbled into the hole. A tidy grave, just dump the dirt back over and say a few prayers.

She grabbed a rider who was close by watching. He gave her a wide-eyed, gap-mouth stare.

"Huh?"

"Let me show you what a horse is for." Then she shoved him from the saddle. She had a foot up in a stirrup and didn't look back. He could've broken his neck, but Claiborne didn't give two shits. In fact, she was all out of shits to give. Unless it was for Thrush. She had one big, smelly turd left for her and was prepared to jam it down her throat.

"I'm coming for you, Thrush," Claiborne whispered, her voice turned to dirt and gravel. "No way you fucking escape this time."

CHAPTER TWENTY-ONE
DEATH IS COMPLICATED

Death is not the end. It is only the beginning.

Ivy wrapped her arms around Thrush's midriff, clinging to her back to keep from being bounced off the horse. Horses still terrified her. She'd escaped nearly being trampled, bitten, and kicked; there had to be an easier way to travel.

"Not so tight," Thrush levered her arm apart. "You don't need to break my ribs."

Ivy pressed the side of her face against Thrush's shoulder blade, pulling back when she heard Thrush's song. She glanced over the woman's shoulder, wishing she hadn't. There was a brief rumble, like approaching thunder and the ground tore open. Rock and stone tore through hard packed dirt, and the Silent Men in their way. As they passed the shattered ground, pieces of flesh and stone rained around them, splattering them in gore that once were living beings. Ivy closed mouth to keep from swallowing any, but she breathed in the stink for a brief moment and then they were past the killing field.

Cacophony would be waiting for her at the stable. The stables where Ivy first threatened to kill the girl who was blocking her song. A different girl with a different set of morales entered that space, prepared to sacrifice all to end the threat. Not to be embraced as a sister, or as a daughter. To be treated like someone important. *It's not too late to stab Thrush in the back and run to him, you know. Trade Thrush's life for Danial.* It would be easy to tell Cacophony about Claiborne's treachery, her ploy to use Danial as leverage against him. With Thrush gone and Claiborne exiled, Danial and her could stay with the Silent Men. Put the world at right again.

Except, she couldn't.

There was no right, or wrong. There was only innocent people being crushed by those who had power because they happened to be in the wrong place at the wrong time. Admitting anything else was a heroic dream. One thing Tym taught her was that heroes died, no matter how hard Ivy tried to protect him.

Better to be the monster and let them remember you longer. Cacophony had said that to her and it sounded about right. Every choice Ivy made always hurt someone. There was no greater good. There was only life and death.

I will stop them from killing Danial.

She snuck a peek past Thrush's elbow. The stables were in view. Choices would need to be made soon. What type of person was she to become? Ivy could take control of them all... could change them into her personal puppets to tug on their strings, demanding they release her, to forget about them. *Let me have them,* her song demanded. Then they crossed an invisible barrier—one moment her song thrummed, warm and comforting in her chest, tingling along her limbs, then she was plunged into icy coldness. No longer nauseas, since Cacophony cured her of it, but her body was numb. Thrush tensed up as well, taking a sharp breath.

"It almost hurts," Ivy said.

"Worse when you've held it long," Thrush said. "Like the death of an intimate friend."

Figures in black armor stood in front of the stables like ants ready to battle. So many with sharp, bristling metal. How could they fight their way past them? Ivy noted a familiar blade rising above the others at the center. Under a golden stream of sunlight, Silent Prayer gripped in both hands by Cacophony. A ring of sharp halberds lowered as they approached, ready to cut apart horses and riders.

"Take the reins," Thrush said, putting them into Ivy's hands and giving her no other choice.

"I don't know how to ride," Ivy said.

"Easy, tug them in what direction you want to go and pull back on these when you want to stop." Then Thrush swung her right leg over the horse's head. She held onto the saddle horn, left foot in the stirrup. Thrush drew her sword and jumped, her arms were crossed and she tucked her head under her chin, rolling like a cast die. Luck was in her favor.

"Shit!" Ivy ducked beneath a halberd, tugging the reins to turn the horse right, at least she hoped it was for the right. The horse whinnied, jerking its head to the right side and Ivy clung on although her body wanted desperately to keep on the same course. Her thighs burned and she grabbed the saddle horn, nearly forgot about the reins, almost dropping them, but held onto them at the last instant. She was headed back to the road, away from the stable.

How the hell do I control this thing?

She leaned back, tugging the reins. The horse's head jerked and it gave another angry whinny. *Sorry, I don't know what I'm doing.* The horse stopped, and Ivy slammed groin first into the saddle horn. The girdle didn't cover that region and she held onto the horse's head, groaning and heart thumping.

I hate horses! She slid, nearly falling from the saddle, and caught her foot in the stirrup. Dangling, one-legged, Ivy got her left foot on the ground and untangled her right. The sound of crashing metal was close. She spun, hand on the dagger's hilt. Took a large gulp of air at the spectacle she witnessed several yards away from the stable. Thrush faced a sharp, pointy forest of wood and steel, looking small, a tiny bird lost among the branches. A quick bird, darting between the lumbering limbs.

Around her, men had fallen, cut down by her quick sword strokes. Thrush's white robe was cut in many places, blood gleaming on the white, but she fought on, five men unable to pin her in place. Behind them stood Cacophony, Silent Prayer in his hand, waiting his turn. Thrush would cut her way to him soon enough.

Danial, she reminded herself why she was there. She couldn't take her eyes off Thrush as the woman skewered another man while deflecting a swing that should have torn her arm off if she was any slower. She was speed and grace, more like a darting hummingbird than a thrush. Ivy shook her head. *Get Danial, toss him on the horse, and get as far away as you can.*

As she took a jittery step in the direction of the stable, she noticed Cacophony no longer was watching Thrush. His eyes were on her. *He knows.* Ivy kept up a steady walk, expecting him to counter her, block her path to the stable. Cacophony watched, men dying in front of him, but it was Ivy who was most important. Observing the choice Ivy would make. His eyes told her it wasn't too late to make things right between them.

Thrush's back was to Ivy, the singer busy concentrating on surviving. *Stab her in the back, end it all.* Ivy drew the dagger. *But it wouldn't end.* The fighting would continue as long as a singer survived to stand against Cacophony. Countless more men and women would die in the war. For what end? Did any of this really stop the Lord of Darkness from taking over their world, or hasten his entrance?

"I'm sorry," Ivy said and moved to the stable. Cacophony gave her a nod. He had expected this, and accepted her decision.

Walk in, get Danial, walk out, so simple. Deal with the consequences later. Simple was not simple. Ivy entered the stables, eyes adjusting to the gloom. She blinked. Breath caught in her throat. *No!*

Some choices were made for you.

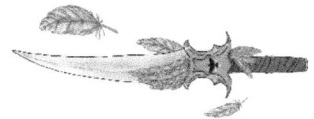

The horse frothed around the bit, galloping along while Claiborne held the reins in her right hand. Her left shoulder hung, dislocated. It was as if hot coals were shoved through a hole in her armpit, pressing where the shoulder and arm should meet. The shoulder no longer had the soft curve, but turned into some misshapen bump. Clash of metal and shrieks of men were loud ahead. Cacophony's guards were doing a great job of giving their lives. *Might as well be a bunch of sheep leaping into the maw of a wolf.* The number standing dropped to two. Thrush would make short work of them.

She spotted Ivy stealing around into the stable. The little bitch betrayed her for a man-child. One whose brains were already pounded into butter long before they had ever met. Maybe he was bigger in other areas to cover his other deficiencies. Claiborne hadn't bothered to look. She hadn't seen a man naked since before Arron died. Mourning and trying to avenge his death took up more time than she had anticipated.

Cacophony backed away, trailing Ivy and leaving Thrush alone to face the last standing guard. Claiborne almost pitied the man. His death would be pointless. The good coming from it being that Thrush would be left alive enough for Claiborne to kill. She heeled harder into the flanks, urging the horse to go faster. *Speeding my way to death.* Claiborne wanted to laugh, but her throat was full of gravel, it hurt to swallow if she had any spit left. Her mouth was dry with curses. This was her last ride. One straight to her lover's arms. Claiborne embraced it, welcomed the end. As long as she had to get to Thrush before Cacophony killed the bitch.

The last man took a while to die. Thrush's sword was rammed up to the hilt under his right arm, but he still swung at her with his left, the wooden halberd pole slick with blood smacked Thrush across the ribs. Claiborne cringed, watching Thrush stumble to the side. The crack of wood on bone usually meant something bad for the bones. Which meant it was something good for Claiborne, whose dislocated shoulder ached like a fire burning, arm jouncing around.

A little closer. A little faster.

The horse wheezed and shook its head at her urging. Bloody foam flew in her face. Thrush recovered, turning in time to see Claiborne swooping down on her, a hawk holding sharp talons to pierce its prey. Thrush had one sword in her hand, her free hand darting beneath her robes and when it came out, a thin object spun at Claiborne. *Shit!* She ducked, veering to the side where the horse wouldn't trample the little bird, yet close enough for Claiborne to dive, or in her case, flop. Luck was a warrior's best friend in a fight. It played a pivotal role in when to duck, weave, and strike. When Claiborne left the horse's saddle, luck served her as she fell directly on top of Thrush.

Luck was also a fickle whore who'd sell you out for a penance.

Claiborne landed directly on her dislocated shoulder. The pain was immediate and intense. *Fuck no, you will not lose consciousness!* Opening her mouth wide, she screamed out the pain, tenuously gripping onto reality. There was a shape, soft beneath her. Claiborne noticed she'd narrowly missed the sharp point of Thrush's blade, scraping against the rings of her armor, but also trapped her own sword arm. Like lovers wrapped in an intimate embrace, Claiborne lay on the smaller woman, face close to enough to kiss. She felt the hot breath rush from Thrush and saw a speck of blood right beneath her left brown eye, smeared like war paint. Smelled the sweat and the death on her.

"Did you miss me?" Claiborne coughed and Thrush's forehead came up, almost like she intended to kiss Claiborne. Instead, her small forehead smashed directly into the bridge of Claiborne's nose. A bright white light flashed across her eyes and the searing pain, intensified by biting her tongue added to her anguish. Her mouth filled with blood and she spat a glob onto Thrush's collar.

One arm trapped and the other useless, Claiborne raised her left knee into the other woman's groin. A satisfying grunt told her she connected, but then a fist cracked her in the eye, snapping Claiborne's head back. She was tossed over her right arm, slipping free in time to catch the smaller woman's arm as she tried to plunge a knife into her side.

"Oh no, you don't!" Claiborne's words came out as grunts rather than tangible sounds. She twisted the arm, hearing the bone click and Thrush squeaked. The knife fell. Claiborne turned on her back, planting her boots in the woman's gut and kicked. Dust flew up, Thrush rolled away and Claiborne managed to dig a stone into her shoulder blade.

"Is this the revenge you want?" Thrush knelt, holding her injured arm. They were equal now, both beaten and down an arm. Her hair was a tangled nest of dirt and sweet covering the right side of her face. The painful grimace was there and it caused Claiborne to smile though her entire face seemed to be a nettle of pain and blood. "Rutting around like two mad dogs in the dirt?"

Thrush was delaying. Trying to catch her breath for another round. Claiborne saw the knife between them.

"Yessh!" Claiborne lunged for the knife and Thrush was a heartbeat behind. Once again, luck warped around her and Thrush caught the handle while Claiborne got the sharp blade. Metal ate into her calloused palms, but Claiborne refused to let go. She grunted, blood slick and the knife slipped free, spraying red droplets across the yellowed-grass. Thrush held the knife pointed at Claiborne. Blade dulled by dirt and blood. Claiborne's arm hung useless, knuckles dragging in the dirt, and her legs refused to move, folded beneath her. Claiborne sucked air through her painfully swollen nose, blood stinging her eye. She sounded like a horse ridden too hard for far too long. *Here is another failure. You never deserved me, Arron.* She stared Thrush in her eyes and held out her throat.

"Kill me," she managed the words and spat a glob of blood at her feet.

Thrush leaned in. The blade close to Claiborne's throat.

"Do it! You bitch!"

A scream came from the stable and the hurt and anger left Thrush's face. She lowered the knife.

"I'm sorry," Thrush said. "I never meant to hurt Arron."

Claiborne lunged for her, hoping for a quick death, the slip of the blade through her throat. Thrush was quicker yet. Stepping back and then running for the stables.

"You bitch! Stupid Bitch!" The words drained her and Claiborne sat, broken and empty of rage. A single tear ran down her dirt-streaked cheek. She lay down, body wracked in pain and waited. It wasn't too late for death to find her. The thing about death, was it never came when one desired it. Death had its own agenda and Claiborne's name wasn't on it.

"What the fuck is this?" Ivy whispered. Her feet were rooted in the old straw, the same moldy stench tickling her nose. Light shone through gaps in the old thatch, centered over two figures.

Danial was tied to a back post, his head down. In front of him, Hyrian knelt, humming a happy song that could have been a hymn to the Creator. The image burned inside Ivy's mind, and she couldn't understand why Hyrian held a knife in her right hand. Or why the pale skin of her fingers were stained a dark red? Like she had dipped them in wine.

The knife plunged into Danial's gut. Danial let out a muffled scream, eyes widening while Hyrian twisted the handle, sawing her arm, carving him up as careful as butcher selling a pound of flesh. When she pulled the knife out, a chunk of flesh dropped into her tiny hands. She lifted it to her blood smeared lips, wrapping around it like it was a sweet she savored. Humming paused long enough to chew. Danial moaned, eyes squeezing tears out, his body shuddering.

"What the fuck?" Louder, thicker, song close to the surface, almost ready to break out. Almost. Life was full of almosts. She hated the word.

Hyrian looked up at Ivy, mouth chewing and grinned, tiny red streaked teeth displayed. Red smeared her lips, beyond the corners to the dimples in her cheeks, and dotted the tip of her button nose. She held out a chunk of flesh in her small fingers.

"Want some?"

Ivy's knees gave way, straw poking her knees. She vomited, heaving at the sight of the innards squished between the pale fingers. Ivy started to scream, but it was caught in her throat, choking her.

Hyrian chewed, watching her struggle. Blood painted her lip red.

"What did you do, you little beast?" Ivy struggled for breath.

"I'm playing, don't you want to play, too."

Danial groaned.

He's still alive!

Hyrian poked her fingers back into the cut, rooting around, her doll, Glorian, nestled in her other arm.

"You fucking disgusting creature." Ivy held the dagger up and ran at

Hyrian.

The girl was quick, dropping her doll and tumbling away from Ivy's swipe. Hyrian jabbed her knife out, the armor on Ivy's shins screeching as it turned the blade away. Ivy leapt back to avoid being stabbed through the foot, and tripped on something hidden in the hay. She lost her grip on the dagger and caught herself before smashing her head into a rotted beam. Her back cracked against it and something fell into the straw.

Hyrian snarled and crawled to her, knife in one hand. Ivy kicked her in the face and the blade plunged into her boot. Ivy gritted her teeth, letting out a screech as the blade cut across the top of her foot. Her right hand dug through the straw grabbing for any object. Hyrian yanked the knife from Ivy's boot, warm, wetness soaking into the sole, and the girl began to climb up her leg. Ivy grabbed something rough and rounded. It had a weight to it and she swung it out of the straw: a rusted horseshoe. Hyrian raised the knife.

"Stop, child!" Cacophony commanded from the stable's opening. Silent Prayer held in his hands.

Hyrian hissed, flecks of blood and bits of skin spraying on Ivy's face. She held her knife out, ready to gut Ivy. Her thin arm was tensed, caught between obeying and following through with her base instinct to kill. The little girl was gone, replaced by some darker, hideous being connected to the world of shadow and death.

"Enough, girl!" Cacophony shouted, his voice softening. "Listen to your father."

Ivy didn't know if she would obey, didn't trust this creature to submit to any human command. She gripped the rusted edges of the horseshoe, holding it tight in her sweat-slicked hands. The girl was strong, stronger than any human of her size and age, though who knew what age the being was in the mummer's outfit, pretending, make-believe. It was all a story Cacophony told in his mind. A carefully crafted tale to maintain his hold on the past here in the present. *Otherwise, he would've dashed the brains out of this creature he called daughter long ago.* Sharp, blue eyes stared into Ivy, and the girl grinned.

"Betrayer," Hyrian said.

"You betrayed me," Ivy said. "Danial did nothing to you."

Ivy lifted the horseshoe and brought the blunted end down with all her strength onto the girl's head. Bone cracked and the skull curved inward as the shoe embedded into the girl's brain. Blood spurted from her blue eyes and nose, spraying Ivy. Then Hyrian fell over, mouth gawping open.

Ivy gripped the horseshoe, ready to strike again. She took a breath. Then another. The light sharpened in the stable, giving everything a thin veneer of a dream.

Is she... Is she...

The power rushed back into Ivy, telling her that Hyrian was dead.

For a moment, she locked eyes with Hyman, but the man was gone. Cacophony was in his place. A low moan, that deepened into a growl crept from his throat. He tore the muslin from his face and gulped in air.

"Is she—"

"Yes," Ivy said, shoving the body off into the straw. She wiped the blood from her face. "She died a long time ago and you knew it. Whatever this thing is, she wasn't your daughter."

The scar twitched and his lips shivered, the defeat in his eyes watered. His voice broke as he spoke. "I...I could have made you into someone. Given you purpose."

"This is my purpose," Ivy said and got to her feet. She stumbled at the fiery pain in her foot. "Destroying you and the monster you created."

Was it?

It was too late to take back what he'd done. No unspilling milk, or blood and brains in this case.

Cacophony laughed, like glass shattering, and his black pauldrons heaved, the metal shrieking.

"I trained you," he said, distant, dreamy. Then strengthening into an accusation. "Made you stronger."

Betrayer. Breaker of men.

"And now you will die by the very weapon you created," Ivy said.

Death. It always came back to me killing others.

Cacophony hefted Silent Prayer and ran at Ivy.

Ivy opened her mouth, releasing the full power of her song. It caught him in mid-stride, fierce hands grappling with him, nails digging their way beneath the tough layers of armor and skin. Cacophony grunted, the weight of his will greater than any she had encountered, like trying to stop a charging bull with a feather. But her song was stronger and feathers turned into needles, pricking and sinking deeper into soft flesh.

The vision was cold, a naked plunge into icy waters. She saw him as a soldier watching helplessly from the hilltop as his companions were swallowed by rising water, thousands upon thousands of corpses floating in an unnatural lake. A flash of light and the scene shifted. He stood in the ashes of his home holding a necklace, gold chain tarnished, and the charred remains of a woman holding a child, watched a shadowed robed man touch the ash and the little girl rise, then Hyman holding the girl on his knee, a sad expression on his face while she sang, endless faces of men and women dying and masked in pain. Saw her sink her teeth into him and tear away the flesh.

This was a true vision, unlike the one he'd shown her earlier. Some Shadow Figure—the same who haunted her—brought him to this moment of reckoning, driving him the way a driver used his whip to force the mule on. Ivy pitied him and in a moment of weakness, her song slipped.

"Get out of me!" Cacophony growled, taking a few steps closer, leaning against the hold Ivy had on him. Silent Prayer was raised, ready to strike Ivy's head from her neck. "You don't know a thing about the world. It is better to be a monster. So be the monster."

Then a single word repeated in verse.

"Glutti!"

Cacophony slowed again. His eyes beckoned for vengeance, but they almost pleaded for mercy. The only mercy Ivy knew how to give to a man who allowed such evil to persist despite the fact it destroyed who he was as a person. Encasing him in a shell thicker than his bug-like armor. Cacophony lowered Silent Prayer. His arms trembled as he turned his wrists so the sharp tip pointed at Ivy, his momentum carrying him down, and down, to impale her...*Glutti! Glutti! Glutti!*...then his wrists snapped back, blade perfectly perpendicular under his chin. He tilted his head back, raised the sword, and opened his mouth. His wrist bent, moving the blade over his lips and lowered it, further into his mouth, beyond the lips that kissed death and let it live. Beneath the mad voice of reason. He swallowed Silent Prayer, choking as the blade cut his gullet apart from the inside, until the hilt rested on his lips.

"Die now," Ivy said, tears in her eyes and shaking. She watched Cacophony drag the sword from his mouth. Red saliva and darker chunks dripped from the blade. The sword clattered to the ground. Cacophony grabbed his throat and took a step. A gush of blood rolled from his mouth and he gagged, dark eyes staring at her. Thanking her, perhaps cursing her, perhaps loving her for the very mercy he had sought, but couldn't achieve because life wasn't always fair. The light slipped from his eyes, they rolled up to the whites, and he went still.

Ivy stumbled past Cacophony's body and dropped to her knees in front of

Danial. He was still alive, barely, a flame holding onto the last bit of wick as it sank into the wax. He smiled, locking eyes with her.

"I just…just want to hear…songs of the nightingale," Danial said, blood bubbling on his lips and he gasped. "One last time."

"Let me sing for you," Ivy said, holding his cold hand in her trembling one. His grip was weak, but she held it tightly. She sang the song her mother sang to her. A lullaby to help her sleep during stormy nights. Danial continued to smile at her, his body shuddering and then going slack.

The song of the nightingale continued until a hand touched her shoulder. Ivy didn't bother to turn and look. Thrush squeezed her gently.

"Time to go, Ivy."

"No," she said, stroking Danial's face. So many people suffered for her. "Ivy died here."

Thrush furrowed her brow. "Oh, Ivy," she said, pity in her voice.

"Nightingale." She stood and held her chin firmly. "You will all call me Nightingale from now on."

Postlude

Nightingale Takes Flight

Failure was never final until you were dead. Cacophony and the thing he called a daughter met their failures and Claiborne nearly headed at a full gallop into her own. She wouldn't shed a tear over their deaths, but she wasn't satisfied. After all the hate, the bloodshed, the killing, punching, spitting, and sacrifice, she found herself back at square one. A beaten and bloody square, shaky in the legs and head, but still square one. The rage was gone, for the moment. The little bitch bird flew away from her enclosed hands, after giving her a good thwapping. Not into a clear sky, since her cats' claws got a good scratching in as well, but the principle remained—Thrush remained alive and she was Claiborne's to kill. At a later time, perhaps. Revenge left unsated would fester, but it wouldn't kill her. It was a corpse bloating in the sun and ready to birth squirming maggots. As long as Claiborne remained alive, she could see to the cleanup of her bad history. A clearing of conscience, so to speak.

I really would make an ugly corpse. She dragged herself from the piss and blood-stained ground, managed to crawl over the saddle and let the horse carry her back to camp. Cacophony was dead. The idea seemed strange, since he had occupied much of her adult life, fighting against and then for him. It was like losing a close friend, one who threatened to kill her more often than she dared count, but more of a friend than anyone else alive.

Time to find a new employer.

Freelance seemed more her style. There were men and women who lacked leadership. When there was a void, something had to fill it.

She returned back to camp. Hundreds of Silent Men watched her slide off the horse. The question plain on their faces: Had they won? One look at her and the answer was evident. They waited for her to speak, to gather the words from her bloody spittle. After a long, long moment, a gap where she might have lost them, she clenched her fists and took hold of the Silent Men. She alone would lead. Cacophony put too much trust in Ivy and as a result, he was dead. That's what happens when you trust anyone that much. They disappoint you.

"Gather what gear you can carry," Claiborne said, leaning against the horse. "We are heading out."

A soldier helped Claiborne to a surgeon who set her shoulder and placed her arm in a sling. He adjusted her nose, but the rest of her face he couldn't do much for. A warrior was bound to bear scars, it was the nature of the game, and Claiborne wore hers on the outside with pride. They were the mark of luck. Luck was never free. It always took its wages.

Claiborne grabbed her bed roll and went to her trunk. It was empty except for a locket on a single copper string. She opened it and looked at the woman inside. It was close to the image of Ivy as any memory could get.

The thing about being a warrior, a servant for the good and blah blah blah, was your work was never done. Not until the last fiend you hunted was put into the ground.

I have another one to add to my mark.

Claiborne slipped the locket around her neck.

First order of business: kill this bitch.

Then she could kill Thrush.

Claiborne limped back into the scurrying camp as they tore it all down. The Silent Men avoided her gaze, head down and hands busy. Claiborne smiled, though it hurt her face. Oh yes, a void needed to be filled and she was the badass woman to do the job right.

"Won't you reconsider?" Thrush stood off to the side, hands pressed together in an almost pleading gesture. Nightingale knew differently. Thrush never begged.

Nightingale tightened the straps on the saddle. The white mare was gentle enough with her, unlike the other horses. She would allow Nightingale plenty of time in the saddle without trying to toss her. Plenty of time to improve her riding skills. She would ride far away from Welksdale. Far away from a past that no longer included her and future that did not welcome her.

"I wish I could," Nightingale said. A lie, since she wished that Danial was alive and they had never encountered the Silent Men nor Singers.

I need answers and I won't find any here.

"We could teach you more about your song," Thrush insisted.

"I know enough to get by," Nightingale said. "That's more of a chance then some people get."

"Ivy, listen—"

"Don't call me that." Nightingale glared at the small woman. Thrush could gut her in an instant, but Nightingale was strong enough to stop her. Her song rested, but not far from reach. Cacophony had helped strengthen her with Sparrow's help. That was the one good deed he did.

"Traditionally a Singer doesn't acquire her new name until after she passes her trials," Thrush said.

"I've passed enough trials to earn a thousand names," Nightingale said. "This is the one I chose. Life is about choices, and I for one don't think you are ready for me."

Thrush went silent. After a moment, she drew a harmonic forged long sword from a scabbard. Nightingale waited for the woman to challenge her. Thrush could whip her soundly, especially since Nightingale didn't believe she'd ever be comfortable with a sword in her hand. Instead, Thrush handed Nightingale the blade.

"For when your song fails you," she said. "There are some dangers you cannot manipulate your way out of." Then she bowed and walked away.

There was no one else to see Nightingale off. All the people who had cared—she counted them on one hand—were dead and gone. She buried Danial out on his farm next to his family marked plot, a pile of stones shaped like a bird, in the best design Nightingale could place them, as his memory stone. She wished she could do more, but one thing she learned, that if wishes were water, she'd be left thirsty.

She had considered Thrush's offer. Continuing to learn what her song could do was tempting, but the image of the Shadow Figure came to her mind. This being ended the life of a little girl, crushed and twisted her father's soul, then brought them both back as monsters. She would not let that happen again.

Nightingale mounted the horse and clicked her tongue. Thrush stood back and watched her leave. Already the ride was much smoother. As she rode past the gates, she refused to look back. That old life, like her name, was dead and gone. There was nothing left for her here.

What remained was the Shadow Figure. A point of light in the darkness. Nightingale planned on following it wherever it led her.

Nazglum could damn her, but not before she killed his minion.

One visit before I begin my hunt.

Her first stop was at the Farlow's pig farm.

As she walked up the steps, the door opened and Crisell stood, arms folded and blocking her way.

"You're kind ain't welcome here," he said.

"You sound like your mother," Nightingale said and regretted it immediately. For an instance hurt flashed across his face. He deserved better than the pain she carried around.

"She died, you know," Crisell said.

The news shocked Nightingale. Ms. Farlow may have despised her, and even tried to kill her, but she was one in a long list of those who had tried and failed. Crisell and Myah were orphaned. She wouldn't wish that sort of pain onto anyone.

Another thing we have in common.

"I didn't know," Nightingale said.

"The night after I took you home," Crisell said. "Where you killed those men. She had a fit of madness, screaming about birds and shadows. Then her heart gave out."

"I'm sorry."

A moment of awkward silence passed.

"What do you want, Ivy?"

"I...I have something to talk to about," Nightingale said, chewing her lip. "About your father. About our father."

Crisell raised an eyebrow, but unfolded his arms. He opened the door and Nightingale went inside.

End of Book One

ABOUT THE AUTHOR

Matthew Johnson is a graduate of the MFA Creative Writing program at University of Riverside Palm Desert. He has published short stories in various genres, a fantasy collection, two fantasy novels and a horror novel. Three plays Wooing the Dragon, Lycanthrope, and Lazarus Rising, a zombie play, entering its third run. He resides in Riverside California with his three lovable puppies.

You can find more about his works at www.professorgrimdark.com

Horror

Plays

Fantasy

Gods War Series

Nightingale Saga